# BLACKHEART

*Paul R. Starling*

*Best Wishes,*
*Paul*

*Copyright*
*Paul R Starling*

*Front cover artwork*
*Chloe Starling*

*First Edition May 2022*

*All rights reserved. No part of this publication may be reproduced, stored in a retrieval system, or transmitted in any form or by any means, electronic, mechanical, photocopy, recording or otherwise, without prior written permission from the copyright holder. Nor can it be circulated in any form of binding or cover other than that in which it is published and without similar condition being imposed on a similar purchaser.*

## Authors Notes

While all the following character names and many events contained within this novel are fictitious for the purposes of creating a thriller, many of the details have been either influenced or gleaned from actual events imparted personally to me, or researched by me.

Spies from all nations all across the globe have always infiltrated their enemies and the character in my story, Anatoly Polivanova, exists in truth in another form. He was an agent who trained with the military of his own country but his actual role remains a national secret. Many female snipers existed throughout WW2, and beyond, and was the heritage of the real Polivanova.

During Perestroika in the 1980's and 1990's there existed much upheaval and dissent within the Russian hierarchy, which resulted in dispersal of lives and assassinations both at home and abroad. During the confusion at the time of the fall of the Berlin Wall - and the subsequent rebuild - materiel, valuables and people were lost, and found, while some items still remain hidden. As mentioned within the text there are many discoveries of once thought lost artefacts which are still being made today and will continue.

The abandoned movie studio mentioned in the text is primarily inspired by the Avala Film studios in old Yugoslavia - I recommend the documentary film Cinema Komunisto directed by Mila Turajlic as a moving tribute to lost and forgotten movie studios. Another poignant source of ghostly celluloid memories is the tragic dismantling to the MGM Studios - explored expertly in the book MGM Hollywoods Greatest Backlot - and its treasures, some saved, many destroyed.

### Thanks and acknowledgments

Firstly I should like to thank Andrew Shearing for his invaluable assistance in the editing of this novel, and inspiring certain directions which the plot takes. I usually blame myself for all the errors within my novels and, because of Andrew's unwavering support, I shall still take that responsibility.

To Bernard Hagon and Les David, both of whom, directly or indirectly, freely offered details and encouragement which have meant this work could not only be made possible, it has a greater depth of their wise experience.

And to you, the reader, for giving my writing a chance. I sincerely hope you enjoy the story as much as I enjoyed the writing and research.

# PROLOGUE

### DECEMBER 20th, 1988

Waltraud Koenig flung open the window of his East Berlin office and the frigid night-time air bit into his skin with its icy spikes. Waltraud needed the fresh oxygen to quell his doom laden thoughts, and his lungs were stung which caused him to cough involuntarily. His heart raced. He was fearful of the consequences should his Russian superiors prematurely uncover his actions. Waltraud had witnessed their particular brand of justice first-hand on numerous occasions over his forty plus years in servitude to them, unscathed himself because he literally ensured he dotted his 'I's' and crossed his 'T's' unfailingly and unquestioningly.

    The functionality of his office wasn't exactly penthouse material despite its top-floor prominence with the view, day and night, of a bittersweet city scape beauty marred by the ever present menace of The Wall and coiled barbed wire.

    Waltraud gazed across the vista where muted lights shone from windows, blinked on the tower tops and from the NATO facility, four miles distant, which was a prominent reminder to aircraft and enemy alike. Berlin was often a bleak and oppressive city, tainted by its own histrionics, mired by an impotent self pity.

Waltraud tried to shake free from the bleak thoughts which mirrored the darkness outside. This path he had chosen to embark upon was precarious yet of his own making and he knew without doubt it was the correct choice.

The Austrian National drew in a deep breath to steady his resolve. Waltraud told himself that he should not be plagued by the cruel histrionics surrounding him. Waltraud had been, and was still viewed as, a trusted and loyal minion within the intelligence gathering community. And rightly so. He had served the Russians unswervingly and with dignity.

When, in 1985, Mikhail Gorbachev succeeded to power, Waltraud had rejoiced along with his colleagues. It was if a veil might be lifted from the rest of the world, an opinion not shared by those voices of dissent, but there were always such voices wherever one lived. There would always be those who understandably claimed the Soviet Union had been successful under a single-party rule. For sixty years the system had remained unchanged and unchallenged but Gorbachev had instigated Perestroika, a bold plan for financial and political reforms of the Motherland. This action had encouraged protests, mainly in favour of a multi-party democracy.

Some were less pleased.

Unrest had swept throughout the Eastern Bloc.

And Waltraud Koenig, secretary, analyst and clerk, could foresee what these reforms might mean to the underlings who had borne secrets which were as twisted as the barbed wire which separated a country.

Waltraud wasn't the only one. Many intellectuals had secretly debated and prophesied the eventual outcome, while some of the dissenting voices were mysteriously silenced.

Twelve months ago Waltraud had set in motion the plan he was now fully committed to. His impetus and focus had prevailed beyond distracted eyes. He was ready to disappear under his own terms.

The fact was that despite his relative position low on the rung of the ladder of importance, Waltraud knew enough secret intelligence information that he was a security risk to Mother Russia. People had been executed for less, or sent to some isolated outpost in Siberia for more. Waltraud had circulated in rarefied air for most of his working life and, despite having an unmemorable face and being a footnote on a long hypothetical list he would, someday, be forcibly removed by Russian forces.

Waltraud shivered involuntarily. He wondered what the air would be like in England. Would it be so frigid? Would the atmosphere be as chilly, both actual and metaphorical, as in an Eastern Bloc country?

Waltraud felt a pang of despair. A nervous roil bubbled in the pit of his stomach.

He would never see his family again.

His wife.

His two children.

Their fate would not be known to him, as his fate would remain forever a secret from them. Waltraud knew his wife would mourn her loss but time would heal her grieving. Maybe she would move on. These thoughts did not bear dwelling upon.

Waltraud was thankful that his son and daughter were grown up and both had forged lives for themselves. They were married. They would heal quickly from their loss.

But, most importantly to Waltraud, they would continue to exist in this world. They would not be hounded or interrogated because Waltraud's disappearance would be utterly complete that death would be his perceived fate.

Waltraud Koenig closed the top floor office windows one final time. His fate sealed in his mind's eye. The vista of Berlin would be forever etched in his memory.

# CHAPTER ONE

### Present Day

"My husband wouldn't hurt a fly." Hayley Wilby declared earnestly, her blue eyes moist and bloodshot from tears and lack of sleep.

Were it not for this young woman's pitiful sobbing Harry Kovac might have brushed off her plea. Not because his heart was cold. Far from it. But too often Harry had heard declarations of innocence from spouses when their significant others were accused of a crime. And Hayley's husband was accused of murder. Which Harry had just been told about on his very doorstep, not in the office of Crane Investigation Services.

Such informality might tick off Harry Kovac more often than not and perhaps if the person hadn't been Hayley he might've asked her to follow the usual procedures. Murder accusations aren't bandied about without grounding. Plus, said private investigation firm didn't deal in cases such as these. But Harry Kovac couldn't help himself. He wasn't about to turn this young woman away from his front door, and besides, this intriguing interruption to what likely would be a routine work day was a welcome change.

Harry Kovac was taken off guard, that was all. His routine had been broken.

He had sprung out of bed not much more than a couple of hours earlier, limbered up, oiled his joints, as it were, and departed his two-bedroom bungalow in Stalton-on-the-Broads, which was in the beautiful heart of Norfolk. The morning bike ride was taken without fail when opportunity favoured him. Harry was a fair-weather cyclist. The journey was a pleasant outdoor pursuit during the long days of summer, such as this mid-August morning, through the quiet Norfolk backroads. An indoor pursuit during the winter. Both were followed by aerobic exercises and a callisthenics routine designed to warm the body and freshen the mind.

After a hot shower followed immediately by a cold burst of water, Harry dried, dressed and partook of coffee, which was black and strong with one sugar, consumed with two rounds of buttered toast and a piece of fruit, usually a banana for the natural energy it provided.

Harry had also tapped a text message which he sent to Parisa Dane, who should be back in Norfolk by nightfall after her business flight up to Scotland.

Harry was ready with his jacket and car keys at promptly seven forty-five every morning. It was a tried and tested routine that suited his metabolism perfectly, honed through service in the police force and a natural willingness to be an early riser. Seize the day was definitely a motto which could be applied to this man.

With nobody to say goodbye to and no pet seeking attention, Harry had unlocked the front door of his bungalow and was prepared for his uninterrupted journey to work, but Hayley Wilby was standing outside his door. The figure was hazy in the frosted glass, like a shimmering wraith. Harry could see an arm extended toward the door bell, mid pause, having likewise seen Harry through the glass and decided it was unnecessary to announce her arrival.

Harry had opened the door and the face which looked back at him was that of a local woman in her twenties. He had seen her in the village. Perhaps the supermarket, perhaps the pub, perhaps the street. Mostly because she was fairly eye catching in a superficial, un-PC way. Hayley was twenty-four, petite and blonde, which was possibly the reason why Harry recognised her because in his younger days she would've been the type of girl he went for. She had been crying, her hair was matted down and untidy and she appeared to be in dire need of sleep. There had been no thought or coordination when she had gotten herself dressed, neither, because the flowery blouse she wore didn't go with the green jeans or white and purple running shoes.

Eye contact with Harry resulted in her sobbing, which racked her entire body.

In his years of experience Harry had built up immunity to people in distress. Or so he believed. But that still didn't prevent him from reaching out a comforting hand, which he placed on her shoulder and squeezed. She was in a bad way and needed support.

Eventually a great big pitiful sigh shuddered through her body. Harry thought she was going to faint and prepared himself to catch her, but instead she lifted up her head.

"I'm Hayley Wilby." She then announced. "My- my husband Karl has been accused of murder." Her lips quavered. "My husband wouldn't hurt a fly."

"Do you want to come in for a coffee?" Harry asked.

Only a truly cold-hearted man could turn away such a distressed person. Hayley clearly knew Harry as a private investigator because it never took long for news that such a person was resident in a village. Any village. But particularly in the close-knit community which existed in Stalton-on-the-Broads.

The village itself was relatively new, having celebrated its fiftieth anniversary only twelve months ago. Straddling the River Bure between Hoveton and Coltishall along the B1138, seven miles north-west of Norwich and at the heart of the Norfolk Broads, at last census the village had just under two thousand residents. There were two pubs, one either side of the Bure, a TAMS Supermarket, five independent retailers, a village hall with recreational ground, and of course housing on different budgetary scales. The bungalow which was Harry's home existed on a new build estate at the southern side of the Bure, and it catered for those people who were financially established or who wanted a quiet retirement surrounded by nature. Harry was fortunate enough to be the former.

Hayley Wilby crossed the threshold and Harry shut the door behind her. He led her into the kitchen where he pulled up a stool at the breakfast bar. She slumped onto the stool, elbows on the bar, body sagging despondently, sobbing woefully.

Harry switched on the coffee machine which he had only switched off ten minutes ago and let it reheat. He gathered two mugs from the cupboard in which they lived, filled the coffee-filter with ground Arabica, and eased onto a stool at right angles to Hayley.

She didn't look at him, at least not immediately. She stared at a point on the windows in front of her, her face running through a gamut of emotions, lost in thought.

"Karl went to his work party last night." She started.

"Your husband?"

Hayley nodded.

"Where does Karl work?"

"TAMS." She said. "But the party was at the village hall in the village."

"Okay. And what happened?"

"The police said Karl murdered Caryn."

"Caryn?"

"She is- was, Karl's boss. But he couldn't have- He- he isn't capable of killing anyone."

Harry waited while Hayley cried some more, getting it out of her system if that were at all possible.

Murder cases were for the police and movie PI's, not real firms, like the one Harry now worked for. There were too many rules and regulations in the real world that private detection of murder crimes were often more trouble than losing your licence over. But Harry knew Hayley would feel much better after telling someone about her situation and he couldn't help but feel a pang of pity for her. She was young and innocent, relatively naive living in the countryside. And she reminded him of his daughter.

Harry would certainly help if he could.

"What did the police tell you happened?" Harry asked gently.

Her eyes flashed brightly and wet and angry. "They told me he lured her into a back room of the village hall where he-" she struggled for breath and it took many seconds for a return to composure. "They said he had sex with her before killing her but he wouldn't do a think like that because he loves me and I know he couldn't betray or hurt me or anyone else."

Hayley stared at the windows again with such a forlorn expression on her face that it was painful to watch. She definitely wasn't acting.

Getting off his stool Harry gave her time while he made the coffee. Both black and strong. She needed it more than he did.

Harry sympathised with her. He had certainly witnessed many occasions when the wife or partner believed their respective other was innocent and incapable of such deeds as cheating and violence. The problem was that nine times out of ten it was proven to be fact. Mostly it involved men cheating on women. The oldest story in the book. But it was unusual that cheating would couple itself with murder unless the attacker was known for violence or psychological issues.

Maybe Karl and Hayley were the exception. The one out of the ten.

Placing the two steaming mugs on the breakfast bar, Harry sat back on his stool.

Hayley looked at the coffee then at him, managing to form a weak smile of gratitude which never reached her eyes.

"Had Karl been prone to violence?"

Hayley shook her head. "No. And I told that to the police and my solicitor. They also asked if he had any psychological problems but he doesn't. He- He is a normal guy."

"Have you spoken to him?"

"No. Not yet. He's in Wymondham. The police said he was in no fit state to talk. Apparently he was taking drugs or something at the party. But that's something else he wouldn't do. He's never done drugs. Not even an ibuprofen for a headache. He doesn't believe in using them."

Harry nodded understanding. It seemed to him Karl probably had a few secrets of which his wife wasn't privy. Unless these two young people had an uncommon relationship, not everything is shared.

"Can you find out what happened?" Hayley asked.

And that was the big question.

Harry knew she hadn't just found him by chance. He knew what her purpose had been. But now the question. And realistically he could find out what had happened but she would hear an identical report from the police and her solicitor, and most probably from Karl, eventually. But looking at her sat on a stool at his breakfast bar sipping his coffee, her hands trembling and small around the mug, her face blotchy, eyes stinging with tears, Harry Kovac wasn't about to abandon her to the inevitable without offering some support of his own. Where was the real harm?

"I will pay." Hayley added, almost in desperation. "I know your help won't be free, I realise that, and I can pay, but I need to help Karl and- and I don't know what else to do."

"Trust that the police will do their job, Hayley. I used to be one myself once, and in my experience if a person is innocent they will surely find out soon enough."

Hayley Wilby looked at him like a lost child, pleading, heartbroken. Once more Harry was reminded of his own daughter. During times when she couldn't understand why some simple task wasn't being done, wondering why those apparently simple things needed to be complicated in an adult world. Now Harry recognised why he was drawn to her plight. Hayley had reminded him of a version of his daughter. She would be fifteen years old now if her life hadn't been taken.

"Hayley, I shall try what I can." A look of hope alighted her face, however meagre. "But I cannot interfere with a police investigation. I know how this works. I've been there myself, frequently, and they will frown upon any action which might jeopardise their investigation."

"I understand." And the look upon her face said that she did. There was hope, too. "Will you at least speak to Karl?"

"Yes. I shall definitely try. Who is your solicitor?"

Hayley told him a name which made Harry inwardly smile. She said the solicitor was visiting Karl later that morning. The solicitor was a guy who owed Harry a favour which could be repaid that very morning, if Harry acted quickly enough.

Harry slid off the stool and pulled his mobile phone from the pocket of his jacket which he had hung back on the stand bedside the door. He tapped out a quick message before sending it to Daphne Crane, the steering-wheel of Crane Investigation Services - it told her that he would be a bit late to the office that morning, nothing more. Harry knew that Karl Wilby would be detained at the Police Investigation Centre in Wymondham, opposite police headquarters where the MIT - Major Investigation Team - would conduct their investigation into the crime. Karl Wilby could be detained at PIC in the first instance for 24 hours, likely extended to 36 hours by the Superintendent in the event of a Serious Arrestable Offence, which murder most definitely was. Harry messaged the solicitor.

When Harry returned to the kitchen Hayley was standing by the breakfast bar finishing her mug of coffee with a look of gratitude in her eyes.

"I'm not promising anything, Hayley." He told her. "I can't. But I'll see what I can do for you. Fair enough?"

She nodded meekly and placed the empty mug down on his table. "Thank you."

Harry could do no more than nod. He handed her one of his personal business cards, before she brushed by him to the front door which he opened. Hayley sucked in some air to calm her nerves, turned back briefly but couldn't find any more words, smiled, and walked down the garden path. She was a broken young woman trying to hold her chin high.

# CHAPTER TWO

Anatoly 'Olly' Polivanova regarded his English work uniform with utter revolt. It lay upon his hotel bed and consisted of a white polyester shirt over which he would put a navy blue polyester waistcoat, accompanied by a pair or navy blue polyester trousers. Pinned to the shirt was a gold name badge which stated that he was Olly and had served the hotel for four years.

It was a typically conformist uniform and the Russian intelligence officer hated it with a passion, but it was part of the cover he had assumed in England, so tolerate it he must. In fact, only his boots were his own. They were polished and sturdy and utilitarian; a reminder of where his heart truly lay.

Anatoly drew in his breath and held it.

This was the completion of his hour-long morning exercise regime and followed five circuits around the entire perimeter of the eighteen-hole golf course, of which the hotel building was nestled in its centre. Both entities were contained within the same acreage yet under separate management.

Shared benefits, different accounting.

The run was followed immediately by twenty minutes of weights and calisthenics in the hotel leisure club, which was a third separate financial department because, like all capitalist businesses, this hotel was franchised out to several entities. Half a dozen entities in the case of Beeston Grange.

Ten minutes under a shower alternating between hot and cold sprays and Anatoly was standing naked in his room and he was poised like a dancer. His chest was out, hard contoured muscles which any athlete in his or her prime would be proud of, but not Anatoly. The Russians body was merely a tool. Pride or ego tended to enter his mind only when he was here at the hotel.

During his calm meditation he had thought nothing of the obsequious day job which would consist of bowing and scraping and pandering to the guests of Beeston Grange all day. Anatoly was effectively a paid slave who carried out the bidding of the fat over-privileged capitalist hotel guests.

Most of the time he was the gracious person indicative of the establishment and he was fluent in English without any trace of accent, so that helped, but if someone utterly obnoxious crossed his path then he pretended to 'no speaker the English' with the best of them. After all, he was paid to do a job the English were too lazy for but that did not mean he needed to put up with rudeness all the time. They should consider themselves fortunate because Anatoly could break their fat neck without so much as breaking a sweat.

Most of the wage Anatoly received was paid to his wife in the Polish city Szczecin. It funded their house build which was not far from the beautiful Park Kasprowicza. It was progressing favourably and should be completed in the next six months. The exchange rate was good although his pay, by comparison to other jobs available, was low.

Two months out of every twelve he returned home, visiting with his wife and their two daughters, his mother and father and in-laws. Plus there was the field training. Anatoly could proudly boast he had twelve successful covert assignments for the Russian Special Services under his belt.

Eleven in Europe.

One in England.

So far.

His training and assignments were unequivocally the highlights of his existence. It would be a lie to himself to claim otherwise. Family was important, of course, but those duties paled by comparison to those in servitude to his country. The training, the order, and the aims of The Party meant everything to Anatoly Polivanova.

The Motherland meant everything.

This national pride was something which the weak-willed English in their dishevelled state of complacency couldn't possibly understand. Ever. But one day in the not too distant future tensions would reach their peak and atrophy.

Some day soon.

But not today.

He slowly expelled air from his lungs and inhaled deeply. One-hundred and seventy five seconds.

He picked up the boxers shorts and slipped them on, one leg at a time, catching a sidelong glance of himself in the mirror. Steely blue eyes looked back at him, clear and bright and dangerous under dark heavy brows and prominent forehead. Clean shaven, his cheeks were a healthy hue of red. In fact his entire body was flush from the fresh air and exercise, promoting pigmentations which displayed his contours, curvatures and musculature.

Anatoly smirked at the face which only his wife and mother could possibly love. But never mind. Vanity wasn't part of his character. And Anatoly was not short on lingering looks from female and male admirers when he wore just a pair of shorts in the leisure club or swimming pool. Then there were the repulsive offers.

His work uniform fitted him snuggly.

A mundane day beckoned and it wouldn't be until two o'clock that afternoon when his smartphone purred, message received. And a simple message it was, too. The only word on the screen was 'thirty minutes'. Nothing more. Because no more was unnecessary. He knew what it meant and he couldn't deny the eager spike of anticipation which welled up in the pit of his stomach. Whatever he was going to be doing at two-thirty would most likely be far more interesting than bowing and scraping to the unappreciative. It might mean his muscle was required. His intimidation would definitely be required. And maybe the possibility of causing pain to someone.

At one-minute past two o'clock a big grin would gruesomely crack on Anatoly Polivanova's face.

# CHAPTER THREE

"I didn't do it."

Harry Kovac scowled at the famous last words which every law-abiding citizen said in the presence of authority. Whether those words were true or not at least Karl Wilby's belief married with that of his own wife.

All the evidence contained in the initial police report which Harry had read five minutes previously leaned squarely toward the contrary. As far as they were concerned Karl Wilby most definitely did do it. But everyone was viewed by the law as innocent until proven guilty so Harry would also give Karl the benefit of the doubt.

For now, at least.

Literally on face value as Harry looked at this naive twenty-eight year old slumped dejectedly in the grey plastic chair opposite, Karl Wilby was as innocent as they came. That innocence obviously was dependent upon judging a book by its previously unblemished cover.

Karl Wilby was a kid who had barely touched the surface of life's possibilities. Country living often provided smaller scope unless a person went further afield. He was a lanky five-feet ten inches tall topped by fair-hair which was slightly receding. Karl's face was unblemished, no scars or visible life stresses, with a pale complexion made worse by the terrified and unkempt state of his current condition. Normally there was probably nothing remarkable about Karl, a point of fact which Harry Kovac surmised upon first glance. This was an average kid leading an average life. Presently the kids eyes were glazed from his extreme and shocking experience of a few short hours ago, and his skin bore the pasty yellow after-effects of alcohol and drugs, plus the signs of sleep deprivation for well over twenty-four hours.

"Okay." Harry said patiently and glanced at his watch which counted down from five minutes, the time frame allotted for this questioning session under the watchful gaze of Karl Wilby's solicitor- but not too watchful owing to the favour being repaid. "I need to know precisely what you did do last night and you need to tell me exactly what you remember. Okay?"

Those blue blood-shot eyes, which before all this happened to Karl were undoubtedly clear and bright, made contact with Harry's sharper brown scrutiny. After making a careful study of his hands, Karl Wilby followed up with a decisive nod to himself at the table in front of him, a darting glance at his solicitor, then almost desperately at the three walls in his line of sight.

"You're no policeman." Karl stated correctly, his speech slurred and dry. "Why should I tell you anything?"

"Because Hayley is concerned about you and time is ticking, kid."

"Hayley?"

"Yes, Hayley. Your wife."

"Hayley." Karl said her name in almost a whisper and his eyes glazed over - if they could do so anymore.

"Contrary to popular belief your wife thinks you are innocent. I'm a private investigator, Karl, and even though this murder rap isn't the usual type of job we handle I've taken it on as a favour to her because I like her. I already said time is precious Karl, so don't be impertinent." Harry pressed, talking quicker than was normal. "I've seen the police report and it's pretty sketchy at the moment but they are piecing more evidence together. They will interview your work colleagues and whoever else was at the party last night and, quite frankly, it's looking pretty grim. Whatever drugs you took might have messed up your memory but that's just temporary, although you definitely had sex with Caryn Krystyva before you or someone murdered her."

The news of his bosses murder failed to shock Karl anymore. He had heard the accusation constantly repeated to him by police detectives and his solicitor and the effect had sunk what seemed a lifetime ago, innocent or not. Caryn had been his boss. Caryn had been the manager of TAMS supermarket. She had been twenty-eight years old, same as Karl, attractive, and murdered at the staff summer party.

"I- didn't take any drugs. I've never taken drugs, not even paracetamol for a headache. You can ask Hayley, feel free, she'll tell you."

"She already did."

"So what does it mean?"

"Possibly a date rape drug."

Karl Wilby baulked at the idea until some vague cognitive process began fermenting behind his heavily glazed eyes, offering the revelation of a silver lining behind the storm cloud.

On the one hand Harry Kovac had to admire the kid because at least he was trying to remember details, the trouble with rape drugs was they had the effect of muddling fact with fiction and, oftentimes, blotting out the event entirely. After all, who wants to remember forced violation? Also to compound matters Karl Wilby was exhausted and hanging like a dog, probably hungry and dehydrated too, so Harry could not blame the kid for his slow responses. Even if time was most definitely of the essence.

"Caryn Krystyva was attractive?" Harry asked.

"Sure." Karl nodded sheepishly, as if an admission was a pronouncement of guilt.

"You fancied her?" Harry asked in a pal-like way, attempting to ingratiate himself upon Karl to pry his mind open.

"Not- No. I love my wife. I would never cheat on her." Famous last words.

Harry continued, changed tact: "We don't have much time, Karl. Was there anyone who might have had the opportunity to slip a drug into your drink?"

"Nobody would- I mean, nobody who was at the party would've. I know them all. I do. They're my colleagues. Why would they? Why would someone want to set me up like this?"

"It's my job to find out. Presumably some of your colleagues had their partners with them?"

"Yes. Of course."

"And you know them all?"

"No."

"So was anyone acting suspiciously?"

Karl shook his head solemnly, sighing with defeat, struggling for memories, tired.

"Is there anyone who can account for your movements? There were obviously lots of witnesses to account for your being there, but anyone specific? A close friend? Someone who you spent more time with at the party other than Caryn?"

"I didn't- that is, I wasn't with Caryn. You know."

"I don't know, Karl. Come on, kid, I might be your last chance and we don't have time to mess around."

"Sarika."

"Okay. Good. What's her surname?"

"Er- Royal."

"Okay. Who is Sarika Royal to you?"

"A work colleague."

"Is she just a work colleague?"

A sly smile passed Karl's lips and the kid averted his eyes and moved his head, trying to conceal his reaction but failing miserably.

Harry gave the impassive solicitor a fleeting, knowing glance.

"Sarika is a colleague." Karl stated.

"And a friend."

"Yes. And a friend. Of course."
"And what else?"
"Nothing."
"You sure, Karl?"

Karl nodded, squirming in his seat and avoiding eye contact, which was tricky with two people in the small white-walled room. It didn't take a detective to work out why.

"Come on, Karl." Harry forced compassion into his tone, which made Karl look back up. "Was she a girlfriend?"

Karl smirked: "She was a girl and a friend so yeah."

"Don't get funny, kid. I can only help you if you tell me the truth. The police think you are guilty. Your name will be soiled in the local press. You will have the media baying for blood soon. But Hayley, your wife, is loyal and she is very convinced that you are innocent. I need to know if you are the kind of kid who cheats on his wife. So tell me, Karl, are you and Sarika lovers?"

The solicitor sucked air through his teeth but said nothing.

"No." Karl shook his head firmly - with a hint of regret?

"What then?"

Silence.

"Look, Karl, your reaction was plain enough for even a blind man to read. The detectives here want to nail you. Your solicitor won't have a chance to save you. But if you tell me what's going on between you and Sarika it might save you a lot of awkward questions later. Think about your wife, Karl. Think about Hayley."

Tears formed in Karl's eyes and his lower lip quivered. A look of guilt blanched his cheeks and contrasted starkly against the paleness from the harsh lighting and his pallor. The kid looked to the ceiling for redemption, his solicitor for hope, and sucked in a breath before resolving his turmoil.

"Okay. Sarika and I aren't lovers and that's the truth. I swear it. She and I are just good friends who-" Karl shrugged. He looked to Harry for some kind of prompt to finish the sentence. Harry held up his watch to emphasise the need for alacrity.

"Hurry up, kid."

"Sarika got me into this adult social network."

"Internet porn."

"Yeah, that's right."

"So you watch porn. Who doesn't?"

"No, it's WalkTank."

WalkTank was not a name which Harry had come across before but it took a minimum amount of deduction to put two and two together: change the places of the letters W and T and the nature of the internet site revealed itself plainly. A more crude name than others available. Face-to-face self satisfaction without being too intrusive. The internet was rife which such sites offering sexual gratification. It was a very big business, too, and catered for all genders and persuasions. It was also a way of cheating without necessarily feeling guilt. Whatever your kink the internet could cater for via high-speed fibre-optics!

"Sarika and I-" Karl continued, "we- separately, not together, we perform sex acts for others to watch."

Harry nodded understanding. This was not the first time he had heard of such things because only the genuinely naive could be unaware of such things. Plentiful domestic disturbance cases came up at The Yard when he was in service there, and plenty which he personally dealt with. Usually it took the form where one partner caught the other acting out an act of sexual gratification over the World Wide Web in what they falsely believed to be secrecy. But as anyone with common-sense knew there was no such thing as a secret when it came to the internet. If hackers can use cyber-space to break through the Firewalls at the Ministry of Defence a civilian account should be a walk in the park. The social network had gone out of control at the exact moment of its inception.

"And did Caryn Krystyva take part in any of these sessions?" Harry asked.

"No."

"Anyone else?"

"No."

"Do any of your work colleagues know?"

"No. At least I don't think so."

"But you don't know for sure."

"Well, no, but the odds are-"

"The odds are favourable that someone might be aware, Karl." Harry stated forcibly. "Word gets out easily when it wants to, let's not be naive, shall we?"

Karl laughed: "None of my work colleagues are murderers!" More famous last words?

"Someone is and if it's not you then who?"

"I- I really don't know."

Harry Kovac glanced at his watch. One more minute to go until Harry's favour came to an end. He was becoming more convinced Karl did murder Caryn Krystyva, even if it had been unintentional. Yet some details still failed to add up. Such as the sullen-faced kid seated before him. Karl Wilby really did not look capable of physical violence under any duress. And a sixth sense told Harry Kovac that Karl was innocent. Yet as the facts stood everything pointed in Karl's direction. WalkTank made it worse. And the secret would only undermine Hayley's faith in her husband. Harry knew he would discover more facts when police forensics discovered them but right now Karl was burying himself. Karl's solicitor listened but offered no comment.

"Maybe you or Sarika wanted to film yourself having sex with Caryn to broadcast on WalkTank?" Harry suggested.

Karl shook his head with certainty.

"Not even on the spur of the moment?" Harry asked. "Maybe you and Sarika made a plan on the night. Maybe you intended to administer a drug to Caryn's drink but that plan backfired. Caryn resisted and you killed her."

"No."

Harry could see that behind the kids blood-shot and teary eyes he was trying his hardest to think, but at that moment in time Karl's mind was as foggy as a pea-souper.

"So you and Sarika liked to watch each other while self-pleasuring?" Harry stated.

"Yes."

"And you both have others watching too, presumably?"

"Yes." Karl sighed in an embarrassed tone, his dirty little secret was out in the open now.

"Does your wife Hayley take part?"

"No. But it's not cheating." A typically naive response. How would his wife react? Would she feel that he hasn't been cheating? A thought which Karl definitely hadn't considered.

"That's not for me to decide."

"It's not cheating. It's just a bit of fun."

"Okay. So is there anyone else who you have fun with online? I'm sure you have your regulars. Maybe some man or woman who likes you in particular."

Meekness masked Karl's flushed face and he looked once more to his hands for salvation, like the answer was hidden in the cuticles beneath his nails. But apparently that was not the case because the kid shook his head slowly from side to side.

"There's this-" Karl said thickly, his mouth dry, his lower lip quivered, eyes wide with fearful admission.

"Go on, kid. We have twenty seconds."

Karl sighed with resignation once more, eyes pleading to Harry for direction.

Eventually, Karl said: "There's this one girl, Jenny Jane, she's only eighteen and I- that is, you know, it's flattering when someone- She's pretty and she likes watching me and-"

"You sure she's a she and not some fifty year old fat bloke jerking off in his bed-sit in California or somewhere?"

The solicitor stifled a laugh, his professional resolve almost shattered.

"No. She lives in England and she-" Karl stopped abruptly as if what he was about to say wasn't something which would benefit him in a court of law if it got out.

Harry glanced at his watch once more.

"She what, Karl? Times almost up."

"She is here."

"Here?"

"In Hemsby."

Harry knew of Hemsby, of course. It was a popular Norfolk coastal resort twenty-miles from Stalton-on-the-Broad.

"Strewth, Karl. This is getting worse and worse. She lives in the County?"

"No, no. She has come here to-" The words stuck in Karl's throat like razors because the bitter unspoken admission would contradict every claim about not cheating on Hayley.

"Okay. Don't panic." Harry said, although he could already see the end result for Karl when the police detectives and solicitor wrung this fact out of the kid.

Karl folded up at the stomach and buried his face in his arms upon the table, sobbing uncontrollably. It was a sorry sight. His solicitor shrugged noncommittally.

A police detective trying to prove Karl Wilby's guilt would only compound the facts. Back in the day Harry wouldn't think twice about pronouncing the sentence and getting his boys to dig up more dirt to bury himself. Sarika Royal would be another black mark against Karl because however much she were to attest to Karl's innocence, their social life would contradict their claims that they weren't having sexual relations. The media would love it.

Yet there remained some facet about this kid which made Harry feel compassion. Something in Karl psychological make-up that forced Harry to question the loosely threaded facts. Plus there was Karl's wife Hayley to add to the equation. Did she genuinely know the capabilities of her husband and having faith in him? Hayley did not seem totally blinkered by love when she told Harry the details.

Innocent.

Until proven guilty.

Harry pulled out a pen and a piece of paper from his right-hand jacket pocket and placed them both on the table in front of Karl with enough force to make the kid jump.

"Your username and password for WalkTank. Now."

Karl blinked back the tears, confused, his whole body shuddering involuntarily.

"Now!" Harry said more forcefully.

Karl scrawled on the paper and slid both it and the pen across to Harry.

The scrape of metal on the blue carpet as Karl's solicitor pushed back his chair signalled the end of Harry Kovac's time with his client.

Harry stood up without further ado.

"Thanks." Harry said to his friend. "I owe you one."

The solicitor grinned: "Yes, Harry, you do."

After a quick nod to Karl, Harry Kovac opened the door and stepped into the brand white corridor with its prerequisite deep blue carpet. A PCO walked along the corridor towards him and nodded.

"Hi Harry."

"Morning, Zach."

The PCO passed by without a backward glance. Harry wasn't exactly an unfamiliar face.

Harry Kovac closed the door behind himself and padded silently, thoughtfully, along the corridor to the reception area. No need to sign out in this modern age where CCTV captured everyone. An automated click of the door unlocked it and Harry stepped out of the PIC building into the forecourt, headquarters opposite him. Karl Wilby had imparted much food for thought and Harry digested everything as he walked to his car.

# CHAPTER FOUR

Crane Investigation Services was located in Stapley Court just off Magdalen Street, Norwich. Housed in a modern three-storey glass and steel cuboid building whose identical twin stood opposite, rent was high but worth the added extras. Accessible through imposing black wrought iron gates via the main street, the backside of older office buildings made up the court itself while the name was derived from the original landowner. The Crane's have operated from these premises for five years and share the same postal address as the eleven other occupants spread across the twin buildings.

    Twenty-five years ago Magdalen Street was a hive of fashionable retailers and awash with customers but since the advent of out-of-town retail parks, which have sprouted up on the City ring road, coupled with online shopping, customer habits have altered the landscape of the road. Now it was filled with charity shops, second-hand emporiums, fast food joints and cafes, culturally diverse food retailers, hairdressers, and one solitary independent supermarket whose main business was located out of town. Even the Anglia Square shopping centre looked tired and old, past its prime, as if the council had long ago given up trying to bring people here, despite extensive redevelopment to provide parking spaces new homes and office space. They had failed to make it trendy and relevant.

Harry Kovac had left his car in his favoured above ground location adjoining a small music and television venue. The pay-and-display parking offered favourable discount to those who worked in the immediate area, such as the Crane's and himself.

The walk took him through Anglia Square, past the bus stops, under the Magdalen Street flyover and a further fifty yards to the Stapley Court gates, which he passed through and, meeting nobody, reached the ground floor entrance to the office building. Harry keyed the six digit code into the numerical panel immediately left of the door and heard the familiar click.

The time was ten thirty and he was well over an hour and a half later than he would've liked to have been, but the time hadn't been wasted.

The small square lobby was empty and the hiss and click of the outer door made minimal sound behind him.

Harry bounded up the two flights of stairs until he reached the first-floor landing, the full length and width glass walls which surrounded the stairs let natural light within the eco friendly building. He strode down the sun-drenched corridor past the first door which was that of the offices of Rodwell Model Agency, a family run independent company who specialised in child models. They had used Crane's services quite often over the years to vet clients. Harry had seen many unusually costumed children pass through their doors in a relatively short time.

Two doors presented themselves at the far end of the corridor. The nearest and window facing door belonged to Crews & Jones Solicitors. A handy practice to have next to the office of Crane Investigation Services.

Harry pushed open the door with the Crane name stencilled upon it and Daphne Crane immediately looked up from her corner positioned workstation, grinned at him and tapped her wristwatch.

"What time do you call this?" Daphne said with the grin pinching her cheeks. Her eyes showed signs of strain and laughter lines were joined by wrinkles, yet she maintained calm efficiency all the time. Daphne was a warm presence facing the troubled souls who sought her office. She possessed a generous hour-glass frame which, when not seated, stood at five-feet six inches and was topped by shoulder length mousy-brown hair, slightly flecked with silver - which was apparently fashionable these days. Daphne's eyes were a light shade of blue, which had been more vivid in her youth, but now they displayed the passage of age, wisdom and much time spent in front of a computer screen. An expressive mouth was lightly shaded by pink lipstick.

"Ten thirty seven, ma'am." Harry replied to Daphne's question. "Or thereabouts."

"That's all right then, nice detective work." Daphne said. "Zero's in his office. Want a coffee?"

"Go on then. Too much coffee has only killed a handful of people I know of." Harry handed a chit of paper with the names Hayley and Karl Wilby, murder victim Caryn Krystyva and WalkTank scrawled upon it in his blocked text, and Karl's handwritten numbers on a separate piece. "Can you check these out for me, please?"

Daphne rapidly ran her eyes across it. "New case?"

"No. at least not officially. Call it a favour for a damsel in distress. Hayley Wilby. I'll explain once I've caught up with the boss."

"I'm the boss." Daphne said and pursed her lips.

"I'm not arguing." Harry held his hands aloft defensively.

Zero's office was through a door on the right-hand side of the reception area, while Harry had the smaller, junior partner office, which was understandable. Harry pushed open the bosses door and behind the desk was the man himself figuratively buried under his usual deluge of morning paperwork. Business was good. Zero looked up at Harry, nodded and smiled his greeting, before he continued reading.

"Anything good?" Harry asked.

"Just the Boothroyd case."

The Boothroyd case had been a relatively simple one: check up on the suitability of a potential employee for a local project developer. These were quite normal cases and Crane handled about two a month for companies who sought not only the best qualified for their offered job but someone who had no skeletons hidden in their closet. Obviously the employee was never aware that a private detective agency had been hired to check up on them, but such searches had become a more common practice in these days of mistrust.

Zero Crane was five years older than Harry and possessed a similar curriculum vitae, if not appearance. Zero was bald, an inch shorter than Harry at six-feet one, stocky of build, fashionably bearded and more casually dressed in black jeans, loose-fitting green checked denim shirt and black trainers; whereas Harry wore businesslike black cotton trousers and lace-up brogues, a pale yellow shirt and black silk tie. He had deposited his charcoal grey sports jacket on the chair back.

Eventually Zero finished reading the paperwork and slipped it into the out-tray on his desk, then looked up at Harry.

"How are things, buddy?" Zero asked.

"Good. Same old same old from last night."

Zero nodded. He knew Harry was referring to the ongoing Churdjiev case: Mrs Churdjiev suspected her husband of cheating and had requested their services to investigate his movements between the times he finished work and returned home. This was to be every day until they came up with a result. Zero had nothing out of the ordinary to report last week, and since Saturday, Harry also had drawn a blank. These kind of jobs continued to be the staple diet of private detectives the world over, and were grist for the domestic mill.

"Typical." Zero acknowledged with a shrug of his shoulders. "I think the wife has a vivid imagination. Nobody would choose to have an affair with her husband, he's a butt ugly hedge funder."

"With money."

"Yeah, but not that much."

"That doesn't matter, old friend. Money corrupts, however meagre."

"Yeah, ain't that the truth."

"Anything new?"

"No."

At that moment Daphne opened the office door and came in with Harry's mug of coffee in one hand and a piece of A5 paper with her handwritten notes upon it in the other.

"A new case beckons." Daphne announced as if on cue. She carefully handed the coffee to Harry and the note paper to Zero, before leaving them.

While Zero read the note, Harry contemplatively blew the steam from his mug. His pursuit on behalf of Hayley was wrong and he would divulge information to Zero when he had any details which might affect the business. In his minds eye Harry could still picture Hayley broken and lost and distraught. He saw her alongside his own daughter, and he knew he couldn't consciously let sleeping dogs lie.

Zero cleared his throat. "Some fella called Stephen Smith has found a letter that he wants us to translate for him."

"Can't he just use Google?"

"Daphne already asked." Zero lifted up the note to emphasise the fact she had written 'Google search suggested' upon it. "Apparently Smith thinks this might offer more investigative work after it's been translated, owing to the nature of the letter and where it was discovered." Zero referred to the note. "And he's paying two grand upfront."

Harry raised a quizzical eyebrow. "Sounds very intriguing. The two grand and the letter."

"That's what I thought."

"He wants us today?"

"Noon."

"He's keen."

Zero opened up a desk drawer and pulled a silver coin from it.

"Heads you go to Smith's." Zero said. "Tails you go to Jones

Harry laughed. "I'd sooner have Smith."

"Me too, buddy."

The Jones case had resolved itself a fortnight ago when the missing daughter they'd been asked to find had turned up. She was dead. Harry or Zero had to go visit their family and offer their condolences along with the awkward delivery of their bill for services rendered, which was never a pleasant thing to do, but if it wasn't carried out soon it would forgotten about. Daphne gave them all the sensitive jobs!

"We have flowers." Zero said.

Harry had noticed earlier a rather sumptuous bouquet in a vase out in the reception area.

"I thought you'd bought them for Daphne because you'd done something wrong."

"I can't afford a bunch a day."

Zero flipped the coin and it came down heads.

"Have fun." Said Harry.

"Thanks a lot, buddy."

"You're welcome." Harry rose from the chair. "I'll see you back here this afternoon?"

"Sure. Don't forget Churdjiev."

"I hope he goes straight home. I'm meeting Parisa later."

"I thought she was in Scotland?"

"Back this evening."

"Young love! How long has it been: one week?"

"Six days. Not that I'm counting, after all, we're grown-ups, not adolescents."

Harry backed out the office and shut the door, coffee still in his hand. He looked significantly at Daphne and smiled.

"You got the new case." Daphne stated.

Harry nodded.

"My poor husband. Oh well, it's all part and parcel of this business I suppose."

"Anything for me yet?"

"Good grief, man, I'm a miracle worker but I'm not that quick. I'll have something for you when you get back from Smith's. So what's this Wilby stuff about anyway? And is WalkTank something other than an internet porn hub?"

Harry briefed her on everything he had already learned about Hayley and Karl and the TAMS murder.

"I guess you're not mentioning this to Zero?"

"No. not yet. Its just a favour I'm doing for Hayley. Like a said: damsel in distress."

"My hero." Daphne said without condescension, while she also nodded acceptance and agreement. "You don't need me to tell you to be careful, you're a big boy."

"I've had no complaints so far." Harry quipped.

# CHAPTER FIVE

At five minutes to noon Harry Kovac patiently waited in the recessed entrance of 54 Queen's Road for the secured glass door to open. He had pressed the buzzer, smiled amicably for the benefit of the fisheye wall camera and tried peering through the glass but could see nothing more than a plain wall painted in magnolia. And still he waited, speculating that perhaps the doorman was taking care of a telephone call or lavatory requirement.

The Norwich office of Stephen Smith's multi-national business was located on the topmost floor of a newly constructed block of units, three storeys high, nestling on top a cheap-jack discount store whose glass-front faced onto St. Stephen's Street, a shopping district. The side Harry was on was pebble dashed onto the lesser used Queen's Road. An old and in much need of repair multi-storey car park rose in dirty grey behind the building. The Norwich City Bus Depot nestled between two buildings further along Queen's Road and it was on one of their inner-city bus links which had transported Harry.

Harry stepped back onto the pavement and looked up, considering the new build atop old and wondered why they didn't just raze the whole block to the ground and begin anew. The post-war disparity somehow cheapened the newness above. Harry wondered if there was some ancient building code which didn't permit alterations to the ground level.

A metallic click emanated from the door when the doorman or receptionist or whoever used an automatic switch to open the lock.

Harry returned to the recess and the door slid smoothly open for him when pushed. Interior air-conditioning hit Harry with its chilliness compared to the mild humidity outdoors. It also tasted and smelled stale. He was pleased he had brought his jacket with him, which he slipped into as the door closed behind him. Harry wasn't a fan of of air-conditioning, it slowed metabolism.

Turning into the interior of the building the lobby opened into a rectangular reception area, its magnolia painted walls adorned with reproductions of famous paintings. Behind a waist-height brushed steel desk stood a man dressed as formally as a five star hotel footman. He was resplendent in pristine white shirt, blue waistcoat and chinos. The uniform fitted tightly against his athletic frame and his build and alert face signalled him as capable in a fight. Not a man to be trifled with. A closed red door was behind him and the desk was free from clutter.

"Good afternoon, Mister Kovac." The man's greeting was clipped, cheerful and alert, his voice a falsetto which jarred with his physical appearance. "You need the top floor. The lift is over there."

Harry looked to where the man pointed. There were a pair of brushed steel doors which could not be mistaken for anything other than the entrance of an elevator.

"Thank you."

The whole set-up was very efficient and secure and modern, which was often lacking in this day and age, at least by Harry's estimation of security. He had observed six small black fisheye cameras. There were no sounds leaking in through the walls or glass-fronted entrance from outside. No doubt the occupants of this office complex paid a premium for the service and it was worth every penny.

The elevator doors opened automatically when Harry stepped up to them, and he smiled to himself. Evidently the security guard come receptionist had total control over his domain.

Harry entered the small elevator car space, located the floor number buttons and pressed No. 3, it being the top floor. The doors noiselessly slid closed. Harry could usually detect movement no matter how imperceptible but this elevator car was pure stillness. It must be serviced regularly to maintain such perfection of operation. A passenger could be moving up or down or sideways and they wouldn't have a clue.

Or maybe it was stuck and he wasn't moving. He had been stuck in elevators before but wasn't claustrophobic so had no fear.

Eventually the doors opened up onto an entirely different and breathtakingly unexpected view.

A bank of windows existed where there should be none because they faced inwards, butting against a wall adjoining the neighbouring block. The view from them was of a striking snow-capped mountain range that receded as far as the eye could see. The sun was where it should be in reality, and had the effect of casting a natural light and shadow into the room as if real, although it obviously was not real. This was a one-hundred percent accurate representation of reality with clouds shifting, wisps of snow falling in front of the sunshine and birds circling around one of the peaks. It was the sort of view to admire and be inspired by, not to mention awestruck by its sheer majesty.

Harry was well and truly taken aback.

He had failed to notice the man standing behind a beverage bar in the near right-hand corner of the long room until he laughed.

Tearing his eyes away from the scenery Harry took in the interior of the room. It was sparsely furnished yet luxurious. Expensive but not vulgar. There were two large cream leather sofas in the middle of a deep-pile red and resplendently patterned Persian rug, parallel to the window, with a dark wooden framed glass-topped table central between them. This area was on a slightly raised stage creating a moat with surrounding blue carpet. A tapestry which Harry recognised as a representative map of Norfolk covered the left-hand wall, very detailed and modern and a fascinating artefact which deserved closer inspection. On the right-hand wall between the faux windows and corner beverage bar were two quite ordinary looking wooden doors.

The room was deceptively spacious. Harry guessed it covered half the depth of the top floor and most of it's width. This illusion of a greater size was created by the spectacular fake view. When the elevator door slid shut one could almost be in an alpine cabin or the Zugspitze.

"Coffee, chap?" Asked his host.

"Black, one sugar, please." Harry answered through gritted teeth: he positively hated being referred to as chap.

A coffee machine ground, clanked and hissed. The host was a man in his late thirties, vertically and spherically challenged but not to ludicrously unhealthy proportions. He had a shiny bald head which he must moisturise to maintain its lustre, friendly dark eyes close together above an aqua-line nose with flared nostrils and a small mouth with barely any lips that showed pearly white teeth and a constantly darting tongue. He was flamboyantly dressed in a bright printed shirt and printed cotton baggy trousers, and would certainly attract attention on the streets of Norwich City. Whether he possessed a unique fashion choice or was a fan of celebrities such as Freddie Mercury or Elton John was impossible to tell, but the curious style somehow suited his frame and face.

Harry stood patiently beside the mahogany bar-top and remained captivated by the alpine view, but his curiosity was soon averted by the chrome and steel drink machine which the man operated deftly, from which a variety of mechanical sounds emitted.

Finally the machine dispensed a generous serving of black liquid into an oversized mug that suited Harry perfectly.

Once completed, Harry asked: "Is that all it does?"

The man laughed jovially and extended a small, almost dainty, hand which Harry shook.

"Climmy."

Harry tried not to raise an eyebrow at the curious name for this curious fellow, who laughed like laughing was going out of fashion and possessed a wet limp handshake.

"I don't need to tell you I'm Harry Kovac. Did you say your name was Climmy?"

"Mum wanted to call me Jimmy, Dad wanted to call me Clive. They settled upon Climmy. Personally I would've preferred Jive." The laughter once more which would've been sustained were it not for Harry's stony expression. "So what do you think, chap?" Climmy eagerly indicated toward the alpine expanse with a flourish of his small hand.

"Very nice." Harry said truthfully.

"Me and Stephen got the idea from Elton John when we met him in Vegas. A mate of ours took us to Elton's suite at the Bellagio and he's got a wall which keeps changing, more like photos and scenery of places he's visited. Elton's a sweet guy, a real old-school diamond. Anyway, Stephen and me incorporated the idea into our Hyde Park HQ and here. They're 8k screens." Climmy nodded wistfully, his bright eyes full of joyful recollection and self-satisfaction, hoping to impress but realised he was hard pressed to do so. "So what's the S.P.?"

Harry was taking a sip from his coffee so didn't feel obliged to respond to the question, if it was a question. S.P. stood for Starting Price and Harry couldn't claim knowledge on the gambling world so concluded this was Climmy's way of asking how things were with a person. Presumably.

"Very good, thank you."

"I bet the private investigation business must be cool. Exciting, I reckon, chap?"

Harry shrugged. "It's the same as any other business, really."

"Except for the guns, I'll bet!" Climmy's eyes brightened with enthusiasm at his own imagination. "And the chases and intrigue and danger around every corner, not forgetting the dames."

"It's not quite like that."

"Yeah, but still-"

"Most of the time we sit around waiting for something to happen or stand around networking."

"But some of the underworld characters you gumshoes deal with must be of the shady variety?" Climmy said, like he had been rehearsing the sentence all morning after researching noir movie detective thrillers.

"A few, I guess. But not every working day is like something from a murky nineteen fifties Mickey Spillane novel."

Climmy laughed so hard that he choked on the coffee, which amused Harry because knowing this man only for a few minutes had grated upon his restraint. Choking would be a good death for him. The man was too cheerful. He was too convivial. Too fake and too Essex! He exuded one-up-man-ship so much so that the surroundings seemed gaudy and out to impress - which was their exact purpose, presumably - but now they palled. Plus Harry really wanted to punch Climmy in the face to show the man what a private investigator could be capable of when in the line of duty and when pushed to patience's limit.

"How does one acquire such trinkets?"

Climmy stared blankly at Harry, not fully comprehending the question.

"What business are you in?"

"A bit of this and that." Climmy replied vaguely, his accent making him sound like a dodgy car salesman. He laughed once more when he realised how vague his answer had been. "We started off running an East-end bookies in the eighties. Those were the days, chap. Yeah. We got into bingo and horse racing after that, and the casinos. Now we got about two dozen different franchises across this fair country of ours. Not too shabby, I'd say."

"What work did you have in mind for us?" Harry asked, not sure he was comfortable with being on first name terms with a man called Climmy who would've preferred Jive. There were a variety of names he would like to call Climmy, but diplomatically he chose to use nothing.

"We can talk shop when Stephen finishes in his Pod."

"Pod?"

"That's right, chap. We've got a relaxation pod out back, along with a small gym. In fact this floor is laid out like an apartment. We've got two bedrooms both en suite and a kitchen. We're only here a couple of months a year so rent the place out the other ten. Not just to anyone, mind. Olly Murs has stayed here, and so's Gary Barlow and Kylie. Not at the same time. And we've even had Judi Dench when she was making that historical film at the city Cathedral. But usually it's footie players who stay here when City are at home, and the occasional City player when they want, ah, privacy."

A noncommittal nod was all Harry gave to this further attempt at oneupmanship. Harry had lived in London for too many years to be impressed by celebrity name-dropping. He had met a few genuine and pretend celebrities around that town, some of whom were visited on official police business. Celebrities are the same as regular folk when is came to law breaking, although their influence and excuses stretched further than those of regular citizens.

"The relaxation pod is extremely exclusive and I don't need to tell you how popular it is in London, right, chap?" No response whatsoever from Harry. "You're from the Old Town ain't you?"

"I worked for Scotland Yard but I wasn't born in London."

"Right, right. I'm from the East End, myself."

"I'd never of guessed."

"Yeah, well, anyway, were was we? Yeah, the pod has got salt water in it straight from the Dead Sea and you lay in it in total darkness. Feels like floating. It's amazing. You'll have to give it a go."

Climmy came out from behind the beverage counter when he once again got an impassive reaction, and led Harry to the sofas. On the table was an A6 sized notepad and black roller-ball pen, plus a used Manila envelope which Harry noticed had a Sutton address upon it and originated from France, judging by the Eiffel Tower postage stamp. It's position signified to Harry that this was what Crane Investigation Services were being hired to pursue.

A second after Climmy eased himself onto the firm sofa one of the twin doors opened and in its frame stood Stephen Smith: entrepreneur, businessman and philanthropist; if Harry believed the claim on the business plaque which had been in the foyer.

What struck a person first and foremost were Smith's lifeless eyes. Almost doll-like ebony pupils and irises surrounded by yellowing sclera. They were unsettling mostly because there was no depth of humanity to them, so one might be staring death in the face or a shark before it tore you apart. Harry could well imagine that any regular person might find them intimidating, frightening, even, but Harry had known people similarly inflicted so was unaffected by them.

Other than those anomalies Stephen Smith's face was quite plain and ordinary, neither handsome nor ugly. He had high cheekbones, narrow lips, a feline nose and a good crop of reddish brown hair which showed no sign of middle-aged greying. Physically his body was in proportion to his generous six-feet one-inch height. The pod had obviously been warm or otherwise Smith had just stepped out the shower because he was sporting a Kimono, wet hair and a red blotchy complexion.

Smith smiled at Harry in greeting, revealing pearly whites similar in brightness to Climmy, but whereas the smile reached Climmy's eyes, there was no reaction in Smith's. Both these men had received extensive and expensive dentistry work, Harry thought, probably in America.

"Mister Smith." Harry said.

"Stephen, chap." Climmy said on the man's behalf, sliding forward to the front edge of the sofa he carefully eased himself to an upright position. "No formalities here.

Without saying a word, Smith nodded toward the envelope on the table and indicated with an effeminate flourish of his left hand for Climmy to give Harry the Manila envelope which was, as already figured, the reason for being there.

"I should've said," Climmy scooped the envelope up and passed it to Harry, "Stephen can't speak. My friend lost his voice at twelve when it broke. Literally." He assumed a forlorn expression. "Doctors couldn't explain why and he's been like it since."

Stephen Smith shrugged in a matter of fact way. His hearing wasn't impaired.

As Harry watched Climmy waddle across to the beverage bar, he couldn't help but think unsympathetically how bizarre a couple these two men were. One needy to help and the other needing help. It was quite clear their friendship had existed for years, maybe even back to childhood, most likely from when Smith lost his voice and Climmy was there to protect him, although if he had been tubby all his life maybe it was a case of two tortured souls finding solace together. If Harry were to be very un-PC he might consider them similar to a freak show double-act at the circus, not that such acts were permitted anymore because of the snowflake society, and rightly so.

Harry turned the envelope around in his hands. Despite being old – the postmark was a faded black from a much used stamper and one could barely read 1989 from it, and certainly no day or month was visible, having completely faded over the years – the envelope was unremarkable. There was no returning address on the rear, so whoever sent it had faith in the postal service of more than thirty years back. Blue ink was used for the addressee Jack Stone and Sutton address, the script being tightly joined, yet neat, and not blocked, unlike what one might expect on the outside of an envelope which had to be read by someone unfamiliar with the handwriting. The written impression of the address was as clear as it had been when it was originally made.

It was unsealed.

Harry carefully turned up the flap and removed its contents, which consisted of a single sheet of very high-grade grained and watermarked magnolia paper. The writer had good taste. Expensive taste. Harry unfolded it to reveal the writer of the envelope was different to the composer of the letter - not only was the script more fluid and precise in the letter, it was also in black ink. There was no address or salutation or signature or date attached to the letter, and it certainly wasn't English except for a string of numbers amongst the words approximately half-way.

"It's Russian."

Climmy nodded, clearly impressed, and smiled at Stephen as if to say that they had chosen the correct man for the task, whatever that task was going to be.

"How is it in your possession?"

"We found it hidden behind an old painting hanging in the bedroom of that house, the one in Sutton, on the envelope."

Harry reread the address: it was in Sutton, not much more than fifteen miles north-east of Norwich.

"Lovely old house it is too, near the river, thatched roof and all."

"A cottage, then."

"Yeah, that's right, chap."

"Other than as a hiding place for the letter, does the painting have any other significant bearing on this?"

"Maybe. We presented it to a local art dealer, friend of ours, Jeremy Devine, and he seems to think it's something special. We dispatched it this morning to a London art gallery whose office is next door to Sotheby's, the auctioneer. Chaps gonna let us know if it's important." Climmy grinned. "Might be worth a bob or two."

"I presume you guys purchased the cottage and just found the painting on the wall?"

Climmy nodded: "Something like that. Our boys found it when they checked the property over after we took possession."

"And you presented it to the seller?"

"No can do. The owner died."

"And you what-? You want us to translate this letter, presumably?"

"That's about the rub of it."

"Why didn't you just use Google to save yourself the money."

Smith stepped up to the table and bent down, picked up the paper and pen, scrawled a few words and handed the pad to Harry, who read: Because I'm a romantic and intrigued where it might lead.

Harry considered the words, looked at Smith, but obviously could read nothing beneath the eyes or beyond the expression. Harry himself could certainly understand the fascination with a letter hidden behind a piece of artwork. He smiled understanding.

"The owner of the house was John Stone." Climmy stated. "Like it says on the envelope, chap. So, yeah, anyway, before we can into possession of the address our estate agent had to carry out all the usual checks, blah de blah de blah. Seems Mr. Stone has only been resident in England since the late nineteen eighties. Nothing unusual there. But before that time he didn't exist. There's no record of John Stone except when he arrived from Berlin." Climmy paused in anticipation of Harry's reaction. "See what we're thinking, chap? He fled Berlin before the fall of the Berlin Wall and he had with him a valuable painting."

Harry nodded: "Oh yes. I follow. An old painting, a man fleeing Germany at the moment of great upheaval, and a Russian letter. You believe there's an intriguing plot to be investigated and you would like us to pursue it?"

"Sure, chap. We thought you'd be able dig deeper than our estate agent could. And if it amounts to nothing you've earned yourself an easy two grand either way."

After a moments considered pondering Harry stood up and carefully slipped the letter back into the envelope, before he tucked it into the inside pocket of his jacket.

"And only a fool would turn down two grand." Harry stated.

Climmy laughed and shook hands vigorously with Harry, and even Smith cracked a smile - a hideous, psychotic smile.

# CHAPTER SIX

Harry took the footpath along the Queen's Road to the roundabout which adjoined St. Stephen's Street, where he continued along the wide shopping boulevard where pedestrians wandered like lost sheep. This was a hub of activity. Buses and taxis collected their passengers. Office workers burst forth from all manner of routes.

Harry was hungry. The nourishment and energy consumed at breakfast had long been burned off but he only had time to get a pastry. Fortunately food wasn't difficult to find in Norwich, and he knew of a very satisfactory sandwich bar just past the discount outlet.

Like pretty much everyone else on the footpath, Harry had a mobile phone in his hand. He checked his texts while walking and deleted two that were junk. He also had a couple of voice messages but they could wait until after his pastry stop.

He purchased a warm cheese and onion slice, paid, and was walking back the way he had come less than three minutes later.

Harry now ate and walked as he checked the first of his voice mail messages. It was from Hayley. She sounded quite calm but drowsy, and told him that she had spoken to Karl who had vaguely remembered Harry's visit. Karl was apparently being questioned further by detectives at one o'clock - adding to Karl's earlier which was taken under, all agreed, excessive duress that might result in inaccuracies. Hayley said that Karl had slept little. She also said she would keep Harry up to date as much as she could. That was all.

The second message made Harry stop abruptly in his tracks, much to the chagrin of a pedestrian who had been following in his wake, head down texting, so had no cause to complain.

Parisa Dane's voice through the miniature phone speaker sounded remote and flat and definitely did no justice to hearing it in person. She apologised for being away and hoped he would be free for their drink later.

Harry took a contemplative bite out of his slice. Text or phone a reply, that was the question. A no-brainer. He phoned.

The dialling tone went on for several seconds, then half a minute. Maybe Parisa was stuck in traffic?

"Hi Harry." Her silky voice emanated from his phone close to his ear. It was music to Harry. He was a gladiator and she his Queen.

"Hi."

"We still on for that drink?"

"Yes, yes."

"Cool. Do you know The Poachers Arms?"

"Sure."

"Eight o'clock okay?"

"Fine."

"Cool. See you then. Gotta go. Bye."

"Bye."

Harry replaced the phone in his pocket. He caught the eye of a man in his fifties who he had never seen before yet the man grinned at him when he walked by. Harry was grinning from ear to ear. Strewth, he needed to get a grip. Six days into his relationship with Parisa and he acted like a giddy schoolboy!

Entering the cube in Stapley Court twenty minutes later Harry bound up the two flights of stairs, strode down the corridor and entered the Crane Investigation Services office, where Daphne remained in the chair behind her desk.

"Haven't you moved at all?" Harry asked.

"You boys make so much work for me where would I possibly be able to go?"

Pulling the Manila envelope with the mysterious letter from out of the inside of his jacket Harry handed it to Daphne with a flourish.

"Sorry," he said, "but are you able to translate this for me? Please. It's the Stephen Smith job."

Daphne looked sternly at him over the top of her glasses, resembling a Head Mistress he knew at high school. But it was, as always, done in good humour.

"Thanks, Daphne. You're a star."

"I know. Zero's in his office dealing with a new case. Go right in, I think he could probably do with the support."

"Oh. Another one of those?"

Daphne nodded. "The stuff you wanted me to look into is on your desk."

Harry poured himself a mug of water from the cooler, drank it down swiftly, and knocked upon the door before going straight in without being invited.

Sat in his chair was Zero, leaning forward, elbows resting on his desk, fingers steepled in the most thoughtful pose he knew.

In the chair opposite was what one might call a cool blonde femme fatale - if this were the forties. She barely wore a red sports bra with matching skirt, fashionable white designer running shoes and very little else. Harry could see a wedding band. Her handbag was hanging lifelessly off the chair back.

When she turned her head to investigate the visitor the movement couldn't be described as a turn in the mundane sense. She twisted at the hip, thrust her chest forward and flicked a stray braid of blonde fringe from her face, which was a far from plain face. Makeup wasn't at a premium in her household. It was applied generously and, in Harry's mind, pointlessly. Why would a beautiful woman want to ruin their natural looks by applying too much makeup? A little was fine. But this attractive face was attempting to cling to the same youthfulness which her body had sustained for forty years. And failed.

Harry caught the look in Zero's eyes during the momentary distraction he had afforded his senior partner. The woman soon lost interest in Harry, who closed the door and moved alongside the desk.

"Will you be able to help me?" The middle-aged woman asked.

Zero released the steepled fingers and lay them flat on the table before he turned to Harry. "This is Adele Parr. She believes her husband is cheating on her."

Harry nodded thoughtfully.

"And the twat is trying to kill me." She added vehemently.

"Really?" Harry said with a raised eyebrow.

"Yeah, really." She replied sourly.

"Have you gone to the police?"

"Course I have. I'm not stupid! I just told him." Adele stabbed a finger in Zero's direction. "Pigs ain't interested. They'll be interested only when I'm dead."

Harry addressed Zero with gravitas. "I believe this lady needs our help, Zero." He turned back to Adele. "If you leave your details with Daphne, and omit nothing, we will do our utmost to discover what your husband is scheming."

"Scheming!? He's shagging some ginger bitch and wants me dead, that's what he's scheming!"

Harry nodded compassionately. "I understand, Mrs. Parr. But there are requirements you need to supply us before we can proceed. We need your address, phone number, and where your husband works and his car registration and, as you clearly have a suspect for whom your husband is having an affair with, we need her name too. So, for us to proceed accordingly, if you would like to see Daphne she can take down all the relevant details." Harry opened the door. "Daphne. Can you process Mrs. Parr?"

"Oh, sure."

Their new client looked from Zero to Harry, weighing them up, probably thinking that all men are the same: cheaters. She wasn't a crier, that was for certain. Unsticking herself from the chair she straightened her minimal skirt material and followed Harry into the outer office where he drew back the chair for her.

Daphne handed him the Manila envelope and the letter with an additional two sheets of hastily written A4 paper, and grinned sarcastically at him.

"Thanks, Daphne, you're a genius."

Adele Parr lowered her contoured frame into the chair in reception, elbows squeezing her breasts fit to burst out the barely there top.

"Be seeing you, Mrs. Parr."

"Sure."

Harry reversed himself back into Zero's office carrying the letter and paperwork, and closed the door behind himself. Zero burst into laughter which he had to stifle to prevent too much noise.

"Come on, Zero." Harry said with a voice of reason, lowered so he couldn't be heard through the wall. "She might be genuinely concerned for her safety and not just an attention seeker."

"Are you kidding? Who would cheat on a woman with a body like that?"

Harry had no answer for that one so he referred to Daphne's paperwork, which was a roughly scrawled translation of the Russian letter. Impressive work carried out in under five minutes. Basically, the author claimed to be one Waltraud Koenig- John Stone's real name, perhaps? - an Austrian who had fled Berlin to protect his family against those who might wish them harm through association. The letter requested that whomever should find it might want to proceed with caution if they pursue the number - pity Waltraud Koenig didn't specify to what the number was pertaining.

Harry handed over the letter and translation to Zero. While the senior partner read through Daphne's words, Harry skimmed over the mental picture of the long number and wondered what it was.

"Smith'll want us to investigate that number next." Zero said. "Any ideas?"

"If it was shorter I would've said the combination for a safe. The painting might be the first artefact in a trail."

"A storage warehouse? Maybe the number is part of coordinates. You know, longitude and latitude."

"Maybe. Except there are too many numbers."

"How about a bank account and sort code?"

"Possibly. Whatever it is, it's obviously located somewhere in Europe."

Zero nodded thoughtfully. The letter had been posted in France so it was safe to assume a European origin for the number.

"Why not a post office box?" Zero proposed.

"The numbers for post office boxes differ wildly across the continent. And this was sent in 1989. Maybe it's a bank deposit code."

"A safety deposit box? But where's the key?"

"Maybe our friend Stephen Smith has it. Maybe it's on a bunch of keys that goes with the rest of the house which Waltraud Koenig or John Stone owned." Harry shrugged. "There are endless possibilities but I'm beginning to lean toward the bank account or safety deposit box angle. I've come across them before and this loosely fits the bill. And if there are more paintings or whatever then where best to securely store them."

"We might be barking up the wrong tree."

"Of course that's a possibility. Anyway, I have an old friend in London who could help. He's an expert on those things."

"Okay. But this-" Zero consulted the translation of the Russian- "Waltraud Koenig who wrote the letter to himself. My wife is trying to find out more about him?"

"Sure."

"What if it's just a load of gibberish?"

"Then Smith is wasting his money. And we're still getting paid."

Zero twisted his mouth into a thoughtful mask. The letter had been a confession of regret and mixed feeling regarding patriotism, written with anger by a man whose only choice had seemed to be fleeing death and starting afresh, and alone. Waltraud Koenig had chosen to sever ties with family and friends and work. A brave decision and probably one not unique to the man himself. Many outcasts throughout history had been required to sever themselves from one life for whatever reason. Why had Waltraud Koenig made that decision for himself?

"It goes without saying," Harry said, "that Daphne will find out as much as she can about Koenig, and you've gotta admit it's an intriguing combination and not an altogether uninteresting situation. A fugitive from Berlin, a priceless painting, and a mysteriously hidden letter written in Russian."

"Sure. But the painting might be something this Koenig fellow threw together himself to make the letter seem more interesting than it truly is. We're not art investigators. We're private detectives who deal mostly with...well, people like that blonde out there."

"Which is exactly why we should tackle this much less predictable intrigue."

Zero nodded. He didn't need much persuasion or encouragement to earn two thousand pounds.

"Time for me to move. I'll contact Smith and tell him the news and find out if he has a bunch of keys." Said Harry. "Although I'll get his friend Climmy. Don't ask. Something about his parents disagreeing on what name to give him. Weird. Both of them!"

# CHAPTER SEVEN

Harry's smaller office space was sparsely furnished: a second-hand oak desk which could have been antique but served its purpose; a pair of leather upholstered and very comfortable swivel chairs, one for himself, the other for a client; an old bureau which was Harry's favourite piece of furniture because he felt it had character within its many compartments and drawers. The walls were adorned with various law-enforcement diplomas and commendations, along with pictures of his daughter. For added quirky comical affect, and the fact that Zero Crane liked movies and the noir genre more specifically, there were framed one-sheet posters for The Maltese Falcon, The Big Sleep and Double Indemnity on the wall either side of the door. They made Harry smile.

He sat, picked up his mobile phone and tapped out a message for Nathaniel Beckley, his banker friend in London who he hoped could identify the number or confirm what Harry thought it might be.

Next Harry dialled the office of Stephen Smith and Associates – he scrawled a message to himself on a notepad while waiting for the connection, a reminder to ask Daphne for information on Smith's precise business credentials, for no real reason other than curiosity.

"Whaddaya know?" The voice of Climmy asked cheerily – too cheerily, in Harry's mind, but everyone is different!

"It's Harry Kovac. Crane Investigation Services."

"Harry, my friend! What's the S.P.?"

Harry winced. Climmy was way too loud in person but he positively shouted down the phone like most people were prone to do - but why when it was totally unnecessary?

"We translated the letter." Harry said and explained what it said. "I've got a friend in London who might be able to confirm what the number pertains to. I've contacted him and will see if he is available tomorrow."

"Sounds epic. You going to the big city?"

"Yes. My friend deals with people better face to face."

"Okay, cool. Any expenses, keep your receipts and Stephen and I will reimburse you with question, chap. Oh, yeah, we've got early news on the painting. It could be a Picasso."

Harry was genuinely surprised. "Truly?"

"Yeah, yeah. The guy we know is getting a second opinion from his mate at the Royal National Gallery. Says this mate is Royalty himself, and in fact, I-"

"Do you have a bundle of keys from John Stone's property?"

"Oh, yeah. Why?"

"Just an idea. We might need one if in fact the number is a safety deposit box."

"Sure, chap. I'll have keys ready for you when you need them."

"Okay. Gotta go, be seeing you."

Harry disconnected the call before he told the annoying fellow to be quiet, using similar words to be quiet, but one word would rhyme with luck and the other is opposite to on. Climmy liked his anecdotes and name dropping and Harry was not impressed by such people. Plus, he had had enough of the conversation.

While Harry read through the information which Daphne Crane had compiled on Karl Wilby and the murder, he inserted some buds in his ears which connected via Bluetooth and selected a random playlist on his phone. Music helped him focus.

Karl Wilby's digital history was quite sparse. Not a bad thing if you want to stay under the radar, although murder flips the coin against you. All this meant was that Karl had up to recently led a pretty mundane existence, which consisted of the usual journey through school, college, work - TAMS Supermarket in Stalton-On-The-Broads from 2004 to date - opening a bank account, learning to drive, getting car finance, getting a passport, setting up home. Nothing spectacular on record and certainly no anomalies. Hayley Wilby had done pretty much the same only she was a pre-school teacher born in Hoveton, the neighbouring village to Karl's, and had travelled more.

The murder victim Caryn Krystyva had moved around as befitted a big supermarket manager. She was born in Hertfordshire, graduated college with a business degree, had started work at her local TAMS Supermarket as a check-out girl and moved up through the ranks, with the Norfolk store being her last. Single. Traveller. Golfer. And out of credit card debts with otherwise no black marks. Caryn was a registered member at Beeston Grange in a Norwich suburb, where she owed a substantial gambling debt at the country club casino: £73,450.

Harry drummed his fingers on the desk and leaned back in his chair.

Could she possibly have been murdered over that debt? Was it enough money to kill for? To setup some innocent guy for? More likely her killing was a crime of passion but Beeston Grange was a fifteen minute drive so worth a visit, and Harry would have time before the last job of the day. Nothing ventured, nothing gained, as the saying went.

WalkTank was exactly as Harry thought: a social network for sex. Daphne Crane had helpfully written a few web links for Harry to try which were relevant to the site, purely for research purchases, Daphne humourlessly added as a sidebar.

Karl's female work friend Sarika Royal was the daughter of a Vietnamese orphan and had a much more interesting background, it was little wonder Karl gravitated in her orbit. Sarika's parents divorced when she was five. She grew up with her Mum but she took her own life when Sarika was seven. There was no information on her school years but evidently she married at age eighteen, was divorced at nineteen, learned to drive and moved from Kent to Norfolk age twenty - probably to escape her old life and begin anew. There was a driving conviction and bad credit score to her name.

Jenny Jane was a much more sketchy proposition. Apparently the only details which Daphne could drag up was the WalkTank profile. No history whatsoever. Which meant that the meeting Karl Wilby was planning to have with this person was definitely a setup. Some entity was going to exploit Karl Wilby on a financial level. Poor, naive fool.

Another motive for murder? Had Karl already gotten himself involved with a blackmail scheme? Maybe he had failed to deliver so this set-up accusation was payback.

Harry mentally shrugged to himself: never discount the improbable.

Daphne Crane had took it upon herself to print a picture of both Sarika Royal and Jenny Jane. Presumably both were profile pictures of sorts from WalkTank. The very real Sarika was a carefree and stunning young woman who undoubtedly had many followers of both sexes. Jenny Jane, or whatever her name might really be, was alluring and sexual and clearly comfortable exploiting people.

Harry absentmindedly lingered over the pictures of the attractive young women, Sarika in exotic underwear was more naturally lit, whereas Jenny was posed and revealed more allure.

When Harry realised what he was doing he promptly put the pictures with the other information which Daphne had gathered for him and slipped them into a desk drawer.

It was two-twenty.

Beeston Grange was to be first on the agenda for Harry, followed by the Churdjiev investigation. There was no time for staring at dirty pictures!

# CHAPTER EIGHT

Crane Investigation Services reception wasn't large but seemed more compact still when Harry Kovac opened the door of his office into it.

Daphne Crane was standing behind her desk, arms folded defiantly beneath her chest, expression stern. Zero stood in front of the open door to his office, a look of innocent objection on his face which was backed up equally by his gesticulation. A tall woman - whose name Harry would later learn to be Annika Smimov - Harry guessed was of Eastern European, possibly even Russian origin, and an even taller and stockier man - Anatoly Polivanova - from a similar region, blocked the entrance and were the reason for his bosses posturing.

Harry wondered how he hadn't heard their arrival then he promptly remembered his ear-buds which he quickly removed.

Harry caught the tail end of a sentence which the tall woman said. Her broken English was accented with a pronounced Russian inflection and truth be told Harry did not understand fifty percent of what she chewed out. When she turned her head to face Harry her impassive dark eyes observed him with total indifference, as if she had trodden in something foul, or he were an unwelcome odour. She wore a severe grey business suit with white shirt and black lace-up shoes. Beneath the clothing Harry got a sense of powerful muscles ready to explode. He could see the sinews in her neck were tight and hard, like that of a wrestler. Her harsh face was makeup free and bore a scar tapering across her cheek from her left ear. She had a matted mop of brown hair which could've been self cut using a mixing bowl, and a small misshapen bowl at that.

The man did not move a muscle. Only his eyes roamed. He regarded Harry like a Siberian tiger might its prey, looking for any weakness before striking. Harry thought that the ill-fitting clothes he sported disdainfully were uncomfortable for the Russian. He he was definitely of a distinguished lineage and more used to the cut of a military uniform. Curiously, though, Harry thought his clothes resembled those of a hotel porters uniform. This was clearly a dangerous fellow. He was the strong-arm and a killer in the literal sense.

"What?" The man said in English which barely contained a hint of an accent, while the resonant timbre reverberated through the air.

"This is Harry Kovac." Zero said tersely. "Our business associate."

The tall woman tilted her head as if she couldn't care less.

"What's going on?" Harry asked Zero and Daphne.

They were both going to answer him but got their words cut off by the Russian woman who was clearly the one in charge.

"I am after Waltraud Koenig's letter." She stated in a tone which afforded no confusion or misinterpretation.

Harry looked at Zero meaningfully, but it was Daphne who responded.

"My translation request was apparently monitored." Daphne said to Harry. "And these nice people want their property back."

Harry raised a quizzical eyebrow. "Their property?"

"Yes." The woman snapped. "We believe it might contain information sensitive to national security."

"Or it might just be some old dead guys rambling love letter." Harry said. "Whose national security are we talking about exactly?"

"Moscow's."

"And you represent Moscow?"

"Of course." The woman replied proudly.

The Russian hulk shouldered forward, he craned his head toward Harry and puffed out his chest menacingly. "You will give it to us." He said it in enough of a matter of fact way that Harry immediately became defensively alert. The man's weakest spot would be his groin.

"No." Harry said. "We shall not."

A hand placed on the man's shoulder by his partner prevented the guy from making a fool of himself. Harry was disappointed that a fight wasn't launched, he had prepared himself for it since entering the reception and encountering the situation.

The woman addressed Harry, producing a grin which would have terrified a child. "May I ask why not?"

"Yes, you may."

After a brief pause the woman asked: "Why will you not let us have the letter?"

"Because its not ours to give and it's not here anymore."

"It's ours to take."

"Like I said: we don't have it here."

The woman sighed in exasperation. "Then who does have it?"

"The owner."

"And-" the woman said with controlled patience, "where might we find the owner."

"That's client confidentiality."

The Russian guy looked at his boss with unconfined expectancy, like he was asking permission to go about this questioning his way, which would probably be through the use of violence. But she was able to stop him with a single glance before she regarded Zero, who shrugged, Daphne, who nodded, then back to Harry.

"Okay." She said. "We shall find your client without any trouble and if he doesn't possess it, then this won't be the last you will hear from us."

Zero snorted a derisive laugh.

Harry said: "Can't you say something a bit more original than that?"

Before she lost her temper the woman brushed out the office and into the corridor. The man stepped up nose to nose with Harry and they locked eyes, neither displayed an ounce of scare at the intimidation.

"I look forward to it." Harry said at the unspoken promise before the man followed his boss.

Harry butted the door shut.

Daphne uttered a relieved curse and sat heavily in her chair.

"Coffee?" Zero asked his wife and Harry.

"Not for me." Harry replied. "I'm pumped up enough!"

"Definitely for me." Daphne sighed.

"So who were those guys?" Harry asked.

"You know as much as we know." Zero said, percolating some coffee in the office machine.

What was it about the smell of coffee which could alter a persons mood? And why was paying through the nose for a cup of coffee in an establishment so fashionable? It's just coffee! Those trendy shops have replaced pubs for social gathering yet in real terms their prices are comparable.

"They show you any I.D.?" Harry asked.

"None." Daphne said.

"We asked." Zero said. "And that's what the argument was about before you arrived. Who do you think they represent? They're certainly not Waltraud Koenig's family."

"Not quite." Daphne laughed.

Harry shook his head in agreement. "You don't send a pair of thugs to collect a letter unless there's the possibility there's something in it which is of value. An what was that about national security? It intrigues me no end because I don't suppose they were from Russian Intelligence, but anything's possible."

"Russian Mafia?"

"Possibly."

"They didn't ask about the painting." Daphne said.

"We don't know if that's significant." Harry said. "Perhaps they knew nothing of it. They were obviously alerted by your internet search for the name Waltraud Koenig. Any more background info on him?"

"Not yet."

"What do you think this is about?" Zero asked the room.

"Whatever it is, it's bigger than a letter." Harry said. "Can you run the picture of those two through a database?"

Daphne nodded like it was a dumb question. "Don't we need to warn Stephen Smith?"

"If those two thugs want to find out about Smith," Harry said, "then it'll be easy enough for them if they're now monitoring our computers."

"True enough."

Zero said. "We had better tell Smith what just happened, as a precaution. We can't afford to lose such a well paying customer."

"You're all heart, darling." Daphne said.

"The plot thickens."

Harry glanced at his watch. "I'd better be off."

"Stay safe."

"Always do."

# CHAPTER NINE

Karl Wilby stood sobbing amidst the tepid spray of shower water. His reason for feeling especially despondent was fully justified, for Karl had been accused of a murder and the evidence was stacked against him. He could not recall the chain of events in their entirety. There was no hope, so the detective had said. His memory was even vague surrounding the work party up-to a certain point. Drink and drugs had been blamed. Karl could certainly remember drinking plenty of alcohol, who wouldn't at a staff party? But drugs? He had never done drugs.

The poured-concrete floor tore a chill through the souls of his feet and he tried to keep moving but couldn't be bothered.

Karl stood alone in the cold stark shower. He thought it was afternoon but truly he had lost all sense of time and couldn't be certain.

And he was dog-tired.

Like his Gran used to say: he could sleep on a linen line.

The prison populace despised those who raped and killed women. Karl believed there existed an undisclosed coda in prison which dictated that men who committed crimes against women or children were the lowest form of scum and summarily judged for their crimes by the inmates themselves.

Karl was accused of the rape and murder of a woman.

This was supposedly a transient time until his case came to trial or something, again, Karl couldn't be a hundred percent certain.

His mind whirled like a turbulent tempest

If he was found guilty, he asked himself if he would be kept away from the populace. Probably except for meal times, which would consist of porridge for breakfast; a hot lunch of mashed potatoes, soggy veg, and fatty sausages; and a dry watery ham or processed cheese sandwich for dinner. Not an appealing thought. Karl had no appetite at the moment, but he figured he deserved none after what he had apparently done.

Karl shivered.

How would he bear the stares from the hardened criminals when in prison. They would make him well aware that he was an undesirable.

Bless his present solitude.

Bless his solitary shower time.

Lifer criminals were intimidating.

Karl had always shied away from confrontation. He positively avoided going places where there was the likelihood of trouble. Karl was mild mannered and friendly. A kindly person. So this environment was anathema to his personality.

He sobbed, eyes stinging.

Rape and murder? Was he really capable of one or both?

Karl had grown up in a happy family. His parents were and remained happily married. His brother and sister lived contented lives. Karl too was content in his existence. He had friends and a social life and enough experience to suit. He was married. Blessed. His wife Hayley was a primary school teacher and a girl guide leader. Hayley was nice and happy and content. She loved Karl and he loved her. They were happily married in their own home in the rural village where they lived.

Their existence was idyllic.

Truly a Norfolk life.

The quiet, outdoor life.

Karl enjoyed his work at the village supermarket where he was liked, respected, and had many friends.

He had no enemies.

It was the middle of August and Karl should be enjoying fresh air and sunshine, not standing cold and naked under a stream of tepid spray with thoughts about a prison he had heard of all his life yet never visited.

Harsh, stark lighting crashed off the white tiled walls against his skin which appeared pale, loose, flaccid and insignificant. Any sense of pride or manliness and self-esteem had utterly drained from his very fibre.

He was unaware of the hour.

He could only guess the time of day.

Karl's mind was frozen.

The party was a surreal, distant and vague memory. Like it belonged to someone else. The accusation like a surreal hallucination. A movie. He liked movies.

Karl's stomach groaned. He buckled at the waist but nothing came, just a pitiful cry of anguish.

His wife Hayley fought his side. A presence flitting across his vision.

Surreal.

Hayley had visited him since the incarceration, at least Karl could recall that memory. She was full of hope and desperation, encouragement and bewilderment. His wife had also looked tired and pale and hadn't eaten.

How was it that Hayley could see he was innocent but no one else could?

People from the courts or police or whoever they were had questioned him repeatedly that morning. Couldn't they see he was tired?

These people demanded an account of the party, facts and the truth, but how could he, Karl, be expected to fill in details when his memory was fogged from a surreal hallucination of events?

His stomach groaned again, their muscles tightening. He placed both hands on the wall in front of him for support. Was he going to be sick or pass out?

Think happy thoughts.

Hayley was fighting his side. His wife. He must remember this foremost. An unimaginable presence herself. But Karl knew without a doubt that she had visited him, however many tricks his mind played, and however cloudy the events of the party.

Tears.

Hayley had cried.

She had told him not to give up. Which was easier said than done.

A Private Investigator was on the case. Hayley had told him. A P.I.! On his case! Such a notion would make him laugh if he could only just remember what laughter was like. And is there really such a service in Norwich, Norfolk, England? No. It was probably some kook exploiting a desperate young woman's plight. But the guy who had visited Karl that morning seemed genuine. And not a figment of his psyche.

Karl clenched a fist in anger.

Someone out there was exploiting his wife while he, Karl, was helpless to protect her. Karl was impotent with fear.

Tears of despair failed him. He cried out. He felt the cold steel of scissors in his fist. They were open. The sharpest, narrowest blade was at his opposite wrist and the vein beckoned beneath his cold skin.

Karl stared trancelike.

He remembered vaguely picking them up in the room where he had undressed. He felt clever. The guard hadn't seen him. They were nail scissors but sharp.

Suicide was an easy way, the cowards way out, some might say, but Karl could see no other option. His life lay in ruins. Twenty-eight years old lived reasonably well, enjoyed in his way and not a slave to conformity, no rules broken.

Until the party.

Murder and rape.

Now the questions, the accusations, the sullying of his name, the embarrassment to his dear, dear wife.

Poor Hayley.

He dropped the pair of scissors onto the wet floor where they clattered loudly. Or was it his imagination?

Karl felt remorsefully impotent. He knew he didn't have the guts to kill himself so how could he possibly commit a crime of passion? Why was the floor turning red?

He hated confrontation and was now exposed to the ultimate proof of his own cowardice.

Karl looked directly into the cold shower spray, the water stinging his eyes. He wished someone would put him out of his misery. Kill him. Or maybe an act of God strike him down. He needed the decision taken out his hands. Why were his hands running with red water?

# CHAPTER TEN

Beeston Grange was a hotel and country club accessible via a slip-road off the westbound A1270, Norwich - the NDR, as it is known locally - although that wasn't always the case. It sat virtually central in a triangle of city suburbs consisting of Rackheath, Spixworth and Sprowston. A serious rethink was in order though because during morning and evening rush hour it was treacherous trying to leave The Grange onto the NDR, so planners proposed an alternative route via Beeston Park, through a new housing development which would be directly attached to a roundabout where motorists could leave in greater safety.

Harry Kovac slowly drove over the speed limiting hump onto the long and straight gravel-in-tar driveway of Beeston Grange, with its prerequisite 'welcome' and 'have a pleasant stay' signage either side of the entrance.

It was four o'clock on a sunny afternoon.

Harry had asked Daphne Crane to keep him abreast of any new developments which might be garnered from the Karl Wilby case. Presently he knew as much as the police, and maybe more, because Daphne had done a thorough job finding out what information was available in the public domain, and via her own ingenuity when digging deep, on both Karl Wilby and his victim, Caryn Krystyva.

The entire one-hundred and eighty acre property was surrounded by tall ash trees four deep, and contained within an eight-feet tall perimeter fence. Originally the entire site was an expanse of woodland until gradual development took place over a timeframe of just over one-hundred years, between 1847 and 1950, that formed the present business. An unmade footpath wound it's way through the trees and was often used by resident joggers or just those wanting a peaceful stroll.

At the top of the driveway was the Grange itself. It was a Tudor gothic farmhouse building designed by renowned nineteenth century Royal architect Jason H. Oxer. Many of the original walls and beams had been preserved, offering forty bespoke bedrooms plus twenty modern, and a unique dining experience in its reconstruction of a Medieval Hall. Although it's shell was considered a National Heritage Site it had its ancient chimneys removed over sixty years ago over safety concerns, and it had been equipped with double-glazed windows, reinforced flooring, an attached rear conservatory and modern heating and electrical system.

New blended seamlessly with old, which meant the frontage and left-hand side of the building had been filmed for period television and film productions, offering an unspoilt backdrop across the first five holes of the golf course.

Harry steered his car along the right-hand gravel drive toward the car park and, as golfers fondly refer to the

Clubhouse, the nineteenth hole. It wasn't difficult to find a space to park up that afternoon.

The Clubhouse was built only twenty years ago on the exact plot of its predecessor. A fire caused by discarded cigarettes had torn through the original construct destroying it utterly. This new building contained a small restaurant, shower block and changing cubicles, plus the Pro Golf Shop. Accessible through the rear was the driving range and practice putting greens.

Harry noted how spotless and well kept the grounds which he could see were. He climbed out of his car and automatically locked the door behind himself.

The gravel crunched beneath his boots, a sound which, for some reason, was one of his favourites.

He reminded himself that this club was quite exclusive and it's rich clientele maintained it by paying the price for luxury. Which was little wonder Caryn Krystyva mounted up gambling debts here. Harry surmised the likelihood that she wasn't the only one to owe management large sums of money. But was that something they would kill for? The idea seemed unlikely, even to Harry. In this day and age wrong-arming someone for their debt was done through the courts, not by murder.

So the question Harry had to ask himself was: what did he hope to learn?

Doubtless he could stir a few people up, find out if anyone would bite against the accusations he could throw at them.

But he couldn't make them too obvious. People were too sensitive these days and he was more likely to come across a whiner who went to the police and the end of the investigation would ensue.

Maybe Caryn Krystyva had a regular playing partner here on the golf course who might have joined her at the casino. Someone who would be able to shed light on her character and be willing to divulge the extent of her gambling.

Either way, Harry was going to dig up some roots and expose the dirt. If there was any dirt to be exposed.

When Harry powered-up his smartphone it nagged at him to check his messages. Three had arrived. The significant one was from Nathaniel Beckley, who said he would be happy to help Harry any which way he could and that it would be good to catch up. Harry texted his reply and pocketed the phone.

Striding through the car park Harry pushed his way through the smoked glass double doors - no automatic sensor - into the Pro Golf Shop. This cube space was naturally lit by its glass roof and contained all the usual golfing apparel, equipment and paraphernalia the most avid player could wish for to improve their game.

Harry couldn't think of a worse sport to waste ones time playing. Why spoil a good walk, as the quote goes.

The shop assistant, if that's the correct terminology for a golf shop assistant, was busy pretending to unnecessarily re-stack a shelf of boxed balls by expensive designer companies which Harry hadn't heard of and didn't care about.

Phil or Nick or Bernard turned his head and forced a grin when he saw Harry walking across the carpeted floor toward him. The carpet was appropriately green. Maybe some sixth sense told him that Harry wasn't a golfer. The guy was in his late twenties, average in height and build, fresh-faced and had an immaculate blonde nest of hair.

The definitely sensed Harry wasn't going to be a paying customer because there was no eagerness to his reaction, so Harry beat the chap to it with practiced fake friendliness: "Good morning. How are you?"

"Fine." Was the cautious reply.

"A friend of mine is a member here and recommended you to me."

"We don't offer a pay and play club, sir. You have to either be a member or guest at the hotel."

"That's fine. She said I could play with her."

"Sure. What's your handicap?"

"Me." Harry laughed. "My friend is Caryn Krystyva. She plays here frequently, so she said."

"Sure. I know her."

"Brilliant. Is her regular playing partner here? Caryn told me her name but I can't remember it for love nor money."

"Georgette Roshier?"

Harry's face brightened, pretending to recognise the name: "That's her!"

The assistant checked the wall clock before he said: "She should be about half way round by now."

"Splendiferous. Thanks very much for your help. Whereabouts do I-" Harry let the sentence tail off and looked toward the entrance.

"It's easy. Left out the door, down the side of the Clubhouse and the ninth green will be in front of you."

"Thanks. Ah- I've not met Georgette before, just heard about her from Caryn. Could you describe her so I know who to look out for?"

The assistant laughed: "Sure. She's quite tall." He demonstrated by putting a flat hand beside his own head height. "Long brown hair, late twenties and wearing golf clothing. Trust me, you can't miss her."

"Thanks. Oh, Caryn told me about the gambling which is permitted here."

"That's the casino in the hotel."

"Right, of course. Is that open to anyone?"

"Anyone with, ahem, money."

"Splendiferous. Thanks again. No doubt I'll be seeing you soon."

"Sure. You're welcome."

Harry followed the directions given him and was facing down the ninth fairway on the edge of the wide, flat green. The flag fluttered and snapped in the breeze atop the pole, before returning to a flaccid state. An avenue of trees reached two-hundred yards distant ahead. On top of a slightly raised hillock two people were conversing. One player was placing his ball. Neither were female.

Twenty yards ahead and to the right was a gap in the trees which, Harry guessed, would lead to the tenth tee. It was a nice morning so a stroll in the countryside would be pleasant and it was a happy coincidence that Georgette Roshier was here anyway, so it was worth tracking her down. On the other hand it might prove to be a waste of time.

Harry took four long strides to his right, mindful of the bloke teeing off on the ninth, thrust his hands in his pockets and approached the opening in the trees. As he got nearer he saw movement on a well trodden plinth of grass which was the slightly elevated tenth teeing position. And he knew this was Georgette setting her white ball on the small red tee stuck in the ground.

As he got nearer Harry was taking in the young woman, and what a fabulous sight she was. Golf clothing wasn't the most flattering apparel but Georgette wore the red shoes, muddy brown slacks and Nike t-shirt very well indeed. Her dark brown hair, which the assistant had described, was tied back with a white scrunchy in a silky ponytail which bobbed jauntily with her every movement. Georgette was indeed quite tall, perhaps five-feet ten, which probably benefited her golf swing. Harry could see that she was quite lithe in her movements, which were almost dance like, all sweeping stance and fluid arms. Side-on Harry could make out the flatness of her stomach and the swell of breasts contained by a sports bra.

When he got within ten yards Georgette must've clocked him out the corner of her eye because she turned her head, before swivelling her body to face him.

There were no other word to describe Georgette but stunning. She was possibly one of the most naturally attractive persons whom Harry had had the pleasure to clap his eyes upon. She had a healthily tanned face and clear skin which highlighted the brown twinkling from her eyes, big and full and mesmerising. He nose was cute, her lips were full and luscious, and she had wonderfully high cheekbones. Georgette oozed femininity.

Standing casually, left leg slightly bent, hand resting on the club handle, fingers curled around the hilt, head tilted with curiosity, Georgette looked demure and strong at the same time. Harry had known femme fatales in his life and career, and almost forgot his purpose for being there.

"Hi." Georgette's voice was husky, confident and musical, and of Mid-England breeding without any hint of a colloquial accent. And she had only said one word, a simple greeting which from anyone else might've sounded ordinary, but from the lips of this young lady it was extraordinary.

"Good morning." Harry said. He knew he was smiling. He couldn't help it, she was infectious. He was a man in his late thirties reduced to a teen again, much like he was with Parisa. "You must be Georgette."

An inline of her head sent the ponytail across her cheek which she swept back: "The one and only. And you are!"

"Harry." He said, extending his hand. "Harry Kovac."

The dark-haired Goddess slipped her gloved hand in his, curled her fingers around and they shook. Harry didn't want to let go. It was a mesmerising experience being beholden to the ethereal aura which extended from Georgette's brown eyes. Her grip was firm, comfortable, like a touch from heaven. Harry's only regret was that her skin was encased in a golf glove.

Before the moment could get awkward Harry reluctantly released her.

"I would like to think you've come here socially," Georgette said, "but I don't think that's the case."

Her words didn't contain any harsh notes and she didn't retreat. Instead she shifted her footing, swinging the club up so it rested on her shoulder. A sign of caution to anyone who might act untoward?

"That's very astute of you." Harry said, dubiously eying the metal shaft which glinted in the sunshine.

"Don't worry. I've never hit anyone with my seven iron."

"That's good to hear."

"So what's this about?"

"Caryn Krystyva."

Georgette's eyes turned fiery, her features hardened, which was a combined blessing and travesty.

"I thought as much." Georgette stated. "Are you a reporter?"

"No. I'm a private investigator."

"A private dick. For who?"

"The wife of the accused."

"Fair enough. What do you want to know?"

Harry felt terrible. This beautiful Goddess before him was now angry at him. All he wanted was to worship at her feet. He had obliterated their initial chemistry, if only such a thing had existed in his mind only. In another life, perhaps. Harry was a grown adult, not some pining love-struck teenager. He was more experienced in life. He should be hardened to the job after twenty years in the police force. There should be no knotting in the pit of his stomach at the regret of what might have been. Which was daft, really, because he had his own blessing in life: Parisa. Harry told himself to grow up.

"I understand you were friends with Caryn. I was wondering if you might know of any trouble she might've been in."

"Apart from being dead, you mean?" Georgette said the words with such contempt they hit Harry like a tonne of bricks.

"Im sorry, I don't mean to-"

"What?"

"I don't want to upset your game. Maybe I chose the wrong moment. I'm an insensitive prick for coming here, but quite honestly, I don't really know what I expect to discover."

Georgette shrugged. Her face remained hardened but something reignited itself in her eyes. The humanity returned. She could see how awkward this had become for Harry and she was regretting her own rigidity.

"I'm sorry." She offered. "I got the news from a friend about Caryn's murder this morning. I was shocked. Deeply. Golf is my way of dealing with things, so here I am."

Relief washed through Harry, which must have transferred itself to to his face because Georgette smiled, and he was once more viewing an angel from his lowly stance, and she knew it, she was well aware of the powers she held over men.

Delving into his inside jacket pocket, Harry pulled out a business card, handing it to her.

"Enjoy your game." He said. "If you have any thoughts, give me a ring."

She turned the card over in her hand, the long fingers teasing it. She read the print, grinned, and turned her eyes on him without moving her head. It was one of the most seductive actions Harry had ever witnessed.

"I will."

And Harry knew there and then that he would be hearing from her. It took all his will-power, all adult common sense, for Harry to turn away from her and walk back toward the Clubhouse.

That was a waste of time.

Mature logic promptly slapped him in the face. Harry had upset that femme fatale and hell hath no fury like a woman scorned. He had given her his card. She now knew who he was and could report him for harassment if whimsy took her. What the hell had he been thinking. He was love struck and love blind. Not by this golfer, Georgette Roshier, that was ludicrous. Georgette was fiery and exciting, beautiful and flirtatious, but she was clearly like that with everybody, including, most probably, Caryn Krystyva.

As Harry walked back to his car he mentally struggled her off and drew back to his actual reason for being there. If there was a link between the murder of Caryn Krystyva and Beeston Grange, he would find out, for Hayley.

A mental image of the Russian guy from the Crane office and his uniform flashed briefly into his head, before being filed under the heading coincidence. It may or may not have been hotel uniform the Russian wore. Maybe the guy had no dress sense or cared nothing about looking stylish.

His smartphone vibrated in his pocket. A text received from Daphne Crane. He learned of Karl Wilby's suicide.

# CHAPTER ELEVEN

Harry was faced with tackling the rush hour exodus from Norwich. Always a challenge because there were so many people in a hurry to get home from work like any other city of it's kind. Invariably there would be heated horn blasts, colourful language, frustrated traffic-light waiting, throbbing engines, and probably thumping sub-woofer rumble from cars not especially designed to impress.

Getting from Beeston Grange through the City outskirts initially proved easy until he pulled into a stream of traffic at Whitefriars, which was heading North. Harry was against the flow, which had its advantages, but not many, as this jam proved. He absentmindedly wondered how many of these motorists were embarking in the type of journey which he was investigating. A surprising number, probably. How many were conducting conversations via their Bluetooth connection? Talking to those who they would be seeing soon anyway and invariably run out of conversation before reaching their ultimate destination. How many were still working, talking to a client or colleague?

All those distractions added to the traffic chaos. It added to the impatience.

Harry's preferred method was to drive alone with the phone switched off and the DAB radio set to Classic FM. This way he could concentrate fully on his driving and employ a distancing from this thoughts. Usually when he reached said destination, whatever was on his mind had ordered itself and meant that dealing with the situation regained calmness.

Another good reason to have the phone off was because of the message from Daphne Crane about Karl Wilby's suicide. Harry knew his phone would be inundated with more messages on the subject, which he could read once at his destination.

Question was: did Karl really commit suicide or was there something more sinister afoot? Yes the kid had seemed at the end of his tether but experience had told Harry that Karl didn't have the guts to take his own life. Yes, when people were pushed far enough they were capable of most things, but there was nothing in Harry's impression of Karl Wilby which added to fatal that outcome.

Either way Harry wasn't going to let it rest now that he had the bit between his teeth. But he couldn't be in two places at once. Tomorrow morning he was going into London, which coincided with the planned meet up that Karl Wilby had arranged with Jenny Jane - or whoever showed up. Harry would just have to ask Zero a massive favour, that was all.

Harry followed the A147 westbound and was immediately snarled up in the traffic which edged forward like a reluctant caterpillar. It was frustrating when a fifteen minute journey on a map took twice that but the soothing sounds of Prokofiev and Saint Saens and the rousing

The Armed Man by Karl Jenkins made the journey more bare-able .

He knew this route well by now, having taken it Saturday evening - the weekend traffic was easier to negotiate - and it was a few minutes before five o'clock when Harry pulled into the Bowthorpe Hall Road Business Park.

Already people were heading out, leaving work for home, not hanging around. But as Harry and Zero had noted this past week, except Tuesday and Sunday, which were Churdjiev's day off, the man was a creature of habit and a dedicated employee. The wife had informed them of his routine, which she said had altered in the last month and caused her suspicions to become aroused. Plus she said a few other indicators and tell-tale signs, such as a loss of intimacy in their marriage and a significant upswing in his personality. Churdjiev had become more health conscious. He now went to a gym with a work colleague, had started playing squash, he went cycling. These were things which his wife was unable to partake with him owing to thyroid and diabetes issues.

Harry parked up, switched off his engine and waited.

Thoughts swerved between Parisa, Georgette then to Hayley Wilby and her husband, and finally to the Russian letter and Stephen Smith. Both those cases were so different from this one. The Wilby murder investigation was the type of thing which Harry used to deal with at Scotland Yard on a routine basis, and he sometimes missed that life. But murder affected so many people, broke so many people, that one had to acknowledge its distressing nature. Dealing with it took a very resolute constitution. Harry wondered how strong Hayley Wilby was, because she needed to harden herself considerably to live with what Harry saw as the inevitable outcome, which was her husbands guilt. Not to mention the suicide. Those kinds of stresses were dealt with dispassionately by people who had to investigate such cases, and giving loved ones the bad news was part and parcel of the job.

   Harry did not miss that.

   In no was did he envy the police officers who would have delivered the news of her husband's death to Hayley.

   The Russian letter, on the other hand, involved an intriguing amount of detection and investigation to get the juices flowing. What caused the Austrian to flee his homeland and change his name? Would Harry's banking friend Nate Beckley be able to shed light on the number code? And what of the provocation prompted by the letter within the Russian community? Might be nothing, might be something, and Harry was going to enjoy finding out which.

   Five minutes after Harry cut the car engine the radio also ceased automatically, so he turned the key and Classic FM sprang back into glorious life.

   And inevitably so did Harry's phone the instant he turned it on. He saw on the caller display that it was Hayley Wilby.

"Hello." Harry said cautiously.

"Karl has taken his own life." Came the reply in a matter-of-fact voice. Hayley had cried herself out and was now in the denial stage.

"I know."

"Our solicitor said Karl was drugged. At the party, I mean. She said there might be", paper rustled in the background- "Gamma-hydroxybutyric acid involved. Do you know what that is?"

"Unfortunately, yes." It was a date rape drug like roofies. Only GHB was worse, if that's possible. GHB can cause memory loss through comatose-like systems."

"Could Karl have taken in accidentally?"

"Somebody would've brought it to the party with the intention of using it. It's an illegal drug but not too difficult to obtain. So Karl was given it or bought it himself. The effects can take up to fifteen minutes to appear. Forensics experts should be able to pinpoint an accurate time Karl ingested the substance and correlate that with the time of Caryn's death."

"Could Karl- Could Karl have killed her, though? Could he have done it without knowing what he was doing?"

Harry didn't like to tell the wife of a dead man the answer was yes.

"Possibly."

A sigh on the line. A sigh of relief or resolution?

Hayley's voice said: "Which means the person who slipped Karl the drug is responsible?"

Or he took it afterwards to hide his crime, Harry thought to himself. He asked: "Have they told you if Caryn had taken the drug too?"

"No. Is that important?"

"Maybe." Harry wanted to tell her that Karl and Caryn might've taken GHB together with the intention of achieving a drug induced sexual high, but refrained. "Did Karl have any close work friends? You know, who he see's socially."

"Yes. Of course-"

From the concrete and glass rectangular structure which served as the business centre for a Norwich hedge-funding and consultancy office, emerged the man whom Harry was going to follow. Churdjiev was tall, at least six-one, one-hundred eighty pounds, fat turning to muscle owing to the new month old regime, well coiffed dyed brown hair, and he bore a vague facial likeness to the television actor Lewis Collins in his prime, only ugly.

"Okay, that's good." Harry said into his phone. "The police will be questioning them and with a bit of digging should soon uncover any subterfuge. If someone slipped Karl the drug they will probably be the type of person who couldn't keep it to themselves for very long."

"Okay." The voice on the line had weakened, became desperate, pleading.

Heart-breaking and heart-broken. "I know- I know my husband has- gone, but you won't give up will you, please?"

Harry watched Churdjiev the Lewis Collins lookalike striding confidently across the park, waving goodbye to a colleague, shouting a friendly departure to another.

"I shall try my best to find out what exactly happened."

"Thank you." Hayley said and there was sobbing in her voice.

Churdjiev got into his brand new BMW six-series, which must've set him back a few quid unless he was part of the fashionable hire purchase schemes which seemed more prevalent than ever these days. People flaunting their faux personal wealth by driving vehicles that stretched their monthly income to breaking point. Harry Kovac was happy with his nondescript Ford Focus whose turbo-charged power was subtle and reserved. Plus it was paid for outright like everything else in his life. Maybe he was just lucky or sensible, or both.

"I'm sorry, Hayley, but I've got to go now. I will be in touch. I promise." A pitiful whimper of despair on the line before Harry disconnected the call. He sighed deeply. He felt sorry for Hayley. Life was a challenge. More so for some than others.

When Churdjiev drove by Harry, the man appeared to be talking animatedly with himself but it was more likely he was talking to somebody on the phone or, less likely, singing full volume at a song on the radio.

    Harry turned the ignition key and his cars engine turned over without hesitation. Giving Churdjiev enough breathing space Harry followed.

    First they turned north toward the City and Bowthorpe Park, going with the steady flow of traffic around boundary roads. The direction was consistent. Churdjiev lived in the village of Horsford, slightly north-easterly and into the suburbs. But when they came upon the A1074 he pulled into the left-hand lane at the junctions, and when the lights went green he took the route north-west towards New Costessey.

    Harry followed. His curiosity was peeked. Maybe today would be the day for Churdjiev to reveal his true colours. Predictably. Like Karl Wilby would eventually prove had he not died. This was the ugly side of life. Blasé attitudes toward relationships were now commonplace. At least the breakdown of Harry's own marriage had been something more earth shattering than discontent.

    Nothing was sacred anymore.

    Housing and shops dominated urban tentacles on the outskirts of Norwich like a concrete overflow pipe gone wrong. There was the occasional green space but until free from the pull of the city the grey and brown seemed endless. Some of the houses were grand but most were privately rented or council properties. Shops offered nothing unique and the pubs were generic, interchangeable with counterparts dotted along the other major outbound routes. There really seemed no unique originality in these suburban estates and Harry was pleased he no longer lived amongst them. He hadn't been sure about the move eighteen months ago from the big city to the countryside, but he definitely hadn't regretted anything since his arrival.

Churdjiev drove through New Costessey on the main road for two-hundred yards before making a right turn into an estate. Harry followed. They continued for a further half-mile, the properties getting bigger and set back further from the roadway. Eventually Churdjiev slowed, signalled right, and turned into Benton Avenue with a new tarmac surface.

Harry slowed.

There was nothing behind him. He indicated left and came to rest kerbside opposite the avenue entrance.

Benton Avenue stretched about a hundred and fifty yards and had just two houses either side and two angled like an apex at the end. All of them were set back from the tarmac with an open lawn out front, double-width driveway and double garage. They had individual touches made by the owners but essentially the properties were of a uniform design. Functional yet pleasant to live in, Harry presumed. Two of them advertised the fact they were business premises: one a physical therapist, the other a carpenter. Maybe Churdjiev was a client at the property he was visiting, which was at the bottom right-hand of the avenue, although from where Harry sat he could not see a name plaque stating what the business was.

The open front spaces meant Harry could see clearly when Churdjiev got out of his car. Harry pulled out his mobile phone, activated the camera, pointed and zoomed in. Perfect.

Harry watched as Churdjiev approached the front of the house. The door was slightly recessed. Churdjiev wasn't acting too conspicuously. There were no furtive glances backward or across to the windows of neighbouring properties. This was obviously a regular haunt.

The front door opened and the occupant appeared and embraced Churdjiev. Their kiss was more than merely from friendship as was the clutch.

So Churdjiev's wife had been correct.

Harry took a few photographs of the incriminating variety like the private investigator stereotype was required, and frowned with displeasure. Harry wasn't entirely sure how the wife would react at seeing her husband in a passionate embrace with a bearded cross-dresser but it took all sorts and Harry had witnessed worse.

# CHAPTER TWELVE

Before Harry drove away from the end of Benton Avenue he swiped and tapped at the screen of his phone to send the incriminating pictures to Daphne Crane's phone. She would no longer be in the office because the time had rolled past six o'clock, but at least she could get prepared early tomorrow with the breaking news for Churdjiev wife. Harry also asked Daphne to persuade her husband to attend the beach rendezvous tomorrow. The one with Jenny Jane which Karl Wilby would no longer be attending.

 Harry cast a contemplative look up the Avenue at the cheating husbands car. There was nothing new which human behaviour could throw up to shock or surprise him. These kinds of things happened everywhere, so it should be no different a world here than in London. But perhaps because Harry had come to Norfolk expecting a slightly quieter existence, sometimes he was reminded that rural living can be equally depraved as city dwelling. Worse, sometimes.

 Not just the cheating in this case but the messed up world which Karl Wilby had introduced his wife to. How many secrets were there hidden in his closet? How many were hidden in anybodies closet? Who knew what happened next door?

 A message received bubble materialised on his screen. It was from Parisa Dane. She would meet him at seven-thirty. Harry barely had time to get home, shower and change.

When he finished typing a reply he dropped the phone on the passenger seat, turned on the ignition and pulled away from the kerb, and with Classic FM as his companion he drove to his home in Stalton-on-the-Broad.

Thirty minutes later Harry had showered, shaved and was dressed in something smart casual for his rendezvous with Parisa, another twenty minutes later at seven twenty-five he climbed out from his car in the car park of The Poachers Arms public house and restaurant. The property was located due north of Norwich on the A146 at the very edge of Newton St Faiths.

Harry had been here not more than three weeks before his first date with Parisa - this was their fourth - when on a case with Zero. He knew the staff to be friendly and courteous. The pub owner was a Norfolk man who could trace his ancestry back to the early eighteen hundreds, which he would gladly tell newcomers, this, in Harry's relatively short time in this county, seemed indicative of much of the local populace. The landlord's regulars had made a tapestry for him a few years back, which included his Great-Grandson who stood to inherit the pub if and when he chose. The food was very good too, all homemade and traditional English.     He compartmentalised work in his brain, the day was over, now it was his time.

Harry hoped Parisa would be as hungry as he was.

Parisa was already waiting for him in her white BMW X7.

She looked spectacular.

Her silky dark brown hair hung loosely, almost haphazardly about her shoulders, cascading in waves across the top of a striking salmon coloured blouse which hugged her figure. Two buttons were casually open at the top displaying a tantalising glimpse of a lacy blue bra and the swell of her breasts. She wore navy blue skinny jeans with a white belt, and white and salmon flats. Everything about her appearance seemed casual, like she dressed without wasted time in selection but still looked coordinated. Parisa Dane was one of those egoless women to whom people naturally found appealing and gravitated toward.

Harry felt proud and fortunate.

When she walked towards Harry her hips swayed hypnotically, and Parisa eyed him with an equal appraisal.

"You look good." Parisa said.

"You look spectacular." Harry replied and they kissed, just a quick peck on the lips but that was more than enough to keep Harry happy, and he soon forgot everything else which had occurred that day. He was suddenly twenty-five again.

They walked side by side, hand in hand, to the recessed beechwood door of the white-washed public house. They were friendly, relaxed, but still in the early stages of a relationship which was unhurried.

"Have you-?" Parisa said.

"Do you-" Harry said at the same instant.

They laughed. Harry held the door open for her.

"Do you come here often?" He asked, tongue in cheek.

"Wow. That's original. You've not been out on a date in a while?"

"Now let's see, what year was Armageddon released at the cinema?"

"Aw, how romantic, you took her to see a disaster movie."

"I thought it was a love story."

"Oh, it is. A love story between men and their testosterone." Parisa teased.

"That was the last time I went to the cinema."

They stepped up to the familiar chrome bar which was brightly lit and adorned by the usual pub signage, accoutrements and paraphernalia. The scheme was surprisingly modern for an establishment which bore a traditional air, but the owner sought to keep apace with the times, a decision which worked successfully.

"What can-" Parisa said.

"What are-" Harry said at the same instant, then continued. "What are you having?"

"A small Archers and lemonade to start with, please. I hope you're hungry. Oh, and it's my treat this time."

Harry nodded and smiled pleasantly: "And I shall have an alcohol-free Peroni, please." He said to the middle-aged woman behind the bar who took their order.

"Isn't he a good boy!" Parisa said to the woman.

"For now." She replied with a wry grin and tended to their order.

"What sort of day have you had?" Parisa asked Harry and leaned back gaily in what turned into an unintentionally demure posture, the bar a perfect posing point, leg crooked with a foot upon the brass shin guard.

Harry thoughtfully considered the question, wondering what to begin with, and grinned broadly.

"Very dramatic." He told her. "And you? How was Scotland?"

"Good. Productive. You'll have to come with me next time I go."

"Sounds good to me."

Their eyes linked, fused, both hoping the other was having similar notions but neither ventured to ask, which was common etiquette in the early stages of any relationship especially when more was hoped for but never assumed. They were adults, not children. Both had life experience. Both were realistic.

Their drinks arrived quickly, were placed on the bar next to them, where their fingers had absentmindedly linked atop the surface, operating automatically.

"Will that be all?" Asked the bar lady.

"Um- are you you hungry?" Harry asked Parisa and hoped the answer would be yes, which it was. He turned back to their server. "May we run a tab and get a menu, please?"

"Of course."

They found a window seat which faced away from the glare of the rapidly setting summer sunshine. They overlooked an ornamental lawn which had decking, seating, a flower bed and small brook with a woodland glade the other side of a low slung embankment. It was a pleasant view, and Harry said so.

"I've been looking forward to this all day." Parisa told him with a contented sigh, menu poised for perusal, not taking her eyes off his.

"Me too." Harry said.

"Pleased your day is over?" She didn't have to be a mind reader.

Harry nodded. "It's been a- day!"

Parisa waited patiently for him to order his thoughts and elucidate.

"I had barely stepped out my front door when a woman stopped me."

"Lucky her."

"Not so lucky. Her husband was accused of murder. I met him later but- well, it's too late for him now because he took his own life."

"That's bad."

"It is that but it's his young widow I feel sorry for because it's not over for her yet. She thinks he was innocent and- well, it's complicated by the fact that he ingested a date rape drug.""

"You think he might be innocent?"

"Yes and no. Only time will tell. He had a lot of secrets. As did the victim. She had gambling debts."

"Enough to be killed for?"

Harry nodded. "A little over seventy-three grand."

Parisa let out a low whistle which, inappropriately, Harry found very erotic. Her lips formed a perfect kiss when she did it.

"Exactly." Harry said.

Parisa sipped the drink thoughtfully, looking Harry straight in the eyes.

"Anyway," Harry said, "we had another interesting job drop into a laps this morning, something less morbid. In fact it's way more unusual that the kind of job we normally handle. An ex-Pat Austrian, a painting, a mysterious letter with a mysterious number attached, and Russian intrigue."

"Sounds thrilling."

"I think so. At least it's definitely better than dealing with adulterers."

"You get those a lot?"

"Sadly, yes. It's our staple business, really."

"I suppose cheating is made too easy these days. People don't talk like they used to."

"Quite true."

They drank and checked their menu's. Harry wished he knew what was going on behind those lovely eyes. He had to admit to himself that he was completely smitten. Harry hadn't known a woman since his wife. In fact he really had not been out on a date for as long as he could remember until he met Parisa Dane just one week ago. And since the beginning of the evening, since she stated this was a date, he had been willing himself not to foul up. But Parisa was such an easy person to talk to that Harry knew by being himself he could not foul up, and yet... Harry was thirty-eight years old, feeling half that age again, uncertain and naive.

"My parents had a very strong relationship." Parisa frowned thoughtfully. "They died six years ago in an accident, which was good in a way, because I don't think one could've lived without the other."

"I'm not sure how Hayley - that's the widow - will cope. Poor girl. She's only in her mid-twenties, whole life ahead of her and now devastated by this."

"I was twenty when my life-changing event occurred. It's difficult, obviously, but somehow we get there."

Harry nodded empathetically. He couldn't tell Parisa about his own event because it involved his wife and daughter. Somehow talking about them seemed inappropriate. One day he would tell her, of course. One day in their future.

Harry drew up his glass to the middle of the table in a gesture to toast.

"To past, present and future."

"I'll drink to that."

They clinked glasses together just as their server arrived to take their food order: Parisa ordered the Caesar salad with a side of fries; Harry chose gammon steak with new potatoes and seasonal veg - although seasonal veg could be anything these days!

The silence during their meal wasn't awkward. They enjoyed their food, commenting upon the quality, but nothing more. They were enjoying each other's company, happy to be together, smiling with mouth and eyes. Both were relaxed after a busy day.

"That was delicious." Parisa said when finished, her plate empty.

Harry had finished a moment earlier, politely waiting.

"Very nice."

Parisa raised her drinking glass to her lips and held his eye contact. The warmth emanated from Parisa's eyes that inwardly Harry cursed his own reticent nature. Why was he always suspicious of his emotions? Why could he not fully open up? Was this to be his fate after years in the police force? Inwardly he was smitten, and her eyes held such promise but was it rehearsed from years of experience? Harry cursed his logic. One second his mind was filled with youthful hope, the next with grown-up cynicism.

Parisa reached across the table and took his hand in hers.

Their server arrived and cleared the table, delivering similar spiel as one expected, and the food had been genuinely good so Harry and Parisa could offer truthful responses - neither were shy about giving criticism, but it wasn't necessary that evening - and they were both lost in thought.

# CHAPTER THIRTEEN

Harry parked up, locked and secured his car after ensuring he had everything which was required for the journey to London in the pockets of his jacket: mainly the Waltraud Koenig letter with its mysterious number. Harry had decided to bring the letter itself to put into context the number for his friend Nathaniel, and that they weren't barking up the wrong tree. Nate Beckley had an innate ability to read between lines where others failed. Not that Harry's friend could read Russian, as far as he knew, but Daphne Crane's interpretation had been very thorough.

A random glance across the car park. Nothing more. Just habit. Casual. Cars had filled three-quarters of the spaces. Random. One car had followed him all the way from the City outskirts. Maybe sooner. Coincidence? The back of the motorists head faced him, short brown scruffy hair, he was on his phone. There was no furtive movement, no turn of the head, no check in his mirror.

Harry shrugged. Just a coincidence.

Striding through the wide entrance onto the broad concourse of Norwich City Train Station, Harry noted on the illuminated board the relevant platform he required, which happened to be number one, and the train was scheduled to depart on time at seven fifteen. He could see the DVT - Driving Van Trailer. The locomotive's engine Harry couldn't see, but was likely a Class 90 and hauled the Mark 3 air conditioned coaches.

Harry popped into the franchise convenience store located just off the platform to purchase a Daily Telegraph plus a bottled water for his journey.

He skimmed through the pages during the smooth journey with an absentmindedly blasé swiftness. Harry was having too many flashbacks to his lovely meal with Parisa. She was an exquisite young woman and he was a lucky man.

One hour fifty six minutes after the London bound train departed it was pulling into the massive space which was Liverpool Street Station. His old home – London, not the train station, although he had spent many undercover hours there in his early days as a Metropolitan Police Sergeant.

When he stepped onto the noisy, stuffy platform with the other passengers who were all purposefully going through their important zombified race against each other, eyes averted from contact, bodies rigid and minds weaving devious webs, Harry knew immediately that converting to a quiet country existence had been the best decision he could've made. Norwich could at times be full of hustle and bustle but on a much smaller scale to London.

Harry strode unhurriedly, head raised confidently, eyes sweeping from face to face to see if he recognised any potential danger to his fellow travellers and humans. He took pleasure in his heightened awareness, it gave him an edge. But none of the hooded, jacketed zombies seemed particularly threatening.

Fish-eye surveillance cameras were in conspicuous abundance, as they were all over London. They offered limited confidence to the weary traveler.

The underground felt positively claustrophobic to Harry. He had become accustomed to the open spaces of Norfolk with its trees and hedgerows and greenery in abundance. Had it really been over eighteen months since he had moved from the oppressive concrete jungle to Norfolk?

All the same he needed not to refer to the maps or signage. Harry simply followed his memory. He knew London like the back of his hand, both its good side and seamy side. Dawdling and uncertainty was what got people into trouble in a big town, with predators looking for any weakness to exploit. It only took a moment. Mere seconds for a mugging or similar crime. But the rats could sense an experienced exterminator and stayed well clear of Harry Kovac.

Harry found the red line, the Central line, and journeyed on the train through to Marble Arch. He decided to stand for the entire trip. He enjoyed the motion. The swaying movement was soothing. And by standing up he was better equipped to observe because old habits died hard. Nobody he saw was particularly interesting except for a couple of animated characters in their mid-thirties whose banter was loud. They were worth closer inspection, but all told there was nobody who threatened to ruin the status quo of the journey between passengers and their destination.

On July 7th 2005 Harry had attended the Tavistock Square suicide bombing. The double-decker bus blasted in half at 9:47am. He had arrived on the scene just three minutes later by a well timed coincidence. Harry had been attending an official visit to the British Medical Association's situation room on Upper Woburn Place with his wife. Now ex-wife. She had been a physician there. Harry was briefing his wife and some of her colleagues on the new response team and available equipment at the facility, placed as a precaution since the 9/11 terrorist attack in New York. The whole civilised world had been on high alert since September 2001. And four years later it was London's turn. The first, but not the last. Harry could still remember the taste in the air on Tavistock Square. He would always remember the shocked faces, the wailing, the confusion. It had been a terrible wake-up call to London security forces and it was inadvertently the catalyst which broke his family apart.

The train rumbled and braked as it rolled into Marble Arch underground station, also breaking into Harry's thoughts, relieving the bitter pain of memory.

Upon striding out the above-ground exit of the underground station into the sunshine, onto Oxford Street, the great shoppers paradise, and the first thing which Harry heard was the siren of a police car. The wail echoed throughout the concrete and glass canyons of hotels and retailers. Pedestrians ignored the siren, accustomed to the familiar sound. They strolled or ambled, their speed dependent upon whether they were local or not, and headed to all points of the compass irrespective of whether anyone was in their path or not.

Harry walked a block west toward Marble Arch before he diverted north into Great Cumberland Place, where he continued a further block until he reached Bryanston Street. From there he turned westward which ran parallel with Oxford Street.

It was quieter there.

Fewer pedestrians, fewer retailers.

The single-Lane road ran narrow though so it felt more enclosed and stifling, not helped by the morning sunshine blazing directly into the heated canyon.

The building Harry needed was on his left, nestled between two six-storey office towers. The shining glass structure reminded Harry of a miniature version of The Shard. It was as if someone thought it would be comical to suggest its design, not believing it would actually be built. But there it was in all its seven-storey splendour - at least it stood above the surrounding buildings even if it didn't quite dominate the skyline. It was a testament to modern design.

The facia surrounding the front entrance to the bank looked for all intents and purposes to have been constructed using cheap plastic. Maybe left over grey construction blocks melted down into one giant archway and placed there by a child. Yet the dichotomy made the overall aesthetic blend with the red name of the bank in curious synergy. This was a bank for rich people but it was dressed like a child's plaything.

Harry walked through the already parting doorways and into a sterile lobby where every sound was amplified. Even the soothing jazz score coming through concealed speakers sounded like an ethereal call.

High-paying customers expected a pleasant view upon entry into this sanctum and behind a highly polished teak desk the red hair receptionist blazed vividly against the white backdrop. She was certainly very eye-catching and Harry surmised that she probably moonlighted as a model - although it was a very un-PC thought which Harry had, the truth was, there's nothing like a pleasant face to greet you wherever you might be.

"Good morning." She said in very husky and precise English diction, which made Harry take back the belief that she was a model.

"Hello. I'm here to see Nathaniel Beckley. Nate. He's expecting me."

"He is." She said with a blazing smile. "I'll let him know you are here. Mister Kovac, isn't it?"

"Harry. Yes."

She nodded approval and touched an angular panel screen on her desk and apparently did not need to say a word into it because she looked up at Harry and said: "He's on his way down, Mister Kovac."

"Thank you."

She didn't bother about him then, instead returning to whatever she had been doing at her desk before Harry arrived. Pleasantries obviously didn't extend to small talk or small fry. Harry wasn't exactly a banking customer, after all.

Harry turned his back and looked out the front door at the passers-by because the lobby wasn't really that interesting anyway. It was a bland building for an unexceptional job, doing all it needed to do. Unless by some miracle the face was just an economical restraint and the floors above where the real work took place, the offices, offered a more inspired environment, there was little appeal.

"Harry Kovac!"

The voice belonged to Nathaniel Beckley and Harry turned to greet his friend from old with a broad smile which faded fast.

Nathaniel did not look well. In fact he was thin in the face and frame. Withdrawn cheeks exposing protruding bone structure inside tight skin, his hair was growing back after being shaven, darkness encircled his eyes. But most striking of all was the fact that his fashion conscious friend now wore his clothing loosely despite the suit being a tailored Tom Ford in dark grey, and the white shirt being crisp and fresh and the shoes being polished to such a high shine they practically flashed in the light. Nathaniel had obviously not been well at all and it did not take a detective to conclude which particular ailment it had been.

"Nate."

Harry didn't lose a beat. He strode forward and embraced his friend as if it were only yesterday, but the frame was more easily crushed so he instinctively hugged more lightly.

When they parted it was with haunted, wet eyes that Nathaniel regarded Harry.

"You haven't aged a day, Harry." Nathaniel said sincerely because it was true. Harry knew he was ageing remarkably well even by his own admission.

"So what happened?" Harry asked.

"Cancer."

"Good God, Nate, why didn't you let me know?"

"What could you have done? You're not that good a detective!"

Harry laughed.

"So you want to grab a coffee and some breakfast, Harry?" Nathaniel asked. "And you can tell me what you countrified tractor boys call interesting."

"Sure. And I've seen better corpses, by the way."

"Thanks buddy, you know how to cheer a guy up."

Harry was pleased his friend still had his sense of humour, although he shouldn't have doubted otherwise. Nate Beckley had always been a strong character and was quite used to dealing with the human effluvia life could serve up with abundance.

They exited the building onto Bryanston Street.

"So what's with you?" Nathaniel asked. "You seeing a Norfolk broad".

"That's funny. A play on words. But yes, thank you."

"Good for you, Harry. Really. I mean it."

"Thanks, Nate."

"You been together long?"

"Seven days, that's all. Not that I'm counting, obviously. How's Sebastian?"

"Amazing. He's been my rock these past few months. If not for him-"

They turned northward into Great Cumberland Place, which was not the direction Harry had anticipated, and he asked: "What's happened to the usual cafe?"

"Franchised."

"You're kidding? What about Pietro?"

"He still works there."

"He sold out!"

"Yeah. Money talks."

"I blame the bankers myself."

Nathaniel laughed. "Me too, Harry, me too."

"So where was your cancer?"

"In my veg."

"So you're no longer a meat a two veg guy?"

"Nope. But Sebastian doesn't mind. We didn't want kids anyway." Nathaniel laughed.

"You shouldn't joke about that, Nate. I understand scientists can perform any miracle you want these days!"

They stopped a block distant from the bank, outside an arched opening to an arcade. The red-bricked outer shell of the building could have been the entrance to an old underground railway station constructed before the Second World War, somehow surviving the worst of the bombing. It stood three-storey's high, about a block wide and one-hundred yards deep.

When Harry and Nathaniel passed beneath the arch Harry looked upward at the ceiling with its wooden support beams running the whole width, supporting a clear glass roof that had been recently cleaned. Natural light introduced a myriad shadows upon the floor but the ambience was unlike any other retail arcade which Harry had visited in London, or elsewhere, for that matter.

Retailers within were not chains or franchises or affiliates. Another surprise. The rent must be quite reasonable. Maybe it was a stipulation of the agreement that only independent businesses be sited there. If that were the case it was a benefit. The store fronts were delightfully old-fashioned, almost bespoke, and were a mixture of clothing stores, a book store, a bakery, a milliner, and bijou cake maker. At the very end of the arcade was an unpretentious no-name cafe with wooden seats and tables made from old railroad timber.

"How come I've never seen this before?" Harry asked.

"It opened just over six months ago." Explained Nathaniel. "And I'm so glad it did. Sebastian and I come here all the time now. It's like a step back in time."

"I should say it is."

Nathaniel smiled, genuinely pleased his friend approved.

They found an empty table just outside the cafe entrance and within seconds of the them taking their seats a waitress was standing between them, her plump rosy cheeks and warm natural smile a welcome change from the often forced smiles found in other establishments.

"Morning, darling." She said, her London accent thick.

"Hiya Tracey, how are you today?"

"Good. Who's the dish?"

"This is my friend Harry."

"Hi Harry." Tracey said.

"Hi." Harry greeted her and couldn't help by smile at the pleasant cordiality. He felt like he was at home, in Norfolk, not London.

Tracey asked Nathaniel: "The usual?"

"Yes, please. Twice." Nathaniel looked to Harry for confirmation." Black coffee and eggs Benedict okay?"

Harry nodded an affirmation and Tracey left their table to fetch their order.

"So what have you got for me, Harry?" Nathaniel asked.

From within his jacket pocket Harry pulled the Waltraud Koenig letter with its hand-scrawled translation attached, and handed them both to Nathaniel, which he studiously sat and read. Harry watched his friend's expression as it altered considerably as he read, and finally settled upon a thoughtful gaze once he had reached the lower half of the letter. That was the part containing the long number. Nathaniel reread it and while doing so Tracey returned to their table with two large mugs of coffee which she set before them, scooting off once again.

Nathaniel nodded, picked up his spoon without saying a word and dug a cube from out of the sugar bowl and turned it into his coffee. He stirred almost absentmindedly, on autopilot, the conscious part of his brain carrying out the task while his subconscious shifted through the number combination and its significance.

"Interesting." Nathaniel said.

Harry was in very little doubt that his friend would pinpoint the origin of the code because this kind of puzzle was right up his alley. Nathaniel had always been into banking details and numbers and the history of the system, in fact he had several published articles on the whole industry. The man possessed an uncanny ability to memorise even the most obscure piece of trivia, something which only a handful of people would possibly know in a million years. And Harry could see that his friend was scouring the very depths of his knowledge.

The eggs Benedict arrived and they ate and drank in silence. Finally, their plates emptied, Nathaniel spoke.

"What did you think, Harry?"

"Delicious. And what do you think?"

Nathaniel steepled his hands together on the table top and considered them.

"After World War Two Berlin was quartered by the occupying nations: us, America, the Soviets and France. Then came the Berlin Wall, which as we all know fell in 1989 and Germany was reunified shortly afterward. Structurally, economically and socially there were great changes. Some of these changes resulted in alterations to banking and postal district codes. Get rid of the old hatred and herald in the new, that sort of thing. An upheaval in the banking community resulted in several relocations. Banks and contents realigned. Very few actually remaining in their original location. Some do, some don't. A bit like the downsizing we've experienced over the past five, ten years. Your number is definitely a safety deposit box. It might still be situated in old East Germany or not, I cannot be sure."

Harry remained momentarily speechless. He had considered the box might be in another country, but not Germany. He had hoped it was in London and they could locate it now, today, and visit it immediately. Evidently that wasn't going to be the case.

Nathaniel said: "Which might at least partially explain why this letter contained a box in East Germany." He lifted up his coffee cup and drained the dregs, a smile upon his face and thought radiating from his eyes. "This is fascinating stuff, Harry. Where was the letter found?"

"Behind a priceless painting."

Nathaniel raised a sceptical eyebrow.

"A lost masterpiece, apparently." Harry added.

"Seriously?"

"Yes, seriously."

"Well, Harry, I wish I could come to Berlin with you. You will go to Berlin? I can put you in touch with a guy there, a banker, of course, who would be able to take you to the very box, probably."

"But wouldn't I need official permission or something? A person can't just gain access to any old safety despot box by using just the number, even I know that."

"You don't have the key?"

"Not yet."

"No problem." Nathaniel shook his head in contemplation. "I can make it happen. Trust me. As long as the box isn't located in the vault of the Bundesbank."

This time it was Harry's turn to nod thoughtfully. This had indeed turned into a very fascinating investigation. A lost masterpiece brought to England by a fleeing Austrian ex-patriot, a letter written in Russian containing an old East German safety deposit box number. What will be unearthed next?

"I suggest you see if our old friend Michel Lomé can help. This would be right up his alley."

"Thanks, Nate." Said Harry, a lightbulb going off in his brain. Michel Lomé was an inspired idea and Harry didn't know why he hadn't thought of the man. Michel had worked for Interpol, amongst other law enforcement organisations. This sort of thing was his hobby in retirement. "When can I go see this friend of yours in Berlin?"

"I'll contact him when I get back to the office and let you know. What do you want me to tell him?"

"Everything. This isn't exactly a secret and your guy might be more sympathetic to our search if he knows what we know."

"Leave it to me, Harry."

Before Nathaniel could pull his wallet out Harry slapped two Jane Austen's onto the table, which covered the food, the drink and a generous tip.

"Thanks, buddy." Nathaniel said.

"It's been my pleasure."

"So don't be a stranger, Harry."

"Sure." Harry nodded. "And don't keep a small thing like cancer a secret from me."

# CHAPTER FOURTEEN

Zero Crane followed the protracted dogleg of the A149 from Norwich passing through Hoveton heading toward Great Yarmouth, his wife, Daphne, beside him. It was a pleasant journey and they passed through Stalham and Potter Heigham and Bastwick with no hold-up, chatting over what they might expect. Sign-posted north-east to Martham was the B1152, which Zero took. The road twisted and turned first through Martham, then West and East Somerton until they reached Winterton-On-Sea, thirty minutes after leaving their office along Norwich's Magdalen Street.

Signage directed traffic toward the coastal parking area east of the church, and Zero negotiated the narrow single-file street where it opened to a field and coastline. To left was a spacious, unmade car park plus a cliff top cafe.

Zero purchased a half-day parking ticket because that was the shortest period of time available, parked up well away from other vehicles, facing the cafe and cliff and other vehicles.

They sat and watched and waited.

"Ten minutes until Karl Wilby's rendezvous." Daphne said. "Poor soul."

"Dirty perve, more like."

"My husband: a prude."

"You know I aren't, right?"

"You never have been, no."

The car was rapidly heating up in the morning sunshine so Daphne opened the door. She undid the bottom three buttons in her blouse and tied the tails in a knot below her breasts.

Most of the arrivals they saw were couples. Young and old. They unpacked blankets, towels, beach bags and supplies. They were dressed in mostly unflattering beach apparel. But it was hot and sunny and promised to be so all day, so why not?

Zero stepped from the car into the glorious east coast air, the sun shining hot but the breeze was a delicious fluttering feather of coolness. He put his sunglasses on, locked the car and strolled through the car park, Daphne beside him. Behind the dark lenses Zero's eyes constantly swept his surroundings and the people. Nobody stood out as an anomaly. Nobody who looked like the video of the young woman whom Daphne had sent him and was the WalkTank babe Karl was due to meet. Not on foot, not by the beachside slope, and not seated outside the cafe.

"I'll get us a couple of drinks." Daphne announced and sauntered to the cafe.

In a plastic chair, back of the cafes outdoor seating area, was a middle-aged man who was people watching while at the same time glancing at the tabloid before him. Not unusual but he did stick out like the proverbial sore thumb, at least in Zero's opinion. It wasn't in the man's appearance, at least not as such. He looked like all the other sun worshippers in shorts, casually flowery shirt and crocs. He wore a baseball cap to keep the sun off his bald head and was very average looking. Nondescript, one might have called him. Not the sort of man who would necessarily attract attention. Which was why he attracted Zero's attention.

The man was too pale for the time of year. In fact the sheen of his skin reflected the sun because of the excessive application of lotion. He was a tea drinker, not coffee. Even on a hot morning. And while nursing his mug, taking a sip, he would people watch in such a way that Zero quickly realised he was looking for someone. But not just anyone. The man was well practised at his job. Zero could tell a person who was well versed in a tradecraft which he himself was adept. Which was what drew Zero to the man in the first place.

Zero and Daphne had bandied the idea of blackmail to Karl Wilby. That possibility became stronger in Zero's mind as he approached the man. Simple as that. The man was local and probably sat in his flat all day until the organisation who employed him sent him on errands similar to this one. The organisation would prey on people like Karl. The women were likely real enough but they most probably lived a thousand miles away under the employ of a global network.

Zero clenched a fist.

Karl would have been more grist for the mill. But now he was dead. His wife Hayley grieving. And the pale tea drinker was the one who unwittingly caused the suicide. Zero was pleased he had come in Harry's place to this rendezvous while his partner had travelled to London. It had been quite some time since he had been afforded the opportunity to mete out a bit of rough justice.

Without further ado Zero sat opposite the man. Before the man could speak Zero produced his Private Investigators ticket and showed it to him. The reaction was priceless. The man slumped visibly, caught out for the first time. But he soon recovered with a sigh and eyebrow bob of resignation.

"Karl is dead." Harry said. No point beating around the bush. "And just because there are plenty of witnesses here don't think you're safe from a similar fate. I honestly don't care. You and your kind are scum and I'm scraping you off my shoe. If you want to leave here intact you better believe what I'm saying and tell me everything I want to know."

The man tried a hard stare as if he too didn't care, as if he were a hard man, but he couldn't conceivably convince himself, let alone Harry.

Zero smirked. "Did you have anything to do with Karl Wilby's death?"

"No."

"Why were you meeting him here?"

"We were going to blackmail him."

"What are you going to do instead?"

The man shrugged, confused.

"What funds do you have at your disposal?" Zero asked. "Right now."

"What-? I don't understand."

"How much cash money could you conceivably lay your hands on in the next fifteen minutes?"

"I don't-"

Daphne Crane placed a drink in her husbands hand and scowled at his table companion. The man was going to look Daphne up and down but thought twice about the potential consequences of his lascivious act, averting his darting eyes which tried to avoid looking at Zero.

"Karl left a grieving wife." Zero said. "She could do with a bit of good fortune coming here way. That's where you come in. There's a cash machine in walking distant. That's where we're now going. People like you carry more than one card. Unless you don't want to get home to your dirty little room, I suggest you comply."

There was obviously no arguing with Zero, it would be a fool who did, so they stood, with Zero towering over the man menacingly and glowered at him. The man assumed his best humble expression despite his trembling hands. Zero smiled, satisfied. This man wasn't going to be any trouble to him. His kind of intimidation were the threats which his organisation told him to make, he wasn't himself dangerous, but doubtful many would resist the blackmail. Zero's kind of intimidation was much more tactile.

"Where's your car?" Zero asked.

The man pointed vaguely in a direction toward the car park.

Zero indicated for the man to lead on, and he and Daphne followed three paces behind him, exchanging a quick, satisfied, smile. Zero wanted to send this seedy organisation a message but in reality the money and the delivery method were only a small part of something much bigger, so it was highly doubtful that ringing this guys neck would have any impact on the whole. But it would make Zero feel good, he was enjoying this, grateful to Harry for bringing him in on the problem. The money was insignificant but it would be put to better use.

"How much was the blackmail going to be for?" Zero asked, and the man's movement stuttered. "Don't hold back now, fella, I'm still considering inflicting pain upon you."

"Twenty-thousand."

"That's the test sum, presumably. More would be asked for next time. It's standard practise. Do you know where you get your instructions from?" A pause. "No, probably not. The top guy is likely thousands of miles away from here. How much is your cut?"

They stopped at a car, a white BMW coupe, not what Zero was expecting. and the man pulled out a fob and deactivated the lock.

"Two-thousand."

"Not bad for a mornings work. Nice car. I'll drive."

Zero took the fob and got in the drivers seat. He waited until the man got in the passenger side before inserted the fob in its dashboard aperture and pressed the ignition button. Zero drove back through the car park followed by Daphne in their car, along Beach Road for four-hundred yards and stopping outside a small Mum and Dad supermarket.

The ATM was wall integrated and it turned out the man had access to ten cards. Zero was impressed as he flicked through the man's wallet before handing it back to him. Normally these lowly guys at the bottom of the chain only had a couple of dodgy cards at their disposal.

Zero didn't let the man out of his sight when he withdrew some funds, and he returned to the car with fifteen hundred in twenties. The machine was probably empty now and had a facial of the man who had drawn out so much. When he got home to his hovel he might have a visit from the police or someone higher up in the organisation who wanted a word.

Zero smiled.

The man passed the money over and Zero grabbed him vicelike by the left wrist, took the money with his other hand, placing it on his own his lap before he presently broke every finger on the man's hand. He screamed like a girl. Zero wasn't concerned if anyone heard. Satisfaction drowned out the concern.

"That was a message." Zero growled. He reached into the man's pocket and took out his wallet, removed the drivers licence and pocketed it himself before dropping the wallet in the footwell. "Get out of this business, little man, you're out of your league. That's the true message here."

Zero left the guy nursing his broken hand with tears streaming down his face.

# CHAPTER FIFTEEN

During the return train journey Harry Kovac was in a retrospective mood, which was a most vociferous thing because he had two hours to mull before the train would reach Norwich Station, at just after one o'clock. It had been the long overdue catch-up with Nathaniel which provoked the introspective state. His friend had beaten cancer into remission. This was a victory. But it was equally a wake up call to the tender grip a person had upon their existence.

Nathaniel was six months younger than Harry.

All the tight scrapes which Harry had survived relatively unscathed, save a few cuts and bruises and scars, whereas a disease like cancer could unrelentingly bring a person down to bear more easily than any criminal. And Nathaniel, of all people. He might work in the banking sector with its predisposed images, but one really couldn't meet a nicer, more unassuming, colourful guy.

Life was a many-faceted thing, and each day had something new to offer so as a rule, unless one was a truly morbid person, the thought of impending doom was never at the forefront of the average persons mind. There's nothing worse than a reminder of mortality, or melancholy, to dampen ones spirits.

A mixed bag of good news and indifferent greeted Harry when he checked his phone once seated on the train - he had chosen to switch it off while in London to give himself a momentary respite from the other workload and aspects of life.

Parisa Dane had been the sender of the message he chose first to open, and he was pleased with that decision because she had invited him to meet her for lunch in the City. Harry replied to her text with his expected arrival time, and they agreed to meet at the Riverside complex, situated opposite Norwich Train Station, and take it from there.

Harry hadn't felt like he did toward a woman as he did Parisa for a number of years. Harry hoped that she felt the same way but he was a realist in his thoughts. He wasn't naive. Far from it. The future would unravel one way or the other.

In his head Harry tried to juggle the time aspects for the remainder of his afternoon. He would have to get to the office first, sort out some stuff with Daphne and Zero and find out what was required of him in the other investigations they were undertaking. If Nathaniel's Berlin connection paid dividends than a trip tomorrow might be on the cards, so he needed to plan ahead for that. And also he needed to find out what had been the further developments in the Wilby murder and suicide investigation alluded to in Daphne Crane's text, which had been the second he had opened. The latter might questionably be the least important because it's an out of work investigation, but that didn't mean he could in all good conscience ignore it. He wondered what Zero had discovered that morning at Winterton-On-Sea.

Included in Daphne's message was the name of one of the Russians, the man, Anatoly Polivanova. She hadn't found the woman on any database yet. Apparently Anatoly Polivanova worked at Beeston Grange, which was too much of a coincidence to be ignored, and at least explained why he wore a uniform which Harry had correctly identified as that of a hotel porter. Harry tried to piece together in his mind the potential connection between Anatoly, Karl Wilby, the murder victim, and Waltraud Koenig.

All he got was a headache for his trouble.

When Harry checked a third message it was from Hayley Wilby. It was a string of words with no punctuation. Typed in a hurry by a young person under extreme duress - as well as being the modern way to text and message and post; omit extraneous punctuation to make a message a meaningless, emotionless jumble of words. Nonetheless, Harry was able to decipher it. Apparently the toxicology report had confirmed the initial verdict that the drug which Karl Wilby ingested at the party was the date-rape drug known as GHB. All of which did nothing to aid Karl's pre-death plea of innocence.

And then there was Karl's fantasy life. His secret life which Hayley did not participate in. WalkTank. Karl Wilby had believed he wasn't cheating on Hayley when sharing online sexual fantasies with strangers who, lets face it, could be absolutely anyone. Harry had stung a few unsavoury people in his time at Scotland Yard by pretending to be a minor.

Maybe Zero's visitation that morning had resulted in the young woman Jenny Jane being a man, and involved what was to eventually be a blackmail operation. Again, not a first encounter with such criminal elements for Harry Kovac. He wasn't easily surprised these days by the depravity of human nature.

Harry needed to track down Sarika, Karl's co-companion on the sexual quest. He might have the opportunity later today. He wouldn't ask Zero to help with this one because that morning had been a favour, and Harry couldn't expect more. The Stalton-on-the-Broad village pub, The Marsh Harrier, was often a reliable hub of gossip. Maybe Sarika would be there tonight, maybe not, but either way Harry could enjoy a drink and some banter before bedtime.

Harry binned two junk messages and while doing so he received a reply from Parisa telling him that one-thirty was perfect.

Splendiferous.

Harry sent a message to Daphne Crane that she should contact Stephen Smith and arrange a visitation from Harry later that same afternoon. The reply came almost instantaneously accompanied by the thumbs up emoji, and a message confirming that Karl Wilby's death isn't suspicious. So it was irrefutably suicide.

Spending the remainder of the journey watching the countryside flash by, with the occasional small town or village or bridge or roadway to break the view, time passed quickly for Harry, and the train was no sooner rolling to a standstill on platform one at Norwich City railway station.

One more text message was the only remaining highlight of the journey. It had been from Nate. It informed Harry that a meeting had been arranged with Nate's Berlin contact in the banking world, a Von Stauffenberg, and all Harry need do was confirm by reply so a time could be fixed. Nate had also took it upon himself to contact Michel Lomé and that Harry should tell their mutual friend what time would arrive in Berlin, so the Frenchman might meet him.

Things were certainly moving rapidly.

Harry typed a message to Daphne Crane requesting that she book him on an early flight the next morning from Norwich Airport.

Once Harry disembarked the train and sent his texts, he switched off his phone and met Parisa for their light lunch at one of the many restaurants situated in the Riverside Complex.

Harry drove out of the train station at just after two-thirty following the quick but nice break from the work routine with Parisa.

He steered his car onto the A147 amidst the traffic which was congested whichever direction he chose. Like his fellow commuters he was well accustomed to waiting and, barring anything unexpected, he anticipated reaching the multi-storey car park along Queen's Road in approximately twenty minutes time. The car satellite navigation told him it was a journey of five minutes, but Harry knew that particular time was only doable when the roads were clear and all lights were green.

Eighteen minutes and thirty seconds later Harry had parked his car in one of the tight spaces on the third floor of the multi-storey car park which conveniently backed onto the office building occupied by Stephen Smith.

Harry was expected.

The doorman permitted his entry, smiled enigmatically and motioned superfluously with his hand toward the elevator.

When the door to Smith's apartment opened Harry was greeted by a wall to wall view of Las Vegas as viewed from an equivalent twenty-storey height hotel. The strip was garishly illuminated whilst the interior of the apartment was bathed in the fake exterior lighting.

Harry had to admit to himself that the facsimile was stunningly realistic even though it wasn't to his own taste.

Stephen Smith and his lackey Climmy were all dressed up in suit and tie ready to hit the town in the middle of the afternoon. When they did exit their building it would seem somewhat less glamorous than present appearances.

"Alright, chap? Anything to report?" Climmy asked cheerily - irritatingly cheerily!

Stephen Smith was his usual impassive and unreadable self but Harry was well accustomed to people like him, his kind did not annoy him as much as the faux joviality presented by Climmy.

"My London friend has confirmed that the number is a safety deposit box, and that it might be located in Germany."

Two pairs of raised eyebrows.

"Possibly on the old Eastern side of Berlin, prior to the redevelopment which took place after the toppling of the wall."

"That's interesting."

Smith nodded his agreement.

Climmy said excitedly: "So what's next, chap?"

"I've already taken further steps."

"What steps?"

"My friend has contacted his friend in Berlin who might be able to help."

"Friends are good."

"Indeed they are."

"So will you be going to Berlin?"

"I thought you might want me to."

Stephen Smith nodded a definite yes.

"We will pay all your expenses. This is exciting stuff. What do you thing is in the box?"

"I have no idea."

"Perhaps another priceless painting. Or some Nazi gold!" Climmy was positively shaking with excited anticipation, grinning broadly at Smith. "When will you be going?"

"Tomorrow morning."

"Excellent. We can't wait to see what you unearth next. This is brilliant. Better than we hoped. Like a treasure hunt. We're treasure hunters on a journey which might lead to hidden Nazi gold. Maybe the Fuehrer's own lost collection of stolen jewels. I saw a documentary on that one time on National Geographic."

"Don't get too excited yet."

"Come on, man, you must admit we're on the trail of something big."

"It might be nothing. It might be another painting like the one already in your possession."

"Which is pretty bloody brilliant."

"I suppose it is, but it's a good idea to remain realistic in your expectations to avoid monumental disappointment."

Realising he couldn't get Harry as excited as himself by the prospect of what may or may not lay ahead, Climmy visibly cleansed the excitement by taking a deep breath and lowering his arms, hands flat, as if pressing downward upon some invisible force.

"Mr. Crane said we might have a visit from a pair of Russian stooges." Climmy said, clearly enjoying the tropes. "The guard didn't let them in. All fun and games." Climmy said eventually. "So we'll be seeing you, chap. Stephen and me are now heading out of town for some Indian food. A joint called the Tamarind in Blofield Heath. Ever been?"

"No."

"Oh well."

"Enjoy the rest of your day, gentlemen."

Harry backed into the elevator car and looked at the floor until the doors closed. He sighed when eventually they did. He was pleased to be away from the annoyance of Climmy because he wished nothing more than so punch the light from his moisturised face!

# CHAPTER SIXTEEN

Harry sat back in his car on the third floor of the Queen's Road car park and shook in head, perplexed. If not for Climmy and his OTT excitement Harry would have indubitably looked forward to this investigation more than he was. The little fat man was just so infuriatingly annoying, with his smiling and breathiness and dancing from foot to foot and Essex accent. All those things combined to create a man who would be easy to sock on the jaw without regret. Harry almost wished the Russians got hold of him!

His phone signalled the arrival of a text. Daphne Crane had booked a flight out of Norwich Airport to Berlin Tegel Airport for first thing tomorrow morning. Early.

Another text came from Nathaniel, whose banker friend in Berlin could meet Harry at eleven o'clock that same day, tomorrow, which was the perfect time for Harry.

Harry liked that things were organised. He didn't appreciate chaos. Although chaos had often been part and parcel of his daily life.

The car ignition bellowed to life with a roar in the confined concrete car park which served as an echo chamber, and made the Ford sound more like a throaty Range Rover - a minnow pretending to be a whale.

At that time in the middle of the afternoon the car park was relatively deserted, which meant Harry didn't have to give way to or play dodgems with anyone when he descended the floors. He drove under the cantilever barrier and out into the sunshine. He pointed the car south easterly onto the A147 on his outward journey.

His plan was to return the office to keep his boss appraised of events, although realistically he could merely message Zero and Daphne. But Harry wanted to check out what exactly Daphne and Zero had found out about Karl Wilby and the WalkTank 'girl' Jenny Jane.

After a couple of hundred yards Harry turned northward into Ber Street, taking him through a series of one-way streets into historic Tombland, passing by the Cathedral and back into Magdalen Street.

But Harry's sixth sense warned him that something was amiss. Something wasn't right. A niggle which the average person might ignore, like perhaps they had forgotten something and could remember what it was. That wasn't it, though, for Harry.

At first he couldn't pinpoint what it could be. The car was performing just fine. The route was sound, he wasn't aware of any newly enforced road restrictions. He certainly hadn't forgotten anything at Smith's. The time was good too. He definitely wasn't late for anything.

What then?

Instinct was born out of experience. A sixth sense was honed through Harry's years in the police force, stretching back years to the training days and through graduation to performing on the job, and dealing with unforeseeable events and unpredictable people.

A danger which was present, or imminent, had set off the mental alarm. Something niggled his brain. As if eyes bored into the back of his head.

Two cars were behind Harry.

Harry instinctively and pointlessly indicated to turn left into Market Avenue.

Both cars followed suit because they had very little choice: the road was practically one-way.

Casting a fleeting in his rearview mirror at the face of the driver in the car immediately behind him and Harry was sure he had never set eyes upon the woman before that moment. She was just a commuter, like the vast majority of motorists in the city right then.

He couldn't see the the driver of the second car. But he had seen the car somewhere before, and not long ago.

Today.

Harry tried convincing himself that he was being irrational, that nobody was following him and everything was just fine. But it wasn't fine and he knew it so the questions were: who was the person, and why would someone be following him?

The Russians?

The traffic flowed briefly eastward through Agricultural Hall Plain before Harry turned northward again, into Upper King Street.

Both cars were still behind.

Maybe he was irrationally seeing shadows where there were none. Nobody should feasibly be tailing Harry. There was no reason. None of the cases he was working on warranted some third party getting worried enough to stick a tail on him and follow his movements.

But Harry trusted his instincts.

Once through Tombland and past the Cathedral the lead car, directly behind Harry, took the right-hand exit at the roundabout, down Palace Street. The second car followed Harry into Wensum Street. Again, nothing unusual there because it was a well travelled route, used mainly by buses and delivery drivers and those heading toward the Norwich City suburb of Sprowston.

Did the driver look familiar?

Harry's eyes kept darting between the road ahead and the face of the driver, but the sunshine glared off the windscreen and obscured the view.

Despite the movement being slow there were many hazards to be aware of so Harry couldn't linger, but finally he got a brief glimpse at a man in his twenties hunched at the wheel, matted down hair, ears which stuck out, a focused stare affixed on the bumper of Harry's car.

If he was tailing Harry, then he was very new to the job.

Over the old brick bridge and they were into Magdalen Street.

And Harry knew he had seen the pocked face kid before. How could he forget? Not only had he followed from the multi-storey car park along Queens Road, but Harry was certain he had seen the guy and his car that morning. The car had parked in Norwich Train Station. Harry had only seen the guy from the back but the shape and ears were one and the same.

Harry's sixth sense had succeeded in alerting him that the guy in the car was no mere coincidence.

Question was: would he follow Harry into the car park under the Magdalen Street fly-over?

Next question: why?

Who was this guy working on behalf of? Harry needed to find out. He also needed to get to the office and if this guy didn't follow that would be that for the day.

Harry memorised the registration number of the vehicle.

Indicating to turn into the road adjacent to the car park Harry glanced back one final time. His pursuer stared forward and did not indicate to follow.

Pity.

Harry drove onto the car park unmolested, his pursuer no longer in pursuit; the guy continued through Magdalen Street without stopping.

Maybe the guy's boss had warned him against conflict? Or maybe it had been a massive coincidence the guy has been in two locations the same moment as Harry?

Within two minutes Harry was entering the outer office of Crane Investigation Services.

Zero was sat in the chair opposite his wife. Both had jackets on as if they had been waiting to leave but couldn't until Harry had arrived, which was exactly the situation.

"So exhibitionisms your thing?" Zero asked with a wry smile.

"It was to Karl Wilby."

"And I can see why." Daphne added. "Although size isn't everything!"

"Sorry, dearest." Zero said. "Your hunch was right."

"Jenny Jane was a man?" Harry asked.

"Sure was." Daphne replied. "And far less attractive than her picture!"

"We set him on a new life path." Zero said.

"Thank you." Harry said.

Dsphne said. "We had a visitor a little while ago. Hayley Wilby."

"And the, er- Russians." Added Zero.

Harry raised a quizzical eyebrow. "Hayley was here?"

Daphne said. "She was a mess, the poor lamb."

"She would be worse still if she knew about her husbands sexual proclivities." Harry said.

Zero said. "She wanted to formally hire us but obviously I said she couldn't. I see what you mean, Harry, she's pretty far gone and very much convinced of her husbands innocence, so I told her you were presently involved in a very in-depth case at the moment, and the police are more than capable."

"Thanks, Zero." Harry said. "She's undoubtedly hoping for some closure after her husband's suicide."

Daphne said. "She's a sweet kid."

"She is, that." Harry agreed. "What did you find out?"

Daphne frowned.

"Nothing from the guy pretending to be Jenny Jane." Zero shook his head sadly. "Although I enjoyed rough-housing him."

"I need proof it was suicide." Harry said. "I won't be convinced until it's concrete. Karl Wilby definitely didn't seem the suicide type. I'd bet my reputation on it."

Harry bent forward and rested his hands in the desk. He had accepted Karl's was guilty of murder but remained angered by the nature of his own demise. Mostly for Hayley, who deserved none of the treatment which she was receiving. Her cause was hopeless. Harry needed to speak to Sarika, quiz her about WalkTank, and soon, before all hope really was lost. Maybe tonight if fortune favoured him. Someone in the pub might know more about her, if she didn't turn up.

"There's a phone number for you." Daphne said, and handed Harry a small sliver of paper. "Karl's best friend at work." The paper had Peter scrawled upon it, with a phone number. "Hayley suggested you give him a shout."

"Which reminds me." Harry said. He picked up a pen and pad and jotted down the vehicle registration number of the pocked face drivers' car, and handed it to Daphne.

Harry said. "Not now, it's not so important, but first thing tomorrow, can you check out the details on this vehicle?"

"Whose is it!" Daphne asked.

"I wouldn't mind knowing the answer to that question myself. Guy followed me from Stephen Smith's apartment here. I also saw him this morning at the train station. It's to much of a coincidence to not have a connection to something, even though I'm in the dark as to which something that is."

Zero said. "Which case is he linked to?"

It was Harry's turn to shrug.

Daphne said. "I'll let you know once I've got the name and address. I also booked you on a six fifty flight to Berlin tomorrow morning, is that okay?"

"I saw that." Harry said. "You're a diamond."

"Can you stake out the bimbo who says her husband is out to murder her tonight?"

Harry had forgotten about Mrs Parr. "Sure." He said wearily. "I don't need sleep."

Zero said. "Daphne and I are having the night off."

"Date night." Daphne confirmed.

"Sure." Harry reaffirmed. "But I've a date myself so I won't be there until after ten."

"That's fine." Said Zero.

Daphne handed Harry two pieces of paper, one which had his flight number for tomorrow upon it, the other with the address to Adele Parr's home.

"The Russians still want Waltraud Koenig's letter?" Harry asked.

Zero nodded. "They eased up on the intimidation this time."

"I've still not found out the identity of the woman." Daphne said.

"It's another funny coincidence." Harry said at length. "The Russian guy working at the same hotel where Karl Wilby's murder victim had her gambling debt."

"It's a bit of a stretch." Zero said. "You think they're connected?"

Harry shrugged: "Yes. No. Maybe. I've tried working the connection but drawn a migraine! Anyway, you two have a nice evening. I'll hopefully see you sometime tomorrow."

"I'll see if I can find the missing link tomorrow." Daphne said.

"Anatoly Polivanova?" Harry quipped.

"Be careful." Daphne told him.

"What she said." Zero offered.

# CHAPTER SEVENTEEN

Harry drove straight home surrounded by a swell of classic tunes to drown out everything else. The day had indeed been a busy one and it wasn't over yet. He put on his coffee machine and took ten minutes under the shower to freshen up. He dressed in a clean white shirt, boxers and khaki cotton trousers. To hell with formality. He was feeling youthful and alive.

The mobile phone beeped multiple times literally two seconds after Harry powered it up, and he couldn't help but grin at the predictability of it. He had received several despondent pleas from Hayley Wilby which had the understandable effect of making him feel guilty for only just checking them. Some just read one word: Hello. Others asked if he had given up on her. But three of the dozen contained a few facts about her husband Karl's suicide: he had cut his wrists in the shower block; somebody else must've helped him because his movements were out of the strict routine of the prison; and she had spoken to Karl's work friend Peter who said he thought somebody had spiked Karl's drink, a claim the police were looking into. These facts led Hayley to believe her husband was innocent and somebody had silenced him in prison. All of which was possible if not probable. Harry thought Hayley's active mind was conjuring cliche after cliche, but who knew for sure?

There wasn't much to say to Hayley which could offer hope. She would have her time taken up comprehensively, with the investigation and media and her own feelings. Harry messaged her to hang tight and that he would continue his investigation and let her know if anything else came up.

What else could he do?

Harry knew how false hope could have a detrimental affect on people. But he wanted to help the young woman whose world had been torn asunder. He ended the message by telling her he was on her side and to keep her chin up.

What little good his words would do her. But it was better than nothing.

Harry looked at the time on his phone which told him it had just gone five o'clock.

He glanced out his window as he sipped the coffee. Scoured the street which ran by his home. A cul-de-sac. Who Harry expected to see was a mystery even to himself. He wondered if he was getting paranoid. The Russians must likely knew where he lived, they could pay him a visit if they wanted, try a bit of intimidation. But nobody was there.

Deciding to pay TAMS Supermarket a visit and see if he could find this Peter who Hayley Wilby had mentioned as being Karl's friend, or Sarika, who Karl himself had mentioned, Harry pocketed his phone and wallet and keys, rinsed his coffee cup, locked up, and strolled the relatively short distance through town to the store.

There was no need to hurry. Harry felt the day had passed by rapidly enough already.

The store was open for business as usual after losing its manager not three days ago. They had remained closed on Monday out of respect for Ms Krystyva and her family. A grand gesture considering the times we lived in, and the frequent apathy shown by big businesses to their staff, who are treated like numbered cattle rather than names.

About a quarter of the available parking spaces out front were occupied. Mothers and fathers on the dinner run and people heading home from work. The situation seemed non-existent. Everyone was acting like normal. Murder was commonplace. The curious would probe in a similar fashion to a sex scandal, tipping their hat with a nod and a wink, not caring how the staff actually felt. Why should the curious care? Supermarket staff are only numbers, only cattle.

Harry picked up a basket at the entrance. He could feel the air-conditioning, cool and refreshing at first, but he knew what it was like to spend all day in an air-con environment and it wasn't as accommodating as the initial impact. He didn't miss it.

What customers there were were focused on themselves and their shopping. Staff were busy, preoccupied with work, subdued. Understandably so.

Harry strolled up to the newspaper rack and slid the local publication, the Eastern Daily Press, off the top of a pile and into his basket. He would read it in the pub and leave it for another patron.

A guy was filling the rack with magazines, he made eye contact with Harry and smiled. But this wasn't Peter. According to his name badge he was Zheng. So Harry nodded acknowledgment and continued into the store toward the produce where two workers were replenishing bananas and apples. Harry picked up a bunched trio of the yellow fruit, glancing casually at the name badges the staff wore but drew a blank once more.

What were the chances the two people he sought out of the hundred and fifty TAMS staff at this store would be working that very evening at that very moment Harry was searching for them? But Harry was a regular, some of the staff recognised him, so obviously the easiest and quickest way to find out if Peter was working was to ask.

"Excuse me guys. Is Peter here today?"

The produce duo look at him, registered the question, recognising Harry as a regular, and the one guy smiled.

"Sure, fella. He's down aisle six filling cereal."

"Cheers."

Harry left the two fillers to their job and strolled along to aisle six where there was indeed a guy filling cereal. Peter appeared to be of similar age to Karl Wilby. He was tall, thin, pasty faced with a mop of coarse brown hair which fit like a tea-cosy.

"Afternoon, Pete." Harry said amiably when three-feet away.

Peter turned his head and settled his baleful blue eyes upon Harry. A flicker of recognition sprang into his face and behind the eyes the young man was trying to place where he knew Harry from.

"Um- yeah, hi, good afternoon."

"You're Karl's friend, right?"

"Um- yeah."

"Sorry. I know it's difficult, especially after what happened yesterday, but do you mind if I ask you a few questions?" Harry could see the hesitation in Peter's expression. "I'm a detective trying to help Karl's wife, Hayley." He omitted the private from detective because responded better to those appeared more official.

"Right."

"Hayley said you might have some information. Like how Karl happened to get drugged at the party?"

"Um- yeah." Peter looked around the aisle nervously, his eyes wandering up to the golf-ball cameras. "I um-"

Harry realised he wasn't going to get any information from this guy right now, he was way too nervous in his work surroundings, so he said, "Tell you what, Pete, I can see you're not comfortable talking here, but I need to know what you know so I can offer some kind of closure to Hayley. How about you and I meet up later?"

"Right."

"At the Harrier."

Peter nodded.

"What time do you clock off?"

"Seven."

"Okay, cool. Shall we say eight o'clock?"

"Okay."

"Thanks, Pete."

Harry left the poor fellow to return to his work under the watchful hidden eye of TAMS management, and he idly wondered if the deceased Caryn Krystyva had already been replaced. Probably, he figured. Big corporations very rarely let the corpse go cold before the position is filled.

Harry finished his shopping without finding Karl Wilby's friend Sarika, paid and left.

# CHAPTER EIGHTEEN

The Marsh Harrier Public House was the exact geographic centre of Stalton-on-the-Broad. It was the second oldest structure in the village to the church, and a place of equally bustling worship, only it was to alcohol which people allayed their sins, rather than the church confessional. Ones own religious convictions depended upon belief as to what the best remedy may be. The pub and church weren't the only places to worship available to people, of course, but every village by and large possessed both so these were the most easily accessible to one and all.

Red brick, brown framed windows, a thatched roof and rear parking and pretentiously monikered Biergarten, The Marsh Harrier had the appearance of being built in the thirties and having served a different purpose in its infancy, but that was not the case. It had always been a public house.

Harry Kovac now stood at the farthest corner of the L-Shaped dark-wood bar at seven-thirty. The EDP was set aside upon his now vacant window table, it's local news consumed with a glass of orange juice, a bowl of chips and a handful of sandwiches.

He watched the patrons as they arrived. Some conversed in their huddled booths or upon stools, or gathered around the pool table and either side the oche.

Fading sunshine and a cool breeze flowed in from an open door to the Biergarten.

Harry had a clear view of the pub interior and exterior. He liked to know where his exits were.

He held a single measure of whiskey in a tumbler in one hand. His face displayed frustration. He had hoped Zero would deal with Adele Parr's investigation tonight. Like Daphne had said, they were paying customers and these kinds of things were part and party of their work, but it didn't prevent him from wanting sleep. And more than the one drink in the pub would've been a bonus, too. But never mind. Work was work and he should be grateful he could earn a living being a private investigator. What else could he do? It was what he was best at.

Harry lifted his glass, toasted his melancholic self, and forgot about his woes.

Pubs were like that!

Music played from ceiling speakers, mini spot-lights created pools of brightness around the room. The smell was of cooked food from the restaurant and hops from the beer. Harry had never been a smoker but he opined the smell of tobacco which imbued character to such establishments. The lack of haze sadly decreased the ambiance of old. On the plus side of things, one could return home without having to immediately dump all clothing into the laundry basket and take a shower to wash the staleness away.

One could not have it both ways.

A barfly who had been regaling whoever would listen to his life exploits was suddenly alone and spotted his next target: Harry. Sometimes these characters could be time-wasters blagging a drink, show-off Walter Mitty-types, or the lonely needing a shoulder. This chap's name was a Jim and every village had one - with a change of name - and was a combination of all three plus a few positive attributes. He was the kind of man who everybody knew on sight even if the name was unknown. An ever-present character who would often know everyone and everything that happened in the village and more than obliged to impart third-hand information like it was the gospel.

Harry had made a point of giving Jim time and plying him with the odd drink or three since he had arrived in the village. People would frequently say things to a Jim which they wouldn't to others, because those he told his stories too would be well aware that half of what they heard was bull while the other half might be shit! Jim was often fifty percent off the mark with his news and gossip but that didn't matter, because it was the remaining fifty percent which mattered most. Information was information and it was up to the individual to sieve fact from fiction accordingly.

"Poirot me old chum." Jim said in the cheery manner of the alcoholic.

"Good evening, Jim. Buy you another?"

Jim didn't need to be asked twice and promptly ordered a pint of the local brew from the barman. Harry unfolded a Jane Austen and flipped it onto the bar.

"Whaddaya know, Poirot?"

"I was hoping you might tell me what you know, Jim."

"Dunno what your talking about."

"Sure you do, Jim. What's the latest on the TAMS murder?"

Jim assumed a conspiratorial look. "Ah, that. You working the case?"

Harry nodded. No point telling Jim the exact truth, it would only produce more questions and take longer for the drunk to spill the beans of his knowledge.

"I heard," Jim began, "he had been banging her for weeks behind his wife's back. It was definitely a crime of passion. Guilty feelings, see? He couldn't bear the strain so bumped her off. Killed himself as well. Yeah, a real classic! That shops just ripe with sex! A year back two girls were caught on camera giving lip service to each other. They were in an office. The footage made the inter web and the media got hold of the story. Made them famous for five minutes. But this one ended badly, didn't it?"

Behind Jim, and through the open door, Peter entered the pub, still dressed in his TAMS uniform. He saw a clutch of colleagues seated around a booth table, shared a brief nodded acknowledgement before he clapped eyes on Harry.

It was ten minutes before eight.

"Thanks for the tips, Jim." Harry said. "Enjoy your drink, and if you hear anything interesting don't forget me. Business is calling."

Harry grinned.

Jim quickly cottoned on and winked conspiratorially. "Oh, yeah, sure."

As Peter approached the bar Harry intercepted him.

"Thanks for coming, Pete."

"Okay."

"Names Harry, by the way."

Peter blinked.

"Buy you a drink?"

"Okay."

"What are you having?"

"Diet Coke." Peter said.

They walked to the bar, Harry ordered for Peter and asked for a glass of orange juice for himself. Peter propped his elbow on the bar top, body slumped like he had worked hard for his pay. Harry reflected that most of today's youth probably wouldn't now what hard work was really like. To much free time is available to them for game play or television watching that tiredness is caused by inactivity and bad posture these days. But maybe Peter had another symptom of society: diabetes. He had, after all, asked for a Diet Coke.

"So, Pete. What can you tell me about Karl?"

"What do you want to know?"

"Sunday night at the staff party."

Peter grinned at the memory, temporarily forgetful of the outcome and the suicide, then his face reverted to solemnity.

"Karl killed the boss, yeah?" Peter said.

"So the police believe. Do you know any different?"

"Well-"

"Come on, Peter. It's too late for your dead friend now, but maybe his widow can have closure. What haven't you told the police?"

Suddenly Peter looked worried, like a startled rabbit caught in the headlights of a car before being run down.

"Relax, my friend. Nobody's perfect. We all forget things and what you might know may be of no importance anyway. I'm just trying to find out if Karl committed the crime he was accused of before he killed himself. I'm thinking only if Hayley, his widow."

"Right."

"Who gave Karl the drug?"

"It wasn't me."

"I know that, my friend. But do you know who did give it to him?"

"I think-" Peter glanced over at the table of his work colleagues, but more significantly was the fact he only looked at one of them, a young woman, pretty, in her mid-twenties, and it dawned on Harry that he had seen her before only with fewer clothes.

"That's Sarika?" Harry stated.

"Er- what? Yeah. She-"

"You think she gave Karl the drug, don't you?"

Before Peter could respond Sarika rose from her chair, said something to her friends and walked across the room. She pulled at the hem of her skirt to straighten it, aware that her actions were being witnessed. The flimsy white blouse she wore gaped, displaying a black lace bra which struggled to contain the swell of her breasts. She had a practised walk, swayed her hips, poised in her strappy black heels.

Harry had to tell himself that she was half his age and he shouldn't stare, but he, like the other red-blooded males in the establishment, couldn't help himself. Sarika was supremely confident in her appearance, proud of her body, and rightly so, judging from the WalkTank footage which Harry had seen of her.

"Hi, big man."

"Hi." Said Peter, even though she looked directly at Harry.

"You're the P.I."

"That's right. And you must be Sarika." Harry responded.

"The one and only. Your name is-?"

"Harry. Harry Kovac."

"Harry." The way Sarika's mouth caressed his name was designed to stir primitive thoughts. They didn't work on Harry.

"Do you mind if I ask you some questions about Karl Wilby?" Harry asked.

"You can ask me anything."

And again!

Sarika looked up at Harry dolefully, the whites of eyes large and innocent and almost pleading to be loved. Little wonder people got themselves into trouble.

"I'll, er-" Peter said, "say hi to the guys." And he sauntered off, knowing when his usefulness had passed.

Without looking at Harry, a coy smile upon her face because she instinctively knew Peter was watching her, Sarika lifted her skirt further up her smooth thighs and perched herself upon the nearest bar stool, back straight, chest thrust forward.

"I'll have a J.D. and Coke." She said and looked with those big eyes at Harry when she added. "Please."

Harry ordered.

"You know Karl didn't kill our boss." Sarika stated.

"What makes you so sure?"

"It wasn't in his nature."

"His widow said pretty much the same."

Sarika ignored the comment. "He was a good guy."

"You and he were more than friends."

"Sure, but I never had sex with him."

"I know about WalkTank."

Once again Sarika was unfazed. In fact, a smile played across her lovely red lips that said she enjoyed the fact Harry knew her secret.

"You've watched me?"

"Sorry to disappoint you, but no." Harry said, then steered the conversation away from where Sarika was attempting to direct it. "Some friends of mine met a guy this morning who had arranged to see Karl. He was a nobody scumbag who worked for a bigger organisation and their aim is to blackmail people. Naive and foolish people like yourself and Karl. Those who use WalkTank without suspecting their actions are being recorded. This makes them vulnerable. The guy they met knew Karl's details because Karl thought he had been making a date with a woman called Jenny Jane."

Sarika listened, absorbing what Harry said, but her impassive expression told Harry that she obviously couldn't relate to Karl's situation. At least that was a blessing for her. This young woman hadn't been preyed upon. Not yet, anyway.

"So, Mister P.I., do you think there's a connection between that and the murder."

The way she asked made Harry laugh. He shook his head. "No. But it meant Karl was capable of cheating on his wife."

"Not with me." Sarika said defensively.

"But you had fun."

"Sure. We enjoyed watching each other. It began as a game between him and me at first, like kids, exploring ourselves."

"It's a pretty big secret which Karl was keeping from his wife."

"Sure."

"And you didn't think it was wrong?"

"Na. We all have our secrets, right."

"You know Karl was drugged the night of the murder, right?"

Sarika nodded. "I heard." She picked up her drink, breaking eye contact with Harry for the first time during their conversation. She knew more. "Some date rape drug, right?" She asked after she licked some J.D. and Coke off her lips.

"That's right." Harry said. "You know something about it, don't you?"

Her eyes dropped to the ground. A complete giveaway. She couldn't be more obvious. Harry could almost hear her mind churning. Sarika was debating the question hard. She realised Harry wouldn't drop it and that he could see through any lie she may spin. Besides, it was too late for Karl now.

"So- a friend of mine gave me it." Sarika's lips quivered, her eyes moistened, cheeks flushed. She looked at the floor, the ceiling, anywhere but at Harry or the corner table where her friends were. She was no longer a confident young woman. Sarika was a child again, trying her best to hold back the tears. She blamed herself.

"Does this friend have a name?" Harry asked softly.

"Everyone knows him as Spock." Sarika told him, looking at her hands, conflicted emotions twisting her features. "On account of his ears and hair."

"And his name?"

"Leo. Leo Forrest." She whispered, eyes furtive, fearful. "Am I in trouble?" Sarika asked, her big wanton eyes frightened now, and despite himself, Harry's heart went out to her.

The fact she had the name of someone who hadn't previously been mentioned in this murder case wasn't insignificant. And from brief description Harry was adamant this Leo was the guy in the car from earlier. Harry weighed up the implications of her withholding the knowledge from the police with implications now that Karl was dead and he, himself, informing the police now he is in possession of the name.

Sarika sobbed. "I should've told the police straight away, but- He threatened me and- It's- it's my fault Karl is dead, isn't it?"

"No." Harry lied. "Of course not." Because the truth was that if Sarika hadn't kept the information to herself Karl Wilby might indeed very well still be alive. Some kids have to learn the hard way, and Sarika has dug a very deep hole to bury herself in.

"Thank you, Sarika." Harry said, and checked his watch. "I have to be going. Don't worry. I'll find the guy who gave you the drug. Don't look so worried. He won't know you told me, I promise. And he won't hurt you, either.""

Sarika nodded meekly and her facade dropped.

Why did Harry feel protective? Sarika was a liar and manipulative person, brazen and sexual. She was also worldly wise enough to fend for herself. But Harry despised men who threatened women and would teach this guy Leo Forrest a lesson…before handing him to the police.

# CHAPTER NINETEEN

Passengers from the eight forty arrival at Berlin Tegel Airport disembarked less than five minutes after landing. Harry Kovac was amongst them and he strode along the rolling pedestrian walkway of Terminal Three, dodging those fellow passengers and travellers who chose a more leisurely pace.

It had been almost three years since he visited Berlin last and that occasion had also been on business. In point of fact he couldn't recall a social visit to anywhere in Europe since a holiday to Disneyland with his family when the kids were young and times had been simpler.

Harry brushed the memory aside. Now was not the time for melancholy.

Much had changed at this airport in those three short years. Security was tighter, fisheye cameras more prevalent and the underlying atmosphere seemed more oppressive. Although, Harry thought to himself, oppressive for a country with such a chequered past as Germany was a bit of a cliche. Decades ago this country knew oppression at its worst thanks to a Nazi dictator and the Kaiser who came before him.

Now Berlin, and the whole of Germany, was a fully integrated multi-cultural society. And it showed in the many different people who he passed by. But like any country there would always be criminals and racists and bigots and sexists and ageists and religious fanatics. He could go on.

When he emerged from the terminal into the main outdoor hub of the airport the early morning freshness hit him like a luxuriant wake-up call. Harry removed his jacket and tie, and loosened his top collar button to enjoy the coolness. He had slept during the flight but the journey was so short that he felt little real benefit from it.

A vehicle rocked up to him and he slid into the rear seat, dropped his jacket on the space beside him and issued instructions to the driver, who bobbed his head and took off the instant Harry had the door closed.

"Do I smell of Bratwurst?" Harry asked the driver in German.

"Yes, as a matter of fact."

"That's a nice way to greet a hungry old friend."

"It's the only way, Harry." Michel Lomé regarded Harry in his rear view mirror with a curious raised eyebrow, a big smile on his face which reached his eyes. "Are we being covert?" Michel reverted to English: he was fluent in German, English, and his own national tongue, French.

"Not necessary, really."

"Then why the back seat, my friend?"

"Just a precaution."

"I am curious. Who might it be a precaution against?"

"The Russian Mafia."

"Ah. Then I thank you for your concern for you friend Michel, but the Mafia and

I go way back, you should remember I told you about my dalliance with them in oh-five."

"Only a hundred times."

"Ah yes, but a good story is worth repeating."

Michel Lomé's laughter was guttural and infectious. It was like old times. Harry enjoyed the company of the Frenchman and had missed the banter considerably, not that he would admit it to the old man with whom he had shared a half-dozen adventures during his service career.

The Frenchman was in his seventieth year but he didn't look a day over fifty, which was a miracle of nature when one took into consideration the myriad stresses life had thrown at the man, all taken in Michel's outwardly nonchalant style - in fact the man was a highly respected intellectual, quick-witted, and the greatest problem solver Harry had ever met. Michel had been bald for as long as Harry had known him, which suited him, and his brow was wrinkle free. His head was spherical, like a football, ears flat against its sides with signs of frostbite to both. Michel's nose was slightly crooked from a career break, and set between vivid thoughtful brown eyes with no lashes or brows. He sported a goatee beard which carried minute flecks of grey. Physically he was muscular and lithe with a flexible, fluid gait that belied his age, and stood upright at five-foot seven. The frame was ornamented with blue loafers without socks, red cotton trousers, a plain white silk shirt and Omega wristwatch.

Harry reflected that his friend hadn't altered a single iota since their fortnight together in the Swiss Alps three years ago, which had been part holiday, part reconnaissance job for an assignment Harry was on at that time. In fact, now that Harry thought it over, the job had been his final overseas task by him served for the Ministry of Defence.

"What time did you get here?" Harry asked, expecting his friend to say he hadn't been waiting long.

"Last night." Michel answered. "I stayed with Kolldehoff."

"Strewth. You must've driven all afternoon."

"Better than a nighttime journey in this country, my friend." Michel replied. "I have brought the meeting forward to ten-thirty." Michel said from the front, a twinkle of amusement in his eyes. "It is a superfluous question, my friend, but are you hungry?"

"You were right, Michel, it was superfluous."

"Good. Enjoy my driving, I am the best, and then you can tell me what's going on in your life right now over breakfast."

"Sounds like a remarkable plan."

While they journeyed in silence save for Michel's occasional impatient cursing and commentary regarding the incompetence of his fellow road users, Harry checked the texts he had received since landing - he was one who chose to turn off his phone on a flight. Daphne Crane had sent one regarding the owner of the vehicle which had tailed him yesterday and the owner was Leo Forrest. Just as Harry had predicted. The pock faced lad lived in Hoveton, which was handy for Harry because it was his neighbouring village.

What was Harry to do with this new information? Sensibly he knew that he should pass the name onto the police. But that would mean putting an end to the Wilby job without a satisfactory sense of closure. Now the decision was made and Harry had plenty of time to think up a suitable means of scare to play on Leo.

Daphne and Zero had company business to tend today, and Harry didn't want to burden them with another task. The office had enough work on its plate at the moment and there might be more after today, who knew? It was frustrating for Harry that he had to be away all day on this case but when the money was as good as Smith's, then refusal was out of the question.

Harry's friend Nate had texted with a message to wish for good hunting and reminded Harry to provide a full progress report.

A message had also come from Hayley Wilby. She had received a call from her solicitor and was meeting him that morning. She asked if Harry had contacted her husbands friend Peter. Harry typed a reply which said that Peter couldn't help, and left it at that.

Parisa Dane had also texted him and this one had him smiling, plus it got his imagination working overtime, so much so that he had to remind himself where he was. Parisa claimed to have thought about him quite intensely last night and she couldn't wait for the real thing from him tonight, if he was available for dinner. He read the text twice.

The car interior grew hot despite its air conditioning.

Harry replied in the affirmative and promptly pocketed the phone.

Michel Lomé had first taken them south then east until they passed the Berlin Zoo and were south again on Augsburger Straße, where traditional architecture mixed with the modern to form an eclectic tapestry. Harry noticed the breeze-block grey buildings where he had been situated as part of the team who brought down the notorious Klauski Dynasty. It was a fleeting glance but it seemed as though nothing had altered on the desolate, robust Herzog Straße. Maybe the houses and retail units remained unoccupied to that day. Maybe the bullet holes and blood had yet to wash away. Perhaps the ownership of the Straße was still under dispute. The Dynasty crimewave had impacted the whole of Berlin and memories were long and not easily erased. Time had stood still on that Straße.

Michel continued a further three-hundred yards until veering slightly south-easterly across a shopping zone with blatant western commercialism at its frontage, before a right-hand turn at a crossroads brought them into ShreckwernerStraße. Here the business fronts were more utilitarian and bore independent names. They were all of a uniform nature except one, which bore the brunt of its chain-store resistance in its broken front window and Bundespolizei ticker tape. Long abandoned in a street run by the German faithful. The old guard redirected into the twenty-first century.

This street, Harry knew, was controlled by a local organisation called Aemaet, whose purpose was essentially to return life to early nineteenth century German values. The authorities permitted Aemaet to go about their business, and despite it being a strictly monitored organisation they were linked to innumerable underworld networks whose sole purpose was to wrest control from those they saw as corrupting their once great country.

It reminded Harry of the old buildings and cobbled streets along historic Tombland in Norwich, much of which had also remained untainted by modern machinations.

Quaint, yet secretive.

Michel pulled up in front of a three-storey structure which was right out of the fifties reconstruction period. Four steps led up to the clean white portico, forming a mouth, with the tall top floor meshed out windows the eyes.

When he turned off the engine Michel twisted about in his seat to face Harry.

"This is the place." Michel nodded toward the three-storey building. "I checked it out this morning before picking you up. Cafes across the street."

"I shouldn't be surprised by your efficiency." Harry said. "But I am. And I presume you're okay to park here?"

"You presume correctly, my friend."

They crossed the street and enjoyed a sumptuous breakfast of smoky Shinkon, scrambled egg and lovely sourdough rolls, with ample black coffee in the proudly pro-Nationalist cafe. Harry filled Michel in with all the details from the Stephen Smith job, omitting nothing because the Frenchmans input would be invaluable. Michel's natural fascination with mysteries kept the Frenchman hooked and he was soon up to speed.

Harry paid the bill, it was the least he could do, and they strode up to big and sturdy brown double doors set in the crumbling red brick wall of the three-storey building. There was no buzzer so Michel turned the handle and they stepped into the reception room, which was a funny shaped narrow rectangle done out to someone's tasteless specifications. The carpet was a deeply rich Axminster centrally ascending a dark-wood staircase with brass grips and redwood banisters.

The left-hand side of the room up to the staircase was glass fronted with a glass door, beyond which was a fully equipped gymnasium where a couple of muscular blonde haired guys worked out in trainers, tight-fitting shorts and vest tops which accentuated their muscles. They were undoubtedly the building's security guards and both cast heavy-browed glances at Harry and Michel when they entered reception, their aim to intimidate.

The wall opposite was adorned with portrait photographs of tweed-dressed mature men with brass plaques beneath bearing their names and the dates which they were resident bankers in the building, but instead of a predictable aesthetically pleasing wood-panelled wall backing the photos, it was garishly decorated with blue and yellow pinstriped wallpaper.

A brass chandelier hung from a pendant and bathed everything with a too-bright halogen glare.

Harry wasn't particularly fashion conscious but even he had better taste than surroundings which were more appropriate to a health spa rather than a banking building. His London friend Nathaniel might work behind a child-built facade but this was worse.

"Lovely decor." Michel's comment mirrored Harry's thought.

Footfalls sounded from the staircase, created under the weight of a heavy step, and indeed it was a squat rotund gentleman in a tweed suit and Party tie who descended them. He was wheezing when he reached halfway down, his bald pudgy face flush from the exertion, his fat nose as moist as his brow, blue eyes shot through with red, and his mouth gaped, displaying pearly white teeth and a big wet tongue which habitually darted across his thin lips.

"Herr Lomé." The man puffed in German when he saw Michel and Harry, and he cracked a smile of recognition that also bore arrogance and superiority. "And Herr Kovac?"

When the fat man had reached the bottom of the staircase he sighed with what could only be described as relief. "I am Adolf Von Stauffenberg." And he extended his hand, which was small with fat fingers.

Harry shook the effeminate grip, wanting to comment upon the unfortunate contradiction of the fat man's name, but resisted temptation. Undoubtedly Adolf Von Stauffenberg had suffered ridicule at the hands of his childhood peers.

"Adolf." Michel said curtly.

"Pleased to meet you, Herr Von Stauffenberg." Harry said in English - in his experience he found that it sometimes paid not to advertise being fluent in a foreign language, that way one could catch a person out at a later date when they spoke offhandedly behind your back.

The fat man nodded and indicated that Harry and Michel should climb the staircase. In the German's eyes was a pained expression that said he himself would prefer not to, like he was about to ascend Everest itself, not just a flight of stairs. Before following, he looked at the two muscular men in the gymnasium and licked his lips lasciviously, which Harry found hypocritical because fully committed Nazis frowned upon homosexuality.

Harry took the steps two at a time and grinned to himself. Michel followed suit. It was wrong to degrade the fat Nazi but

Harry knew the man would find some way to redress the physical imbalance with his own condescending intellectual superiority.

Herr Von Stauffenberg followed slowly, and when he reached the top landing he led them both into a typical wood and leather bankers office which reeked of body odour and old books, of which the shelves were plentiful - books, not body odour.

They sat opposite each other with a solid oaken table between them.

"You have the letter?" Von Stauffenberg asked bluntly.

"Let's dispense with pleasantries," Michel said, "shall we, old friend?"

"You- want a drink?"

Michel shook his head.

"Nothing for me, thank you." Harry said and produced the letter from the inside pocket of his jacket.

The fat man opened it in his greasy hand and cast a glance over it, nodding with superiority, furrowing his brow and smiling with arrogant knowledge as if everything had been totally obvious in the first place.

"I know it." He stated. "And it's a fascinating history." With that claim he proceeded to bore Harry and Michel with a dull ten-minute long lecture on the history of banking and deposit boxes and their relevance to the German economy. Eventually he got to the points of interest which Harry required. "The box you require was moved in the early nineteen-nineties - October nineteen-ninety two, to be precise – when the building it was in was demolished to make way for what is now the capitalist monstrosity Potsdamer Platz. The old bank was situated in the Russian quarter of East Berlin before the wall fell in nineteen eighty-nine. All their boxes were moved to their present location in the vault of the Geschichte Bank."

"Are you able to gain entry there for my friend and I?" Michel asked. "We don't possess a key."

Von Stauffenberg stroked his chin thoughtfully. In Harry's mind, the German was playing the game to the full. He was bound to be as intrigued as they were, only his stoic expression was giving away nothing. Maybe Von Stauffenberg's heritage had chiselled the reticence into his psyche which he displayed.

"Ya." Von Stauffenberg said. "Of course. It will be a favour to you and our friend Herr Beckley. First I shall have to make a phone call, but it can be arranged."

"I understand." Harry said. "And thank you, Herr Von Stauffenberg."

"I shall, of course, accompany you." Von Stauffenberg informed then.

"Of course." Harry agreed.

"I would expect nothing less, Adolf." Michel stated.

"Shall we take my car?" Von Stauffenberg was telling them, rather than asking.

## CHAPTER TWENTY

Harry Kovac and Michel Lomé sat in the wide forward-facing rear seat of the chauffeured Mercedes Limousine opposite Adolf Von Stauffenberg. It had been a clipped ten minutes after the German banker had called through for the car. They were whisked into Berlin's Banking District and it was a smooth and comfortable drive as the streets flashed by outside the window.

"Have you visited our country before, Herr Kovac?" Von Stauffenberg asked perfunctorily.

"Yes. Many times."

"Recently?"

"A few years past."

"You like our country?"

"Yes. And the people. You have a no-nonsense approach to things which, well, from my point of view it makes life less complicated. If you know what I mean?"

"I do, Herr Kovac, I do. I am from the old establishment. I have traced my ancestry back over two hundred years. My family were of noble birth. They were honoured patriots. They protected and respected the traditional German values."

Harry wondered which family connection the German was talking about but chose not to broach the subject. "I can empathise. My family were the same."

"Do you not agree that it is becoming increasingly difficult to perpetuate traditional values in these less tolerant times, Herr Kovac? Patriotism is often coupled with extremism. Passion for ones country is seen as racism."

Michel, who had been quietly listening, finally spoke up: "The popular phraseology is snowflake generation. Although ironically it is politically incorrect to use the phrase. We exist in a society today where caution is the byword. Caution regarding actions and words. Caution against racial contact lest we upset others. Society today has narrowed because of the internet, but it has also broadened the cultural divide because people don't have to be present when making their views. It's a technological mask whereby the snowflake or troll can perpetuate fake news and hatred by proxy. And it will get worse before it gets better."

"Well said," Von Stauffenberg agreed.

Harry nodded. He could definitely see the reality in what Michel and Von Stauffenberg said. Upholding beliefs in patriotic values were often upended by the moral high ground. The value of law and order themselves were shadows unto which those of righteous indignation frowned. Harry knew injustice. Harry knew many of the persecuted patriots. The trouble was, plenty of those patriots chose violence as their tool.

"What do you hope to find in the vault when we get there, Herr Kovac?" Von Stauffenberg asked casually.

"Hidden treasure." Harry laughed, half joking. "Did Beckley tell you where the letter with the box number on it was discovered?"

"Yes." Von Stauffenberg's eyes lit up briefly. "It was found behind a priceless, long-lost piece of art."

"That's right."

"Very....Hollywood." Michel commented, tongue in cheek.

Harry laughed. "Isn't it just."

"And intriguing." Von Stauffenberg added.

"Quite true."

They spent the remainder of the journey it companionable silence, which wasn't for long, as it turned out. The Mercedes sliced through the traffic between garishly bright fashionable store frontages and pulled up to the kerbside between the soaring glass and steel skyscrapers in Berlin's Banking District. Business was obviously good where German investments were being made and deals were brokered. The sidewalks and road were litter free and unspoilt, most probably cleaned every morning before start of business - like a somber Disneyland. The buildings radiated newness from their every modern angle.

Harry and Michel followed Herr Von Stauffenberg from the car across a wide sidewalk, up a flight of four granite steps onto the raised marble plaza which encircled a spectacular white and glass thirty-storey oval shaped skyscraper, that tapered the further it rose being tipped with various antennae. It was more refined and architecturally exquisite than anything back home in London, unobtrusive yet dominant.

Men, women and the undecided walked in zombie like trances or animated conversation, with their prerequisite phone in one hand, typing with the other. People here were mainly dressed in anthracite or charcoal coloured business suits. Not all, of course. It would be wrong to pigeonhole all business people the same, or tar them with the same uniformity brush, but certainly seventy-five percent of those milling about the business plaza whom Harry saw seemed to come from an identikit.

The Mercedes pulled away from the kerb and drove off, no doubt parking elsewhere until called upon to collect them.

A doorman of the Geschichte Bank pulled open one side of the big double doors by its thick steel bar, and he nodded curtly to Von Stauffenberg, merely cursory interest to Harry and Michel.

The entrance lobby had a vaulted ceiling which spiralled toward the glass frontage and drew in light from outside, providing natural lighting and generating power via a series of solar panels artfully attached to the wall. The floor was a hardwearing grey resin composite. There was a circular eco-friendly wooden service point with two building clerks in attendance centrally positioned, and four elevator shafts next to stairwells.

Security, Harry noted, was discrete and high tech. He could barely see the abundant fisheye cameras, while two guards concealed themselves equitably amongst the workers.

Harry could see they were alert and vigilant. He was impressed. And why not? Germany was renowned for its efficiency.

A woman strode toward the trio with an impassive scrutiny, heels clicking rhythmically on the floor. A smile of greeting briefly flickered from her pursed lips alighting her dark eyes, and she extended her right hand in greeting.

"Herr Von Stauffenberg." She said, her German rich and deep. They shook hands.

"My friends," Von Stauffenberg said to her. "Herr Lomé and Herr Kovac."

She took Harry's hand, her grip firm, confident. Harry thought wryly that she could probably trace her ancestry back two-hundred years, like their host, Von Stauffenberg.

"Welcome to the Geschichte." She said.

"Thank you."

"I spend more time here than at my real home." She said in an attempt at humour. "You understand?"

"I'm retired." Michel said when it was his turn. "But I can sympathise, Madam."

Harry nodded. Typical arrogant banker thinking nobody could possibly understand the joke, and pretentiously believing that she was the only one who worked long hours. This woman was efficient in her dress, makeup and mannerisms and would no doubt prove exemplary at her job.

"You can call me...The Concierge." She said cryptically. "You understand?"

"I certainly do." Harry replied. She was using a nom de plume so there would be no come back on her if Harry revealed details about what she was about to permit them access to, which was totally understandable. Hence she wore no name badge.

Von Stauffenberg said. "Thank you."

The Concierge nodded and smiled almost imperceptibly but enough, and led them across the lobby into the nearest elevator car which had arrived, door open, as if on cue - which it probably had been. She selected the sub-basement and the door closed.

The elevator car and it's occupants descended in silence, and when the doors slid open they looked into an utterly nondescript breeze-blocked cuboid space with just a mirror opposite - so they faced themselves.

And that was it, at least to the untrained eye.

Upon stepping out of the car, which hissed shut behind them, Harry grinned from the corner of his mouth. At first glance the mirror appeared to be perfect, unmarked, and exactly what it was: a mirror. But reflected from behind and above him were pinpoint red diodes which strobed imperceptibly. Again Harry couldn't help but be impressed by the level of security. He had seen similar in an especially modern London vault so he knew what to expect, and wasn't at all surprised when, from the middle section of the mirror, a man appeared as if he had passed straight through it.

The armed guard made eye contact with the trio, utterly unconcerned by their presence, because they posed no threat to the six-feet four inch, two-hundred and fifty pound hulk with an Uzi. He stepped to one side of the entrance to the vault to permit their continued passage.

Harry and Michel followed The Concierge and Von Stauffenberg through the hologram, unfazed and unharmed, into the vault which resembled the interior of a silver golfball. Before them was a small pedestal with a touch screen terminal atop it and a dispenser for thin latex gloves. The floor was flat and circular with a waist high circular dais in the middle, a step-up, and the silver deposit boxes from floor to ceiling in the shiny round room. It was immaculately clean, there wasn't a fingerprint in sight, and it bore a distinctively futuristic appearance.

The Concierge handed the trio a pair gloves each, which they pulled on, while she took the piece of paper with the box code from Harry and stepped up to the terminal, where she deftly tapped in a password followed immediately by the code. Harry saw a box number appear on the screen and a sixty second countdown began.

One of the boxes on the wall, approximately shoulder height and to their right-hand side along the globe interior, emitted a purple point of light which the trio walked up to. The Concierge took hold of the small silver handle and tugged out the box. The purple aura ceased, the terminal made an audible double-beep, and The Concierge placed the oblong box, roughly two-feet wide, three feet deep and six-inches thick, on the small circular dais which was in the centre of the round vault.

"No key required." The Concierge announced proudly.

Von Stauffenberg rubbed his hands together in anticipation, his breathing coming in rapid wheezes. "This is very exciting." He said without displaying any excitement on his face. "The grand reveal." He added pompously.

"And not altogether legal." The Concierge reminded the trio sternly.

"Which I very much appreciate." Harry said. "And I thank you greatly for allowing this." Followed by the winning smile which never failed to work.

The Concierge bowed her head slightly, one corner of her lips twitching briefly, eyes fleetingly registering a positive reaction to Harry's smile. She gave indication with a hand for Harry to proceed with the opening like this was indeed the grand event which Von Stauffenberg suggested.

"May I be permitted to remain?" She asked.

"Of course." Harry confirmed.

Harry took the front of the box squarely in his hands and lifted and turned it toward himself, careful not to drag it across the metallic surface for fear of causing damage, and placed it back down. He turned the two catches positioned left and right of the handle and the click which came from the box signalled it's unlocking. Harry pulled the handle upward and the hinged lid came loose, folding back onto itself.

Von Stauffenberg and The Concierge craned their heads to see what was inside the box before Harry lifted out a wrapped package the size of a small book. He could immediately tell that it was indeed a hardback book beneath the brown grease proofed paper, tied with string which had seen better days but hadn't deteriorated owing to the conditions of storage.

Harry placed the package on the table next to the box and drew out a further, similarly wrapped, but larger, package. This one was the size of a painting but, to Harry's mind, it felt too weighty to be artwork. He placed this package beside the first and tilted the deposit box up by its back corners. Nothing slid out. The two packages had been sole contents.

Von Stauffenberg, The Concierge and Michel all watched silently.

Harry picked up the book-sized package and carefully untied the string, which he dropped back into the box. Next he removed the paper, placing it also in the box. The book was a leather bound claret coloured diary dated 1988, with gold script of the date bearing no sign of its age. A quality product, not a cheap freebie, with it's storage having preserved it.

"Just over thirty years." The Concierge whispered close by. "I somehow expected something much older."

Von Stauffenberg nodded his agreement. He didn't hide the disappointment.

Harry opened the diary up to the first page. An illegible name was scrawled in black ink in the top left-hand corner.

When Harry turned the next page it was revealed that this diary had belonged to the Austrian, Waltraud Koenig.

"You read Russian." Harry said to Michel and handed him the single volume when he saw it was written in that country's language.

Michel Lomé carefully flipped it open to the first page and began reading it, while Harry picked open the knotted string around the bigger package before he carefully unwrapped it. Michel closed the diary, a thoughtful expression on his face, but said nothing as he watched Harry's actions.

A box slightly larger than A3-sized paper and an inch and a half deep, royal blue in colour, was revealed by Harry. It had a faded manufacturing mark upon its felt lid. Harry carefully lifted the lid and beneath was diaphanous pink silk, which he promptly removed.

The quartet let out a collective variety of awed sighs and sounds, comically loud in the man-made sound booth, and it Michel was the one who laughed. The exquisite piece of ornamental jewellery, a necklace, was truly stunning.

"It's called an Opera Necklace." Michel told them, recognising it immediately. "I'm sure of it."

The chain was thirty inches in length, which would rest on the breast bone, and was formed by five-millimetre thick linked gold ringlets. The pendant which hung from it was a tightly formed golden Star of David about three inches in diameter with a dazzling diamond at its centre, itself ringed by twenty equally dazzling but smaller black jewels.

"Black diamonds." Michel said, his eyes studious like a pinpoint directed at the smaller stones.

"Surely they're onyx?" Von Stauffenberg suggested.

Michel shook his head and stooped lower to get a better look. "They're diamonds all right."

"But-"

"It looks old." The Concierge commented. "And valuable."

"I wonder where it's from? It looks Napoleonic." Harry added. He was no expert but the nature of his previous employment meant he sat in on a varied degree of training courses, so his statement wasn't unfounded.

"Yes." Michel said. "Quite right, my friend, very good."

"Maybe the diary contains something to explain it's origin?" Harry suggested.

"It would be intriguing to find out." The Concierge offered, and Von Stauffenberg nodded his agreement with renewed enthusiasm.

Harry carefully replaced the silk and closed up the jewellery box. He placed the book on top and picked up both.

"Thank you," Harry said. "When I get back to England I'm sure my employer will pass the necklace onto a jewellery expert, and when I know it's origin and value, I will inform Herr Von Stauffenberg," then to The Concierge, "and he can inform yourself."

"And the diary?" The Concierge asked.

"If my employer wants it translated," Harry said, "and if he wants my people to do it, then I shall let you know if there's anything interesting written in it, but in my experience diaries are usually filled with mundane musings."

"Then why was it locked away in a deposit box?" Von Stauffenberg asked.

"That is indeed a good point," Michel said, "my inquisitive friend. Perhaps Herr Kovac will discover if there is more to this than first meets the eye." He wasn't asking the question that he wanted to ask. "I, too, am intrigued to know more, but that is not for us to decide."

Both Von Stauffenberg and The Concierge looked vaguely disappointed because they had no say in the matter, but on the surface they accepted Michel's words nonetheless.

"You will be returning with it to England now?" Asked Von Stauffenberg.

"That was my plan." Harry said.

There was an awkward silence. Von Stauffenberg and The Concierge clearly wanted to argue and protest, as if the ownership of the diary and necklace was in contention. But both remained silent.

## CHAPTER TWENTY-ONE

Harry Kovac felt like he was carrying the Crown Jewels or Mona Lisa. In his mind all eyes were upon him and the two packages which he had tucked under his left arm - he had instinctively freed his right arm with which he could more confidently defend himself against attack. Although who the attackers would be and from where they might appear was anybodies guess.

The Concierge bade them farewell, a missive which curiously held a foreboding warning prophecy. She stood stoically as she watched them depart the Geschichte Bank.

When the trio strode across the marble surfaced pavement outside the bank there was nothing amiss, yet Harry's hairs on the back of his neck were up, as if he anticipated danger. He told himself that he wasn't transporting a bomb which might explode any minute. Nobody but the three of them and The Concierge knew of the contents he carried. Neither Von Stauffenberg or The Concierge had had time to inform anyone of what they transported, even if they were inclined to do so.

Harry decided that it was his distrust of humans generally that had made him edgy. It was the way The Concierge and Von Stauffenberg had reacted to the contents, coupled with the suggestion that he take them to the rightful owner. Maybe they both believed that Germany was the rightful owner because that was where they had ended up. And maybe they were right.

The Mercedes Limousine awaited them kerb-side. There were no suspicious characters laying in wait.

Harry smiled at his own distrusting paranoia. Years of expecting the worst from people had mostly been a benefit, and there was no reason to dismiss the ability to detect danger off-hand.

The trio climbed into the backseat and their driver engaged the accelerator and they were away without incident.

Harry sighed out loud without realising it, and placed the packages on his lap.

"Relax, my friend." Michel said.

"I must be getting old." Harry quipped.

"Don't worry. I shall soon have you on a plane back to England. You have nothing and no-one to fear. Isn't that right, Adolf?"

Von Stauffenberg looked startled as his thoughts were disturbed. He smiled, briefly, and mumbled an affirmation. "My only interest is that these artefacts get into the proper hands, and not some dealer who is only out for their own greed. They should go to the rightful owner."

"I agree." Michel said. He exchanged a knowing look with Harry. "Hopefully the painting behind which the letter was found, and now this necklace, will end up in a museum for all to enjoy and not in a private collection."

"One can hope, Herr Lomé." Von Stauffenberg said out of politeness only. He definitely believed the latter more than the former. "And what of the diary?" He added as an afterthought.

"That's up to my client." Harry said wearily. "He's a man of wealth who is just as fascinated by this escapade, as he calls it. I think you can rest assure, Herr Von Stauffenberg, that my client will offer these trinkets to a museum."

"There you are." Michel slapped his thigh. "Your concerns are over, Adolf. The next time you visit the Pergamon Museum you might see that necklace." Michel nodded to the larger of the two packages on Harry's lap.

Von Stauffenberg nodded acceptance but was clearly still unconvinced.

They arrived outside the office of Adolf Von Stauffenberg, and the limousine smoothly pulled up to a standstill behind Michel's car, which seemed to be dwarfed by the large, black German Mercedes.

The trio climbed out, exchanged pleasantries before the German banker left them on the sidewalk.

"Greedy banker." Michel muttered under his breath when the German was out of earshot. "His day will now be spent checking the value of diamonds and necklaces." He laughed. "Come, my friend."

Harry climbed into the passenger seat of Michel's car. The Frenchman expansively stretched his arms before getting in the drivers' seat and turning the key in the ignition. The engine burst into life before ticking over.

"I have," Michel said, "some devious minded friends, no?"

"Herr Von Stauffenberg was more interested in the contents of the diary than the necklace."

"I noticed that too."

Michel released the handbrake, indicated to pull out and promptly did just that. Ahead the road was clear the three blocks to an intersection. A hundred-yards back were two cars which were joined by a third car, a red Audi RS e-Tron GT.

"This Waltraud Koenig fascinates me." Michel said, eyes on the road. "He flees Europe and assumes a new name. He had a priceless painting in his home with a letter he wrote to himself hidden behind it. We find his diary with a necklace dating back two centuries. Maybe more. He was obviously an important fellow."

"You think there might be something in the diary which leads us to more artefacts?"

"Yes, my friend, I do. I think these two items, the painting and the necklace, are to whet one's appetite. Koenig probably realised that if somebody like yourself set off on the hunt, then whatever gold lies at the end of the rainbow might be discovered."

"Which may explain why the Russians had the name Waltraud Koenig on a watchlist."

"Precisely so." Michel drummed his fingers thoughtfully on the steering-wheel. "If Koenig is wanted for some unspecified reason by the Russians and the safety deposit box was originally located in old East Germany, it might be safe to assume that our man worked for them. That is to say the Russians."

"I'm sure my client wouldn't object to me leaving the diary with you." Harry hedged. "If you're interested, that is."

"I thought you would never ask." Michel laughed.

Having made a few lefts and rights at junctions Michel had become accustomed to seeing the red Audi in his rear-view mirror. At first he thought maybe their being there was a coincidence. It wasn't as if they were hassling the traffic. Plus the car did stick out like a sore thumb so wasn't exactly discrete for a tail. Maybe the occupants had been told by their boss to ensure Harry arrived at the airport unscathed. Perhaps they had been warned off engagement. Or maybe they were unmarked police.

"It might be nothing, my friend," Michel said at length. "And don't look back, but I think we have grown ourselves a tail."

Michel indicated to turn left, which wasn't exactly a diversion from their route to the airport but it certainly wasn't the most direct path.

"Two cars back." Michel said. "Now."

Harry looked in the wing-mirror and saw the vivid red Audi. He got a brief glimpse of the driver in a white t-shirt and a passenger in blue. Both had blonde hair.

"They aren't exactly trying for a subtlety award." Harry quipped.

Michel laughed: "Not at all, my friend."

"I wonder who they work for?"

"It might be useful to find out. Open the glove box."

"What?"

"You will find a gun."

Harry found the weapon, an old Walther PPK which had probably been fashionable in the 1940's but was now an antique. At least it looked clean and in good working condition.

"Seriously!?"

"We live a rough world."

"You're retired. Is this legal?"

"It's a collectors item, my friend. I'm taking it to a dealer, of course! At least I am if anyone should find it and ask. Besides, I still have my licence. Do you?"

Harry nodded and instinctively turned the gun in his hand, released the magazine and slid it out. The mechanism was smooth. He palmed it back in with an encouraging click, released the safety and thumbed it back. It had been many months since Harry had handled a firearm but once learned, never forgotten, and it was a reassuring man-stopper.

"Happy?" Michel asked.

"Never better."

The street which they were on was a busy shopping district. People milled around every corner, crossed sidewalks and generally got in each other's way. There were plenty of roads left and right and much stopping and starting of traffic, which offered Michel ample time to locate the type of road which he required: a single-lane, one-way street which might primarily be used for unloading. The kind that might be quiet and less frequented by the average motorist. Identical to the one fifty yards beyond a crosswalk.

"Question is," Michel said, mostly to himself, "will they be stupid enough to follow us?"

Michel nudged the indicator just as they moved beyond the crossing. He slowed, waited for a man and woman to pass the entrance of the street, and drove onward.

The street ahead was a block deep, open ended, it's buildings two-storey's high either side. There were twin fire-escape ladders either side. A big loading door was set half-way on the left wall, while half-a-dozen doorways were open on the right with various vendors on the sidewalk.

No traffic blocked their passage.

The business vendor proprietors watched the unfamiliar vehicle with puzzled annoyance. They didn't get much traffic this way so assumed the driver had lost his way.

Michel deliberately dawdled along at five miles an hour.

The Audi had been only fifty yards back. It's nose appeared. They too had slowed down. Harry looked in his mirror and could imagine the debate, the back and forth arguing over what they should do. But they rolled on past the entrance with barely a glance from the passenger. Clearly, they weren't being drawn into an ambush.

"It might be a sound idea if we parted company here." Harry said. "They cannot follow us both, and I can catch a bus to the airport along the street back there." He put the diary into the glove-box beneath the Walther PPK."

"Sounds a solid plan." Michel agreed and drew the car up to a standstill. "Call me when you are in the air, my friend."

"Safe journey to you, Michel."

Harry got out the car and gave Michel a quick wave as the Frenchman drove off.

# CHAPTER TWENTY-TWO

Harry Kovac hopped onboard a shuttle bus to Berlin Tegel Airport within ten minutes of leaving Michel to go on by himself, the valuable parcel plucked securely under the crook of his arm nobody was wrestling it from Harry's grip.

He wondered if Michel would catch up with Audi, or vice versa, and if so would he discover who they were representing. Harry had pieced events together how he saw them unfolding. Whether he was right or wrong mattered not. He concluded that the Audi had been waiting at Von Stauffenberg's after a phone call from The Concierge of the Geschichte Bank. She had been working in some capacity for Russian Intelligence, which explained her reaction to the diary. Although Herr Von Stauffenberg had reacted similarly, he hadn't had the opportunity to phone ahead. Unless the Audi had been waiting longer, then it was Von Stauffenberg who worked for the opposition.

It was a tangle of what-if's and Harry left them dangling in his subconscious to fight it out amongst themselves.

The air out front the airport was stifling after the coolness of the air-conditioned bus and Harry was pleased to be inside the main terminal moments later. Hardly a surprise but the terminal had a steady flow of foot traffic. Harry's senses remained on high alert, despite the unlikeliness of something bad going down here. Certainly the Russians had no jurisdiction here.

Harry joined the back of a small queue of people waiting at the British Airways desk. Daphne Crane had taken the liberty of pre-booking three probable outbound flights for him ahead of time. The next was due to liftoff in thirty-minutes time. When it was his turn he requested that particular flight and was handed his tickets without any delay.

"Have a good flight."

"Thank you." Harry replied cordially.

Next was the customs desk, where Harry anticipated a delay due to the package with the necklace he was transporting. He was prepared, though, for the inevitable.

"You have proof of receipt?" This was less a question from the customs officer, more a stoic statement. The officer didn't really care either way. In fact, Harry knew that delaying passengers was often the highlight of a custom officers shift.

"No." Harry smiled, and produced his private investigator license along with a business card which The Concierge of the Geschichte Bank had given him. "But if you would care to telephone this number and explain who am I and the package I carry, I'm sure she will verify my credentials." At least Harry hoped she would. Either way at least it would be revealed who was working for whom.

The customs officer studied both license and card, his expression one of well trained boredom. He regarded Harry, considered him and what he said at length.

"Come with me, sir." The sir was added as an afterthought.

Harry was led through a door marked 'Customs Private' which opened into a ten by ten boxy room. The only furniture was an aluminium tête-à-tête table and chairs. An unmarked door in back led to the Customs nerve centre, a facility which Harry was familiar with from old.

"Wait here." The customs officer said and disappeared through the unmarked door, along with Harry's license and the business card.

Harry accepted the cold invitation and decided to sit down in one of the chairs. He placed the re-wrapped package atop the table in front of him.

Accustomed as he was to bureaucracy, and fully aware that security was paramount, especially these days, Harry expected to wait not much more than five minutes to be cleared for travel. Ten, tops. Enough time to catch his flight.

Ten minutes passed.

He began to feel anxious. He might not make the flight if it took much longer. What was keeping them? Maybe the phone call to the Geschichte Bank was the delay. Maybe The Concierge was the duplicitous one.

Fifteen minutes passed.

Harry was definitely going to miss his flight unless someone pulled their finger out. But unlike the average commuter he had alternatives. This customs stalling tactic was designed to make a person impatient, antsy, especially if they were guilty of something. At least now, Harry knew what it felt like to be on the receiving end of this kind of treatment.

He forced a mental shrug. Matters were out of his hand. If The Concierge had painted a negative picture of Harry Kovac then his private investigator license meant nothing in the grand scheme of things. Harry would be tied up with the local authorities in Berlin as he tried to explain his actions. One consolation was that Michel Lomé had the much sought after diary, and by the time Harry got back home, hopefully the Frenchman would have made a good start on the translation.

Twenty minutes passed.

The unmarked door opened and it wasn't the customs officer who returned with his license and the business card.

"Detective Serge Cheklovich!" Harry said without hiding the surprise in his voice, and he rose from his chair.

Detective Cheklovich smiled and shook the extended hand which Harry offered. The Interpol officer was about Harry's age, of a similar height and build, but that was where any similarity ended. His face was pale from various skin grafts, results of enemy action, he sported a scruffy beard which attempted to hide the disfigurement, and failed, and he was bald. He was dressed in black.

"Am I in trouble?" Harry asked.

"Big trouble with Russia, my old friend." Cheklovich said with the best grin his grafts permitted. "Have you been stirring the pot from across the pond in little England?"

"Funny you should mention it."

"And with our friend Michel in tow. Do I need to worry?"

"Not necessarily, Serge." Harry said at length, and explained the visit to the bank and the tail they had after leaving the office of Herr Adolf Von Stauffenberg.

"The good Von Stauffenberg is your leak, old friend."

Harry nodded. It had been a fifty-fifty chance but he had hedged his bets on the banker, rather than The Concierge. The duo in the Audi must have been patiently waiting their return.

"There's a first." Harry's said. "A banker openly cooperating with Russian Intelligence."

If Detective Cheklovich had eye brows he would've raised them: "Who said anything about Russian Intelligence?"

"So. Mafia then?"

Detective Cheklovich nodded.

Harry nodded thoughtfully. That would confirm the two back home in England who didn't want to show their identification at the Crane offices.

"And what does Interpol suggest I do next?" Harry asked.

"Officially, Harry, I am to advise you try to avoid travelling back to Germany for the foreseeable future. We do not need the trouble. And you would be detained for your own protection. There are many ongoing operations taking place at present, and your stirring of the pot would be undesirable."

"Too many cooks." Harry said. "I understand. How about the unofficial angle?"

"Be very careful, old friend. Michel was able to lose his pursuers with our intervention. And my presence here at the airport scared others away. This organisation is very well protected and monitored. I don't need tell you how dangerous these kinds of people can be."

Harry nodded: "Thank you, Serge."

Detective Cheklovich nodded his acknowledgement: "Your next flight leaves in an hour. Join me in a drink?"

"That's an offer I cannot turn down."

## CHAPTER TWENTY-THREE

Harry and Detective Cheklovich avoided all shop talk and spent their drinking time reminiscing about past glories and indignities, until it came time for Harry to catch his flight back home.

"Be careful, old friend." Were Serge's final words. "It would be good to see you again."

It didn't take a scholarship in prose or psychology for Harry to read between those lines.

The flight from Berlin to Norwich was uneventful, but Harry's subconscious was dialled up so high that he couldn't relax. There were lots of loose ends which needed tying up on the two main jobs which played through his mind. Karl Wilby and Waltraud Koenig. Could they be any more a disparate pair. Yet both cases arrived on the same day from entirely different sources. And both cases were a change from what had become normal for Harry Kovac. Normal did not necessarily mean mundane, but it was definitely a splendid and welcome mixture.

And a week ago along came Parisa Dane in his life.

There was no connection to these three events - except Beeston Grange - but Harry wistfully thought it was funny how, as the saying went, that things often came along in threes.

And occasionally in pairs.

Anatoly Polivanova and Annika Smimov were standing impassively beside Harry's car when he strolled through the above ground car-park of Norwich Airport. Anatoly had obviously been to work, while she sported the grey suit with sleeves rolled up to expose muscular arms.

Good news travelled fast, Harry thought wryly.

"Good afternoon." Harry said amiably.

Annika nodded her head toward the package which Harry had tucked under his arm, the veins prominent on her sinewy neck: "You had two."

"You're well informed." Harry said. "For Russian Intelligence, I mean"

Annika grinned mirthlessly: "Everything we do is for our Motherland."

Anatoly stood proudly in place, chest out, head high, eyes front. The true patriot, or missing link.

"What have you done with the diary?" Annika asked.

"Wouldn't the necklace be a more valuable asset?"

"We are not interested in mere trinkets. You and Stephen Smith can keep that and the painting. We want the diary."

"I left it with your friend Herr Adolf Von Stauffenberg."

From beneath her heavy brows Annika studied Harry hard. Harry stared back implacably. If she wanted to play that game Harry was an expert. They might be used to intimidation tactics, and Harry admitted to himself that Anatoly would be a challenging adversary in a fight, yet he wasn't the sort of person who felt easily threatened. What was the age gap: ten years? Wisdom over youth?

Anatoly was yet to move. Presumably he would do so on command from Annika.

"You gave it to your friend Michel." Annika stated bluntly. "It was a pity we didn't know that before…"

"Before your organisation let him get away?" Harry said. "Look, I don't have a clue what might be in it but it's clearly a probability there's some juicy stuff you and your friends are frightened might get discovered. Better stuff than this necklace or a long lost piece of artwork. If it's something of value to the Russian people then naturally my client will hand it over, presuming he wants to continue the pursuit."

Annika grunted dismissively. "Why did your friend Michel get involved if you know nothing about the diary?"

"He's a translator."

"And ex Interpol."

"Among many other things."

"Just so." Annika said. "How can we ensure you and Michel will not pursue whatever he finds in the diary?"

"You can't." Harry couldn't help but grin because he knew there was no way any intelligence agency could find Michel's home. They would have to stop him en route, which again would be no small task, because Michel Lomé would have numerous car changes available to him. There was no man more capable of eluding people than the Frenchman.

"Unless we offer to purchase the diary once it is in the hands of Stephen Smith."

"I suppose that would be an option to you. I can ask him next time I see him, if you like?"

Annika laughs dryly: "Thank you Mr Kovac but I think not. But, if you should interfere..."

"Is this where your silent but deadly strongman comes in? Is he going to break an arm or a leg or just a finger? Does he talk?"

"He does."

Harry directed his next question to Anatoly: "You must hate being lumbered with an English name for your hotel job? It must make you feel humiliated to bow and scrape like a servant, Olly."

Anatoly was starting to bristle with anger. It didn't take much. The glare from his eyes would be enough to drop an ordinary person. In fact, Harry himself was questioning the wisdom of riling such an individual. Undoubtedly Anatoly would do anything which his superior instructed no matter the consequences.

"Is the name Karl Wilby familiar?" Harry asked Anatoly.

Anatoly churned out a few words in Russian which Harry couldn't understand, but assumed they weren't overly friendly. Harry tried reading some kind of reaction to the name, but there was none. That was the trouble with professionals. They knew their job better than anyone else and were skilled. Hence being a professional. Harry was butting up against one right now. Nothing was going to be learned except the man's boiling point.

"I'll take that as a no?" Harry said.

"Take it how you like." When Anatoly spoke in his deep voice the ground seemed to reverberate. The Russians expression didn't alter. He shifted forward, right foot forward, one stride, and it was as if he had covered the entire distance separating him from Harry.

"Take your best swing." Harry said. "It'll be the only chance you have."

Anatoly bellowed with laughter.

"Not here." Annika told Harry. "But we will keep you in check. We know about the Crane's. Should some accident happen to them, then you will know it was our doing. Or perhaps your girlfriend. We work without prejudice. So, make sure your friend Michel returns the diary promptly, Mr Kovac, otherwise I shall be forced to send others to retrieve it."

To mock, or not to mock. That was the question in Harry's mind. But he decided not to test his luck too far. Mention of Parisa, his girlfriend, was enough to quell any urge he might have to engage in unarmed combat. Harry couldn't put her in jeopardy. Mention of her had been enough. The only thing to do was play along, pretend to have been rattled, then proceed from there.

"I understand fully." Harry said compliantly. "And you have my word that I shall contact Michel at once."

"Good." Annika seemed happy and, most importantly to Harry, convinced. "You have common sense, Mr Kovac. I am pleased by that."

Without another word, Annika turned and walked away. Presumably in the direction of their car. Anatoly hesitated only briefly. Enough to stamp his perceived superiority, before following his boss.

Harry gritted his teeth. He wasn't a person who threatened easily but protecting Parisa had prevented him from from acting rashly. Harry would definitely have to settle the account with these Russians sometime, but first he had to take the necklace to the Crane office before they locked up.

# CHAPTER TWENTY-FOUR

Parisa Dane lived in a detached bungalow on a desirable estate in the equally desirable Norwich City suburb of Thorpe St. Andrews. Many of the properties in that particular hamlet offered spacious front and rear gardens, either open or walled and gated, generous driveways, and what shops were there were boutiques rather than common place retailers. The three sides of the village which didn't adjoin houses were surrounded by fields and trees.

Addy Avenue had only existed for ten years. A farmer had chosen to sell some of his land which now accommodated the twelve bungalows, one of which Parisa snapped up not more than six years past.

Harry parked his Ford next to Parisa's top of the range brand new white BMW X7 in the oval-shaped turning circle through the open wooden gate of her property.

The oval flowerbed was perfectly tended, the circle was blue and white stone RonaDeck resin, and the front lawn was a lustrous green - fake grass. The bungalow exterior was whitewashed and oak beamed with dark-wood framed windows, a recessed doorway and sported a beautiful thatched roof. This could almost pass as a show property for perspective buyers rather than a lived-in home.

When Harry climbed out his car he realised his stomach was twisted with nervous anticipation and he didn't know why. He had been married and had relationships before marriage. He had much life experience. It was not as if Harry were a giddy schoolboy. He had received blatant offers of sexual favours from men, women, and those who weren't entirely sure. But Parisa was different, and he couldn't really put his finger on why that was.

His muscles, which had ached earlier, were tense and he couldn't shrug off the feeling of the days momentum. Harry had been moving all day, one way or another, and his mind continued to race ahead. To tomorrow. To tonight, and the next relationship stage. He was still angry after his confrontation with the Russian. Having relayed the warning to Michel had made him feel better, and the Frenchman was as determined as Harry to crack the puzzle. But where would it next lead?

Harry shrugged it off with smile to himself, loosened his neck and shoulders, picked the flowers off the passenger seat - pink roses, which he hoped Ms. Dane weren't allergic too - locked his car and strode to the front door.

Parisa had obviously witnessed his arrival for she opened the door before he could press the buzzer. Perhaps she had a miniature motion activated security camera which activated a phone app to alert her of visitors, that way she could choose who she opened the door to, or not. A very modern conceit in this paranoid avoidance society, but a useful tool nonetheless. Harry saw the discrete doorbell-cam.

"Hi." She said and smiled at the roses then at Harry.

Harry held out the bouquet which she took. Parisa looked particularly ravishing, a beautiful figure in skin-tight denim jeans and a flimsy white blouse tied in a knot, over which was a yellow-checked kitchen apron. He hair hung loosely about her shoulders, glossy, as if she weren't long out the shower. She was flush faced from working on their dinner and, backlit by the sun, which was setting behind her bungalow and cascading its orange hue through the hallway she was a heavenly vision. That's how Harry would describe the scene.

Harry's nostrils detected a lovely aroma wafting through the door. "Something smells good." What he wanted to say was too corny, because he wanted to say that the aroma was as good as she looked. But this wasn't the seventies, when corny one-liners passed muster.

"Come in."

Harry stepped over the threshold and onto the wood-decked hallway. Parisa closed the door behind him. She kissed him on the lips, a peck, but the fire burned passionately behind her eyes and she muttered a curse before locking lips with him.

Minutes, or hours, later, Harry couldn't tell, they came up for air.

"I love it." She panted, before taking a step back as if willing herself to wait, which took a great deal of discipline to accomplish. "I hope you're hungry."

"Famished. I haven't eaten since breakfast."

"Busy day?"

"Yes. Stressful. And you?"

The way Parisa looked up at his face made him think he had something unsightly about him. His quizzical look drew her toward him.

"Allow me." She reached behind his head and pulled his lips onto hers and she kissed him more firmly. Her lips were moist, soft and warm. She tasted of citrus and white wine. When they parted she was smiling. "Is that better?"

"Much better. Thank you."

"My pleasure."

Harry felt warmth under his collar. Parisa's eyes twinkled. A fire burned in his stomach which spread outward. The stresses of his day had melted away almost instantly.

Parisa took him by the hand and led him into the kitchen from where the delicious aroma came. Her hand felt tiny in his own, but not delicate, she had a good, confidant warm grip. It was reassuring. He should be exhausted but wasn't, and Parisa looked fresh and awake.

"I hope you like Cantonese?" She asked.

"Very much."

"Good. Would you like some wine?"

The implication and expectation in her question, and the way she stood hand poised at the handle of her fridge was unmistakable. They hadn't arranged for him to stay the night, there had been no preplanning or assumptions. Harry was an old-fashioned guy like that. He could only have hoped. But there was no need for Parisa to ask.

"A large glass definitely wouldn't hurt." Which was true in Harry's case. He carried with him a rare chemical condition that prevented him from being intoxicated for long. His metabolism rejected the effects of alcohol. Harry received the initial hit but it wore off quicker than it would in a regular person, meaning he felt no hangover or side effects.

She nodded, read between the intonation of his words, happily satisfied, and refilled her own glass whilst pouring one for him.

"So, have you been investigating me, mister detective?"

"No."

"Oh. I'm disappointed."

"I prefer questioning you in person." He told her when she handed him the wine. They chinked glasses. "Wait until you see my interrogation tactics."

She laughed. "You haven't found out my name yet, then?"

"Isn't it Parisa Dane?" Now that he thought about it there had been no such question asked during their previous dates. She asked him about Kovac, but obviously something else had cropped up in their conversation meaning he hadn't asked her.

Harry concluded that for Parisa the wine was talking. And maybe nervousness. A curiosity in this day and age, especially from someone who exuded confidence.

She indicated for him to be seated at the head of the dining table and turned her back but they continued the conversation.

"Dane." Harry repeated and shrugged, no clue as to the names origin so took a stab in the dark. "Scottish?"

"Irish."

"Close."

"Not really."

"You have the Irish fire."

"I'm half Italian on my fathers side."

"Ah, that makes sense."

"But I'm an orphan." She explained. "My mother was Elizabeth Maccudyn." She held up her hand, seeing that Harry was confused. "Maccudyn is an anglicised name derived from a Gaelic surname based in County Donegal. My father met my mother at Spivey Point, a fishing village, and couldn't conceive so I was adopted. And that's as much as I know."

Harry was impressed. Most people had no idea or didn't care where their name came from or what it meant. "You've looked deeply into it. I'm going to guess that Parisa has Persian origins."

"Well done. And it means like a fairy."

"Ah. That makes sense. Do you speak Italian?"

She nodded. "Plus English and German."

"Zweisprachig."

Parisa laughed at that.

"Ya. Bist du bereit fur das Abendessen?"

"Ya, bitte."

"Your German is good." Parisa offered.

"Better than my English sometimes."

Parisa served up the Cantonese in ceramic bowls. The meal was delicious and they ate and drank with companionable small talk, making eye contact and acknowledgement with smiles, much as they had on previous dates, but there was a palpable feeling of anticipation.

"What was Berlin like?" She asked.

"Hot. Stuffy. And unchanged." He grinned at some other distant memory. "I felt like the outsider cop going back into an arena of oppression. They're very efficient, the Germans, but there still exists a Fascist underground movement. One might think that by now, based on their history over the last hundred years, if any nation were to have banished subversive behaviour, it would be the Germans. But that's not the case. A bit like us in England, to a smaller degree, with our fading National Pride which is often considered to be racist or elitist or worse."

"Did you achieve your goal?"

"Sure. They're very efficient in their work, I'll say that for them." Harry didn't tell her everything, he didn't want to ruin the best evening he had experienced in years. Once the bowls were empty and glasses drained, he said as much.

"I'm pleased you enjoyed it."

Parisa got a second bottle of wine from the fridge, filled their glasses, and they repaired to the lounge and seated themselves on the three-seater sofa which looked across the back lawn, lit by stars and moonlight, sipping their wine, patio doors swung wide open. The cool night air was wonderful as it wafted indoors, as if it complemented the food and drink.

"This is wonderful." Harry said. "Thank you for dinner."

"You're welcome."

Parisa leaned toward him, placed a hand on his thigh, and they kissed passionately.

"Mmm." She moaned contentedly and licked her moist lips. "I love it. Now let's see if I can't help ease away the rest of your stresses."

# CHAPTER TWENTY-FIVE

Harry and Parisa made love again next morning and when they dragged themselves free of the sheets to the shower it was seven thirty. Scrubbed and dressed, Parisa sorted coffee and orange juice and cereal for breakfast which they could enjoy on the back patio.

Parisa had a morning meeting in Norwich City's Millennium Library at nine o'clock, and Harry had a rendezvous with Sarika Royal's friend, Leo Forrest, who had supplied her with the date rape drug and used intimidation. The lad wasn't yet aware of this rendezvous.

Harry watched Parisa admiringly in her thin blouse which was of an almost diaphanous red material with a black bra beneath, and a black skirt which showed the right amount of thigh and proved distracting - at least it was to Harry, the red-blooded male.

She was radiant like the new dawn, or the cat which had got the cream.

"What time does your meeting finish?" Harry asked, then downed the remnants of coffee from the bottom of his large mug.

"I should be back home no later than one o'clock. We're still on for the rest of the day...I hope."

"Most definitely, yes." Harry pushed himself off the sofa. "The proverbial wild horses couldn't keep me away."

"I'll get some extra food in so we don't have to leave the house."

"Sounds good to me. After my jobs are all finished I can get a change of clothes and ablutions from home then I am all yours."

"And I, my darling," Parisa said, unfolding her legs and rising from the sofa, "am all yours."

Their final kiss before parting was explosive with the promise of what was to be in store later. Harry reluctantly tore himself away from her.

"Behave." He said.

Lowering her head, she looked up at him in the most submissive, coquettish manner possible which took his breath completely away. "I shall try, darling." She said. "At least until this afternoon."

He mouthed a curse and grinned and left her in the lounge. She would be safe from harm that morning. There would be plenty of people with her. And then all afternoon he would be with her. Harry didn't need to concern himself with the Russians.

He was grinning like the Cheshire Cat all the way to his car, eventually shaking his head clear, attempting to bring his senses back to reality and what lay ahead that morning. He had to get the lad who set up Karl Wilby and teach him a lesson or two. A task with mixed unpleasantries. Nothing to be proud of.

But Leo Forrest's lesson would be fully deserved.

Stupid kid. He deserved to get caught. Harry chuckled. Fancy using your own car to tail somebody. A real pro would've stolen one!

His stupidity was Harry's gain.

The messages received alert beeped on the phone, which was to be expected, of course. He ignored most of them. Replied to one from Daphne that he was taking the afternoon off, which wouldn't go down particularly well, but who cared?

Michel Lomé had sent him a message at two o'clock in the morning. The Frenchman never required sleep when something had piqued his curiosity, and the Waltraud Koenig diary had most definitely done that. Michel mentioned a township in Austria, Nazi gold, and had attached a file to the message. Michel suggested they meet at the township which had been Koenig's birthplace and where his last known relative still resided.

Harry sent a condensed reply, effectively telling Michel to wait for Harry's phone call before proceeding, and reiterating his caution about the Russians.

Next Harry rechecked the address of the lad he was seeing that morning.

The address was one which Harry didn't recognise in Wroxham so he entered the postcode into his sat nav. Of course Wroxham was the most misinterpreted village the opposite side of the bridge from Hoveton - the neighbouring village to Harry's own, Stalton-on-the-Broads. People often confused the location, believing themselves to be in Wroxham when really most of the life and businesses were, in fact, in Hoveton. The reason for that was because the train station was originally supposed to be in Wroxham - where the local football club was based - and ye olde mapmakers marked Wroxham as the dominant village before the station was built. Thus the first village store, hotel, and boatyards were all addressed as being in Wroxham, despite being in Hoveton, because this was the village on the first map!

Simple!

Harry did not know the layout of the village of Wroxham very well, hence the need for sat nav. Hoveton, he was fine with.

The route from Thorpe St. Andrew to Wroxham was north-easterly and took Harry through Rackheath and Salhouse, twisting and turning, downshifting and never getting into fifth. The sat nav nagged him to take the first turning on his right after he had driven through the dip beyond The Lodge restaurant, which is what he did.

The Avenue, which the road was called, was definitely not for first time home owners. The houses, bungalows and chalets were mostly set back from the road with either sweeping lawns and driveways out front, or gated walled-off perimeters. The homes were impressive in size and of many varying styles, some newer than others, some better maintained than others. Quiet, secluded, and perfect for his objective.

Harry took the drive slowly. The sat nav remained silent. On the small LCD screen his vehicle made steady progression to the dot which was his destination.

He hoped Leo Forrest was home. Otherwise this was going to be a waste of time.

All thought of what the lad had or hadn't done prior to passing the date rape drug to Sarika Royal was moot. Harry knew without doubt that the kid was involved in Karl Wilby's incarceration and suicide. Caryn Krystyva owed money to his fathers business so she had been murdered. Yes, that was detailed in Daphne Crane's message. There was the possibility of more motives for what the lad did and Harry could soon out, if anything, what those motives had been. The lad new Karl's work colleague and friend Sarika Royal and had set him up. Leo Forrest was scum, basically.

It was increasingly likely that the lads father was responsible for getting his son to do these things. But the amateur way they had gone about this just beggared belief.

Yet still the facts had been well concealed from the police who thought that Karl Wilby had been the guilty party, hence their case was practically closed. Chance had come to the welcome assistance of Harry, plus some plain old-fashioned leg work, plus sticking his nose in the correct troughs.

The proper course of action now was for Harry to contact the police, tell them the facts and have the lad brought in for questioning.

But that could wait until later.

The sat nav had announced the address he required was fifty-yards on the left.

Harry silenced the nagging voice and rolled slowly until he crawled opposite a six-feet high panelled fence made of reed. A wide wooden gate, half the height of the fence, broke the centre and was a quarter width of the entire front length. Beyond was a two-storey home with a pretentious white front portico, wide eaves, a solar panel visible on one side of the tiled roof and a balcony with presumably ran around to the rear.

An attached carport contained one vehicle. In it was the lads car. And leaning across the bonnet with a hosepipe in his hand was the lad himself. His skinny frame was bare except for loose fitting hi-vis beach shorts which were in need to pulling up, and a pair of bright orange flip flops. Leo Forrest deserved a kicking for his fashion sense alone.

If looks could kill the lad would've dropped down dead on the spot.

This was obviously the family home. There was no way a scabby lad could afford such luxury.

Harry stopped the car on the opposite side of the road from the gate, turned off the engine and climbed out. The air was humid amongst the avenue of trees, the scent of pine and cyclamen hung heavy. Harry was pleased he was dressed comfortably.

The lad failed to look up when Harry shut the car door and locked up, nor when he carefully opened the gate. He was wearing air-buds and bobbed and weaved to the beat.

Harry paused. Cautious. Just in case the family had a dog. They had no security cameras.

Leaving the gate hanging open Harry walked across the tarmac forecourt. His eyes flirted to the front windows just in case anyone else was home, but the absence of a second car made him conclude early on that the lad was in fact on his own.

Harry appreciated he was riding on a wave of good luck. He was stealthy when required but anybody else would've already clocked his presence.

He was within twenty-feet of the lad when he must have sensed Harry's presence, or saw his reflection in the car.

Leo Forrest turned and his whole body went rigid. He recognised Harry and knew he was out if his league, although if he were with his mates, he would have confidence. Yes, he was one of those kind of bullies.

"Good morning." Harry said without trying to sound menacing because he didn't need to try, he was menacing by virtue of the situation.

The kid didn't know whether to drop the hose, scream in rage or flee in terror. So he just stood stock still and tried his best cool and calm facial expression, but failed miserably.

"You might want to turn that off." Harry said. "You're wasting water."

The lad gradually registered the words spoken and put the hose down. He was wisely being very careful. He didn't know if Harry carried a gun. When Leo turned off the hose at the wall Harry had gotten within three feet of him.

"I should kick your teeth down your throat. Don't you agree?"

The lad opened and closed his mouth like a fish, unable to find any words.

"And I still might. But I can see you're a pussy and I don't like seeing a grown man mess his pants as badly as I think you will. So how about telling me about Karl Wilby and the rape drug and how you murdered Caryn Krystyva?"

"I don't have to say squat to you. You're no more than a private dick. You lay a finger on me and I'll go to the real pigs."

Harry admitted to himself that he was surprised by the brave words from the lad because he really had pegged him as a bit yellow, only capable of intimidating women.

"Wrong answer, Leo."

The kid let loose a stream of curse words which he believed made him the big man. Unfortunately the bigger man socked him on the jaw hard enough to knock him to the ground, dazed, but conscious. Harry followed through with a firm kick up the backside which made the lad yelp and consider himself lucky, because it would've hurt far worse had the position been reversed.

When Leo had caught his breath and emptied his breakfast over the floor, he sat slumped against the wall, glaring angrily at Harry, and let slip a couple more expletives.

"If that's the extent of your vocabulary then this is going to get frustrating, boy. But count yourself fortunate that I have an ounce of compassion. Let's try again. Last Sunday you supplied Sarika Royal with a date rape drug."

The lad looked at Harry and must have realised there was no point in keeping quiet because there was plenty more pain where that came from.

"Sarika wanted the stuff for herself."

"Why?"

"How should I know."

"Come on, really!?"

The lad sighed. "Look. I gave it to her because she asked me too. She told me she wanted it for a guy. Guess it was that bloke who killed that woman."

"Okay. Fair enough. He killed the woman as a result of you passing a drug to Sarika."

"Yeah, exactly."

"So why were you tailing my car the other day?"

"I weren't."

"Yes, you were."

"No I weren't."

"A bit of a coincidence then, is that what you are suggesting?"

The lad shrugged.

"Look, I don't have all day, so I'll make this simple for you. You like to threaten women, which makes you the lowest form of scum. You told Sarika

Royal to pass the drug onto Karl and Caryn, so you could kill the woman without either of them being aware, because she owed your father lots of money and couldn't pay up."

Leo Forrest laughed in derision and told Harry where to go using colourful language. But Harry could see the truth plainly written across the lads face. Harry had most definitely hit the nail on the head and felt supremely satisfied.

Harry took a step forward and kicked the lad in the groin. The result was spectacular. He screamed, curled up into the foetal position, cried, retched and quivered.

All at the same time.

Patiently Harry waited for the lad's long recovery and grinned at him when he was moderately better composed. The hatred and pain in the kids bloodshot eyes was priceless. Worth admission alone.

"Come on, boy. You don't want any more. Spill the beans before I spill some of your red stuff instead of the piss!"

"It was Dad's plan, like you said."

"Good boy. Does that include Karl Wilby's faked suicide?"

"Dunno. Like I just told you, it was all Dad's plan."

"Okay. So how did you slit the woman's throat without leaving a trace of any evidence that you had been there?"

"Easy." The lad told Harry the intricacies of getting away with murder like he was describing the average persons daily chores. He might be slow but he was very conniving and easily impressed by his own cleverness, although Harry suspected his father was responsible for the plan. Why do fools fall so easily?

"What hold do you have on Sarika?" Harry asked.

The kid sniggered. "Her parents would freak out if I posted all the porn stuff she does on the internet."

"Fair enough. You know you're going to jail."

"No I ain't." He sneered. "I got mental health issues. They can bang my Dad up but I'll be taken away in an ambulance and see doctors for a while then be home by Christmas. That'll be nice. Home alone."

"You might need an ambulance right now."

The quizzical expression on the kids face lasted two seconds because it was soon replaced once more by agony. Harry stamped the heal of his shoe into the palm of the lads hand, breaking the bones against the hard tarmac. That wiped the smirk off the cocky little brats face for good.

# CHAPTER TWENTY-SIX

Harry Kovac chose Salhouse Road as his route back to Norwich and arrived at the office of Crane Investigation Services just before ten o'clock. The outer office was empty but movement was visible through the frosted glass of Zero's office. Harry closed the door and the one opposite opened.

Daphne Crane studied his appearance in a brief second and seemed satisfied that Harry was in one piece and unscathed.

"You look like a cat who has got the cream." Daphne said when she saw something in his eyes which obviously gave him away. A sly smile turned one corner of her mouth as she walked to the coffee machine. "Coffee?"

"Yes, please." Harry replied and deliberately avoided looking directly at her. He didn't tell her about the double satisfaction. "Zero not here?"

"Nope. He's paying Mrs Parr a visit, but-"she glanced at the digital wall clock display- "he shouldn't long. Good night last night, was it?"

"Yes, thank you."

"I presume your Russian friends weren't involved?"

Daphne glanced at him sidelong and grinned, fully aware of his aversion to discussing personal matters, but she loved to wind Harry up.

"I've not seen them since leaving the city airport yesterday. Yes, it was a busy day." Harry said at length. "But not altogether unpleasant. Has Stephen Smith collected the necklace yet?"

"Yes. First thing."

"Any mention of the diary."

"Yes. But Zero can fill you in when he gets here."

Harry nodded absently, then said: "Good. I've got to make a phone call and read some stuff. Oh, and I'm going to take the afternoon off."

"I got your message."

"There shouldn't be anything else for me today which can't wait."

"You did have a good night!" Daphne smiled knowingly.

Harry grinned and for emphasis he widened his eyes and raised his eyebrows, took his coffee and turned into his office. He closed the door, stepped to his desk and put the mug onto a placemat. While he picked up the office phone he simultaneously sat down. Harry speed-dialled his friend at the detectives desk of the Norwich City main police station. The detective was assigned to the Karl Wilby murder suicide.

"Morning, Harry." Came the familiar joviality to Harry's ear, which was not at all indicative of the detectives status in the force, or the seriousness with which he conducted himself.

Following on from his own greeting, Harry told him about his own findings on the Wilby case. He also told the detective about the lad who supplied the date rape drug, the fact that Leo Forrest's father was manager at Beeston Grange, plus the information which Sarika

Royal had withheld. Harry omitted nothing and even included WalkTank and Jenny Jane for good measure.

When Harry finished he felt a distinct relief at the unburdened load. As far as he was now concerned the favour asked by Hayley Wilby was now behind him.

"Obviously all this is anonymous." Harry said, not that it was entirely necessary because it would be a big ask for both Harry and the detective to explain how both came about the information. "It's up to you how you act upon these details but I might suggest quizzing Sarika Royal some more first, she was quite forthcoming with a bit of persuasion and she will definitely lead you to the Leo Forrest."

The line was briefly silent and Harry did, for a second, wonder if the connection had been lost. But the officer was digesting all the new stuff thrown into the mixture of the official police investigation. Harry could almost picture the detective drumming fingers upon the desk while cognitive processes were apace.

"Thanks for the tip off." The voice eventually said. "I shall try my best not to mention your name but I can't vouch for Hayley Wilby, nor this Sarika Royal. I presume they both know you by name?"

"Yes." Harry replied. "But we can cross those bridges if or when you reach them. Have fun."

Harry disconnected the call. He was totally confident the detective would know precisely what to do. The problem for Harry's friend would be the red-tape and protocols. But if there was any natural progression that meant Harry's name was avoided a mention then that way would be found. He had consigned the Anatoly Polivanova connection with Beeston Grange to the coincidence pile. It was, after all, a small world.

At least for now Harry could get on with other, more pressing, matters.

The Waltraud Koenig diary, and what it might contain which had stirred up the interest of the Russians. At least, that was, the Russian mafia. Although logically if the diary writers name was on some kind of watchlist it was the Russian government who had been notified, surely? The two who kept entering Harry's life were clearly playing both sides of an age old game of double-dealing.

Harry picked up his mobile phone, found the email which Michel Lomé had sent him in the unearthly hours of the morning, and opened it up. There was no perfunctory salutation just straight to the point, which was a brief biographical background on Koenig, followed by a paragraph on anything of significance which Michel had so far garnered from the diary.

The Frenchman's idea of brief was the equivalent of many an authors short story. Harry skimmed through the facts, digesting pertinent points of detail.

Waltraud Hannes Koenig had been born in 1925 and was raised in the family home in the Austrian village of Spital Am Pyhrn - Michel had added a point of note about Hungarian gold being secreted in the village during World War Two; Harry wondered if maybe that was reason enough for the Russians interest. Koenig was conscripted into military service in 1941, allied with Germany at that time, and saw action in the Mediterranean and Eastern Europe until his capture and internment as a prisoner of war by the USSR. Young Koenig learned the Russian language and eventually became a bookkeeper and translator for them. His work in various capacities continued for the Russian government after the war right up to 1989. He was a filing clerk and helped them set up notable archives in the old Czech Republic, Poland, and East Germany. Koenig married in 1950 and settled his family in his ancestral home at Spital Am Pyhrn, where his oldest living relative, a sister, still resided. Waltraud's wife and children were no longer alive.

As a footnote to the text Michel Lomé had suggested a visit to Spital but would wait on Harry's reply before he proceeded further.

By the time Harry had finished reading he was in need of more coffee. Reading always made him feel slightly lethargic. Desk work was certainly something he did not miss.

Harry stood and stretched. He picked up his mug and opened his office door at the precise moment Zero returned.

"Give me strength." Zero said and closed the outer door. He looked harassed and tired.

"How about a coffee?" Harry offered.

"A strong one, please. Oh. Good morning, by the way."

"And a pleasant one to you."

Zero raised a sceptical eyebrow at that, before he sank into one of the office chairs.

"How was Mrs Parr?" Daphne asked.

"Hard work." Zero told his wife with an exasperated sigh. "While she badmouthed her husband, her neighbours and friends, she practically offered herself on a plate to me. She's a tiring, hypocritical, person!"

"I told you to take care." Daphne admonished. "I knew she was going to be trouble."

"Believe you me," Zero said, "I soon left when she suggested that she and I relax in the garden because it's her private space."

Harry and Daphne laughed. Zero eventually saw the funny side and joined their mirth.

"Stephen Smith's-" Zero hesitated before he found an appropriate word- "friend Climmy collected the necklace this morning."

"Daphne already told me." Harry said.

"We told him about the diary, of course. They're both keen that we should continue investigating Waltraud Koenig as much as possible. Climmy said that he would get his people onto the Russian concern, whatever that means. He also stressed that money was no object."

"That's fortunate. Next port of call is going to be Austria. It's Koenig's place of birth and his only remaining relative, a sister, still lives there in a village called Spital Am Pyhrn."

"You don't plan on going today."

Daphne said to Harry: "I messaged Zero and told him you require the rest of the day off."

Zero nodded, equal part confirmation and consent.

"Thanks guys." Harry said.

"When do you intend going?" Zero asked.

"Tomorrow. We need to act swiftly, just in case the Russians try standing in our path and press for the diary."

"Won't they just go see your friend whose got it?"

"No. Michel is a very difficult man to track down."

"Fair enough."

"Be careful." Daphne warned. "The Russian Mafia aren't exactly short on resources and the duo who we've met are just part of a much bigger cell. It's not only yourself who you have to consider now, Harry."

Harry nodded wearily. "I know. I think I placated them for a while. Things should be okay for now, at least."

"Why the diary anyway?" Asked Zero. "Does it contain some dirty state secret?"

Harry shrugged. "In his message my friend Michel mentioned that the village where Koenig grew up was a storage site during World War Two for Hungary's gold supply. Who knows if other countries didn't use it too, and maybe there's a possibility Koenig somehow knew where it was deposited."

"And if its unclaimed?" Daphne suggested.

"Precisely."

Harry checked his watch. "I'd better go, if that's it?"

Zero nodded. "I can't think of anything else. Daphne can message you if anything crops up."

"Enjoy the rest of your day." Daphne said with a silly grin her face.

# CHAPTER TWENTY-SEVEN

Parisa Dane stood completely stark naked in the doorway of her bungalow casually holding the door open for Harry, smiling, the blazing sun radiating around her. It might be rude to stare but he couldn't help himself, her body was posed erotically and charged with lustre from exposure to the elements, with lines of shadow because she was lit from the rear. Harry's adolescent younger self would've experienced an involuntarily reaction.

It was undeniable that Parisa was not only savvy and intelligent, but also gloriously carefree and confident. Her figure Harry could admire all day long and then some, and not in a shallow sense.

Her breasts rose and fell with every breath she took, which seemed to quicken as Harry approached. Her waist muscles fluttered involuntarily when Harry put his arms around her.

Practically dragging him over the threshold by his collar, Parisa pressed her body into him and pulled his mouth onto hers, tongue exploring, tastes exploding, deliciously charged with passion in a kiss which lasted uncountable minutes.

She was panting when they parted, her skin flushed dark around her neck, nerves fired and exposed.

"I could really do with a shower if that's okay?" Harry need not have asked.

Parisa's eyes lit up at the idea and, kicking the door shut, she helped him to undress as they made their way to her bathroom, clothing scattered along the corridor, into the bathroom.

The water lashed upon Harry's skin which felt great after his morning, when they were under the shower. What made this better was Parisa. She took control. Her small hands and fingers scrubbed shower gel into his back, kneading away the stress and making him feel equally powerful in the process. Parisa washed him all over, thoroughly, took her time with her small fingers lingering and removing any tension and memories of his morning like that time of day never existed.

Afterward Harry carried her across the hallway, water dripping from them both, their lips and bodies interlocked as one being, into the bedroom, where he lay her gently upon the King Sized bed and they made love slowly, deliberately, until satisfied and slick with sweat.

They lay spent above the sheets, her leg draped over his, arm and hand caressing his chest, hair tickling his neck. Harry had been like a wild enthusiastic younger version of himself, revelling in the sensation she produced and giving back equally in return.

Parisa had a smile of contentment upon her lips. She had expressed herself well enough during their lovemaking that no words were necessary.

Harry stared at the ceiling like an unbeliever who had suddenly witnessed his first miracle.

The time was two o'clock.

She stirred and slipped off the bed, took his hand and led him into the kitchen where she pulled a bottle of wine and two bowls of prepared salad from out of the fridge.

Harry laughed without mirth at her preparedness, and followed her through the spacious lounge at the back of the bungalow. The open French windows looked out across the lush fake lawn which was bathed in the high sunshine, a few wispy clouds floating gently. A small orchard of trees slightly obscured the eight-feet high panelled fence at the rear, the sides of the garden were completely enclosed. A gentle stirring to the air was caressingly cool on their bare skins.

Plates and drinking glasses were already awaiting them at the set of Rattan garden furniture, and they sat side by side on the two-seater sofa, where they ate.

"And how has your day been so far?" Harry asked.

"Better now." She replied, eyes twinkling brightly.

"Oh?"

"Definitely."

"Same here."

"Stressful day in the detective world?"

"Overworked and underpaid. Lots of interfering busybodies." He paused briefly before adding: "But this is all right I suppose."

"Charming."

Harry didn't need to look at her to realise she was grinning.

He asked. "That scar on your thigh?"

"Car accident three years ago. How about the two on your back."

"In the line of duty."

"My hero."

"My fault."

"Oh?"

"I walked into an ambush."

"My car accident was my fault too, but not an ambush, so we are like peas in a pod."

"Scars and accidents add character. They prove we aren't perfect."

Parisa cleared the table, refused his help because he was the guest, and returned with two bottles of water which dripped with condensation. She sat down. Harry twisted off the cap from his bottle and drank down half its contents immediately. The salad and half-bottle of wine had made him thirsty.

Harry looked at her now, her head down, eyes up, she radiated wanton passion. And perfection. At least he thought so. Harry couldn't really quantify how incredibly lucky he felt right there and then because postcoital bliss and alcohol played their part in his mindset. Parisa was beautiful, funny, successful, and had given herself to him. What more could he possibly want?

"What are you thinking?" Parisa asked.

"How lucky I am."

"Me too."

"Good morning at work I presume."

"How did you guess?" She laughed throatily.

Parisa uncurled her legs from beneath her and reached around his neck, pulled his mouth onto hers and kissed him long, sighing when they parted.

"I bought some more land today." She said. "We are going to redevelop it."

"Housing?"

"Yeah. But just one eco-home with a small orchard at the back of the garden. A bit like mine. I try to be as environmentally friendly as I can."

Parisa brushed his lips with her index finger before she kissed him again, hard, passionately. She draped her left leg over his right thigh while their lips were locked. Harry's hand found its way to her knee, traced a circle then stroked a path up her thigh. She moaned.

"How do you fancy a trip to Austria?" Harry asked.

Parisa was sat upon his lap facing him, wrists draped languidly over his shoulders, her body resting and glistening in the sunshine with droplets of sweat.

"Sounds lovely." Parisa looked thoughtfully into his eyes, and smiled.

"Tomorrow."

She nodded: "Sounds like fun. I've not got any plans which can't be altered until next week."

"We can stay overnight in a hotel."

"I'm guessing it's a trip tied into your work?"

Harry nodded: "Is that okay?"

"Of course it is."

"Marvellous. Thank you. Can I ask you a big favour?"

Parisa leaned forward on his lap, she kissed him, eyes open, hair gently brushing his face, before resting her buttocks on his thighs.

"I'll, um, take that as a yes."

"Anything, darling."

"I shall give you our destination if you don't mind booking it under your name. I will pay, of course, but I need to...travel under the radar, as it were."

"Sounds exciting." She told him, slipped off his thighs and stood in front of him, hands on hips. "Fancy another bottle of wine?"

"In the middle of the afternoon? How decadent."

When Parisa had left him Harry considered the wisdom of asking her to travel to Austria. It was a foolhardy decision on his part owing to the euphoria of the moment. But she would be with him. Harry could protect her better than if he were away for a day or two. He hadn't told her of the Russian threat, nor would he. No. He had made the correct decision.

When she returned, Parisa carried a bottle of wine in one hand, electronic tablet in the other.

"Probably a good idea to book our trip right now." Parisa said. "Before I'm too drunk and we end up in Siberia."

They spent the remainder of the day and night chatting, drinking, watching a movie, and making love.

# CHAPTER TWENTY-EIGHT

The morning flight from London's Stansted Airport touched down at the Wolfgang Amadeus Mozart Airport, west of Salzburg, two hours after its departure time, with the morning sunshine burning through a haze of cloud cover. The journey had been relaxed and uneventful and, owing to the early hour, without a complimentary breakfast.

Harry Kovac and Parisa Dane were vomited from the departure tunnel with the gaggle of fellow passengers into the main concourse, from where they collected their compact solitary suitcase before breaking free from the snatching crowd.

Unhindered by the gift shops, duty-free, restaurants or security checks, they were soon standing at the Hire Car counter where Parisa collected the keys for a car she had booked at the same time as the flight. The car had sat-nav which, as far as Harry was concerned, they would use as a last resort. Parisa programmed their course just in case, and silenced the electronically processed voice. Harry had memorised the route they required.

Bill paid, car fully fuelled and with Parisa at the wheel, they exited the airports sprawling complex and took the second exit off the first roundabout they reached, which took them into Kasernenstrasse, bearing right one-hundred yards until they were on the A1 autobahn and bypassing Salzburg, circling north easterly into the heart of landlocked Austria.

"I'll give us an hour," Parisa said, "then find a cafe."

"Sounds like a plan."

The six-lane macadam snake traced a swathe through the spectacularly undulating countryside, often a view which which kept much of the journey silent save a few remarks pointing up various worthy sights, such as one does when travelling to new places, or old for that matter, should something unique strike out from the land. And presented here were numerous points of interest. Harry, who was normally quite taciturn, particularly when working, and after countless excursions into foreign territories during his career, couldn't help but join the light-hearted nature with which Parisa treated this visit.

And why shouldn't he? Harry had to admit to himself once more that any time spent with this young woman was well spent, and something about her spirit lifted his own.

"Here, I think." Parisa announced and tipped the indicator.

They drove onto the elevated exit road and found the typical motorway service area. It was a franchise, but beggars couldn't be choosers, and their adequate breakfast was accompanied by unlimited refills of coffee.

Forty-five minutes after stopping, they continued their scenic journey through the rolling landscape.

Eventually the sat-nav visually nagged Parisa to take the next exit, 195, off the west autobahn - Harry agreed. They were taken onto the A9 Pyhrn-autobahn, and swept them south-east towards Limestone Alps National Park.

Majestic greenery and snow-capped mountains dotted by the occasional sloping roof and small hamlet were their company on the A9 southward, with vast swathes of lush forest blanketing the land. The view was made all the more spectacular because the sun was high and shone brightly down upon them. Wisps of cloud and high mountain mist drifted like diaphanous wraiths in the sky. It was picture postcard perfect.

This was rapidly becoming Harry's new favourite European region, which was no small complement when he adored the French Dordogne so much. Here was a location one could retire to and never grow bored with - not that he was considering retirement any time soon. Little wonder this region was an inspiration to so many artists of various crafts.

The municipality they sought was called Spital am Pyhrn and was situated in the Kirchdorf an der Krems district, clearly signposted off the autobahn.

Nestled between the Warscheneck-Massif and Haller Mauern mountain ranges at the foot of the Pyhrn Pass was the village of Spital am Pyhrn which, of particular interest to Harry, during World War Two was the deposit for Hungary's gold reserves. Converted farms, villas, guest houses and hotels spread themselves throughout the countryside and form a knot of scattered hiking trails on the outskirts of the village, and the adventurous walker on his travels could explore mountain huts which had existed for centuries.

The village itself had the late gothic spires of the Church of St. Leonard as its centrepiece, and maintained a very distinct Alpine ambience because building regulations stated that any new construction must be ergonomic with the local landscape. Other plus points for the visitor were the Art Cafe, frequented by many who sought inspiration from the undulating landscape, and a Gingerbread Village which was a quaint museum with two-hundred miniature houses.

Parisa drove them into the village as a sedate pace and easily located the Hotel Bosruck, whose traditional two-storey chalet style with wooden and white interlaced beams had a definite Alpine feel about them, and was where their overnight stay was booked. A car park with twenty spaces, half occupied, was at the rear, itself backed by lush woodland and surrounded on two sides by spectacularly colourful flowers which Harry couldn't identify if his life depended on it, but appreciated nonetheless.

"Lovely." Parisa said with a sigh as she turned off the ignition, clearly relieved the long drive was successfully over with, despite them both revelling in the glorious landscapes.

Parisa climbed out the car and stretched her arms above her head, sucking in the invigorating fresh oxygen. Harry watched her, smiling, as he got out the passenger side. She was in fine shape and every curve was accentuated by her tightly fit denims, short-sleeved chequered blouse and black leather thigh boots.

It was a warm summers day with a light northerly breeze, and Harry was happy he had chosen taupe chinos, a white cotton shirt and sturdy walking boots. The air was clear and refreshing on Harry's bare arms and in his lungs.

"You okay?" Parisa asked.

"Sure. You?"

"Definitely. The air is lighter." Parisa said brightly and twirled playfully while sucking in a lungful.

Harry drank in her gaiety and their surroundings.

Beyond the flower gardens were equally fine structures in traditional Alpine design, white and bright and inviting, with the mountains visible beyond. The woodland was lush, and only broken centrally behind the car park by a footpath which would evidently lead into its heart. Birdsong sailed on the air and a cow mooed from somewhere. There was the sound of distant running water, a stream perhaps. No traffic or pedestrian noise reached them at the back of their hotel.

"Lets check in," said Parisa, "and dump our case with reception and take a look around the village."

"Sounds like a great plan." Harry agreed and popped open the trunk to retrieve their compact suitcase. Parisa locked up. They wouldn't require the car anymore until their departure the next day.

"I hope they have a big bed." Parisa said.

Fifteen minutes later they were walking along the pedestrianised street away from the Hotel Bosruck, their suitcase deposited courtesy of the pigtailed, blonde-haired fresh-face young woman who had booked them in, and informed them their room would be available after two o'clock that afternoon. The receptionist was apparently the owners daughter on summer break from studying art and design at a Viennese University, so she had informed them.

Spital am Pyhrn had a very definite Alpine village old world romanticism in its architecture and streets, the most prominent features being the twin spires of a former monastery, which certainly gave the view from the southern direction of the Hotel Bosruck a picturesque quality. As Harry and Parisa walked the graduating route they could do nothing but get caught up in the moment. Parisa put her hand in his, smiled without saying a word. This was supposed to be an information gathering journey for Harry but presently he was once more enjoying the moment. It had been many years since he had walked hand in hand with a woman, too many to count, in point of fact.

Parisa was of such exquisite beauty and his chest swelled with pride from a sensation which was both familiar yet long forgotten. Harry was initially aware of the intimacy and felt slightly self-conscious at first, but he soon relaxed.

Life really couldn't get any better as far as Harry was concerned.

They strolled unhurriedly along the pedestrian street, glancing about them like regular tourists, nodding an occasional greeting to passers by. There were plenty of sightseers, hikers and hardened skiers walking about the village, drinking in the splendour of it all. The main thoroughfare wasn't garishly commercialised and subsequently made their walk all the more enjoyable.

Harry wondered where the author of the diary, Waltraud Koenig, had lived. He pulled the piece of paper supplied him by Daphne Crane - he had ignored her suggestion about destroying it because it contained too many unfamiliar foreign place names and surnames that even he, with his photographic memory, wouldn't possibly be able to recall. Daphne had even made a diagram indicating that the Koenig home was situated along a narrow track running beside the entrance to the cemetery, on the village outskirts. Apparently trees concealed the burial ground so that the tourists don't see it, and the view wasn't spoiled. Waltraud Koenig's sister and her husband still resided in the old family home and Harry could only hope they were open and friendly to strangers wanting a chat and, also, that they hadn't lost their faculties like some elderly folk did - they must be in their eighties, easily.

There was a small locally run coffeehouse at a raised section of the street, with Koenigstrasse Alley running from its east side. Koenig was a popular name, it seemed. There were a handful of seats outside the front and a small awning over top. It looked very inviting and the smell from within seemed to make Harry's stomach rumble. Funny how an inactive car journey can still work up an appetite.

"Fancy a coffee and cake?" Harry asked.

"Very much."

They disengaged hands and sat themselves at a circular steel table with matching corrugated steel chairs, tasteful yet artistically unique, as if someone had designed them specifically for this coffeehouse. The owners wintertime hobby, perhaps?

A quartet of patrons sat together at a table inside the establishment, chatting and laughing audibly in German, empty plates and cups on their table. The girl behind the counter, who might be the Hotel Bosruck receptionists sister, watched the group with amusement and leaned across the countertop. She clocked Harry and Parisa outside as they picked up the menu and perused.

"Coffee and honey biscuits." Harry promptly announced without too much consideration of the various mouthwatering confections on offer.

"That was quick." Parisa responded from behind her menu card.

"Good afternoon." Their server had appeared beside the table silently and addressed them in English with a very strong Middle European accent.

Harry smiled and replied in German. "Good afternoon." Then reverted to English. "Is it that obvious we are English?"

The girl wasn't sheepish or embarrassed when she replied with an affirmative.

"May we have a large cafetière of coffee, please?" Harry asked.

"Of course." The girl didn't need a notepad to take down their order.

"A cinnamon croissant for me, please." Parisa said.

"And I'll have some honey biscuits." Harry added. "I image you are busy this time of the year?"

"Oh, sure." She replied, using English phrasing probably picked up from tv or college life. "But most of our trade is early morning and later afternoon. Hikers and skiers and artists. Some daytime tourists, such as you nice people."

"I can imagine lots of painters visit?"

"Oh, sure. And poets and musicians too. The beauty is...inspiring." She looked wistful, her eyes drifting to some indeterminate point in the distance.

"You study in Vienna?" Harry asked.

"How did you guess?"

"I have a sixth sense for these things. Like you knowing we are English."

She nodded. "I'm on summer break right now. My parents own this place. It's useful. I get to chat with interesting people. Sometimes writers like myself. What brings you both here?"

"Two birds with one stone, really." Harry said, and received a puzzled look. "My lovely lady here is a property developer and hoped she might find some interesting homes here, and I'm doing some research into my family tree."

"Sounds interesting. There are a few chalets down by the cemetery road which need a bit of attention. Half a dozen of them with a good deal of land. Older residents who passed away and never lived anywhere else, mostly. You might want to try those first."

Parisa nodded interestedly. "Thanks for the tip."

"My great-great-Uncle Waltraud Koenig lived in your village until the late nineteen eighties." Harry said. "Then he moved to England. I believe my Aunt might still reside here somewhere."

The girl nodded thoughtfully. "They'd be quite old, no offence. Are you staying in the village tonight?"

Harry told her they were.

"In which case if you go to The Bockshorn later - it's a public house - you might find them there, or at least somebody who knows them. It's a regular gaming night there for the old folk."

"Thank you. You've been very helpful."

The girl grinned and tended their order.

"Might be useful if the Koenig's aren't home this afternoon." Harry said.

"You think there's more treasure to be found!" Parisa asked.

Harry gave a vague nod and a shrug. "I'm not entirely certain. It's most likely that whatever was deposited here in the nineteen forties is long gone. But as I told you before, there is a possibility that the previous finds are just the tip of the iceberg. At least my client hopes so and he's paying big so I've nothing to lose."

Parisa nodded thoughtfully.

Harry didn't say, but he was more intrigued to find out why the Russian Mafia were so interested. What claim did they have to the diary and what it may reveal?

# CHAPTER TWENTY-NINE

The Bockshorn public house suggested by the coffee house girl was situated beside an old Town Hall at the most southern quarter of the village, the ancient quarter, and had stood the test of time with crumbling dignity. Without its modern refurbishments the Bockshorn would've crumbled to decay in the Austrian extremes, but with much love and care and money the old building had been shorn up to modern comfortable expectations. The decor was duck-egg blue walls, rich red carpet, sturdy oak beams and typically Alpine blandishments.

When Harry and Parisa arrived it was just after six o'clock, when the restaurant half of the establishment began serving food.

Harry ordered the Tafelspitz, which was boiled beef with mixed vegetables and spices served with horseradish sauce and minced apples, while Parisa chose the hot Gulasch with locally sourced crusty bread. They rinsed it down with a nice bottle of white wine from the region. Neither required a dessert after the hearty main course.

During the meal they chatted amiably about their day like regular folk, which to a degree they were, as far as any observer could tell, their real reason for being there remained a secret. That afternoon they had scouted the village, found the cemetery along with the six properties located down the lane from its eastern perimeter. The coffeehouse girl hadn't been wrong in her assessment of the buildings. They definitely needed renovation and modernisation, although the land attached to all of them was remarkably well maintained. Harry hadn't learned anything further pertaining to his assignment because Waltraud Koenig's relatives hadn't been home when Harry had knocked upon the door.

But it hasn't been a complete loss. Harry relished any opportunity for spending time with Parisa.

"That was delicious." Parisa stated truthfully after their meal and reclined in her seat, satisfied. She puffed air as if to cool her face. "Plenty of Paprika in it. Phew."

"Shall I fetch us another bottle?"

Parisa nodded after draining the last drop of wine from her glass.

"I love it here." Parisa said, face rosy and gleaming from the heat of food.

"It's definitely a change from Norfolk and Norwich."

"I couldn't live here, though. It's too quiet for me. Nice for a break but it's too far from the City and the world."

"This is the world."

"You know what I mean."

Harry reluctantly agreed. Norwich was quieter than London, no argument there. Norfolk had hamlets in the middle of nowhere much like Spital am Pyhrn, minus the mountains. Harry had lived on the outskirts of London, worked in the town, and with the quicker pace came experience, encounters and largess, which a person definitely couldn't attain from a rural life. If one wanted life on the doorstep one did not live in rural hamlets. Although a murder mystery had occurred in the village where Harry lived life did, otherwise, tick along at a much more sedate pace than he had been used to in his career with the police force. But that was to be expected. Did he enjoy the relative quietness? Partly. Did he miss the life in a city? Sometimes. But certainly not enough to move back.

"Do you suppose the sister is here now?" Parisa posed.

Harry surveyed the room.

There were thirteen people at the tables in the bar area of the pub. A group of five were around a six-seater and were all too young, under forty, and had obviously been hiking all day, downing beers tonight. A group of four were seated together and were a mixture of ages and dressed lightly, so hadn't travelled far, and probably weren't walking home. The Alpine temperature was dropping rapidly despite it being late summer, and a cold wind with showers had been forecast overnight according to the bulletin board behind the bar. A pair who sat nearest the heating were of the correct age group and had big coats hung upon the back of their chairs, so were a good possibility, and the table seated eight easily. The other couple, a young man and his younger girlfriend, weren't a possibility.

Just as Harry was wondering when the older couple's friends would show up the door opened, letting in a bit of chill, and six men and women of maturity entered. Most carried hiking sticks but weren't frail. The Alpine air in these parts was clearly very healthy.

"I think they've just arrived." Harry said and strode to the bar where he ordered another bottle of wine and, when a pair of the new patrons approached the bar.

"The usual, Carla?" The man asked in a hoarse voice barely above a whisper.

"What else, dear, what else." The woman told him.

"Excuse me." Harry said to lady, using his most ingratiating voice accompanied by a sincere smile. "Would you happen to be Carla Koenig. Waltraud Koenig's sister?"

The lady called Carla looked Harry up and down with a quick bob of the head and alert eyes. She might be a small and fragile lady on the outside but her darting movements and keenness where evident, and they belied her age.

"I am." She told him. "But I'm already married to this gentleman man, although I could go for a younger handsome model like yourself, so I shall consider any proposal you might offer."

Harry grinned. He took an instant liking to the lady. She reminded Harry of her Nan on his Mother's side, she too hard a keen wit about her.

"My name is Harry." He extended his hand. "Harry Kovac."

She shook his hand and nodded, impressed.

"A nice name and a big hand." She said. "I bet they can work magic, hey?"

Parisa, who had joined Harry's side and looped her arm through his other, laughed.

"Oh yes." Parisa said.

"You're a lucky lass." Carla told her. "Now, if you aren't too proud to join a group of oldies, how about we sit down and you tell me what can I do for you, Harry Kovac?"

Harry and Parisa took the spare chairs at the table, and he told Carla briefly about himself and Crane investigators so she could understand his position better, and wouldn't withdraw when he asked prying questions. Harry provided a condensed version of the events over the past few days, because there really was no point trying to hide the truth from this astute, wise lady who would immediately be able to see through a tall tale. For his efforts she, and her husband and friends, listened with rapt attention.

"How exciting, young Harry." Carla said once he had finished, and there followed a murmur of agreement all around the table - even Parisa seemed to enjoy the story, and she had witnessed some of it first-hand and heard it told already. "But I don't know if I can be of much help, my dear. I'd not seen Walty for a good ten years. Not since my husband and I visited him. Even then Walty insisted on our meeting being a bit cloak and dagger. You know what I mean?"

"I do."

"It was quite exciting though, really."

"Has anybody else been to see you this week?" Harry asked. "And asked about your brother?"

"No. Nobody." Carla answered.

Her husband put a hand on his and asked: "Will there be anyone else?" He tried hiding the concern in his voice.

"No. Not now. Anybody else who wanted to ask about your brother would've done so by now."

Which was probably true, Harry reflected. If Waltraud Koenig had been employed by the Russians for forty years then they would surely know of the man's family. And if that were the case and they believed his sister might have knowledge of interest to them, then they would not have wasted time.

"Did your brother write to you often?" Harry asked.

"Oh yes, my dear. Every month without fail we received a letter from him telling me that he was okay. We would have to send a reply to a post office box. All very clandestine it was."

"Don't exaggerate, dear!" Carla's husband said and received a dirty look for his efforts. He went on to explain to Harry that they only discovered Waltraud's passing when they heard nothing from him. They assumed the worst, rightly so, and conducted a private ceremony on the family plot because of course Waltraud couldn't receive a proper burial owing to his change of identity until the time was right, which was probably now.

"Did he mention the Hungarian gold?" Harry asked. "It was stashed here, in your town, during the last war, wasn't it?"

"Oh yes." Carla answered without pause. "But only as a point of fact, not to do with his job, if that's what you mean. There was a made a film about it. But Walty never talked in much detail about his job. It was all very secretive. And there was certainly no mention of the painting or necklace you talked about finding."

"Remember the film studio, dear?" Her husband prompted.

Carla Koenig's eyes suddenly lit up at the memory, which was obviously a fond one and she appeared momentarily lost in deep reminiscence.

"Film studio?" Harry prompted.

"That's right, my dear." Carla said with a wistful look in her eyes. "I can't remember exactly what it was called but it definitely wasn't Hollywood, that I am certain of. But I know Walty absolutely loved it there. He was in his element rubbing shoulders with old-time movie stars. Oh, dear, here I am talking about old-timers and I'm one myself." She laughed. "Walty brought home several trinkets, I suppose you would call them film props, and he had his picture taken with so many people I've got a suitcase full in his old room back home."

"The studio was in old Czechoslovakia." Carla's husband said. "You young folk call it Czechia nowadays. That's always been a problem with Europe, hadn't it! There has always been land disputes and segregation. I was stationed in old Yugoslavia when Marshal Tito was overthrown. They broke the country afterwards, too."

"He liked films too, if I recall." Carla said insightfully.

"If your brother worked for Russian military," Harry said, "why would be at a film studio?"

Carla's husband rolled his eyes: "More secrets!"

"Walty was posted at the military training site at the studio." Carla explained. "He volunteered to help there because of his love for films and he wanted to mingle with the stars."

Carla then talked amongst her friends about the good old days and films, they got quite enthused and consumed by the topic. Harry and Parisa listened with interest, but Harry knew that there was no more real information to be garnered.

"Well, thank very much." Harry said and pushed himself up from the. "It's been most enlightening, but we have an early start in the morning."

"Do you have Walty's diary with you." Carla Koenig asked.

Harry regrettably shook his head: "A friend is translating it on behalf of my client. But I promise that when the work is done I shall try my utmost to get it into the rightful owner. You."

"Thank you, young Harry." Carla said. "That would mean a lot."

# CHAPTER THIRTY

Next morning Harry awoke fully sated and rested after a glorious night of vigorous, passionate exercise and the fresh air. He felt ten years younger. The food and wine had been better than average, home cooked, and filling. His conversation with Waltraud Koenig's relatives had been relatively fruitful on later reflection but not too revealing at the time. Harry had decided that once he and Parisa were back at the airport he would send her home, and intended to take the train to meet his friend Michel Lomé outside Vienna. Harry wanted Parisa back in England where it might be safer for her. Not that there had been any real sense of danger but one could never predict what might occur, particularly where the Russians were concerned.

It was seven o'clock in the morning and Harry stared up at the ceiling, absently counting the dots of light cast through the top of the window blinds. He grinned and snaked his hand across the bed sheet expecting to tough Parisa's skin but connected with nothing. He couldn't hear the shower running. The room was empty and silent without Parisa's presence.

Harry vaguely recalled her telling him that she was going to rise early and go for a jog in the woodland which was behind their hotel. Sounded like a splendiferous idea to Harry, but he had obviously been sound asleep and she hadn't disturbed him.

Sun streamed in the window when Harry threw aside the curtains and twisted open the blinds. The forecast of over night rain evidently hadn't materialised.

He showered, dressed, scooped up his wallet and keys, putting them inside his jacket pockets, and trotted down the flight of stairs to the ground floor reception.

A receptionist who he hadn't seen before was behind the desk. A young man with a mass of unkempt mousy coloured curls. Harry nodded a simple greeting to the youth before exiting the hotel.

The breeze was light and fresh and felt good in Harry's lungs. A few people in groups strode purposefully up the road with their hiking sticks and rucksacks and all-weather clothing, boots clomping, chatting amongst themselves about their day ahead or events from yesterday.

Mist swirled at the foot of the mountains, over treetops, and impaired total visibility of the landscape.

Harry walked round back of the hotel and put on his sunglasses to reduce the strong glare, which he was probably noticing more courtesy of the wine and lateness of hour he and Parisa had slept. His mind went back and he marvelled at the seemingly boundless energy which Parisa possessed. Had he really been the same ten years ago? Would he have gotten up so early and gone for a jog before breakfast? The simple answer was: yes. And he still could when so inclined but certainly more limbering up was required than in his younger days. But not this morning. He would follow up the footpath at a walking pace until he met her return journey.

The hire car was tucked between two gleaming Range Rover's and the car park was now full. Parisa had been fortunate indeed to be able to book them a room there during peak season.

The ground was littered with tree debris, and a branch had splintered during the night and was resting upon its neighbouring tree. But that wasn't what drew Harry's attention. Resting lightly against the bonnet of a blue family saloon, one foot upon the bumper, phone in hand as he was swiping and clicking, was the big Russian Mafia guy - Anatoly Polivanova.

Harry locked eyes with him as they connected. Anatoly guy stopped typing, dipped his head lugubriously, brows heavy, dark emotionless eyes penetrating.

They shared a nod of acknowledgement.

Harry stopped dead in his tracks, scanned left and right, in the car, up the footpath. Nobody. Just the big Russian guy, fit and young and mean looking, who didn't move from his casual stance. Harry knew he only had a minimal chance in a fight against this highly trained, younger guy, especially as no weapon was at hand. And the Russian knew it too, hence a superior smirk.

Anatoly languidly slid off the car bonnet, fully erect, and stretched his muscles, yawning. He was like a tiger displaying his dominance to the rest of the pack. He made a gutter disparaging curse which Harry could barely translate.

"Where's my girl?" Harry snarled in his best tough guy voice, the one honed over years which put fear into most perpetrators. The Russian giant wasn't fazed.

"With my boss." Anatoly's sneered reply was given in perfect English. In fact, it was uncanny in its perfection, and false upper-class mockery.

Harry rapidly strode forward and halved the distance between them. He looked for a concealed weapon on the Russian, not that the guy needed one.

"No harm better come if her." Harry warned.

The Russian shrugged.

"I'm not joking."

"What...ever." Anatoly said mockingly.

"You got life insurance?"

"Why?"

"You got a family?"

"What if I have?" The Russian sneered as if Harry's posturing was inconsequential.

"Because they'll need to make a claim if your boss lays a finger on my girl."

"My boss is not that way."

Harry stopped about ten paces in front of the big Russian who hadn't made any move, offensive or defensive, because he believed there was no real threat from the Englishman.

"That was actually quite funny. I didn't realise you guys had any sense of humour."

"We don't."

The silence around them was broken by a car engine in high revs, changing gear, gaining nearer. Well tuned, moving fast. Would it pull into the hotel car park or drive by?

The Russian didn't move because he was totally unconcerned.

Harry looked from the guy to the woodland pathway, clenching his fists, willing Parisa and the Russian woman to appear right now. He hoped the car he could hear would arrive. He hoped a hotel guest might stumble upon this scene and diffuse the rising tension. Harry knew he wasn't helpless, far from it, but he would do everything in his power to diffuse a situation to avoid a fight. That was the way of his training. But with Parisa in jeopardy a primal instinct had engaged in his brain. Harry wasn't yet seeing red but the haze was creeping like a weed through his sub-conscience.

Suddenly there was movement and a flash of white from the woodland pathway.

Two people appeared. They were Parisa and the Russian, Annika Smimov. Walking and talking like a friendly couple of women but they couldn't be more chalk and cheese. The frumpy woman was dressed for winter in drab greys and browns while Parisa looked athletic and gay in running shoes, skintight white leggings, and a bright pink long sleeved top.

Harry noticed instantly that Annika Smimov was holding the unmistakable shape of a gun in her jacket pocket - no two-finger ploy from her, that was for sure.

The car had stopped, the engine silenced. Harry hadn't noticed when because he had been enraptured by the arrival of the women. There was to be no interruption to this scene.

Parisa couldn't manage even the slightest smile of acknowledgement when she made eye contact with Harry. She was terrified, but unharmed. Harry wondered how easy it had been for the Russian woman to carry out her inevitable interrogation. Verbal threats and the display of a firearm would surely have been enough. And why not? Parisa didn't need to put herself in harms way unnecessarily. Best to comply.

"Your friend has told me everything." Annika said as if predicting Harry's thoughts. "Give me the diary, tell me what you know, go home, forget you ever heard the name Koenig, and you can live a safe and happy life together." There was no emotion in her tone.

"That's a pretty tall order." Harry asked.

"That's not your concern. Your lives are. We know your business partner has been paid by Stephen Smith and it is he who we shall be dealing with in any further matter. Give me the diary."

"And how do I know I can trust you?"

"Come, now. Don't ask such a naive question. You are experienced. You know that what I say will happen."

"True." Harry replied and held out an open hand then, looking directly at Parisa he said: "Come on, sweetheart." It was the first time he had used the word sweetheart as an endearment and to his ear it didn't roll off the tongue naturally, so he decided to discard it in the future and find another.

"The diary first." Said Anatoly in a voice which broached no discussion. "Then tell us what we want to know."

Parisa was hands down more important to Harry than the diary. No contest. Apart from he didn't have the diary. He cursed himself for not coming here alone. Zero Crane had been right in his advice and Harry had ignored it. Be careful, he had said. Well, at least Parisa was going home today while he met with Michel Lomé. The Frenchman had the diary. Harry had told the Russians that. How had they located him so quickly? Is the Hungary gold deposit during World War Two the link? What do they know? They could simply get the information themselves by talking to Waltraud Koenig's sister, like Harry had. This was his address before moving to England. Too coincidental, perhaps? Maybe the gold remained unclaimed, or at least some if it, and the precise location is mentioned in the diary.

Harry became aware that the trio before him were suddenly not looking at him, but past him, preoccupied, and Anatoly had tensed up.

When Harry turned about he could see the nature of their distraction and he himself felt a sense of happy relief. Two people, one male one female, who couldn't have been more obviously Interpol Agents if they had tattoos declaring as much.

Their standard issue clothing, standard issue haircuts, and standard issue stances were badges enough. This altered the situation considerably. Surely the Russians wouldn't dare incite an international incident, especially if the diary contents were so important. This isn't some action movie where people shoot each other to compensate for lack of a plot!

Partly Harry wanted to grin but his professionalism overruled emotion.

"Good morning, Mister Harry Kovac and friends." The male officer said in English with a hint of Polish in his accent. He was in charge. His partner was a fresh-faced eager rookie out to impress.

"Its a small world," Harry responded, "Detective Cheklovich."

"That it is. Who are your friends, Harry?"

"The lovely young lady is Parisa Dane" Harry said and made a gesture in her general direction, no need to make it to obvious who he meant because the Russian woman could be called neither young nor lovely. "And these are our friends from Russia, Annika Smimov and Anatoly Polivanova. They're on holiday." The next was directed to all three. "This is Detective Serge Cheklovich of Interpol. He and I go way back." He turned back to the Detective: no need to announce their meeting once already that week. "Breaking in a new partner?"

Cheklovich nodded, hiding his scepticism. It was obvious to him that he had interrupted at the right moment and diffused some situation although he wasn't entirely sure what that situation was, of course. He introduced his partner to all concerned and she was well versed in playing along with the niceties too.

"Definitely an improvement on her predecessor." Harry complimented her and she didn't blush. He called out: "Parisa! Come say a proper hello to my friends from Interpol."

The decisive moment lasted no longer than a split second. The Russians made no attempt to stop Parisa from returning to Harry. They could see both Agents were armed and knew how well honed their skills were. They would undoubtedly try again for the diary and Harry some other time.

"It's been fun." The Russian woman said. "Thanks for the chat."

"Enjoy the rest of your holiday." Harry threw back.

The duo got into their car, Annika in the drivers seat, and neither of them made eye contact when they drove off.

Harry had his arm around Parisa and wasn't paying any attention to the departure of the Russians.

"You all right?" Harry asked.

Parisa nodded meekly, still shaken from her ordeal but she was a strong woman and Harry could sense a quick recovery from the shock, particularly after they had some coffee and breakfast.

"What was that all about?" Detective Cheklovich asked.

"I'll tell you over breakfast." Harry said. "And you can tell me to get outta town. I guess that's why you've come from Berlin?"

"Town and country, Harry. You know it." Cheklovich said with a smile. "Seems you're persona non grata in Europe now."

"And only yesterday I was considering retiring here." Quipped Harry, and he took Parisa's hand and they led the Interpol detectives to the Hotel.

# CHAPTER THIRTY-ONE

The quartet sat at a six-seater table in the restaurant of Hotel Bosruck to allow adequate room for their copious pots of coffee, racks of toast and tray of assorted jams and preserves and pastries. They were all very hungry and a long day was spread before them.

It transpired that the Interpol Detectives had driven from Salzburg since arriving by plane in the early hours to collect their Company Car. Interpol had plenty of Company Car's at their disposal all over Europe which any agent could use should the need arise. It was a useful arrangement.

The conversation about how picturesque Spital am Pyhrn and Austria and the hotel was didn't last long, because it was soon down to business.

"Who were your friends?" Cheklovich asked.

"Russian Mafia." Harry told him, which raised an eyebrow, not of surprise, but as if the news was expected. "You recall I mentioned a diary which Michel has? It's apparently something which they covert."

"The one you retrieved from Berlin?"

Harry nodded. He wondered who had talked and how much digging had been done by Interpol since his meeting with Cheklovich in Berlin. Harry updated Cheklovich with most of what had transpired since they spoke last, except for the name of the diary writer, his client, and what he intended to do next.

"Now what beef have Interpol got with me here, in Austria?" Harry asked. "You being here isn't just a happy coincidence, that's for sure. Although your timing couldn't have been any better, that's also for sure, and I thank you very much."

"You're welcome." Cheklovich said. "Apparently your visit to Berlin and the contents of the safety deposit box has raised several diplomatic eyebrows. There are people who believe the necklace should be in a museum. There's been chatter on the wires about a diary. The one you found. And based on your past, my people are frightened you might start an incident."

"I thought we had sorted that out years ago." Harry laughed. "The other day I was doing the bidding of my employer. They are paying my firm to find hidden treasure for their own fortune and glory. It's all on record back home at the office."

Cheklovich nodded. "And then you come here. You use Miss Dane as a decoy on the booking form and to hire a car. This implies you wanted to be here incognito. Or at least as incognito as is possible these days."

"Which worked well."

"Sure it did." Cheklovich laughed.

"I didn't think you people would be that interested or that quick."

"As quick as your Russian friends." Cheklovich stated. "You are taking a big risk, Harry, you know that. My people know about the Mafia connection but they didn't bother telling me in Berlin. I had to check that myself and have since dug a bit deeper. They're afraid you are kicking up a hornets nest."

"They need not worry." Harry said. "We're leaving right after breakfast."

"And we will be right behind you to make sure you do." Cheklovich said almost apologetically, because despite his orders, it didn't mean he had to like them. "Don't go breaking any speed limits though, otherwise I might be pulling you over."

Harry laughed. "And you keep an eye out for our Russian Mafia friends. I have a feeling they definitely won't be far behind."

"Hmm, yes, that's a foregone conclusion."

"It's been a pleasure." Harry said to Cheklovich's partner. "Don't let this guy teach you any of his bad habits."

"Like not adhering to the book?" She suggested.

Harry nodded. "That's one to avoid at all costs."

Back in their hotel room it took no time at all for Harry and Parisa to pack their few things, and it was no small relief when Parisa became more talkative, finally snapping out of the reverie she was feeling after her ordeal with the Russian woman. She put a hand to Harry's mouth to silence him when he was about to apologise for getting her into this mess.

"I'm trying to understand all this intrigue." Parisa told him. "It's like something out of an adventure movie and it's kind of fun."

He kissed her on the forehead gratefully.

"That's not the best you can do, is it?"

After proving to Parisa that a quick kiss was indeed not the best he could do, they dressed, collected their things, paid the bill and thanked the chap on reception for a genuinely delightful stay.

Cheklovich and his partner sat patiently in their car outside the front of the hotel and exchanged a friendly smile with Harry and Parisa.

The hire car was under Parisa's name so she drove the way back to Salzburg, their escort not far behind them.

Harry couldn't tell if the Russian Mafia duo were also tailing them, but he presumed they were back there somewhere.

It was almost three hours after their departure from the Hotel Bosruck at Spital am Pyhrn that Parisa parked the car back outside the hire firms airport office, from where they had collected it not much more than twenty-four hours ago. They had an open ended ticket for the return flight so all they had to do was find the next departure time to Stansted.

Interpol parked a few spaces up from them, nearer to the main entrance of the airport, as a precaution. Cheklovich was taking no chances, evidently.

"Are you okay?" Harry asked Parisa when she had returned the car keys.

Parisa smiled and nodded, and as if to cement her assurance she kissed him on the lips, long and hard.

"Cool it, you two." Detective Cheklovich said with a wry smile on his face when he idled up to them. "There are laws against lewd conduct."

"You really throwing us out?" Harry asked.

Cheklovich nodded by way of apology.

"Cool." Said Parisa. "I've never been kicked out of a country before."

"This isn't Harry's first time." Cheklovich told her.

"You aren't seriously following us to the departure lounge?" Harry asked Cheklovich. He needed to persuade his friend that he could be trusted to get both himself and Parisa on the plane without the help of Interpol, otherwise his plan wouldn't work.

"No." Cheklovich said. "But I am under orders to ensure you board, so I shall need to find out what time your departure is and stay out here until your plane leaves."

"Better come with us, then."

Harry took hold of Parisa's hand and, followed by the vigilant Interpol agent, they booked two tickets for the next available flight to Stansted, which meant just under one hour of waiting. Harry hated to waste money but he had to keep up the pretence he too would be on board.

"Happy?" Harry asked Cheklovich.

"Of course. Be seeing you. Although hopefully not too soon." Then, to Parisa: "Make sure this bum treats you properly ."

"I've no complaints so far." And there was enough of a twinkle in her eye to silence Cheklovich further.

The agent doffed an imaginary cap and left them.

Harry watched his friend until he was out of sight.

There were many mixed groups, families, couples and singles who milled around the airport or walked with purpose. A middle aged woman was crying, she waved to a young man, her son? Excited children chattered ceaselessly or played on the ubiquitous mobile phone. Anxious adults, impatient people.

Harry had taken all this hubbub on board while singling out the various exit strategies which might get him free without being made be Interpol or the Russian Mafia. He smiled to himself. He hadn't realised how much he missed the thrill of adventure until that moment.

"I'm not going with you." Harry said.

"But-"

"I've got to find out more about the diary and I'm meeting my friend Michel in Vienna later today. He can help. It's already been arranged."

"I understand, and I'm not surprised, but it's not going to stop me from worrying about you. So please be careful, for my sake, if not your own. Okay?" Parisa pulled his mouth onto hers and kissed him like it might be the last time. "Something for you to think about."

"I'll phone you once you're back in England. Go straight to my office. Zero and Daphne Crane can protect you, not that I think there's any real danger to you, but, if our Russian friends need some leverage, they might try something."

"Don't worry about me," Parisa said. "I'll be fine. But you take care, okay? You know...this isn't just something temporary we have, right?"

Harry smiled. He was pleased to hear her confirm what he had hoped. Wrapped up in the euphoria this lovely woman brought to his life he had suspected she might not feel as deeply about him as he did her. Such was life. These were the early days in their relationship. Neither of them were naive youngsters any more.

"Absolutely. Yes."

"Then come back safely."

Parisa squeezed his hand, took the suitcase from him and didn't look back when she walked through the security checks.

It was with effort and an enforced sense of gritted determination that Harry found his own departure point. He used the crowds to obscure himself from any watchers, joining a group of eleven young tourists as they made their way outside, and slipped away from the group when a shuttle bus drove by and blocked Harry from Cheklovich's view.

Harry remained in stealth-mode when he purchased a baseball cap, which he despised, to blend in, and a burner phone, a bottle of water for the journey and a sandwich, all from a shop which sold everything located between the airport and train station.

Keeping his head down to avoid the ubiquitous surveillance cameras, Harry couldn't take the chance. His picture had most likely been circulated everywhere by now and he wondered how long it would take in real time for Interpol to discover he wasn't onboard the outbound flight.

Luck was on his side because he could board a train directly from the adjoining station immediately after he purchased his ticket to Vienna, and the train would depart fifteen minutes after.

Harry located the correct platform, ensuring he wasn't followed by waiting a further five minutes on a bench, and boarded the train from the very last carriage.

Harry Kovac strolled in what appeared to be an aimless fashion through the train carriages, but he was searching for faces which might be onboard undercover security, a necessity in these troubling times. By the time he reached his forward facing seat he had counted none. Maybe tightening budgets meant cutting personnel and, should something occur, point the blame elsewhere. Harry didn't mind one bit. It meant he could relax. Trains didn't possess onboard surveillance cameras linked to a police network, so the journey would pass by without worry. At least that's what he hoped.

Harry's seat was near the back end of the carriage, close by the connecting door, and there were barely a dozen other passengers sharing the journey with him, although he knew not how many stops they would en route.

A barely audible announcement in German was repeated in English informing the passengers that the train from Salzburg to Vienna, which stopped at only two other stations en route, was now departing.

# CHAPTER THIRTY-TWO

As if on cue a whistle blew and the Vienna bound train started moving forward, wheels rolling along their rails, speed building gradually, the platform slowly receding. The internal lights flickered, dimmed, then brightened once more as the power discharged. Motion was laboured at first but soon built up as the train broke out of the station canopy into bright daylight, the multiple tracks leading to various destinations soon became just the twin pair of their route, and they were thundering along.

Harry soon grew bored with the scenery, obscured frequently by poured concrete or gravel embankments. Instead he broke the seal on the burner phone and connected the battery that was already three-quarters charged, topping the credit up with a prepaid international top-up card. He didn't doubt International calls would cost a fair premium, but he wouldn't need the phone long so cost mattered not. Phone features mattered less. It was a basic keypad, certainly old fashioned by Smart Phone standards, but it did what Harry wanted and after phoning Michel Lomé with his estimated arrival time in Vienna, and being told where to meet, he dialled the number for Crane Investigation Services. The connection was made within seconds.

"Crane Investigation Services." The level soothing voice of Daphne Crane came loud and clear from the earpiece. "How can we help?"

"I'm tempted to give some sordid reply but I know Zero would punch me!"

"Harry!" Daphne said, laughter and relief in her voice came down the line. "It's about time. How goes it?"

Harry told her everything as concisely as he could, mindful of the credit running down on the phone and the allowed time, and the possibility that the office line was tapped. He finished off with the same instruction that he had given Parisa: to call by the office.

"Don't worry, we'll look after her." Daphne told him. "Now for my news."

"We might have company, don't forget."

There was a brief pause, then Daphne continued: "Stephen Smith's representative Climmy contacted us...what sort of a name is that!? Anyway, those guys should now be in the States, so Climmy said...at length and beating round the bush. They have heard from the Russians but told them nothing. They're too savvy an outfit to be coerced by the Mafia and now they're well out of contact range anyway. The guy, the one who you thought you recognised...well, get this...he works as a porter for Beeston Grange."

"Small world." Harry said without pause.

"And he's a member of The Party."

This drew Harry up short. Mafia weren't The Party. They had entirely different agendas and motives. So were he and the woman lying about their connection? Why? There was no need for the Russian State to hide its interest in property which might belong to them anyway. Equally, the Russian guy might believe he was working for the Motherland without realising he was being manipulated.

"Harry, are you still there?"
"Yes, sorry. I was thinking."
"Where are you going to now?"
"I can't say. It's easier this way. The less you guys know the less danger you will be in. Anything else going on I should know about?"
"No. Just the usual."
"Okay. I'll be in touch."
"Stay safe."
Harry hung up.
Stay safe? What an anachronism.
If the office was being listened to then he hadn't said anything which the Russians, or whoever, did not already know. And at least the Crane's weren't compromised with additional information, so long as the listeners believed what Harry had said. If there were listeners. Modern technology might locate his signal by satellite from the call to the office, so Harry fully deactivated the phone and dropped it into the bag. When he reached Vienna he would contact Parisa and she could relay his whereabouts to the office in person. It would be safer that way.
Harry spent the remainder of the journey watching the grand vistas and majestic mountains they passed through, and clearing the job from his mind, as a sort of recharge function. It was a long

practised technique. Something new might occur to him later. And he couldn't sleep right then.

Before the train hissed into Vienna station Harry had consumed the sandwich and water, depositing the rubbish in the correct recycling receptacle. He considered that the inward journey skimmed by picturesque parks and homes and did well to convince a new arrival that this city was bereft of lower class society and poverty. Like cities the world over. Who were they trying to fool?

With no luggage or loose possessions - Harry had pocketed the phone and wallet - he was able to assist a gentleman and his wife with their two big bags off the train, and placed them on a trolley. He asked if they required any further help, which they politely declined. He walked with them, chatting amicably while at the same time he watched for any surveillance cameras or watchers. The couple made good cover because if anyone were on the lookout for him they would have been told about a man on his own. This was an old trick of subterfuge but remained effective.

Wien Hauptbahnhof train station was much like any other the world older although it was definitely grander than sooty Norwich. There was plenty of light and a high ceiling made it quite airy. Mosaics highlighted the white tiled walls, there were newspaper sellers, a busking musician, confectioners and souvenir pedlars. The smell of food and metal dominated while the ubiquitous soot clogged the sinuses. Clanking machines, chattering voices, the musician and stomping feet echoed off the walls and created quite a cacophony of sound.

Harry strode unhurriedly with the couple until they were halfway across the concourse where they decided they needed a newspaper. He bid them goodbye and went on his way, fully focused and aware of his surroundings.

Nobody stood out glaringly as a potential concern.

Directly outside the entrance of the train station was the taxi rank and bus lane - what else!?

Harry quickly caught the attention of an available driver, got into the rear, told him his destination and off they sped into the busy streets of central Vienna.

It took thirty minutes for the driver to negotiate the route to Naturpark Eichenhain. They slowly passed through unfavourable traffic-lights and unforgiving pedestrian crossings and, to Harry, much chaotic vehicular activity. During the journey the driver had reeled off so many facts and statistics about his home city that Harry felt he could seat a history lesson at the local University and pass with flying colours. It had been a thoroughly pleasant drive, and Harry gave the driver a generous tip on top of the fare as a thank you.

Harry had been deposited into a parking lay-by with an elevated concrete parapet that descended to a huge acreage of lawn, sporadically dotted with groupings of grand oak trees. A parkland roadway etched a route around the lawn, and to the left and right was a car park. A wooden cafe was in one corner, a lake in the other, and more trees beyond. It was evident this was a popular destination for families, for there were plenty. There were ball games in progress, kites being flown, frisbee's being thrown, dogs being walked, plus a variety of other pastimes being enjoyed.

    While Harry strode through the middle of this melee he mused about the leisure time, and how, all around the world right then, similar activities were taking place. He was people watching himself, to a degree, but his was a more clinical approach. A professional eye view, one might say. Once a policeman, always a policeman. Although here the only criminals of whom one need be aware were of the opportunistic variety. Slim pickings for the professional criminal at a country park, although even they might descend in their droves like locusts from time to time.

    Michel Lomé stuck out from the crowd like the proverbial sore thumb in this regard, but only because Harry knew who he was looking for and this crowded location wouldn't be the man's preferred ground. Although the Frenchman was trying his best to blend in, eating an ice cream purchased from one of the mobile venders, his demeanour was not that of a relaxed tourist.

The Frenchman clocked Harry when a hundred yards away and started walking toward the car park off to Harry's right.

Harry changed his own direction to match that of his friend. Thirty seconds later and Harry had caught up with the Frenchman.

"Bonjour, Michel."

"Harry, mon amie! It's been too long." Michel said and he cast a sidelong glance, a twinkle in his eye and grin on his lips.

"Im getting a strange sense of deja vu because I seem to recall you saying the same thing not more than three days ago!"

"Ah, yes, but this..." Michel made a sweeping gesture with his free hand which took in the parkland. "This is much more pleasant than Berlin, Oui?"

Harry nodded because he had no arguments there.

"I am indeed excited to tell you what more I have discovered in the diary." Michel said. "You see, I have also been carrying out my own research into this man, Waltraud Koenig, using my vast library and I have unearthed many more fascinating facts which you too shall find interesting, I feel sure of it."

"I thought you might, somehow. I shouldn't be surprised and I'm not, but all the same-."

"Of course, Harry. But we must hurry to my home." Michel said, and looked around at all the people nervously. "Your Russian comrades are likely not far away. Word is it they have an entire network searching for you right now."

Harry smiled. Again, he shouldn't be surprised by Michel Lomé's declarations. The Frenchman should never be underestimated. So he didn't ask how his friend knew so much because all would be resolved later, most probably over a lovely home cooked meal and a bottle or two of wine from his own vineyards.

The two hour drive to the north-eastern corner of Austria took them to within twenty-five miles of the border with Czechia, where Michel's remote bespoke villa was nestled in twenty acres of private land nowhere near civilisation. It was a location which suited the Frenchman's need for total privacy and anonymity - he Michel had acquired many enemies, and some friends, whom he would prefer to avoid contact.

Villa Inconnu was a beautifully constructed bespoke building which nestled ergonomically into the valley. The building was of a seamless shape and design which wouldn't suit an urban location, and it's edged grey breeze-block, glass and oak beamed construction should be incongruous amongst the Austrian foliage, but somehow it worked. This was a case of modern design in a natural setting serving its environment but with an eye-catching beauty at the same time.

Harry liked it. He wondered what Parisa's more acute eye for property design would think. To Harry, she seemed more of a traditionalist whereby a thatched cottage or completely wooden house might suit her tastes better than brick and glass. Harry made a mental note to mention it to her when he called on the phone. She would be home by now and made contact with the Crane's, but Harry would wait until later to talk with her.

# CHAPTER THIRTY-THREE

Two bottles of red wine were opened, as Harry predicted would be the case, one of which was already three-quarters consumed while the other breathed on the countertop behind them. Harry and Michel sat upon the kitchen veranda drinking in the spectacular valley vista and the delightful French wine, produced in the Lomé vineyard in the Dordogne region, which was why Harry adored that specific French region so much, having visited his friend numerous times on business and pleasure before the Frenchman had to leave his country of birth. The family still owned the estate, though, hence the continued supply of wine.

The villa's kitchen and lounge were on the first floor, with sliding Perspex doors open to the veranda that created a very large and airy space. The pitched roof was constructed of interlinked glass panels, some of which could be opened from beneath.

The ground floor was devoted to the two en suite bedrooms and extensive library, which Michel mentioned earlier and Harry was able to briefly see while he phoned Parisa. She was safe and Harry allayed any fears which abounded his own.

Harry sat in an imitation Rattan chair, which Michel had designed and created himself. It was a set made from reclaimed plastic and the Frenchman had used his ingenuity to repurpose the waste. They were unique and unconventional. Certainly they were the most sturdy and comfortable patio furniture Harry had lounged in, and he complimented Michel upon them, while outwardly ruminating that the wine was hitting his empty stomach and that created a false sense of awe, such was the euphoric ability of alcohol.

At that particularly euphoric moment Michel handed him a lap tray upon which was a saucer of steaming oxtail. The aroma was mouthwatering. The Frenchman sat in the chair next to him with the same.

"Bon appetit." Michel said, smacking his lips.

They devoured the starter in respectful silence, sipping at the full-bodied red wine between mouthfuls, their tastebuds revelling in the splendiferous flavours beholden them.

Earlier, while Michel was preparing dinner, Harry had told Michel everything in the precise detail becoming of a police officer, omitting nothing about what had transpired since the acquisition of Waltraud Koenig's diary. The Frenchman had listened intently without interrupting, logging the details for future reference, and collating facts with what he had already learnt.

"Waltraud Koenig was essentially a secretary." Michel said after the oxtail was but a gnawed husk in the bowl. "A privileged secretary, to be sure, according to the records which I have unearthed on him. A lot of sensitive information passed through his hands yet he remained a secretary, nothing more. Each successive boss he served trusted him implicitly, that's also for sure. And during his time he processed much sensitive information given him by numerous high ranking officials, both in the German and Russian commands. The stories he might have told-"

Michel let the sentence trail off and collected Harry's bowl.

"Waltraud's sister Carla seems to worship her brother."

"Hindsight, perhaps?"

"Romantic hindsight. To her his life was exciting and adventurous."

"Maybe it was."

Michel carried the bowls to the kitchen and placed them in the sink. He refilled their wine glasses and brought from the fridge two plates of prepared salad with fillets of wild red salmon.

"This looks good." Harry said when the plate was placed on the tray upon his lap.

"Do you need any condiments?"

"No, thank you. This will be just fine."

When Michel returned it was with his own plate and tray and he sat back down.

"Waltraud ostensibly lived in whichever facility he was working at." Michel explained. "His movements were relatively restricted depending on who his commanding officer was, but I doubt he was able to fraternise much with his colleagues, if at all. It's on record that he attended several official functions and met diplomats from other countries but I don't think he was especially involved in anything like spying or espionage work. Waltraud might have dealt with many secrets and sensitive material in the years he was employed by the highest level commanders in Russia, but he saw no real action after the war."

Harry nodded. Waltraud's sister Carla had sketched a picture of the man which made him sound almost like a hero, a spy involved in secret espionage work, almost. But the facts which Harry knew already had pegged Waltraud Koenig as almost a pacifist soldier who shied away from confrontation. Hence he was mainly stationed at facilities where his skills as a clerk and runner were better suited. It was all a matter of record although like many people who saw little combat they would frequently embellish their involvement. Call it embarrassment or a false sense of pride, but Harry knew several men similar to Waltraud, his Grandfather on his mother's side being a prime example - the man had seen no action during World War Two but never told anybody that, often placing himself in locations he never visited and migrated tales to his own life from those who fought on the frontline.

"Waltraud Koenig was very fortunate to live out the rest of his life like he did." Michel stated. "You just have to look at the fates of Weinstrau and Goiberitz for proof of how the Russian regime during the Cold War years treated their people."

It took a few seconds for Harry to recall the names from history. The duo had been loyal mistresses to a couple of Russian diplomats in East Germany but were executed when the wall fell and the diplomats were stationed elsewhere, to be executed themselves not long afterward in the cleansing which took place during the Glasnost reforms in the Motherland. It was feared that some of the information the women overheard could compromise the state. Many others suffered the same fate and few, such as Waltraud Koenig, successfully fled and lived a happy life.

"Maybe Waltraud wasn't a high profile risk like he thought." Harry suggested. "Maybe changing his name was a pointless exercise in the end,"

"Maybe."

"But-?"

"You said that his sister Carla only ever received correspondence from him since he fled Europe?"

"That's right."

"Did she ever see him?"

"She visited him just the once and never had his new address. I suppose he was effectively trying to disappear, like those Nazi's who fled to South America after the War. Waltraud obviously believed he was at risk."

"And he left a trail of clues to hidden treasure." Michel's eyes were bright from wine and intrigue. "Do you know the origins of the necklace you found?"

Harry shook his head. "I half expected you to unearth the details."

Michel laughed and, with a flourish, pulled a sheaf of folded A4 paper from out of his shirt pocket which had been visible to Harry all evening.

"I thought that was a handkerchief!" Harry said when he took it from the Frenchman's hand. "Always the dramatist!"

The brief chronological report on the history of the bejewelled necklace made interesting reading and offered an intriguing premise for what else might be discovered. The necklace had originally been made at the behest of Peter the Great for his wife Catherine I, who was Empresses of Russia for three years from 1724 to her death in 1727. After then it was believed the necklace was entombed with her body until it mysteriously resurfaced in the late nineteenth century on the black market. Emperor Alexander II then commissioned jeweller Peter Carl Faberge, famous for his Faberge Eggs, to endow the necklace with the fine black-heart diamonds which now adorned it, for his wife Princess Catherine Dolgorukova. Shortly after the Emperor's death the Necklace of Catherine, as it became formally known, was archived in the deep chambers of the Kremlin for fear of the historic artefact being broken down and sold off, as had happened with many other items prior to, and during, the Russian Revolution. It had been forgotten about for thirty years until Josef Stalin came into power and the archives were emptied for an unspecified reason. Scholars speculated that its intended use might be for payment of arms to the Nazi's, hence the necklace was last recorded as leaving Berlin in 1944, after which time it disappeared completely. That was, until a few days ago.

"How did it come into Waltraud's possession?" Harry asked.

"Spoils of his labour, perhaps."

"Very nice spoils."

"Or maybe his commander asked him to store it and the commander was subsequently killed and Waltraud could do absolutely nothing with it, of course, so it remained undiscovered. We don't even know for sure when it was put in the deposit box." Michel got out of his seat, put down the tray and empty plate, and picked up a notebook from the central service top. "My memory isn't what it used to be." He said before he sat back down. "The deposit box originally belonged to Herrkommandant Albrecht Foring of the new German army, and was registered as being his in 1953."

"So really the necklace could've been placed there any time after that date."

"That's right."

"And it didn't have to be Waltraud Koenig who put it there. He was aware of it, of course. He must've been."

"Most certainly, yes." Michel nodded. "And the box was only registered in Waltraud's name two days before he placed the diary there. Herrkommandant Foring died three days later of old age."

"Old age!"

"Yes, one has to take these official reports with a grain of salt. It is most likely that foul play was involved."

"Because it usually was!"

A priceless painting and an even greater priceless piece of Royal Russian jewellery. Harry wondered what else they might find.

"Did this Foring hide Nazi gold!"

"Possibly. Nothing would surprise me."

Michel removed Harry's tray and poured them both another glass of wine from the second bottle, smacking his lips in satisfaction.

"It's amazing these treasures have remained hidden for so long." Harry said.

"Yes it is, my friend, especially when one considers that we live in the age of the internet and quick cash."

"The world is smaller for it."

"It fascinates me that anything could possibly remain secret, now, but one has just to look into ones own back yard."

"Quite true. Dinosaur bones and ancient Roman artefacts and World War Two bombs are still being discovered."

"Yes, yes, my point exactly. Just look what they found a few years back: a perfectly preserved Spitfire which had crashed in a Norwegian mountainside and been undiscovered for over seventy-five years. It seems impossible something that size could go unnoticed for so long, but it was. I visited the site because I was in the area and it was indeed an amazing scene to behold."

It wasn't easy to impress a man like Michel Lomé who had so many life experiences an autobiography would read as far fetched, so Harry wasn't taking lightly anything this man said. The man had, when all was said and done, signed the Official Secrets Act in a dozen countries, received numerous honours and citations which he wasn't permitted to publicly acknowledge, and was barred from entering half a dozen European countries, including his homeland, France. All because in his capacity as a lawman Michel loved nothing more than making new and unique discoveries which Governments and big business sometimes didn't want exposed. Harry could only be happy to be a part of this new adventure.

"Unfortunately, my friend," Michel said ruefully, looking into his glass of wine, "technology is making these discoveries few and far between and the world a smaller place, although the powers elect tried briefly to turn the tide."

Harry knew precisely what the Frenchman was talking about and it was a subject they had only discussed in emailed messages

"Twenty-twenty was a bizarre year." Harry said.

"And I'm still unearthing more facts. As if the truth weren't terrifying enough but they followed it with such an ill conceived reaction. It was preposterous."

"Why do you think I left the police force?"

"Ludicrous! It was like the plot of a poorly executed action movie villain in real life!"

Harry laughed: "Waltraud's sister, Carla, mentioned that her brother had been stationed at a training camp in a movie studio somewhere in Czechia."

"Which, by happy coincidence, my friend, is where we shall be going tomorrow."

They sat in companionable silence, caught up in their own ruminations. The world was a crazy place filled with crazy people and along came COVID-19 to highlight that fact. Everyone had been effected by its shadow on one level or another. Harry's mind went to Parisa Dane, as it invariably tended to do these past few days. They hadn't mentioned the spectre of the pandemic in their conversations once, which had indeed been a blessing. Maybe she wanted to distance herself from it. Harry sighed and shut his eyes. He had known several people globally whose lives had been taken. It's bitter taste would linger on. Unless it was the wine. The delicious fruity wine. Harry's eyelids were heavy, his body fatigued, the hour later, and he fell into a wonderfully deep sleep.

# CHAPTER THIRTY-FOUR

Harry and Michel departed the Austrian villa immediately after the Frenchman had served a breakfast of croissants, fresh fruit and strong coffee - two flasks of the black wake-up drink were brought along for the journey.

The Czechia border was only a thirty minute journey and Michel had declared that this was their destination. Apparently after Harry had dozed off, Michel had proceeded to read more from the diary of Waltraud Koenig. Harry knew that his friend could survive on little sleep but he didn't want the Frenchman to push himself too hard. Nonetheless, that was what had happened, and after reading the diary Michel had realised their next point of call would definitely be the abandoned Russian archives in something called Vyrobni Zarizeni Remeslnika - Artisan Production Facilities - in what is now Czechia, but when the movie and television studio had been formed over eight decades ago the country was still known as Czechoslovakia.

Michel had a friend who would be stationed that morning at a particular border crossing but they had to be there no later than 07:45, and it was indeed he who permitted them pass through the gate with a minimum of fuss when they arrived.

Harry had to use his passport as proper formality dictated. He was reluctant to do so because it wouldn't take long for an Interpol alert to go out across the European country. How soon or how efficient the local police force reacted would remain to be seen.

At least their drive into the green and gold Czechia countryside avoided populated areas, and they had no active mobile phones or possible tracking devices in Michel's 1980's Land Rover. At least that was small consolation for revealing his passport.

To Harry the drive in the bumpy old vehicle through the wilderness felt very much like a step back in time to his youth, specifically journeying into the Highlands of Scotland with his family. Pre-mobile phones and a slower lifestyle. It occurred to Harry that maybe his choice of moving from London to Norfolk had been a subconscious decision, almost a yearning to return to those halcyon days. Or was he reading to much into it? Certainly he had no regrets.

While Michel drove he explained the purpose of the facility which they were going to, and its history, which somehow the Frenchman had memorised in detail in the early hours that morning. Michel explained that APF was now a lost and forgotten movie studio and had been formed in 1931 by the Polish Vyrobni Brothers for making Partisan entertainments. It had been financed and controlled by the Government, like many other European bloc entertainment industries during the early twentieth century. Michel explained this was a similar approach later adopted my Marshal Tito in the old Yugoslavia in 1946 - whom

Harry recalled Carla Koenig's husband had mentioned - although history records the Dictator was a genuine movie buff. A similar fate to that of APF befell Marshal Tito's beloved Avala Film when he was deposed from power.

The APF studio compound covered fifty acres of real estate. It was surrounded by woodland on two sides, had a mountain view from its third, and production buildings and entrance on its fourth side. It's perimeter was protected by an eight-foot high steel mesh fence that was barbed and inverted at the top. What state of disrepair had befallen it they would discover upon arrival.

In the mountain woodland behind the studio ran a rail link and, in another large clearing, a military outpost and airstrip. Both still in use.

Despite both complexes covering swathes of ground from the road one wouldn't know either existed, which was the secrecy behind the construction in the first place. The studio grounds had provided an ideal training area for the military when not in use for filming, the comings and goings so regular as to raise any concern to what might really be occurring behind the fences.

Michel said that what had caught his attention upon reading Waltraud's diary was his declaration that there was an abandoned and long forgotten storage facility in the studio grounds. Waltraud visited it regularly and the mere mention of it in the pages of the diary were enough to declare its significance.

"We may or may not find any gold," Michel had said, "but it might be a stepping stone, or treasure map, as it were."

As they drove onward through the rugged hills the sun burnt its way through the misty clouds and poured sunshine upon them. The reds, greens and golds became a lush blanket of colour all around. It was beautiful and bare in equal measure.

Michel had turned on the radio and dialled into a local station which played a mixture of popular English music and more traditional Eastern European fare. The sound was very eclectic and enhanced Harry's feeling for the nostalgic. They were heading to an abandoned movie studio whose heyday had long passed, a factory for producing the unreal, while the vehicle they drove in was a throwback to a similar era. Plus the countryside they passed through wasn't totally blighted by modern contrivances.

"Can you get the map out of the glove box, please?" Michel asked. "The route gets a bit challenging from here."

"I'm impressed you got us this far already without checking." Harry said and reached forward in his seat, pulling the map and handwritten route Michel had scrawled.

Twenty minutes of winding tracks and decaying road surfaces and they came upon the boundary fence, which was tangled with riotous thorns and unruly gorse, bowing in places but still upright. The occasional whitewashed building and rooftop was visible beyond. Left untended the trees had reached their maximum and tangled branches formed a strong barrier, and a perfect natural environment. The place looked exactly what it was: abandoned.

The faded name of Vyrobni Zarizeni Remeslnika was a ghostly etch in faded grey script above the crumbling arched entrance to the facility. Tarnished steel double gates were padlocked, a wooden security hut had almost collapsed, and wires which had presumably once connected to a telephone line and electricity generator were hanging loosely in empty space.

Michel drove up to the gate and cut the engine.

Beyond the gate, set back fifty-yards, a huge white soundstage seemed to grow out of the poured concrete ground, grass and mildew lending natures hand to the decay. The link road ran left and right where other buildings were out of sight from the entrance.

They climbed out of the Land Rover.

Harry stretched his legs alongside their vehicle while Michel examined the padlock securing the gate. Picking it was an impossibility, so Michel withdrew a pair of meaty bolt cutters from the back of his vehicle which made short work of the task.

Harry heaved one side of the gate, Michel the other, and they soon had it open and Michel drove the Land Rover through, turned a corner to hid it from sight. Harry closed the gates. From the back of the Land Rover Michel withdrew a hold-all which he slung over his shoulder before locking up.

"I'm surprised travellers haven't claimed this place for themselves." Harry remarked when he joined Michel.

The building's were shells with broken windows, doors hung off hinges where there were still doors, and nothing but dilapidated furniture was visible inside.

"This isn't England, my friend." Michel said with a wink.

"All the same-"

Leaves and branches littered the ground along with occasional animal faeces, which would have been unheard of in the heyday of the facility. There was also an eerie silence like that cast in a ghost town, which was what this place had essentially become.

Harry wondered what variety of wildlife might have flourished since its abandonment apart from rats, rabbits and birds.

"Why haven't the army procured the site?" Harry asked as he followed Michel's lead northward into the maze of production buildings, which were more extensive than he had imagined. It was like walking through a vacant industrial complex before modernisation took place. "It seems a real waste of land."

"That, I can't answer." Michel told him truthfully. "Maybe the ownership of this land got tied up in red tape litigation and the military gave up pursuing its use. Wouldn't be the first time, and probably not the last. One day somebody will realise it's here, though, and develop it. They usually do."

They passed by a two storey structure which resembled an apartment block. Ten rooms at the bottom, ten above, a rickety looking outside corridor and stairwell. Probably old dressing rooms or a residential area for employees. Opposite that was the Commissary, looking like a forlorn husk, it's once bright and welcoming facia now faded and pocked from age. Alongside it was the hull and cabin of a small boat, incongruous against the building, but curiously in better condition than its surroundings despite being weather damaged. A movie prop, perhaps?

"Do you know movies, my friend!" Michel asked as they walked through the ghost town movie factory.

"Not really."

"Pity. This would be a fans dream. Walking through here. Nothing like this exists outside Europe. When the major studios crumbled their land was apportioned and developed for housing or industrial use. Those which still exist are working studios. Imagine the stories this place could tell."

Harry nodded, although he couldn't see beyond the ruin to days past. He had no real point of reference, no romanticism for such things. Leaving such a place unused for decades seemed wasteful to him, nothing more.

At the end of the link road they turned eastward into an avenue of tall, broad warehouse-like buildings with huge elephant doors and a pedestrian door in their front facia. There were twelve of these identical structures in total, six each side, and numbered one through to twelve. Michel explained that these were sound-stages where fake sets were constructed, like those used for theatre only on a much grander scale, where filming could more easily take place without interference from the noise of the real world. These were gargantuan buildings and the mind boggled at the scope and size which a filmmaker had at his or her disposal.

Even the alley-ways between buildings had once been utilised judging by the equipment, vehicles and props stored or abandoned. Here was a clapboard tenement facia, there a three storey office block, all flush against the walls.

They reached the end of the avenue and butted up against an overgrown hedge with a pitted grass track continuing east, which they followed until it opened into a meadow that covered roughly ten acres of land. There was movement as a few wild deer scattered and birds flew aloft from some carcass they had been scavenging.

In the western corner of the meadow was a pile of lumber which might've been holdovers from a western movie, and a wooden bell tower without the bell held up by rickety two by fours. It was the pillbox type structure opposite which interested them more.

# CHAPTER THIRTY-FIVE

The northern corner of the film studio meadow was dominated by a more permanent single storey structure made from sandblasted breeze blocks with a corrugated iron conical roof. Mildew crawled up it. The structure resembled a military pillbox with oblong openings instead of windows and a chunky wrought iron door. Next to it were corrugated iron uprights that barely resembled Quonset Huts. Timber fragments and boards were scattered on the perimeter of these buildings, and Harry decided they used to be upright to conceal this miniature army outpost while something other than a war movie was being filmed. It might also have been used as a catering post or another filming requirement.

"What we require might very well be beneath that pillbox." Michel announced. "It doesn't look like a movie prop to me. It's too solid and permanent."

"Makes sense."

The hinges on the door were rusted but the bolt slammed across easily. A flatter of wings preceded the departure of three birds from the box. It took both men some heaving too and fro before the heavy door finally creaked open, dust and oxide particles fluttering into the air.

A scent of animal droppings mixed with mildew filled their nostrils when they tentatively stepped inside the low-ceilinged, round room. Meadow hay, twigs and grass were scattered in nest-like structures upon the ground around the edges, and various other debris filled the floor area.

On the far side was the handle of a trapdoor, mostly concealed by hay. Together they cleared the trapdoor and it took both their efforts to haul the concrete slab open, which boomed like a massive bass drum in the confined space, and scattered a bit more hidden wildlife.

A dark opening with stone steps gaped at them.

Michel unzipped his hold-all and produced two torches, one of which he handed to Harry.

"Everything including the kitchen sink?" Harry quipped.

"Be prepared. That's my motto."

Beams from the powerful torches pierced the darkness as they cautiously descended the steps, taking care as they trod, not knowing if any Cold War boobytrap might still be active despite the years of disuse. A short corridor and another closed door were presented to them once they reached the very bottom. A hollow sound rebounded their voices when they spoke.

"This will be like a hidden bunker." Michel said.

"Everybody should have one!"

"I don't know the extent of this place. Maybe a dozen rooms. I don't suppose we shall find any bodies!"

"That's reassuring." Harry laughed.

The door opened with surprising ease and a long bare corridor stretched out before then, ending abruptly after about fifty-feet. Five doors were either side, all shut. They were the first two people who had ventured down there in over thirty years. Would there still be files and records down there? A question Harry had raised on their drive which could only be answered upon investigation. The chances of their day being wasted remained fifty-fifty. The original owner might have cleared everything out when he left.

The high gloss white walls splashed their torch beams wide and revealed no adornment or obstacle to obstruct their passage, and the air was earthy but not damp, which bode well because it meant dry rot wouldn't have damaged any potential paperwork left behind. The bare walls made Harry think that they were unlikely to find anything. Whoever was stationed here had plenty of time to depart. They hadn't just abandoned the place and fled.

Harry and Michel walked to the end and worked backwards. Michel took the left-hand side doors, Harry the right.

The first door Harry tried opened inward with a squeal of protesting metal hinges. He stepped into a bathroom which he could smell before he saw, and it took only a few seconds for him to realise there was nothing of value inside so he exited and shut away the stench, which lingered faintly in the corridor afterward.

Michel was still inside his first room when Harry tried the second door. Again it opened inward and was accompanied by a scraping metallic whine. This room had obviously been a break room - the Russians had at least some care for their people, Harry mused, despite their hard exterior and the Cold War. A long wooden bench table, like one in an eighties school dinner hall, ran down the centre of the room, with four smaller ones either side. A service hatch abutted the far wall. The room bizarrely hadn't been completely stripped of utensils and looked ready for use, apart from the dust and cobwebs. Maybe recycling wasn't a priority to the Russian military.

When Harry re-entered the corridor Michel had finished his search of the first room.

"Sleeping quarters." Michel said. "Nothing but beds and mattresses."

"Bathroom and break room for me."

The next door Harry opened was that of an office. This was deeper than the two previous rooms with eight shoulder-height metal filing cabinets on the side walls, wooden trays, empty, on the top of each one, and a steel table and chair on the back wall facing the door. A half dozen framed headshot photographs lined the door wall from Lenin to Gorbachev, plus those in-between who were considered significant enough to whomever operated this facility.

Harry wondered if this might be the room where Waltraud Koenig worked. He had been a clerk so it made sense that this would be his workspace. Although he likely shared it with others during its time in operation.

Harry tried the first top drawer, right-side cabinet, and it easily slid open on well greased runners.

Empty.

All the others on that side were the same.

When Harry turned to do the same to the left-side, although he expected the result would be identical so it would likely be a waste of time, he saw the second door. It was nestled in the right corner beside the last cabinet and wasn't visible from the entrance, but it was to whom ever was at the desk. Was it possible that when this facility was abandoned they forgot about the area beyond the door? Or maybe Waltraud Koenig deliberately left something behind.

Gold, perhaps?

"Michel!" Harry called into the hollow darkness of the corridor and within five seconds his friend appeared in the entrance. "I might've hit pay-dirt." He nodded to the door in front of him which only he could see.

Michel stepped into the room and up to the cabinet and the concealed doorway.

"It might be a private bathroom." The Frenchman suggested with a shrug.

Harry knew his friend was joking.

Michel turned the handle but the door was locked. He examined the keyhole thoroughly before turning to Harry: "We shall need the key. I don't have the right pick for this lock!"

"Okay. So where will the key he stored?"

They finished searching the remainder of the rooms and in the very first one was a sealed cabinet, along with other furniture long since forgotten about. Michel broke open the cabinet with a miniature pry-bar from his holdall and they were presented with one-hundred nearly identical keys.

"This might take some time." Michel announced superfluously.

"No kidding. They're not even numbered."

Michel leaned in closer to the mix. "Maybe they are." And he went out the room, returning in fifty seconds looking victorious. "Voila!" He bent back to the keys and selected one which looked identical to all the others. "There is a tiny box etched into them all and in that box are Roman Numerals."

"As simple as that?"

"Oui. But it takes a proper detective's eye to see it."

"Very funny."

They returned to the room with the secret door, the key fitted, and Michel smiled at Harry expectantly before he slowly turned the key. The locked clicked satisfyingly. The door opened smoothly, a rubber seal around the interior rim helping its movement.

They both shone their torches into a room the size of a large closet, but instead of cleaning equipment inside, three walls were lined with narrow cages and boxed files top to bottom.

"Success!" Michel declared.

"Not quite gold bars!."

"You cynical British never look on the bright side."

"Not cynical, Michel: realistic."

Once again Michel began at the left-side and Harry the right, but they started door-ward in so they might meet in the middle. The boxed files were alphabetised but as neither of them really knew what they were looking for they decided it made sense to go through them all if necessary. A long job, to be sure, which might prove ultimately fruitless.

"Hmm." Michel uttered an hour into the search, where the only sounds had been the movement of cardboard and shuffle of paper.

Harry turned to see what it was that had caught his friends interest. Michel was reading a letter.

"It's in German." Michel said. "It's a letter from Lenin to Kaiser Wilhelm. My friend, this is staggering. Lenin offers his support to the Kaiser in this letter."

"But I thought-"

"I know. We should give this to a museum."

Michel briefly left the room to put it on the office table.

Their search continued until it was Harry's turn to find something. This time it was linked to Waltraud Koenig. Attached to a file were a set of blueprints which resembled a hotel.

"Yes, it is a hotel." Michel said when he studied the plans with Harry. "One that was to be built in...1961...in East

Berlin. But there's more to it than that. What else was with this?"

Harry, perplexed, handed Michel a half-dozen hand written letters from various heads of state. They had been addressed to high ranking military leaders and marked as Top Secret.

Michel quickly read through the letters, his brow furrowing when he came upon something significant.

'Well?" Harry prompted.

"The construction was bigger than the hotel. There's mention of machinery acquisitions and chemicals. Who knows what was being planned?"

"Something underneath?"

"Most probably a network of secret tunnels to other sites across Berlin. They used them for spying, a bit like Hitler had during the war."

"Do you suppose there are more artefacts hidden in them?"

"More than here, you mean?"

"Yes, exactly."

"Who knows. It's too early to speculate but it's certainly a possibility."

"At this point, anything possible."

"Let's carry on with our search, my cynical friend. There might be more."

It took a further hour to complete their search which was fruitful. Michel found a catalogue of items which included the necklace. They were all in the same file with Waltraud Koenig's letter. The list had no mention of the painting, and no indication where these items had ultimately been stored. The catalogue was filed along with more letters from numerous Russian and German officials, so Michel took them all and, along with their other two finds, slipped them into his hold-all.

Soon they were back outside in the daylight.

"This is better." Michel declared. "Now, my friend, you and I need to go to Berlin."

"That's going to be a bit tricky. Interpol are after me, don't forget. Not to mention the Russians."

"You have become a very popular fellow indeed, my friend. But I think the next step of our treasure hunt is Berlin. Specifically the old Eastern Quarter. Let's go back to my car and I shall think the matter over while we walk."

Their route back was very much the same as their outward bound walk only perhaps more contemplative. Something which Harry noticed this time because they had been hidden by the buildings from the opposite direction, was the dilapidated uprights, some of which were two storeys high, of what presumably once depicted buildings. This was the backlot, tarnished through time and corroded by the weather, another tattered remnant of the sites previous days. Surely this site couldn't remain like this for much longer in this era of development. It seemed impossible enough as it was that it could still be this way after over thirty years disuse.

"I have friends," Michel began, "who can get you across the border without being discovered, but then it shall be up to you to reach Berlin. We still have friends there. I shall tell Kolldehoff to expect you. He's never got anything better to do all day than sit in his garden and paint."

"Is he still under house arrest?" Harry queried.

"Yes. I shall take you the outskirts of Prague. We don't want to test our luck to much. Then I shall go home and check out all this paperwork we have unearthed. You should get a new phone. Don't use that burner. Leave it here. Technology is to easy to track."

Harry agreed.

"My friend." Michel said. "We need to be very careful. And by we, I mean you."

# CHAPTER THIRTY-SIX

Michel Lomé did as he said he would and Harry Kovac was left standing roadside in a less than desirable district of the Czech capital, Prague. He watched the old Land Rover with his friend driving recede the way they came. Prague was a very beautiful city but like all others across the world it had its seedy underbelly and lower class who suffered poverty. Which meant there was a very low possibility of there being surveillance cameras on the streets. And it was a good area for Harry to move unnoticed and from where to catch a bus.

En route the Frenchman had told Harry the name and address of his friend of dubious character who could get him across the border. All Harry needed to do next was get to the hamlet of Doubice, which was located outside the Bohemian Switzerland National Park that also cut into Germany. This would deposit him barely four miles from the border where his friend could assure a safe and unnoticed crossing.

The journey to Doubice would have to be via public transport.

Harry consulted the map as he walked to the nearest municipal bus stop. His journey would mean lots of changing and waiting but it was do-able and presented less risk of his face being captured on camera. He didn't feel that he needed to worry about local law enforcement recognising him. Harry doubted very much that he had become such a wanted man, despite Interpol being on the look out, that his photo had been widely circulated. And the Russians too would be out of the picture for now unless they could trace him to Michel, which was exceedingly doubtful.

Helpfully the first bus-stop was a sit-down shelter at a crosswalk and had a timetable, but most importantly it was in good condition. Harry supposed that to local residents public transport was essential, hence no vandalism except for some colourfully graffitied language. The next bus to a town on the route Harry required wasn't due for twenty-five minutes, so he crossed the street to a convenience store and purchased a cheap new burner phone and credit for same.

Harry returned to the bus-stop and while waiting he sorted the phone and called Parisa, who answered hesitantly because of the unrecognised number.

"Its me." Harry said.

"Where have you been all day?" Came the reply, which sounded distant and hollow, like the network signal wasn't that great where Harry was calling from. "I've tried not to worry like you told me but I can't help it."

"I know." Harry replied. "And it's nice somebody cares, believe me. I'm in Czechia at the moment. I cannot say where precisely, just to be safe. Can you tell the office I'm onto the next lead which might be the last and I should know more later tomorrow."

"Okay." A pause. "I love you."

Harry wished he could find something more profound to say than he felt the same way, but words failed him. It sounded soppy and predictable and insufficient to reply "I love you too," - at least to Harry's mind - but he said it anyway because he meant it, before he deactivated the call and powered off the phone. Should anyone be able to monitor Parisa's smartphone they wouldn't have had time to locate the incoming call, and to their ears he hadn't said anything significant. Czechia was a big country, after all.

Twenty-five different changes later Harry Kovac was stepping off the final bus at the village of Doubice. The centre of the village consisted of a church, a shop and a few homes, but mostly there were scattered far and wide around the municipality itself, and the population being statistically low considering it covered an area of almost eight square kilometres.

Unchanged over the last fifty years, very rural and rustic and scenic, the countryside was not dissimilar to that which surrounded the site of the Vyrobni Zarizeni Remeslnika film studio. Lots of greens and browns with a few early autumnal flourishes of colour.

This was definitely unlike many villages located so close to a border. In Harry's experience they were usually seedy places populated by undesirables who exploited those fleeing their country, especially in this territorial region of Europe. Those who had perhaps attempted to flee the tyranny in their own country typically settled there, hence the frequent unrest and creation of similar predicaments to that from which they were fleeing in the first place.

A vicious circle, no less.

But none of that was in evidence here, at least not in the surface. The border was a relatively short hike from where Harry stood, but it looked like an arduous hike not to be attempted by an amateur. The region was full of valleys and rugged terrain.

Despite the outward appearance of a sleepy little village in the middle of nowhere, Harry remained weary and alert as he walked through what might be dubbed as the High Street. He knew how close-knit communities could be more dangerous than larger ones. There are fewer secrets in small places but those secrets can often be greater and the people more protective towards them. Strangers often stood out like the proverbial sore thumb.

According to Michel's instructions the home Harry needed to find was two miles beyond the church, an uphill trek through woodland via a narrow, winding single-Lane road. The home was called Smrt Farm. Not the sort of name which inspired confidence in a visitor or, if it was a livestock farm rather than agriculture, in any animals. Smrt was the Czech word for death. Death Farm. A good name to ward off the curious.

The road was a single-lane unmarked grey-top with plenty of potholes and sloping verges, and snaked upward as if reaching toward the National Park which loomed forebodingly ahead of him. The gradient increased and became more of a labour with every step.

The sun was low in the sky behind him and cast long shadows.

Harry saw no-one.

Smrt Farm announced itself with an inglorious fencepost sign scrawled in black which seemed hastily written and assembled. Which maybe it had been. Perhaps Michel's friend had erected it after being contacted by the Frenchman, and it was for Harry's benefit. All Harry knew was that he was grateful for it as he turned into a haphazard small-stone driveway, which ended at a thatched cottage which took Harry's breath away because it was utterly incongruous. The cottage was beautifully adorned with pink paint, the oak beam sidings were fresh, the roof looked brand new, and the windows and door were light-brown plastic offset by decorative flowery inlays. Borders of red and yellow flowers caught the remainder of the sunlight either side of the cottage.

This farm with the name of death was remarkably vibrant with life.

A woman dressed in a flowery blouse matching the gait of the property opened the door. She had brown hair cut in a bob without product and gave it body. She had a healthy sun kissed complexion, stood at five-foot four and possessed physical contours which went with the outdoor environment.

"Hello." She said in German, her voice neither harsh nor warm, businesslike, but also it wasn't the unemotional drone Harry expected. This was becoming a curious moment of contradiction. First the building and now this woman.

"I'm Harry." He announced himself. "Michel said you would be able to help me."

"And he was right." She replied, breaking into a sunny smile of white teeth. "He described you well. Come in. Have some food, get some rest, and we can begin before sun-up."

"Thank you."

All business and no banter was the order for the following morning. Harry Kovac was able to sleep better than he had for days, and following a breakfast of fruit and yogurt and strong black coffee, was feeling refreshed and ready for the day ahead despite the time being five a.m.

Despite the chill air his hostess was dressed in denim shorts, a loose blouse and hiking boots. She equipped them both with a metal hiking stick each and a hunting knife, and gave him a small holdall with food and drink inside because his journey would inevitably be greater. She had a rifle slung across her back because, as she said, they might came across some game she could claim for her lunch, not as a precaution against predators.

They trudged silently up the hillside and followed an invisible pathway through the trees which she had presumably used on many occasions, because Harry could barely see in the encroaching dawn, let alone an obvious route. But she negotiated the way with ease. He assumed she regularly smuggled people across the border this way. In fact the woman was perfect cover. Her home and outward appearance belied this line of work, although he had noticed her exquisite paintings which were presumably her main line of income.

After forty minutes of hiking upward they reached a bare hilltop. The sun had begun to crawl into the sky and the view was truly spectacular. Rugged grey stone-sided valleys, waterfalls, pine forest and heathland was spread before them. Thick rain bearing clouds roiled in the skies about ten miles in an easterly direction, but the valley which they looked upon was gradually bathed in early morning sunlight, the foliage seeming to bow toward the warmth.

"Don't worry about that." She said to him, and nodded toward the clouds. "The wind is tracking the rain southwards and shouldn't hit this region until well past noon. You should be at the West Saxony Park station before then, if you don't stop on the way. Just follow the stream at the bottom of the valley and my directions and you can't possibly go wrong."

"Erm- thank you." Harry replied, while thinking about famous last words.

She nodded, smiled, and started her return journey without a backward glance.

The time was a quarter to six in the morning. She obviously had faith in him that he could negotiate this terrain in under six hours. A formidable task indeed, but perhaps the National Park covered less area than at first it looked upon a map. Oh well, he thought, no time to waste wondering, just wandering.

# CHAPTER THIRTY-SEVEN

Harry Kovac was tempted to take a rest at the Saxon Switzerland National Park cafe situated on the outskirts of Hinterhermsdorf and Neudorf, Germany, and perhaps grab some hot food and coffee. The route he took through the Bohemian Switzerland National Park might not look a staggering distance on a map but the hike had been slow and undulating, over cobbled stones and rough terrain, through paths trodden by hikers but unspoilt by an abundance of people. Some part of Harry had enjoyed the walk, another part was glad that it had almost ended.

The woman whose name Harry hadn't found out had packed him food in the hold-all for later and time had been of the essence so he consumed most of the food and all the drink en route, and although he could do with a coffee, he better not dally on the way.

The scenery at the cafe grounds was dutifully grand and picturesque, as had been the case on his hike, and Harry almost mourned the fact he couldn't spend a day here. Note to self, Harry thought: bring Parisa here in the future.

Interpol's machine was efficient, and even though he couldn't be a high priority target for them, it was best to err on the side of caution and not dither. Harry's likeness would be in their database and circulated, and the Russian Mafia too would be on the lookout. Harry had been off the grid for over twenty-four hours and people would begin to wonder why.

Harry was very tempted to contact Michel Lomé to learn the present state of play at his end, but to do so would place his friend in jeopardy. Undoubtedly by now Michel had been questioned about Harry - it was inevitable when the Frenchman returned to the border crossing - and consequently his phones would be monitored. Possibly Michel's travel options would be restricted for the duration until Harry was intercepted.

There really was no time to dither.

Three signal-strength bars illuminated themselves on Harry's burner phone when he walked down the exit road of the National Park. Not bad, all thing's considered. He couldn't see a visible mast. He touched in Parisa's mobile number and it took no time at all to connect.

"Oh, Harry, it's good to hear your voice." Parisa replied after he announced himself, and he professed likewise. "Where are you now?" She asked eagerly.

"I'd rather not be too precise, just as a precaution, but I'm in Germany."

"A precaution?"

"In case your phone is being tapped."

"They can really do that?"

Harry wanted to tell Parisa to stop being naive but instead he confirmed that yes, they could and would and most likely were.

"You're okay, though?"

"Yes, fine." Harry replied, trying to hide his irritability. "Has there been any word from the office?"

"Nothing."

"Are you okay?"

"Yes, I'm fine, darling. When will you be back?"

"A couple of days. Certainly no longer."

"Okay. Be careful. I miss you." There was a yearning to her voice which made Harry want to be with her right there and then and collect her in his arms.

"I miss you too."

It was nice to hear a familiar voice.

Once Harry disconnected the call he took out the battery and placed the components in his hold-all. It wasn't totally impossible in this technological era that if someone badly wanted to track a phone by satellite they could. He wasn't taking the chance.

Harry departed the National Park and walked through the outskirts of Neudorf until he reached the Neudorfstrasse. He knew from his map that five miles further along the main thoroughfare was a service station which linked up with major routes out of the area. Harry hoped to find a truck and driver there was willing to take him at least partway to Berlin.

Five miles on the flat road surface took him three-quarters of an hour, which was much longer than normal for Harry, but it had been many years since he had participated in a hike such as the one that morning and his legs ached something wicked. He ate the remainder of food on the way.

Neudorf Service Station consisted of a car- and truck-park abutting a franchised combined filling station and cafe. It was bleak and sooty but it was busy and there were a few small trucks and vans parked up. Harry could see no surveillance cameras in operation, which was a good thing for him.

Caffeine deficiency was taking its toll, so Harry dispensed a couple of bursts into styrofoam cups at a vending machine affixed to the external side wall of the cafe. Clearly the liquid was meant to be grabbed on the go by undiscerning coffee drinkers because it was tepid and weak. He could've bought an energy drink from the machine next-door but Harry had delivered a seminar for senior police chiefs on the product, the drinks harmful effects and undesirable chemicals, which had put him off ever consuming the stuff himself. The youth of society were easily led into believing the wrong thing was fashionable.

Harry strolled across the car-park and leaned casually against a back wall, drinking the questionable warm beverage, facing the truck-park.

A guy who could only be a trucker emerged from the cafe, hitched up his jeans and concealed the pink belly hanging over them and under his dirty white shirt, and approached an unmarked long-wheelbase white van which had seen better days.

Harry weighed up his options. This guy would be amicable enough but the state of his truck might add to the risk of being pulled over by the police. The vehicle barely looked road worthy or legal. And who knew what he was hauling in an unmarked vehicle.

He chose to let the guy go.

Eight minutes passed when another guy appeared. He was short, thin, young, and dressed in the colours and sported the logo of the van which he approached, which bore an animal motif.

Harry made the decision and started across the car-park toward him.

"Excuse me." Harry said in German, hedging his bets on the language through pure observation: the company logo declared it was based in Germany.

The guy didn't seem to hear him. He looked about as if unsure where the sound came from. Harry saw he had a hearing aid, so smiled amicably and nodded at the guy to gain his attention.

"I was wondering if you might be going in the direction of Berlin?" Harry said. He wondered if it might be against company rules so thought up a new strategy. "And if so, may I pay you for a ride?"

"Sure." The young trucker said without hesitation in his native German tongue. "I would be glad of the company."

When Harry climbed up into the passenger seat he noted no onboard camera, which was a definite plus. The cab was clean and tidy and had anew-car smell about it.

"I just had it cleaned." The guy said as if reading Harry's thoughts.

"Ah."

"I haul pet food so I get it done regularly otherwise it stinks up here."

The young guy said he was going to the port at Greifswald, north of Berlin, but would be taking the E55 Berliner Ring autobahn to the east of the capital and would happily drop Harry at a service station. This suited Harry perfectly and could not possibly had been any better, so he settled in for the three hour drive.

Pet food was their cargo, the trucker explained, and went on talking about the animal trade in general, the fact his wife was a veterinarian, they lived in Leipzig and he had just come from Prague - if only Harry had known! For a young guy he was both knowledgeable and passionate about his work and the industry in general, and hoped one day to combine his work with that of his wife's into a business of their own. Harry listened intently, not that he had much choice in the cab, and would've liked a snooze but the trucker's spiel was curiously compelling, plus Harry enjoyed it when people talked about a subject they were passionate about. At least Harry could relax in the knowledge he was neither Interpol or Mafia, and didn't ask Harry about himself.

They joined the E55 and followed the great curving beast north to Berlin and it seemed no time before that they reached the Berliner Ring.

When they reached the Karlshof Interchange the trucker took the eastern route which they then followed for a further eight miles until they came upon a service station at Fangschleuse, where he pulled off the carriageway.

Harry could not have been more perfectly located had he planned this himself. His friend Kolldehoff resided in the lakeside town of Woltersdorf, which was located just a few miles away. Walking distance, if necessary, although Harry cringed at the mere thought of any more walking.

The entrance road of the service station ran through a bend between trees and hoardings which stated what was available at the service station: fuel, food, drink, toilets, sleeping accommodation. All very efficient and organised and tidy. They followed arrows clearly marking the way for trucks and pulled into a space between an eighteen-wheeler and a huge motorhome.

Harry thanked the driver profusely, genuinely grateful and paid him appropriately before he bid him a safe journey and a blessing on his ambition, which the trucker appreciated.

It was going to be extremely challenging for Harry to leave the area of the service station without being caught on camera. He had noted several black domed surveillance bubbles on the drive through the truck parking lot and there would be no way of avoiding them. A high perimeter fence encircled the area, meaning the only way in and out was the official entrance and exit. And then after that he would need to travel five miles through the suburbs of Berlin to reach the home of his old friend, Kolldehoff.

Not only would he have to avoid the surveillance cameras, but he did not doubt that in the German capital there would be a greater network of Russian Mafia aides, all of whom would be keen to report his presence to who ever was in charge. The duo of the Anatoly Polivanova and the woman had probably made a calculated guess that he was heading here after tracking his route. Harry couldn't be complacent surrounding their intelligence and resources. In fact these Mafia people might be better at finding him than Interpol. But Berlin was a large city for them to cover so it might work more favourably for Harry.

Harry needed to contact Michel Lomé to gather a situation report. If the Frenchman hadn't been detained to long on the Czechia border for questioning he should be home long ago, and done his usual thorough job of going through the material they had gathered from the Vyrobni Zarizeni Remeslnika yesterday.

Yesterday!?

Harry shook his head. Had it really been over twenty-four hours?

To him it didn't feel like that many hours had passed.

Harry's only contact over that time period had been Parisa, who had had no new information for him. Who knew what else had transpired while he was away from the loop?

Finding a secluded area amidst the trucks, away from discovery or observation, Harry snapped together the relevant components of the burner phone which the artist lady had placed into his hold-all, and powered it up. He touched in the numbers for Michel's mobile phone and the network soon connected.

"Harry?" The familiar voice of the Frenchmen can back at him through the earpiece with static.

"Yes." Harry said without preamble, and moved slowly out of his truck hiding place to improve reception.

"Have you arrived?" The voice sounded harried, tired, and urgent because the line was being monitored.

"More or less." Harry raised his voice to be heard, ambling through the parking lot.

"Good. Our friend has the information you require."

"Thank you." The signal improved.

"Your Interpol friends know you are going to Berlin and I suggest cooperating with them before their Russian counterparts find you."

"I understand."

"You are creating a political stink, my friend, and I regret I cannot come help you."

"Thank you."

"Good luck, my friend."

Phone disconnected, Harry dismantled it, snapped the Sim card and put all components in the nearest dumpster. There had been little time for a trace to be made of the call, but Harry knew first-hand how efficient the system could be and wasn't take anything for granted.

    Harry need not worry about the traced call because as he had absentmindedly walked and talked on the phone he had inadvertently been caught on two bubble-cameras and an Interpol team were just two minutes away.

# CHAPTER THIRTY-EIGHT

Detectives Beckmann and Markowitz sped through the late afternoon traffic onto the Berliner Ring in their police issued BMW M3, red and blues flashing front and rear, siren shattering the air the wail echoed through a valley of concrete. Beckmann was driving hard in total concentration, eyes bulging on stalks if such a thing were physically possible, while Markowitz had one hand firmly on the dashboard in front of him, radio mic in the other, mirthless grin on his face.

Both these German detectives looked their part for the job description. They sported similar haircuts, similar dark glasses, shirts and trousers which differed only in colour, and police-issue lace-up Doc Martens. They had gone to school together, joined the force together, and lived together.

The exhilaration of a high-speed car chase was beyond the comprehension of the layman, and a definite plus point as far as Beckmann and Markowitz were concerned. Blasting among the traffic doing over a hundred mph without breaking the law, weaving and dodging between cars and lorries like something out of an action movie, crossing intersections without giving way or waiting for the lights to change, all while in pursuit of a dangerous criminal. It didn't get any better than that!

Ninety seconds out.

Up ahead were the barriers assembled by a construction crew. For most road users this would be a problem, a delay. To the police officers it was a definite irritation but not much of an inconvenience.

Beckmann was required to brake abruptly, much to his chagrin, but the squeal followed by burning of rubber as the tyres gained purchase was very gratifying.

A driver whose music obviously filled his car interior and deafened his awareness to the siren pulled out at a green light in front of the police BMW M3, forcing Beckmann to swerve left to avoid a collision and he narrowly scraped their car through a gap in the construction traffic. The music lover stamped on his brakes and watched meekly as the police car sped by, while Markowitz gave a glare which the driver would never forget.

Sixty seconds out.

Never a dull moment. They sped onward.

Sixty seconds before Detective Markowitz had responded to the radioed alert, Brigadier Annika Smimov of the Russian Kumarin Bratva had received a text. It told her that Harry Kovac had been located, along with his whereabouts. She was annoyed beyond words that she and Anatoly Polivanova were too far out to respond directly. They had absolutely no hope getting to Kovac's destination in time.

But all wasn't lost.

She put in a call to the Berlin Pakhan of their particular section of the Bratva, gave the prearranged code sign, and told him where Harry Kovac could be found. She stressed in no uncertain terms that Harry was to be taken unharmed, or at least able to communicate verbally. She also told the handler where he should be brought upon capture. There was an abandoned warehouse on a disused industrial complex - of course there was! - fifteen miles from her present location, twenty miles from Harry Kovac's location.

The Pakhan had better than good news: two new guys were on site who could identify Kovac instantly because they had seen him before, and could take Harry well before the police arrived.

Annika grinned to herself. Their organisation really was one of the best structured in the world. Annika told Anatoly the good news when she hung up the phone, whose stoic reaction told her that he too would be pleased to meet Harry Kovac for a further time.

Poor idealistic fool, Annika thought as she looked at the big Russian, whose heart and soul served the Motherland like the conditioned soldier he had been trained to be. The longer he remained unaware of who he really served the better. Annika knew him to be a dangerous man, and if Anatoly discovered he was acting for the Kumarin Bratva, a section of a much wider Russian Mafia group, then hell would indeed be paid.

Harry Kovac was saved by the dumpster into which he had deposited his burner phone. The mirrored lid flap had swung back and forth at the precise interval. On its return swing the flap had revealed the pair of hard-men as they tried their conspicuous best to not look like the thugs they invariably were, and failed miserably at it!

Both guys were dressed identically in blue jeans, black running shoes, and t-shirts which stretched the material to its limits. One logo-devoid tee was blue, the other red. They sported blonde buzzcuts and fashionable goatee beards. They might be twins, thought Harry - he would soon discover they were indeed - and looked familiar.

It took a split-second for Harry to recall where he had seen these two before: Berlin. He had had only a fleeting look at them but they were unmistakably the same duo who had tailed himself and Michel Lomé through the streets.

The mirrored swinging surface didn't exaggerate their distance from Harry, which he estimated at fifty-feet.

Ten seconds to react, tops.

Harry could discern no concealed weaponry. They were big, fit guys. Fast and strong. They were confident enough to not carry a piece.

Eight seconds.

Both these hard-men weren't as professional as they might seem, not to Harry's experienced eye. They weren't spaced far enough apart, for one thing.

Too close to one another to make an effective tag team. This fact displayed their first training deficit. And the running shoes! What were they all about? Soft shoes begged for broken toes in a fight.

Six seconds.

Maybe these two were newbies. Harry was their proving ground, perhaps? An average person would be intimidated by their presence. Harry grinned to himself: he wasn't an average person.

Four seconds.

Blue shirt would reach Harry first. He had a pronounced Adams Apple. That would be target number one. A kick to the groin would be target number two, no question. Dirty tactics, perhaps, but very effective on any male of any stature.

Two seconds.

Harry continued to play unaware. He pretended to straighten his shirt front, but really he was preparing for the first strike. His back was toward them. They wouldn't know what had hit them until it was too late.

And it worked.

The squarely aimed punch struck blue shirt in the throat hard and the follow through weight took the guy down, leaving him coughing and rolling in pain.

Before red shirt had the opportunity to register anything other than surprise, Harry delivered the second strike to him instead of his twin. The hard tip of Harry's boot sliced up between the guy's thighs and connected hard with his pelvic bone.

The poor man's agonised scream shattered the air and he dropped to the ground in blistering pain, curling into a protective foetal ball where he laid.

When Harry checked the state of blue shirt he discovered the guy was passed out, but he was breathing, at least. Harry rifled through the guy's pockets and found car keys but nothing else.

Their vehicle was the Audi RS e-Tron GT from the other day, which they definitely wouldn't be capable of driving anytime soon.

Detective Beckmann didn't bother to slow the BMW when he drove onto the Berliner Ring off-ramp at the Fangschluese junction and up the slip-road for the Service Station. The tyres hit the rumble strips full pelt and they soon reached the sharp forty degree bend into the roundabout.

Markowitz gritted his teeth. Not because he was nervous at the velocity his partner chose, but he was anxious to nab their quarry. His eyes were fixed determinedly ahead as if he could see through the foliage and concrete and steel to Harry Kovac, a crystal clear picture of whom was displayed on the BMW's nine-inch LED dash screen. There would be no difficulty identifying the Englishman.

The detective cut off the siren but not their red and blues. He didn't like giving criminals advance warning of their arrival but the lights at least warned civilians of their presence.

More rumble strips bounced the suspension as they approached the junction.

"Nothing." Markowitz said as he craned in his seat to see if they were likely to be hit broadside by any traffic.

Beckmann threw their car into the approach road for the service station without a second thought, foot to the floor, straightening up in the middle of the dual carriageway. The power and control of the BMW felt like an extension of Beckmann's body.

Markowitz leaned forward in the passenger seat anticipating their arrival, seatbelt straining, as if he could egg on their BMW to move quicker. It was like when he was kid with his Dad in an old car, a Lada, leaning forward to help it up a steep hill, his Dad would say to him and Mum; "All lean forward", like it was going help. He had always wanted to be a cop, and Beckmann had too, which was why they remained friends and more for all these years.

Cars which approached on the carriageway behind slowed at the red and blues flashing before them, not wanting to get in the way of the law or become witnesses.

"Come on!" Beckmann hissed between pursed lips as they reached the entrance to the service station, fully focused on his driving and the road surface and obstacles.

"There!" Markowitz suddenly shouted and pointed and bashed the dashboard simultaneously in frustration.

Harry Kovac was driving a carbon vorsprung red Audi RS in the opposite direction. A nice car which Markowitz coveted. It passed them by, the raised central reservation obscuring the vehicle number plate from Markowitz, who cursed the service station for not having an exit barrier which could be lowered and locked to prevent such an incident like this from occurring.

# CHAPTER THIRTY-NINE

Harry briefly saw the strobing red and blue headlights of the unmarked police car and, when he drove by, glanced at the driver and passenger, before he shot across the exit give-way markings onto the carriageway.

The car he was driving possess awesome acceleration and the manual transmission responded fluidly when he changed up as the revs piled on. It was a very modern car which had all the bells and whistles one might expect, and thankfully whichever twin owned it was evidently a petrol-head. Sport-mode was the new default and many of the manufacturers safety regulators were switched off, elevating a simple drive to an explosive experience. Steering was very responsive, power was in abundance. It suited Harry's needs perfectly.

Harry chose to ignore the Berliner Ring carriageway this time.

That route was the obvious choice for a quicker escape but it would also be easier for the local police to find him.

Instead, he peeled off the carriageway before he reached the slip road.

The right-turn was blocked by bollards and signage declaring the road closed and diversions were in place, so he carved a path eastbound through the Underpass. He followed the L38 into Fangschleuse town and was forced to gradually ease up on the gas. This car was distinctive enough, there was little point attracting any more unnecessary attention if he could avoid it.

Harry was heading east. He needed to be heading west. Back toward Berlin, not away from it. But he had no real choice.

Presently he was in a suburb of the capital. Homes on his right and left, signage indicating Werlsee, a lake with historical value - primarily the hundred-year plus old boathouse, if Harry's recollection served him. Other town facilities probably hadn't altered since Harry had last visit this place with Kolldehoff and Michel some five years past. Relatively, Kolldehoff's home was not far from Harry's present location.

The police were not in evidence tailing him presently. No wailing sirens or helicopter support. But they wouldn't be long.

Harry definitely had the advantage of timing and speed. If an APB went out there was only the description of the car to go on, not the registration plate. Trouble was, they had a twenty-five percent chance of choosing the same route out of the service station he had taken. Narrow odds.

There was also a possibility the Audi had a GPS tracker in case it was stolen - like now - but the twins would be in no condition yet to report that to their superiors.

It was clear that the Mafia were as well informed as the Berlin police, but should come as no real surprise. Unfortunately there were always informers on both sides of the law. These facts would mean Harry now more than ever needed to act more cautiously which, again, was no surprise.

Harry needed to change vehicle somehow and head back across the Berlin ring-road without being detected.

Before reaching the Neue Locknitz he turned down a road called An der Fangschleuse, found an entrance to one of the boatyards located lakeside, and parked up between a wall and a camper van. Out of plain sight, although the Audi stood out like a sore thumb if observed from above.

Harry reckoned he had about ten minutes before police air support would be circling the area.

It was eight miles by river to Woltersdorf, a journey of about an hour, depending upon the amount of river traffic. There should be no worries from the police or Mafia. Plain sailing, one might say. But first Harry had to acquire a small boat. One which was easy to steal and even easier to conceal when he reached his destination. Basically, nothing at all fancy was required.

Steinweg was an Avenue leading to the water with several private moorings because these were riverside properties. Primarily seasonal lets.

Harry strolled confidently down the track like he belonged there, noting that many of the wood-clad holiday lets appeared to be unoccupied. Through the open spaces between them he could see a couple of hopeful prospects.

Upon reaching the end of the unmade road, Harry decided to backtrack to the first of the two likelier options, a house on stilts raised about two feet on the ground, with a porch running its perimeter and circular. It was a single storey affair painted eggshell blue with a conical shaped roof. It resembled a yurt, or ger, but was made of wood instead of tent fabric.

The property had a square-cut lawn of equal dimension, probably eighty feet each edge, with low hedges either side separating it from its neighbour. Wooden decking came inland twelve feet, summer seating in temporary position upon it, and included the jetty where a twenty-foot pleasure cruiser with plastic canopy was moored.

Harry brazenly strode beyond the house and immediately movement and an open door caught his eye. He cursed inwardly.

"Hallo." A breezy female German voice said from the porch.

"Guten Tag." Harry replied, and continued in his fluent German: "Mister Koenig not here?"

"No."

"Oh, sorry. When do you expect him?"

"I don't." The woman in her twenties smiled. Her eyes were heavy. Clearly the roll-up she held between her left thumb and index finger contained weed.

"Okay. Bye."

Harry turned about and left the woman, smiled to himself, because she was probably laughing behind his back in a drug high. She had been pretty far gone and unashamedly naked. Harry was just annoyed with himself that he hadn't detected the smell of her weed around the property, but the more he tried when he walked back to the road, the more he came to realise the scent of the few pine trees was stronger.

Oh well, Harry thought, second time lucky.

Aspidistra Lodge was more bold and pretentious than its neighbour and, from the looks of clean lines, polished surface and modern appearance, it hadn't been there long. Maybe an older building had been recently knocked down for this two storey chalet to replace. It was white and glass with a plastic roof that sloped from front to rear. Very ecologically friendly.

The drive was a small beige stone affair between the chalet and a row of aspidistras.

This time Harry walked more cautiously, but there was definitely nobody home.

The lawn was surrounded by bamboo fence panels, and was AstroTurf. An outdoor set of rattan furniture was central in the fake lawn, and a chunky stone barbecue sat to one side. Decking and a jetty, much like its neighbour, joined the waters edge, and to it was tied a small boat.

The ten-feet long craft looked nearly new with a red and beige livery. It was moored up on its private jetty and in appearance was similar to a sleek Waverley Dinghy. Its mast rested upon the grass, presumably because there had been no wind when the owner last took it out. The outboard motor was fitted in place of the rudder on the transom thanks to an ingenious quick-release mechanism. Even a mere novice could operate it.

Which was perfect for Harry.

He checked the tank was full, untied the craft and boarded it. Shoving off he pressed the very modern, and very convenient, starter on the expensive outboard motor. Obviously theft wasn't rife in these parts and the owner was a very trusting person. Maybe from now on he, or she, would think twice before making theft of their vehicle so simple.

The craft puttered along steadily along the winding, narrow river, and soon Harry had left the outskirts of the village behind. Harry permitted himself a relaxed sigh. This was the life, he thought. At least for now, anyway.

# CHAPTER FORTY

Kolldehoff's generous estate in the town of Woltersdorf wasn't so much of a hideaway as that of Michel Lomé's, but gaining access to it was just as difficult. Harry couldn't arrive by river because the boathouse and entire riverside was like an enclosed wooden fortress, so he carefully dumped the undamaged Dinghy-type craft at a boat-hire mooring where everybody had finished their days work and gone home. The craft would be safely returned to its owner, Harry was certain.

Harry walked for twenty minutes until he reached the whitewashed concrete wall standing nine feet tall which surrounded the entire property to where Kolldehoff had retired, except for the Flakensee River side, of course. Unseen at the top of the wall was razor wire. Nobody was getting in announced.

Retired was too strong a label to affix to Kolldehoff's existence. Only a handful knew his whereabouts. Fewer still knew his real name. Harry was privy to the former, Michel to both.

There was no nameplate visible on or near the sturdy iron gates, which were wide enough for two cars to pass side by side, and it was level with the top of the wall. A solitary gold letterbox set flush into the wall indicated that somebody might reside there.

Harry knew there was no doorbell or visible means for attracting the occupants attention, even the hidden surveillance cameras were disguised.

So he just stood and waited patiently.

He tried to recall the season five years ago when he was last there. Many things had occurred in his own life and around the globe since then that it was difficult to remember. He knew the weather had been temperate. Maybe it had been autumn, maybe spring. Definitely not summer or winter. He knew it was at a time when he required a hideaway from the New Pro-Nazi Party while he, with Michel, had been assisting the Berlin secret service. It was at a time when there had been a surge of attacks attributed to Islamic State terrorists. This had been fabricated, a lie told by the press to deflect attention away from the real, and homegrown, culprits. These people were extremists but their cause was flexible and fewer such radicals now exist, although factions do occasionally raise their heads just as a reminder they're out there. Organised groups with belief systems were okay by Harry. It was once they started killing innocent civilians that he found their system abhorrent. There were less violent ways of expressing ones self, but until some miraculous utopian solution was discovered, these would never alter.

A magnetic bolt clicked.

The right-hand gate unhurriedly swung open wide enough to permit Harry's entry, and immediately after he had passed through, the gate swung back with a secure click.

The brick-weave driveway ended at what appeared a dead-end not forty feet from the gateway entrance.

All three sides of the driveway were bordered by virtually identical hedging, perfectly trimmed to the same height. To anyone unfamiliar with the layout these would leave a baffled question. But Harry knew this was an optical illusion, and a very good one, at that. Kolldehoff was a specialist in his particular artistic field and renowned for his often illusory tactical instinct. The hedge looked authentic but was a durable synthetic compound.

When Harry was twenty-feet along the driveway the whole dynamic perception of the driveway changed. The brick weave continued to the right, beyond the hedge, with enough space for a big car to drive through, and the hedge in front revealed itself to be incomplete, an illusion of space and a trick to the eye.

It was a brilliant if elaborate concept and another way to fool any unwanted snoopers.

Tiny LED's shone from the bottom edges of the driveway as guide through the darkness caused by overhanging trees for thirty feet, until it opened into the parking circle which itself was surrounded by trees.

A thatched bungalow had a porch and two bay windows faced front, with nothing of the property visible either side owing to the trees being right up to the edge. Inside Harry knew the home was a spacious three bedroom property- each with en suite - a kitchen lounge combo, while the largest room butted up-to the rear garden and was Kolldehoff's sanctuary, his workroom, where he spent much of his time.

Kolldehoff himself stood in the doorway, framed by internal lighting. To Harry's eyes the tall man hadn't aged in the slightest. He was six-two, two-hundred pounds, no fat, healthy brown complexion, smooth head. He was relatively nondescript. It was hard to reconcile the life this man had once had with the seventy year old.

"This is very unorthodox, Kovac!"

Harry gave a wry apologetic smile. It was a relief for him to have arrived without further trouble. What a day. He said: "Thank you for helping."

They shook hands like old friends. Kolldehoff's grip hadn't lost any of its firmness, and the grey, lined eyes had lost none if their spark. This man was a walking testament to growing old gracefully.

"I presume you want some supper?"

"I don't want to put you to any trouble."

"Too late to worry about that."

"I suppose it is."

"Well come in, man! I'm sure you can remember how to find the kitchen."

Harry crossed the threshold into the warm home and slipped out of his shoes, placing them tidily on the rack. The smell of freshly baked bread wafted under Harry's nose and his stomach groaned at him as a reminder to how hungry he was.

"Staying overnight, too!" Kolldehoff said when he had the door closed and locked behind them. Harry grinned because it seemed an utterly superfluous act to lock a door on a highly secure property.

"If it's no trouble?"

"Beds ready. You want to freshen up?"

"No. I'm too hungry. Your bread smells delicious."

Kolldehoff emitted a dismissive harrumph and followed Harry into the spacious kitchen lounge where, on the central counter, was a freshly baked crispy baguette, a selection of cheeses and chutneys, crisps in a bowl, a jug of water and an unopened bottle of wine.

"Expecting company?" Harry asked.

Another harrumph from Kolldehoff before he said: "The stuff Michel sent you is printed off and in your room. There's a shredder when you've finished with it. I presume it's ridiculously top secret! I don't need to ask you to tidy up when you've finished your supper, I know you'll do it. Nothings changed when you were last here."

"Thank you."

"Glad of the company."

Kolldehoff promptly backed out the kitchen into his workroom and closed the door.

Firstly, Harry poured a tall glass of water from the frosted jug and downed the cool liquid gratefully.

He smacked his lips with satisfaction.

Next he opened the red wine with the corkscrew to let it breath before he tore off a hunk of baguette and buttered it.

There were half a dozen cheeses to choose from and Harry selected a Bavarian Obatzda, which he found had a generously robust taste with a bit of a kick that required the compliment of red wine to cool his palate.

The butter melted on the warm baguette and the cheese melded to it. Harry temporarily forgot everything but this delicious meal, which he took his time over. Kolldehoff was a mind reader because when Harry finished he had concluded that it was exactly what had been required after the last two days.

After covering the cheese he put it and the butter in the big refrigerator, tipped the water away, poured the last drop of wine into his glass and took it with him to his bedroom.

Everything he might require for the night and tomorrow was present: towels, ablutions, shorts for swimming if he wanted to use the pool, and a change of clothing. A bottle of unopened water rested upon the dresser next to a stack of printed A4 sheets of paper. The stuff from Michel Lomé.

Harry stripped and went into the bathroom. He scrubbed his face with cold water and a flannel, before returning to the bedroom and opening the bay window, feeling the cool night air wash over his skin. He got his wine and sat in the window seat. It was going to be a long night and he needed to remain awake so he could digest everything which was in the printouts.

The first page was a cover sheet from Michel. Apparently the Czechia border police had held him for several hours and questioned him about his acquaintance with one Harry Kovac, and they wanted to know where Harry was going. Michel was more adept than most people at cross examination and they gave up in the end, but told him he was effectively under arrest. On his way home Michel had made the acquaintance of the especially well informed Mafia duo, but circumstances were in Michel's favour and he was able to lose them, although he didn't go into much detail on his escape – these Mafia people were proving pretty inept!

Michel went on to say that scouring the documents had proven invaluable and he envied Harry's adventure. He named the Hotel Pils in Berlin and a maze of underground tunnels as Harry's next destination. He had included a brief list of missing treasures, and signed off by wishing Harry good hunting and begging that he, Michel, be the first to know what Harry unearthed.

The next sheet contained a history of the Hotel Pils: it was once a stately home in the Friedrichshain district of Berlin. It was purchased in 1913 by Max Zoller and his family and opened up as Hotel am Kiesel, and it rapidly became a cultural hotspot. After the October Revolution, and Max Zoller's death, it became a meeting place for Berliners and prominent Russian travellers. During the Second World War it served as an officers' barracks and received some bomb damage but somehow survived the ravages of destruction around it. It received a major facelift during the fifties and was often visited by spies and high ranking officials visiting East Berlin. It's luxury status, and name change, came about after the fall of the Berlin Wall, and it is now part of a multinational conglomerate.

There were names of current employees and contact numbers for the hotel, plus a detailed schematic of the tunnel system with helpful amendments from Michel suggesting where might be best to search. A further ten sheets of paper listed complete names and descriptions of what might be buried there, if the fact that Waltraud Koenig had kept these papers grouped together was significant.

It would not be an inconsiderable task to get beneath the Hotel Pils, yet beneath it might a considerable haul worthy of constructing a new museum to house it all, if it was all there.

# CHAPTER FORTY-ONE

Cafe Moskau was situated directly opposite Hotel Pils in Hagon der Platz, and Harry Kovac was seated in a wicker chair with an ice cold bottle of alcohol free Liebfraumilch on the glass-topped wicker table in front of him, enjoying a clear view of the entire square. He wore a Homburg, dark glasses and tailored navy blue shirt, black trousers and brown leather brogues. A disguise of sorts. His face was fairly well concealed from facial recognition cameras and the clothing was bland enough to blend in with the trendy casual surroundings.

    It had been noon when Harry arrived at Hagon der Platz after a bus journey from Kolldehoff's estate followed by a short walk. Harry had mused over the three mile stroll that at least it was a shorter and more comfortable stroll than the day before.

    The Platz was a perfectly symmetrical square pretentiously brick-weave paved to give the appearance of a diamond when viewed from above, or from the church tower on the northern side. It was surrounded by a mixture of fashionable boutiques, hair salons, restaurants and cafes, a prominent bank, the main entrance frontage to the Erstes Museum of science and history, and the Hotel Pils. Alleyways darted between the buildings to boutiques and cafes, the Volkspark Friedrichshain and other areas of the district. This was a tidy, busy place to be and otherwise pedestrianised except for the one-way road running right to left past the Hotel frontage.

The outdoor seating areas were jam-packed. Lunchtime trade was brisk. Sunshine blazed into the square through diaphanous clouds, and a soft breeze felt comfortably warm.

Harry knew that he definitely blended in here. And he needed to. High positioned globe surveillance cameras were ubiquitous, monitored by a computer, no doubt, which reported instantly via facial recognition to the local authority. It was a good system - when it worked - which Harry was well acquainted with so he knew to be careful and avoid any flourish which my draw attention to himself, whether they were watching him or not.

The only risk he took was when he phoned Parisa, but the reaction alone was worth it.

"Harry!" The voice on the other end of the line had been elated, almost breathless from relief, as if Parisa hadn't expected to hear from Harry any more. "Promise me you are all right." She pleaded.

"Yes. I'm fine." Harry said. It was the truth, for now. "Anything from the office?"

"They send their love. And so do I."

"Are you okay?"

"Yes, yes, I'm fine. Sorry. I'm just excited to hear your voice. I must sound like a silly schoolgirl."

"You're not silly." He was relieved to be reminded despite their relationship being in its infancy that she felt for him as strongly as he felt toward her. "How's business?"

"Oh fine. I've had a morning with a property developer who wants me to join his team, but the truth is I like being my own boss, so I said I'd think about it. When will you be back?"

"Tomorrow."

"Brilliant."

"See you soon."

A pause before: "I understand. Bye my love. Be careful."

Harry disconnected the call and pocketed the phone, grinning to himself and blessing his good fortune for the umpteenth time . He toasted himself with the Lieb before composure resettled him.

The job at hand was paramount.

Harry refocused his mindset and sat patiently, thoughtfully, drinking the wine unhurriedly, consuming a sandwich, all the while studying the coming's and going's of the Hotel Pils.

It took no small amount of focus to get thoughts of Parisa Dane off his mind.

Harry felt that he knew the exterior of the hotel well enough by his mere study of the schematic which Michel Lomé had supplied, and the interior too, but there was nothing quite like first-hand knowledge. Flags fluttered in the breeze out front. A window opened then closed. People occasionally appeared at windows. Birds settled and rose.

After ninety minutes Harry dropped some Euros on the table which covered his bill plus a generous tip, not because he was dazzled by the service, but he had taken longer at the table than a person alone deserved.

Time was very much of the essence. He would reconnoiter now and do the job later that night.

People bustled to and fro. Sightseeing tourists, workers, locals, criminals and plain-clothed law enforcers. Who truly knew what life lurked in any street in any part of the world?

Harry was able to pinpoint a few likely candidates up to no good as her strolled through the Hagon der Platz. He identified a pickpocket searching for a mark; there were a couple - or two - conducting elicit love affairs; a drunk who would be up to no good pretty soon if he didn't find a lavatory; and a store detective on his lunch break.

But who was Harry to judge others when he too was plotting to enter the premises of a hotel under false pretences to case the joint for later. He had given great thought to the reconnaissance he was about to perform.

Con means confidence, and to successfully pull off a job one must exude total comfort with one's surroundings, and confidence in abundance, so you didn't stick out like the proverbial sore thumb.

Harry bound up the three wide steps into the hotel like he should be there. And why not? Why shouldn't he be there?

The interior layout was memorised so nobody bat an eyelid when he boarded the nearest elevator without hesitation, pretending to be moving to his own rhythm. He boarded the elevator, held the door for an overdressed lady and asked which floor she required, hit the button and they ascended together.

"Danke." She said when the door opened and she stepped out.

"Bitte schon."

"I've not seen you before."

"I arrived yesterday."

"Maybe you will be at the party later?"

"I expect I shall."

Harry grinned a killer smile and headed off down the corridor in the direction opposite to the woman. Confidence, like you belonged, and total familiarity with your surroundings. The ingredients to a successful job.

He strode up the corridor which was empty except for a couple of breakfast trays awaiting removal - such a thing wouldn't occur if he were in charge, they would've been removed straight away. Sloppy service.

At the end of the long corridor it became a T-shape, left and right. Harry went left, found the stairwell which he descended two steps at a time. He wondered idly if there was a security guard monitoring the cameras and if they had noticed his movements, or perhaps the guard wasn't paid enough to be that observant. Only time would tell. If they were onto him quickly then Harry would know other options were required for consideration later. If not, then the world was his proverbial oyster.

Harry had met nobody save the woman since first entering the elevator so staff were occupied with work, guests with other things.

The very foot of the stairwell spilled into a shallow service corridor with two doors and the service elevator for staff only. One door was clearly marked as alarmed and not to be opened unless there was an emergency - what did the door have to be alarmed about?

Harry opened the second door into a broad and airy, brightly lit, carpeted lobby which serviced the kitchen, the dining-room and ballroom, the leisure club, the main elevators and a double door leading into reception. The fixtures were gilded gold, small chandeliers served as lighting, paintings of previous managers adorned the wall along with a photographic timeline of the hotels history.

There was an ambient hum of a vacuum cleaner from the ballroom, clatter of steel from the kitchen, and voices from reception.

A couple of red-faced women in their forties, dressed in the latest trendy sports wear, exited the door to the leisure club chatting in German about their morning workout routine. They passed Harry just a cursory glance before leaving via the reception door.

It's a hard life for some, thought Harry wryly.

A member of staff exited the kitchen.

"Guten tag!" Harry said as he pretended to be going somewhere.

"Guten tag!" The Porter replied and Harry held open the door to the ballroom for the fellow, who was precariously balancing a large silver food tray in his hands. "Danke."

When he had gone Harry turned to the kitchen door, which swung on two-way hinges, and pushed it open. Inside, the kitchen staff were busy prepping food for later, washing dishes and cutlery. It was a clean white tiled and shiny stainless steel kitchen run with typical efficiency. They had received a recent delivery of food judging by the non-perishables stacked on a counter, and there was a lot of it. No doubt catering for the party which the woman in the elevator had mentioned. All the more reason for Harry to attend. It would be busy and noisy and he could pass through unnoticed.

Harry walked right in and straight to where he knew the cellar door was. Nobody bat an eyelid yet. They were too engrossed in their workload, which wasn't too surprising. If they did see him, he could act like the stupid lost guest with the best of them. So much for a kitchen being a secure environment. What if he was an extremist about to poison the entire guest list at that nights party? He should report them for negligence!

The cellar-door had no lock and the handle turned with ease. Terrific. His job should be relatively easy. He released the handle and was halfway across the kitchen toward the exit when a member of the team saw him.

"Hey! You!" It was an English voice. A chef learning his trade overseas.

But Harry didn't stop. He was already out the kitchen and by the time the staff had reacted he was back in the foot of the stairwell, out of sight.

Harry headed back through the hotel reverse his original route. This would be a good test of security. The chef would alert reception. Harry was dressed distinctively so there could be no mistake.

Back up the stairs, along the two corridors, down the elevator and across the reception lobby until a smart looking chap with an old-fashioned walkie-talkie blocked his path.

"Are you all right, sir." The question was in German and asked in a customer service friendly way, no aggression, not challenging, just polite courtesy.

"Ya." Harry replied and walked right around the security guard and out the door.

Confidence was key.

Getting into the cellar would be easy.

Harry walked through the Hagon der Platz and smiled to himself with satisfaction.

"Herr Kovac!" The voice was deep, male, authoritative, and not one he recognised, but Harry did recognise trouble when he heard it.

# CHAPTER FORTY-TWO

When Harry Kovac realised the utter stupidity of the action which had given him away he first cursed himself then figured his lackadaisical stupidity served him quite right. He deserved to be found. It was amateurish. His action and lack of thought was totally and utterly dum - to use modern gaming parlance.

Hagon der Platz was busy with people and Harry's only possible saviour was the crowd. Would the man be Interpol and take him in quietly? Although if they had to take Harry down hard it didn't matter to Interpol. Or was it Russian Mafia, who wouldn't necessarily want to cause a scene?

Harry slid a hand into his right-hand pocket and squeezed the phone like he could wring it to death. The device was his idiotic mistake and he had been fortunate to have lasted in the open for so long. How much time had it taken? Thirty minutes, perhaps? Only in the movies were people in the right place at the right time to react in seconds. Yesterday afternoon had been Harry's unfortunate anomaly. The twins had been in the right place at the right time. Despite the time lapse it still proved technological surveillance was the bane of everybody's life. They could monitor any conversation, locate any human on the planet if that person had an active mobile phone.

But who were they, this time?

Harry continued walking. He had not turned around. Why should he? Maybe they were hedging their bets and to acknowledge them would be his next giveaway. A stab in the dark. Or, more appropriately, a stab in daylight in front of a few hundred witnesses.

There were no sirens, which meant little, really, because if he had been in charge he would've tried to be as covert as possible.

"Herr Harry Kovac."

Second time, the voice was more insistent but the distance from it and Harry hadn't faltered, neither nearer nor farther.

The phone was active. If this person were the Mafia then at least he had the phone for Interpol to find him if he was taken. Maybe the phone would be a saving grace after all.

Maybe's and if's and but's were not reliable.

Harry was mid-turn to confront his companion when a hand lay upon his shoulder, but it was too late for Harry to register any kind of emotion or the slightest thought, too late to retaliate or loosen the grip, because his senses departed and he blacked out.

A hollowness and the smell of industrial grease greeted Harry when the dark fog of unconsciousness began clearing from within his head. Daylight filtered through the red and interlaced veins of his eyelids. His mouth was dry in an unnatural way, caused by a fast acting drug which his captors had surreptitiously injected into him.

Harry felt no pain. Which was both a relief and a curiosity. Even if his captors had stopped him from hitting the pavement when they took him he should at least feel some sensation of discomfort. Surely he was tied to a chair? But he drew upon a blank when he tried to use will power to force his senses to seek out his nervous system and skin, because nothing registered against them.

He opened his eyes because at least they were working but the diffused sunlight seared into them and he crushed them tight. Although he subconsciously knew his eyes watered he couldn't feel tears upon his cheeks.

They say the sensation of complete paralyses was gut-wrenching, but that was an understatement, and not altogether true, because Harry could not even feel that he possessed a gut.

More cautiously the second time, Harry opened his eyes and blinked away reactionary tears before he took in his surroundings. He was in a warehouse - of course he was! - which had a corrugated plastic roof to let in the light. He could see no windows but equally he couldn't turn his head so knew nothing of what lay behind him. What he could see was a stack of packing cases against the furthest wall, an orange trolley-jack, a yellow scissor-lift, and about ten big old printing presses. They appeared ancient and disused, covered in dust and cobwebs, yet the other equipment and boxes were new. It was a curious disparity of stuff.

His peripheral vision was excellent so he could make out a wood and glass hut, obviously the office, to his right, and a white Transit van to his left. He couldn't ascertain the state of the van, whether it was new or old, just that it was there.

Harry could judge for himself that he was seated. He could see his hands and arms on the rests of the chair. There were no restraints he could see, but that did not mean there were none.

While Harry wondered where he was the wail of an emergency services siren broke into his thoughts. It was distant but distinctly in street environs. Which meant he hadn't been taken too far. He was still in Berlin, or at least a suburb. An industrial complex on the Berliner Ring, perhaps. Hopefully.

Harry needed his circulation to begin registering. He needed his limbs to begin functioning.

His facial muscles started to work.

What kind of drugs had his captors used? There were some, he knew, that his system could cope with better than most people. Some which wore off quicker than others.

Another thought struck him: had he already been questioned? Were his captors already in their way to the Hotel Pils because he had spilled every bean?

Was he alone?

Panic struck him at that moment. He was helpless. They had left him because he was of no use. What if this paralysis wasn't caused by the drug? What if this was permanent?

Movement on Harry's right-hand side periphery caught his attention.

The Russian Mafia woman Annika Smimov paced deliberately across the floor in an arc, an almost euphoric expression on her face. She had won and was proud of the fact. Her crisp business suit swished expensively as she walked. There was a bonus on the cards for her when she extracted all the information her superiors required. And now it was a case of when, not if.

Harry could at last feel his heart pumping in his chest. This was a good sign for him, bad for them. Especially if they had injected him with the drug these people normally used. The effects were identical. Harry's panic had ignited his metabolism and it was slowly pushing the drug to one side. He was in the one-percent category of people on this earth whose system reactively rejected most forms of truth-serum. Lucky for him, not so lucky for them.

Annika waved an arm to gather a reaction from Harry and the effect was a ghostlike image in front of his vision.

She laughed at his perceived total incapacitation.

"Is your name Harry Kovac?" She asked.

"Yes." Harry's speech was slurred, mouth dry. He tried to focus his thoughts to ensure he didn't reveal too much, not that he cared, because in about ten minutes time he was going to kill this woman.

"Good. And you are a private detective?" Annika Smimov said the words with utter disdain, like it was an effort to lower her vocabulary.

"Yes."

"Tell us what Waltraud Koenig stored in the vaults at Vyrobni Zarizeni Remeslnika."

"Paper."

"What was on the paper?" She glanced fleetingly beyond Harry's left shoulder. Now he knew the Russian guy, Anatoly Polivanova, was also in the room, and probably not far from his back.

Harry methodically ran through for them the details of what he and Michel Lomé had discovered, his words slow, drawled and drugged, trying not to move his head or body while he pretended to think things through. It took an effort to constrain himself because now he could feel motor functions returning to his joints, which ached. It was going to be an effort to eventually move but his life depended upon it. Harry would make them regret their oversight of using no restraints. Their confidence in the drug would bite back badly for them.

Harry finished his meandering story by telling the woman about the Hungarian gold which was stored in the Austrian town of Spital am Pyhrn during World War Two, and his belief it was taken by the Nazi's to Berlin, and had ended up in hands of the Russians who kept its whereabouts secret until even their history forgot about it.

"And where are you looking next?" She asked when Harry mentioned the possibility of more treasure.

"What was once called the Hotel am Kiesel is now the Hotel Pils, in Hagon der Platz. Beneath it is a long forgotten maze of tunnels used during the Cold War."

"And is the gold there?"

"Yes."

"Your friend Michel thinks so, too?"

"Yes."

"Does anybody else know about this?"

"No."

"Just Michel and yourself?"

"That's right."

"Good."

Harry's circulation had by now fully returned while he kept up the pretence of being under the influence of their drug. He had been able to move imperceptibly without them having noticed. His limbs needed stretching before he acted but he couldn't do much about that, for obvious reasons. On the plus side he would most definitely be taking the Russians by surprise. They were treating him as an insignificant threat by being amateurish themselves. What came would serve as justice for his own stupidity for being captured.

The same moment Harry launched himself forward he pushed the chair back hard and was rewarded by a startled cry of pain when it connected solidly with legs or shins.

The look of surprise on the Russian woman's face alone was worth it, despite it being short lived. Harry swiftly removed Annika Smimov's life with a brutal front punch that had his full force behind in. Sinew and bone crumbled, teeth were uprooted, and the woman fell to the floor.

Harry disliked killing but he had no choice. This was a case of kill or be killed and his preference was the former.

Harry dropped down beside her, mostly because inactivity gave him no say in the matter. He yanked the gun from out her waistband, flicked the safety off and pivoted onto the balls of feet, expecting the big thug Anatoly to be back up, but evidently the chair had caught Anatoly better than Harry thought because the guy was still writhing in pain on the ground. If it was a bluff, Anatoly was very convincing.

Harry took aim at Anatoly.

No time to shoot.

An open door at the end of the warehouse had its light partially blocked with the silhouette of a man, a gun raised.

Harry tipped backward onto the floor as bullets shattered the near silence, bellowing from the handgun which was more powerful and rangy than Harry's.

Bullets exploded behind him, ricocheting furiously, sending up clouds of ancient dust.

Abruptly the burst of gunfire ceased.

Harry heard conversation from afar in German. There were at least two of them.

Their boss was dead. What would they do next?

As if answering Harry's thought, the silhouetted men entered the warehouse.

Harry slithered across the grimy concrete floor, hidden from the twin shooters by machinery and packing boxes, toward the left hand side, away from the door and towards the van. He needed to eliminate them as quickly as possible before they thought to call for backup. Harry snaked along on his belly now, gun arm ready, remaining low. His body ached something furious, he desperately needed to stretch, and this wasn't the way to do it.

The twins weren't being very quiet at all so Harry knew precisely where they were. One of them was edging along the front wall while the other moved across the middle of the floor into the room.

Harry rolled onto his side and eased into a crouching position. He was very well concealed. It was now or never.

Red-top was slammed against the wall when the first round struck him. Blue-top got off one shot before Harry caught him in the shoulder and chest in rapid succession. Harry swung back to finish the job on blue-top.

The twins hadn't been cut out for this kind of work anyway. If Harry hadn't put an end to their lives then their chiefs most definitely would've.

Harry stretched his legs in a long stride to the exit, rotating his arms and flexing his neck muscles. Anybody watching might think his actions were those of a madman.

Harry left the gun behind, found the car, which was the Audi RS had driven not much more than twenty-four hours ago, and was satisfied to discover the key had been left in the ignition. Too late for them to learn the error of their ways, he started the engine and pulled away from the warehouse.

# CHAPTER FORTY-THREE

Daylight was getting old and the night was young by the time Harry Kovac pulled his newly acquired car off the main road into an amber lit retail park. There were six large shops including a fashion outlet and hardware store, both of which he required, and two fast-food franchises, both of which he wouldn't dine at even if he were held at gunpoint. The twins had helpfully stashed his wallet in the glovebox of their car with an very thick envelope stuffed full of cash, for which Harry offered a posthumous thank you.

It took Harry twenty minutes to make all his purchases - tools and torches - and be back on the road again. He wore black lace-up soft leather brogues, dark blue cotton chinos with a crisp seam, a white cotton shirt and casual deep blue suede jacket that had plenty of pockets. He could easily pass as a businessman or party guest for that night at Hotel Pils.

From the hardware store he had purchased several pieces of miniaturised tools which might aid him later. If they didn't, he was screwed, but he had no time to return to Kolldehoff's for some proper preparation.

Five minutes on the road he discovered he had sprouted a tail. Obviously the Audi RS had been recognised, it did stick out a bit like the proverbial sore thumb, but Harry was prepared for the event.

He floored the accelerator pedal and the Audi lurched forward as if shot from a canon.

The streetlights flashed by in streamer blur as Harry tore through the Berlin outskirts at breakneck speed. It seemed as though this was another capital city which never slept, although it was still relatively early. His pursuer lagged behind until Harry had successfully lost them but Harry was under no illusion that his escape from prying mafia eyes would last long, so when he had the opportunity he drove down a quiet back alley, parked up and dumped the conspicuous motor.

When Harry Kovac strolled into the Hotel Pils reception lobby he was composed, collected and refreshed after his two-mile walk in the cool evening air and, most significantly, he was totally unrecognisable from his persona earlier that day. Not only because of his attire but he carried his posture differently.

Confidence was once more the key to success.

The party wasn't by invitation only, which he discovered when standing in the ballroom entrance, and it wouldn't be to difficult to blag his way amongst the crowd. Through the busy reception area he searched the faces to locate the woman in the elevator from earlier that same day, but hadn't seen her yet. It would be useful if she sought him out as a beau for the evening, if she recognised him. She had been older and she was charmed by him and would probably enjoy showing him off to her friends. Heaven only knew why charm still worked in this age of equality but there was no denying it, a person with charisma could more easily woo.

And there she was. Done up like a dogs dinner and thoroughly enjoying being a widow.

The instant she clapped her eyes upon Harry her whole face lit up, and the caked on make-up cracked.

"Hello." She said to him with a faintly seductive twang to her German, and she eyed him up and down. "You scrub up well."

"I was in disguise earlier." He replied truthfully. "I didn't want to be recognised."

"I knew it!" Her face lit up once more at this unexpected revelation "I thought I recognised you. You're on television, aren't you?"

Harry nodded, playing along. So long as he wasn't on television as a wanted criminal he was more than happy to play up to this case of mistaken identity.

"You're an actor." She said.

"That's right. Call me Heinrich."

"Heinrich." She swooned, then realised her faux pas. "Sorry, Heinrich, I've not introduced myself. I'm Irma."

"It's my pleasure." Harry said, took her right hand and kissed the back of it, tasting the moisturiser. He needed a drink. "What are you drinking?"

"Gin and tonic."

"Of course."

Harry took her arm and led her into the ballroom. The party was in full swing. He estimated two-hundred and fifty well dressed people in the well lit, dome-roofed space. A partition had been rolled back against the side wall that previously was used used to separate the ballroom and dining room. An eight-piece jazz band were playing an uptempo beat from the furthest corner, tables and chairs were situated on the perimeter, and a longer table was adorned with an exquisite buffet which reached up to the bar.

Harry ordered the gin and tonic for Irma, and a bourbon and cola for himself. She insisted upon billing it to her room and Harry shuddered involuntarily from the blatantly suggestive look she gave him. The implications for what she hoped might happen in that room later were as plain as the fake-up splattered over her face.

"Come on, handsome," Irma said, "let's mingle."

Irma spied a group of her cronies across the crowded room and led Harry by the arm hurriedly, proudly, through the people to them, all of whom were of similar age to Irma and similarly done up to the nines.

"This is Heinrich." Irma introduced him and they shook him by the hand when she told him their respective names. "He's on television."

They all coo'd and fawned over him, asked him various questions about the industry which he was able to blag answers to quite easily. It took Harry thirty minutes of this fakery before he was able to get away from them under a pretext of needing the lavatory, and he was in the hall.

Human nature loved routine and Harry was adept at studying the patterns which formed and breaking them down. The hallway was busy. Hotel staff were going about their jobs efficiently, calmly and generally doing the company proud. Back and forth from the kitchen to the ballroom, smiling amicably, allowing Harry ample opportunity to spy out the chefs and caterers within. Nobody suspected him of any ill-doing. Humans in the main were trusting, especially when there was a party going on to distract their attention, with many people generally milling around. A group of four were chattering amongst themselves in the hallway, having temporarily spilled out of the ballroom. Harry easily blended in.

Ten seconds was all that was required to get through the kitchen doors unseen, open the cellar, step through the entrance, close the door softly behind him and descend the stairs into the bowels of the Hotel Pils.

Harry now had all the time in the world. Although patience wasn't his strong suit it was a waiting game for him until the party finished and the general to and fro of staff down to the cellar ceased. He found a corner at the back behind a large rack of vintage wine, contemplated opening a bottle, and waited.

# CHAPTER FORTY-FOUR

Harry Kovac had no way of knowing what time in the early hours of the morning that the party ended and no more visits to the cellar were made, only that the time now was ten minutes past two and he felt refreshed after catching forty winks. Harry had dreamed of a stakeout in Manchester he had been on during the early days of his career, a long waiting game where there had been no resultant successful conclusion. A portent for things to come, perhaps?

He had memorised the schematic provided by Michel Lomé and located the area of wall where the long forgotten entrance to the hidden tunnels should be. Harry ran his eyes and hands over the smooth white plastered wall, but could find no subsidence where the hidden door might be positioned. Obviously the wall had recently been treated with a new coat of paint and plaster.

The skirting board was more revealing. There was a seam running the average width of a doorway, a two millimetre crack between it and the concrete floor which the most recent hotel renovation had failed to conceal. Harry wondered if the team of builders who renovated the place had explored the tunnels and decided they were unimportant. Could that be possible? Perhaps they were told to ignore the entrance and hide it by a higher power. That was most likely.

Harry felt the tingle of anticipation rising in his belly.

He took out the various tools he had purchased from the hardware store and placed them on the ground nearby with the pair of power Maglite torches. Drawing out a miniature chisel and hammer, Harry tapped away at the skirting and prized it off the wall in one complete length. Behind, the wall was plaster free and, lo and behold, there was the very bottom of a brushed-metal door which was set flush in its cavity. No wonder the plaster work on the wall revealed nothing.

It was cold in the cellar but Harry took off his jacket and hung it nearby before he began the task of chipping away the plaster on the wall, which proved a long and dusty task, one which he had to step back from every fifteen minutes to breath air, and brush himself down, but eventually the metal door was revealed to him in its entirety.

A panel about waist height slid across and inward to reveal the keyless handle.

Taking a deep breath and anticipating some resistance, Harry pulled down on the handle and leaned his weight against the door. Much to his surprise it opened easily on hinges which hadn't been used in decades.

Blackness gaped at him from beyond.

A cold air like that of a church, or graveyard, wafted from the tunnel.

Harry shivered, pulled his jacket on and picked up the pair torches, one which he pocketed, the other he activated.

There was no point hiding his tools should someone venture down to the cellar because there was a big gaping hole in the wall, so he left them on the ground, pocketing the screwdriver set, just in case.

The powerful torch beam pierced the darkness without obstruction save for floating dust particles. The tunnel wall was of red brick which curved at its roof, much like a long, high archway. It had miraculously survived intact. There was no visible gapping or loosening through the years, and Harry wondered if it had a strengthened outer shell to protect it from natural movement. Maybe the tunnel had been preserved with a steel encasement for histrionics sake by the Russians.

Harry moved along the tunnel at a steady walking pace, trying to guesstimate the distance until the gradient shifted almost imperceptibly downward. The only sound from within were his own footfalls. Harry knew that Michel's schematic had indicated this first section of tunnel extended almost a mile and he could well believe it.

A shiver ran involuntarily down his spine. The tunnels had been traversed only by ghosts of the past until Harry's arrival, and he could almost feel the chill presence of the men who had used them. Violent men. Men of action who had perhaps been bent to the will of Communist rule.

Abruptly the tunnels ambiance altered and Harry stopped in his tracks. His footfalls had began echoing rather than being lost. Ahead the torch beam seemed brighter, wider, as if the tunnel surface was changing.

Harry continued walking and the tunnel walls did indeed change from brick to a half-cylindrical steel with the concrete floor unaltered. The cylinder broadened the further Harry walked until it branched off.

Harry pondered which direction to take. The schematic had shown the fork in the tunnel and the fact this underground facility was donut shaped, so it really mattered not one bit which direction Harry took.

Choosing the left-hand fork Harry proceeded to walk, torch held waist height, beam illumination brighter now that the walls were a polished metal.

He checked his watched: 0312.

How soon would someone need to go down to the hotel cellar? Somebody was required to make a stock inventory and purchase replacements for the alcohol consumed at the party. When was that likely? A couple more hours perhaps?

After he had walked what he estimated to be one-hundred yards from the fork there was a sunken doorway along the right-hand side of the corridor, followed by an identical one twenty-yards along the stretch, then another, then another until what lay beyond was lost in the blackness.

An underground hideaway for Russian soldiers, perhaps?

And, Harry hoped, fruition.

The handle turned with ease and the door opened on well-oiled hinges despite their decades of disuse. Russian and German engineering was indeed the most reliable.

The room revealed itself to be a commissary when Harry shone his torch inside. The tables and chairs, untouched for many years, were arranged tidily as if their patrons might return any time. Shutters were over the serving hatch, hiding a kitchen beyond. He tried the light-switch but there was no power.

Another abandoned underground ghost-town much like the film studio in Czechia. It's residents departed in an orderly hurry. This area had empty coffee cups atop the tables alongside salt and pepper shakers. Abandoned but not messy. Used but efficient. Just like the military machine.

Harry lingered only a moment more before moving along to the next door, which revealed itself to be sleeping quarters. When Harry walked around the rectangular space he estimated two-hundred bunk beds. That was four-hundred troops, minimum. A reasonable sized hidden force under the streets of Berlin ready for the Cold War to become hot.

The schematic definitely hadn't conveyed the size of this place.

He wondered who had knowledge of this facility. And what had become of the soldiers based here? The Russians are a secretive lot but word spreads and yet nothing had been revealed of this location. Harry didn't dwell upon the fate of the men stationed here who, at best, were likely sent to Siberia for the remainder of their commission.

The next room was some kind of multi-purpose training hall with white boards, chairs and boxes of stationery. Nothing of importance to Harry's investigations so he moved on, but the next room was full of exercise equipment.

Next was the shower and lavatory area, the smell of chemicals mingled with sewage prevented Harry from making a thorough search.

Harry opened the next door expecting tedious repetition but his hopes rose. This oblong room was stacked on both sides with wooden packing crates half-way up to the roof. They were of various shapes and sizes but neatly placed. On first glance Harry guessed at perhaps fifty crates in total.

Harry couldn't control the grin which broke upon his face. The crates were of the type used to package valuables or weapons or something breakable. Usually they were padded with shredded paper for protection, depending upon what they contained. He went to the first on his left, a cube about a foot on all sides. It was unmarked. Tiny nails held the lid on. When Harry carefully lifted it up, it was quite heavy, the weight of a watermelon, although that was unlikely it's contents.

He took out the largest flat-head screwdriver from the set he brought along and slipped its wedge into the framework seam.

Buried in straw was a haphazardly wrapped package which, when pulled apart, revealed an Imperial egg which could have been made by none other than Faberge. Nestled in the centre of the ornate gold and silver latticed egg was a Flamingo formed from precious jewels intricately joined by rose-gold foil.

Harry admired the object for all angles, loath to put it back, but did so carefully.

The treasure in the next package was a cameo painting identical to the fresco Coronation Of The Virgin, contained in the Pinacoteca Vaticans but Raffaello Sanzioda Urbino. When Harry turned the cameo over he noted the gold-sewn date: 1518.

This had indeed proven a very fruitful hunt across Europe. Two hidden packages open, two long lost treasures, and that was only the tip of the iceberg.

Harry looked at his watch: 0418. Early. Very early, plenty of time.

One more package, then he would leave.

He opened the box in the same careful way a the previous two and dug into wood shavings. Harry pulled out a finely carved wooden goblet which had seen better days but might be Roman or Egyptian, undoubtedly important to someone but less impressive than the egg or cameo.

Harry felt no sense of the anticlimax he had anticipated once he finished the three of boxes. Experience prepared one for the reality of disappointment. Not this time, because the discoveries up to now were priceless, and he knew that whatever else was hidden in the remaining cases would be worth waiting for.

# CHAPTER FORTY-FIVE

Time was becoming very much of the essence and he needed to get topside to report his findings to the kind of people who wouldn't act with financial greed, those who would appreciated this find for its historical, not commercial, value.

Harry hesitated outside the room which reaped rewards. The corridor yawned at his torch beam, both left and right. Deserted for all these years, soon to be swarming with historians and representatives from various authorities.

It seemed a shame to Harry that he should be the one to ruin this ancient calm by instigating a mass brawl for discovery. How many more places were there like this? Long forgotten secrets faded from memory.

Looking at the corridor not travelled Harry wondered where there would be other entry points to this facility. And how many? The layout was doughnut-shaped with these rooms branching inward, but nothing on the schematic, which had been faded and sketchy, indicated where the remaining exits were.

He consulted his watch: 0359.

Maybe an hour, hour and a half, until the cellar door was discovered.

Nothing ventured, nothing gained.

Harry proceeded to complete the doughnut. He didn't have any idea how far he'd already come around the facility anyway, and it certainly wasn't going onward infinitely.

He tried the doors, identical to all the others, as he went, but most were empty except for the occasional table and chairs. The place was immense and it still seemed utterly inconceivable to Harry that nobody had discovered it already, what with all the modernisation that had taken place over the years in Berlin. Maybe he was deeper underground than he realised.

When he opened a further door the unexpected happened: overhead fluorescent strip lighting flickered into life. The self-powered room was a command centre. A wide circular metal table on sturdy wooden legs was the centrepiece of the room. Flat against the left-hand wall stood aluminium filing cabinets with a similarly designed table and two chairs between them. The right-hand wall consisted of plasma-screen monitors, long since rendered useless over time, and a set of control panels with chairs. In front of Harry, light from the room filtered through clear windows and although not all was revealed, what Harry could see caused his heart to figuratively leap into his mouth.

Harry walked through the room and up-to the window, shining his torch into a cylindrical silo, the white torpedo from tip to base must've been more than forty-feet in length.

This was the first weapon Harry had seen that had survived the evacuation of this facility, and it was a ballistic missile capable of being launched…where? It looked like a long range device, although Harry would be first to admit he was no expert. But the markings on the warhead were quite unmistakable, one could be a layman and still distinguish the symbols denoting a Nuclear or Atomic weapon.

At the heart of this device was a black orb of utter devastation which, even in the right hands, could be used to deadly effect.

Harry was no expert. He knew that long dormant weapons could still be live. He knew that atomic weapons didn't need to be launched to be lethal, even at the depth it was at right now. Harry also knew that it took a certain skill set to activate such a device, or instructions detailed to a mind capable of such an act.

It was a terrifying sight and made Harry forget about going around the donut shape, instead he left the room at a quick stride, which turned into a fast jog back along the corridor and tunnel to the cellar exit and took him half the time as earlier.

The cellar light was on and Harry could see the unmistakable form of Anatoly Polivanova standing about ten-fect into the room, effectively blocking his path.

Harry couldn't possibly know how long the Russian Mafia assassin had been at the hotel, or how he had been able to track him, but the man was there and Harry needed to think fast. How much did the Russian know? Did his boss know what might lay at the end of this hunt? The

Mafia were a remarkably well informed outfit but surely if they had known about the potential nuclear device then they could've located it for themselves. So it was safe for Harry to presume that, at this point, they had been seeking saleable items to finance their operations, and not a weapon of utter devastation. If they chose to use the weapon, if it was in fact still useable, then they could send a great swath of Berlin back to the dark ages.

Harry must stop Anatoly from reaching it, but how to incapacitate this intimating man. He could see the Russian wasn't armed, not that that made a significant difference in a fight, but at least Harry had a chance.

"Hello, little man." Anatoly said with a palpable menace to his tone.

Harry knew he must stall, give himself time to concoct a plan.

"How did you know where to find me?" Harry asked.

"You'll find out soon enough."

"Was it Von Stauffenberg?"

"No." Olly slowly shook his head.

"Okay, thanks for the information." Harry sighed. "So who do you work for? I mean, who do you really work for? That woman you hung around with before I killed her was Mafia, and she probably just a small pawn in a bigger organisation, but you look like a true patriot. Are you working for the enemy of your country or Mother Russia?"

The big Russian was stoically silent, meaning Harry couldn't tell if this was new information to him that he was now digesting, or just that he didn't care what Harry had to say because he figured the Englishman would do anything to stall.

Either way Harry had had enough standing around. Anatoly Polivanova, the Russian assassin, would least expect Harry to take the offensive move, the first action where the bigger guy felt superior. This wasn't quite a David versus Goliath clash because Harry lacked a slingshot.

This would be good, and long overdue. Harry thought. Even if it was a slight mismatch.

Three long, fast strides forward and Harry planted double-tap rabbit punches to the man's throat and solar plexus. No point aiming for bone, go for the soft spots where pain was immediate.

Anatoly wasn't slow to react but he was taken by surprise, his confidence in his own superiority working against him. The pain burst sharply against his Adams Apple, the second blow was more slow in taking full effect and was one that his training allowed for its absorption, more like a focus point to explode outward from. Normally that was what he would do. Anatoly could take down this Englishman easily despite him putting up a sturdy defence when the Russian rained blows upon him. He wouldn't think twice, usually. But Anatoly had an ace up his sleeve, one which Harry couldn't possibly expect and when revealed it would know the Englishman down more assuredly than resorting to a fist fight.

"Halt!" Came a booming German voice from atop the cellar staircase.

Two armed Bundespolizei officers quickly descended the steps, their big leather boots pounding loudly. They were followed by Detectives Beckmann and Markowitz, both armed, looking incongruously like movie characters in their fashionable clothing and shades.

The Russian smiled arrogantly at Harry. "Your luck has run out, little man." Then he said to the two detectives. "This man is yours, gentlemen."

"Thank you, Agent Polivanova." Beckmann said.

"Wait!" Harry tried to protest but was ignored and swiftly cut short.

"Might I borrow your two officers?" Anatoly asked. "They can help me investigate that." He nodded toward the tunnel entrance.

"Do what you like, Polivanova." Markowitz told him, deftly taking out a pair handcuffs and considering Harry contemptuously. "We just want him!"

# CHAPTER FORTY-SIX

Harry Kovac sat cuffed and chained to the restraining seat in the rear of the Bundespolizei van. Detective Markowitz sat opposite him, happily chatting away on his smartphone, expressively getting across his arresting prowess, praising his partner, too, but claiming most of the credit for himself. The detective was apparently up for promotion thanks to the capture of the criminal in his charge oh, yes, Beckmann too, of course.

Harry sighed. Showboating was nothing new and he hadn't expected any pleas he might've made at that point to fall upon anything but deaf ears. He needed to wait to make his phone call to Detective Cheklovich of Interpol to straighten things out and explain the situation so a team could be sent after Anatoly Polivanova.

Special Agent Polivanova of Russian Intelligence had really pulled off a coup, at least according to the local police. He was a hero. The man who captured the renegade Englishman who had been causing havoc across Europe. There was no point in Harry arguing his side of the matter yet. He had time on his side. It would take at least thirty minutes at a brisk walking pace for the atomic weapon to be found, and unless the double-agent had a working knowledge of 1980's atomic weapons, there was little chance that the abandoned device could be activated, at least not in such a relatively short time frame.

Harry felt he could relax.

Interpol would swoop down on the underground facility in no time at all and prevent any action on the part of Anatoly Polivanova, whether the Russian was working for the Mafia or Motherland.

It seemed to Harry an inordinate amount of travelling to the large Wittenau District police station. He reasoned they had chosen this large principal station, far away from where he had been picked up, purely because it contained the largest concentration of Crime Investigation Bureaux, and could more secretly and swiftly expedite foreign legal matters. Harry had visited the place upon opening not more than six years ago when it's modern facilities seemed brutally high-tech.

The police van rolled to a stop in one of the parking slots outside the front of the big grey and white building, it's tarnished and aged appearance was sad and forlorn. At least that's what Harry thought, but maybe it was just the situation.

Detective Markowitz levered open the back doors before releasing the locking mechanism on the restraining seat, which allowed Harry to pushing himself off the bench, hands behind him. He stepped gingerly from the rear of the van not wanting to fall out, like he had seem some prisoners do accidentally, and deliberately.

Detective Beckmann joined his partner, eyes lit up like a child who has received the best present he could wish for.

"We caught you eventually." Beckmann said.

Harry just looked on placidly. He knew his rights. He didn't have to say anything without a lawyer present. Not that he was bothered, but he had to make the phone call first.

Beckmann shrugged at the unresponsive prisoner and motioned Harry toward the station steps.

Harry walked like the subjugated person they expected. He wasn't going to spring any surprises, which seemed to disappoint the two detectives who were alert and on guard. These fellows were very enthusiastic professionals, Harry realised, who were undoubtedly popular team players and would go far in the force if they kept their noses clean. He knew their kind well, he had seen and nurtured their kind in the Metropolitan Police Force and at Scotland Yard, years back. Heck, he had been one if them once, even further back.

Behind the booking desk was an experienced Sergeant, bored and long in the tooth waiting to be pensioned off. Harry grinned at him.

"I'd like to make a phone please." Harry asked in his best German.

"Of course." It was Markowitz who responded, and the detective indicated an old-fashioned button press wall-phone. "You have two minutes."

Harry picked up the handset and touch-dialled the number for Detective Cheklovich. The dial tone purred six times before his friends answering message told Harry the person he required wasn't available right now but he could a message after the tone.

"Serge, it's me." Harry said and left his contact details, hoping the Interpol agent would be swift in returning the phone call to the station so this could be cleared up.

Harry replaced the handset.

"Feel like talking to us now?" Markowitz asked.

"Why not." Harry replied.

With Harry sandwiched between them, the Detectives kept a watchful eye as they marched him through the foyer and gained access via a secure door to the main station corridor. A few police officers gave Harry a cursory glance, while the Detectives received acknowledging nods. There was respect, and no small amount love, for these two hotshots who were evidently the examples of aspiration to their peers.

Markowitz opened a door to an interview room and indicated for Harry to step inside, which he did without any resistance. There was no point being awkward. He would need their help soon, once his Interpol friend enlightened them on the work Harry had been on. Time was ticking, but there was still plenty of opportunity to apprehend Anatoly Polivanova before it was too late.

Harry didn't need to be told which chair to take, he had been in this situation from the opposing end on many an occasion. He sat in the chair which faced the mirrored wall, knowing that beyond was a camera and probably an officer watching this interview. It made Harry laughed how politely correctness had substituted interview from interrogation.

Beckmann shut the door. Markowitz slid casually into the chair opposite Harry.

"Harry Kovac." The seated Detective began, grinning assuredly. "I won't bother reading your rights because for now this is off the record. Your history is known to us and we are respectful of the position you attained in your country, but what we don't know is the exact reason why you have been breaking the law in our country. Would you care to tell us?"

Harry smirked. "I'm shocked. I thought you knew it all."

"Enlighten us." Beckmann said when he propped himself up half-on the table.

Harry gave them a brief outline sketch of the assignment he had embarked upon for his client, Stephen Smith, including the Koenig diary and Russian Mafia. He was conscious of the time, gradually becoming concerned that Interpol detective Serge Cheklovich was yet to contact him. His friend was never far from his phone. Maybe he was already on his way here.

"And your friends?" Markowitz prompted.

"I have several." Harry retorted. "You need to more specific."

"Let's start with Rene Kolldehoff."

"He used to be one of you guys…only better." And Harry thought the old guy had dropped completely off the radar, but apparently that wasn't the case.

"And he was your friend?"

"Like I already told you, I have several friends. But, yes, Rene is one of them and he helped me out."

Beckmann leaned on the table, looked down at Harry and asked: "So why did you kill him?"

Harry was shocked. He was stuck for words. Anatoly Polivanova had obviously killed Rene but how had he found out where the man was and, also, how had the Russian actually gotten to him through all the security obstacles? Michel Lomé was safe, Harry knew that, so the Russians couldn't have got to Kolldehoff through him. Which meant it had to be the German banker, Von Stauffenberg. The banker had been connected to the Mafia and got them onto Harry and Lomé outside his Berlin office four days ago, and it was he who had led the Russians to Kolldehoff. It would've been a struggle for Polivanova to extract information from the old pro, unless Harry had left something incriminating in his room. Damn! That could be the only explanation. No way would Rene Kolldehoff give anything away no matter what duress he was under.

"Okay." Harry said, looking from one Detective to the other, composed. "I didn't kill my friend so you need to ask yourselves who did. Anatoly Polivanova-"

"The Russian guy?" Markowitz said.

"The Russian Secret Service guy." Beckmann added.

Markowitz nodded to his colleague.

"That's the one." Harry said. "Only he's not Secret Service, or maybe he is, I'm not sure. He's playing a dual role here. He's Russian Intelligence, for sure, but he's also been working alongside the Russian Mafia. But either way, he is the one who murdered my friend, Rene Kolldehoff. His people have had him in my tail from the beginning of this thing because they wanted whatever was found for themselves, to make money, no doubt, only what I found at the end of the rainbow wasn't just a put of gold, it was far more deadly and if it got into the wrong hands, their hands, it would be devastating. Now, when I get in touch with…" Harry let the sentence tail off. Something else has occurred to him. The reason why Interpol agent, Detective Serge Cheklovich hadn't answered his call. "Who is your Interpol agent here?" Harry asked briskly.

The German duo looked impassively from one to the other.

"This station has its own Interpol section." Harry's voice was almost at a shout, it had become difficult to reign in his patience because time was suddenly contracting itself like a noose. "You need to find the officer in charge and find out where their Detective Serge Cheklovich is. I think our Russian friend has murdered him also, and…and most probably a banker by the name of Adolf Von Stauffenberg."

Another look was shared between the duo, this one Harry could interpret.

"Look," Harry said, "you need to tell your men at the Hotel Pils that Polivanova needs to be arrested but to handle him with care. He's a dangerous man, obviously."

"I'm sorry, Herr Kovac." Markowitz said without any hint of apology in his voice. "But Agent Polivanova told us that is what you would say."

"And he also told us," added Beckmann, "that you were responsible for the murder of Adolf Von Stauffenberg and Serge Cheklovich."

Of course he did, thought Harry. It made perfect sense the Russian would state such a claim. And it also made sense these German detectives would believe the credentials of the intelligence officer rather than a registered private detective. Anatoly Polivanova was severing all loose ends, it seemed.

"Okay." Harry said. "I can fully appreciate that you would listen to the Russian, that's fair enough, but if you contact Interpol and tell them what I've told you, and also warn them about the nuclear device in a silo beneath Berlin."

This registered mild surprise shared between the two detectives. Harry had omitted to mention that to them earlier, preferring to tell Cheklovich, but as that was no longer going to happen Harry had to throw his hat into the ring.

"At least tell someone." Harry urged. "If I'm feeding lies to you then you haven't lost anything. If I'm telling the truth then you become bigger heroes than you already were when you caught me."

It took the two showboating Detectives little time to decide because Beckmann left the interview room without a word.

Harry grinned. Yes, these Detectives were your typical glory seekers who had watched too many cop shows as kids, but at least they were listening to him. They didn't have to. Harry had known many in his lifetime who followed due process to the letter. But, in case there was no progress, Harry needed a backup plan. He couldn't rely solely upon the Polizei to act in the way Harry desired. They might choose the predictable route and follow correct procedure, report to hierarchy, wait for their orders and paperwork and a court appointed solicitor to be in on a more legal questioning session with Harry.

All those scenarios might takes hours. They didn't have hours. Who knew what Anatoly Polivanova was now doing? Was he reporting his findings to his own superiors? Who were his superiors? If so, what would their course of action be? Was the device something which an individual with the appropriate knowledge could activate?

Harry recalled that the Russian woman was initially dismissive of the painting and necklace. She had been interested in the Koenig diary. Had she had an inkling of where the diary might lead? Had she and her people known the information which Waltraud Koenig might have been privy to and the secret hidden with the diary? They just hadn't known the location of the nuclear device. But now they knew, or would pretty soon if not already.

Markowitz grinned at Harry.

"I'm not wasting your time." Harry said. "I know that's what you're thinking. I know there are proper channels you need to to go through but... You need to act, otherwise-"

"What?"

Harry shrugged. "Truthfully, I don't know. If Anatoly Polivanova is capable of activating and firing an ancient nuclear device then I would hate to think what will happen. It's deep underground so maybe the effect will be minimal. I'm no expert. But if he finds it and you give him enough time, maybe he can remove it to...who knows where."

"What if we do believe you?" Markowitz asked.

Harry shrugged again. "Then we all save the day, like I told you already."

Beckmann returned with a stoic face. "The hotel people say they've secured the cellar but I can't raise our guys on the radio."

# CHAPTER FORTY-SEVEN

Harry Kovac looked from one detective to the other, their fresh faces young and unlined, lacking the experience of seasoned officers. Their enthusiastic showboating would only get them so far. Harry could tell that neither one of them wanted to make the wrong judgment call, but time was of the essence. What would he do in their shoes? They were juggling the risk to reward ratio. They were wondering if they should go directly to a superior officer, who might take over the case and reap the glory, or pursue Harry's claim for themselves. The question was: by the book, or not by the book?

Beckmann matched Harry's studious stare with his own, cogs of contemplation whirring behind his eyes.

"What are we doing?" It was Markowitz who spoke first.

"We need to check out what this guy is saying." Beckmann tells his partner. "If it's false information we can be back here in a couple of hours, nobody else needs to know, and we save face. Kovac isn't exactly going anywhere."

"Okay, but there are rules we need to stick to."

"I'm not forgetting the rules. We will be acting on a hunch and we don't want to waste the Chief's time by reporting to her first. Look, this is the smart play. I know we can't base our careers on glory-hunting but I don't want someone else stealing our work away from us. Not this time."

Harry caught the meaning of that last statement. These guys had been stiffed before by a superior officer and didn't want burning again. He could empathise with that. Early in his own career Harry had learned from that kind of mistake. There was always someone more than willing to step up from midfield to claim the goal.

Beckmann turns to Harry. "Look- This isn't television or the movies so you're obviously not coming with us. In fact, we're locking you up in a cell until we get back. But I promise that as soon as we get back and your story checks out then you're free to fill in any of the blanks you didn't tell us earlier, and I'm sure there are some to fill. You were one of us not long ago and we found out that in your day you even conducted an operation with our guys, so out of that respect, I shall make sure you get some coffee and breakfast while we're gone. Fair enough?"

"Fair enough." Harry agreed. "I know I don't have to tell you but I'm going to anyway: be careful. This guy Polivanova is very good at his job and probably won't hesitate to betray you."

"We aren't too shabby ourselves." Markowitz said.

"Be that as it may," Harry reiterated, "you're up against a trained and hardened killer, not some street punk. He will try to deceive you, throw you off his scent or just blow your brains out if his mission is to set off the atomic device beneath your city. He really won't care, believe me."

"Okay." Beckmann said. "We appreciate the advice. Now come on-"

Harry Kovac sat alone in the temperate cell and sipped slowly at the steaming mug of black coffee which had been brought for him, along with a greasy plate of bacon, scrambled egg, sausage and fried bread. He wasn't especially hungry but he learned years ago in his business to eat when the opportunity arose because who knew what might occur between this meal and the next. So he ate.

While he sat there he contemplated what lay ahead for the two detectives when they reached the underground facility.

It was feasible that Anatoly Polivanova had been instructed to use his own judgement when he found the treasure hidden within the abandoned rooms. Maybe his superiors had realised there would be objects more valuable than the painting and necklace, which was why they cared not about the initial find. The diary had been their priority.

Harry could only hope they knew nothing if the atomic device, and when Polivanova found it he would first contact his people. The Russian might initially be torn between loyalty for his handlers, the Mafia, if he had known that was who the woman represented, and the Motherland.

As if global tensions weren't enough already without a terrorist group setting off a bomb in the heart of Europe.

Harry had no idea about the time frame required to activate such an old atomic weapon and it's impact. He knew the bare minimum information required when he served in the London Met. Presumably if Polivanova were instructed to activate it he would have to contact his people. Harry had already discovered that however smart one's phone were there was no signal beneath the concrete. The Russian would lose time. The German detectives would benefit. And they could avert potential disaster. If not for the fact that they were up against an opponent out of their league.

Somehow, Harry was determined to find a way to be there.

Harry stood, paced the confines of his small cell. He needed to be there, helping, not helplessly trapped like a caged animal.

There was no way out the cell except with help. There would be a gaoler at the small table. A bored gaoler, most probably. His job would be a purgatory sentence what lasted a shift until he was relieved. Harry seemed to be the only prisoner that morning. Times were lean.

The cell itself offered up no assistance. There was no possible weapon, nothing loose. In fact, the porcelain toilet and hole in the floor were the only redeeming features!

Harry was right about the gaoler, he was bored. He unenthusiastically collected the tray, cup and utensils. Harry tried to talk to the gaoler, address his concerns, but the man was a mere functionary and close to retirement and offered no reaction or response to Harry's words. He pleased to speak with the Custody Sergeant.

The cell was locked once more and Harry paced the small confines. After several minutes it became clear the gaoler had either ignored Harry's request or hasn't heard him.

Abruptly an idea sprang into his mind, an idea brought about by desperation.

The cell had an intercom system so Harry pressed the buzzer and waited, but there was no immediate answer so Harry tried repeatedly until finally there was a reaction.

"What!" Came the gruff German response.

Not exactly professional, Harry thought, before he launched into what he hoped was an award worthy performance: "Help. I'm having a stroke."

"Ya." Was the disinterested reply.

Harry let out an abrupt scream of absolute agony before crashing to the cell floor in a controlled fall, causing himself no injury, by raising enough ruckus to attract even the most bored gaoler.

The cell door was opened and the gaoler was greeted by Harry writhing on the floor in feigned, contorted spasms.

"What is wrong?" The gaoler asked, still unable to register concern, and if

Harry hadn't been acting a part a part his answer would've involved sarcasm!

Saliva spluttering from his mouth, Harry repeated the word "stroke", which caused the gaoler to act more appropriately by closing the cell door and running off along the corridor to the custody desk.

Moments later and Harry can hear two sets of running feet, the cell is open, and the prisoner looks up and the returned gaoler and a Sergeant. This one looks near retirement age too, like the gaoler.

"I need," Harry slurred and sputtered, "a medic." By this stage in his acting, Harry was having flashbacks to his childhood and terrible inspiration for the believability of his present actions. His mother had suffered a fatal stroke in front of Harry when he was just nine years old, the memory of her a heartbreaking one that had taken years for him to come to terms with, profoundly affecting his youth. Adulthood and his profession had hardened him, but it didn't prevent him from reflecting upon that now and being angered by his decision - a stroke was no joking matter.

"This is serious." The Sergeant said.

Harry listened to their conversation. They were having their own difficulties. Neither the gaoler or nor the Sergeant had the experience to deal with this situation. The Medical Examiner had her own work cut out in another custody suite so couldn't Ben called upon, while the stations own Health Care Professional, who should've been on duty today, was off through sickness.

Harry was now inert on the floor of his cell, breathing, but motionless, his performance utterly convincing.

"We need to get him to a hospital." Was the Sergeants decision, almost said in desperation like he wanted nothing to do with the responsibility for this prisoners death – too much paperwork and explaining and he with only two weeks before retiring.

The Sergeant and gaoler stepped either side of Harry and hooked the arms under his shoulders and lifted the seemingly unconscious body up. Not the most orthodox action they could've chosen.

They carefully dragged their charge along the corridor, grateful that nobody witnessed their desperation and took him out the back way, before they loaded Harry into the rear if an unmarked police car. No restraints were applied.

The Sergeant took the drivers seat, the gaoler his reluctant passenger, but neither wanted to be next to a man who might be dying.

Harry was barely able to restrain the rolling motion he experienced on the backseat of the car as they proceeded apace. The Sergeant was unhurried at first, until on the open road and away from the station. After about five minutes of unabated driving the car slowed.

"Scheisse!"

Inevitably they have been halted by traffic. Harry could hear the unmistakable warning bleep of a van reversing.

The Sergeant shouted in German for the obstruction to hurry up, his bark falling on deaf ears.

Harry chose this moment to escape. He was lucky that the car he rode in wasn't a squad car because otherwise the back doors would've been locked, so all he had to do was be quick! He opened the passenger-side rear door, a warning on the drivers display warned the Sergeant immediately, but Harry was sprinting away on unshod feet as fast as he could - his shoes and belt had been removed when he was placed in the cell - holding up his trousers in what might've been a comical fashion were it not for the seriousness of the situation.

An exclamation elicited from whom Harry didn't turn around to find out, and was the last he heard from the car before he vanished into the hubbub of the city.

# CHAPTER FORTY-EIGHT

Harry Kovac was pretty intimidating when he wanted to be and as he strode through the Hotel Pils lobby from Hagon der Platz his eyes were focused rigidly forward. He was well aware that people were observing him and reacting to his determined stride, employees and guests alike, but he was putting out a powerfully antisocial vibe - at least now he had shoes on his feet and belted trousers, regrettably forced to steal the required items. No doubt the shift manager would be alerting the Polizei soon enough but Harry would be far along the underground corridor by that time, and too focused to care.

When Harry reached the entrance which he had forced open less than twelve hours prior, Hotel security had seated himself in a folding chair beside the yawning opening.

The guard wasn't armed. He wore body armour which was essentially just a stab vest and the standard body-cam, but physically he posed no threat or hindrance to Harry.

"Don't!" Harry put up a warning finger when he had reached the bottom of the staircase and the guy was ready to react after his initial surprise. "I will hurt you."

The guard didn't move. He was wise with experience to know when he was outmatched.

"Has anyone come out of there?" Harry asked.

"No."

"Okay. Thank you."

The news to Harry was a mixed blessing. It could mean the two hotshot German detectives had the Russian pinned down in a stalemate with nowhere to go. It could also mean that Anatoly Polivanova had found another exit, the device had been activated and Harry was now striding towards his own destruction.

Harry picked up a torch off the floor near the entrance, the beam led the way but Harry was on autopilot, barely aware of the now familiar cylindrical corridor, the face of his object arrogantly taunting him. The big Russian wasn't just a threat to Harry now, he was a potential threat to Europe. Innocent people would be killed, not to mention the vaporising of all the treasures within these vaults of history.

In what seemed like no time at all Harry had reached the branch in the tunnel. Without hesitation he veered left, retraced his steps. He doused the torch, slowed his pace, figuring he would see or hear what was transpiring in the bowels of this facility.

Harry proceeded cautiously.

The corridor was eerily quite. More so than earlier when Harry had been alone in the depths. The knowledge of the presence of others was clearly heightening the tension of the moment.

A feint glow lit the corridor up ahead and when Harry could see what it was, he saw a male Polizei officer lying dead on the floor with his stab-vest light skewed out beside his chest. His colleague was an obscene dark sharp on the floor not ten feet further along the corridor.

It was challenging to get perspective when the corridor and doorways all appeared identical, but Harry possessed a good sense of special awareness and recall.

A shout from ahead. The sound was hollow, disconnected, impossible to judge from where it emanated.

Harry removed the unused gun from the downed officers hip holster and picked up his pace, feathering his fingers along the wall for guidance as he plunged into blackness.

He wondered when the two hotshot German detectives had engaged Polivanova. They had obviously and wisely assessed the situation before engaging him. Harry also allowed time for the detectives to negotiate the unfamiliar tunnels. It would have taken them longer to reach this point. Plus they might've taken the wrong fork at the junction.

Had Polivanova contacted his people? Had they instructed him to arm the weapon?

Harry increased his stride, reached a point along the tunnel where he could see the light spewing from the control room, and Markowitz and Beckmann standing outside, shielded, guns raised. They weren't taking any chances.

Harry approached no further. He assessed the situation while teasing the safety catch off the gun in his hand.

The gun battle ended abruptly when Detective Beckmann was knocked to the ground and all ammunition was spent. Before Detective Markowitz could react to the change in circumstances Polivanova barrelled from the room into the corridor and knocked the German detective off his feet.

Without hesitation Harry fired at the big Russian, the unsuspecting man spinning away from the detective, crashing into the corridor wall. Harry's mind was filled with nothing but the desire for revenge for his friends, Rene Kolldehoff and Serge Cheklovich, the lives which Anatoly Polivanova had taken from him, plus the threats made to Parisa. Harry dispassionately squeezed the trigger and pummelled Polivanova until he had emptied the magazine, and the Russian was nothing more than a lifeless corpse.

"Thanks." Markowitz said and picked himself up off the floor before tending to his parter, who was bleeding from a shoulder wound but otherwise okay.

"I warned you that he was dangerous." Harry said.

# EPILOGUE

Harry Kovac could not possibly be more satiated than he was right now on the patio lounger in Parisa Dane's garden. Her bare right leg was draped over his left, her right hand held his left. Her hair gently brushed his shoulder when a gust of wind jauntily lifted it in his direction, and caused Harry to shiver from the touch.

An empty bottle of White Zinfandel was on the table in front of them along with a half-filled quartered bowl of various savoury snacks. Parisa's full wine glass rested on the tabletop, while he held his in his hand - it was positively half-full.

A second bottle of wine was chilling in the fridge, a more exquisite Bordeaux picked up from his home en route, which Harry had been given years ago by a grateful client and had saved for such an occasion as this.

Splendiferous sunlight spilled over and through the trees which barely rustled beyond the lawn in front of them. The temperature was cooling imperceptibly but it was still glorious enough to be able to enjoy being outdoors.

To be enjoying life.

And what a life-

A full week had passed since Germany and the endless stream of bureaucratic and diplomatic meetings and paperwork. Harry had lost count of the numerous grateful hands he had shaken and invitations received. The interviews he had given to the local German authorities would fill a three volume opus, if not for the repeats! Not all had be congratulatory. There were still a few legal formalities to take care of but none of these things were too major, really, at least not in the grand scheme of things. All in all, the discovery of the treasures and avoidance of an atomic device reaching the wrong hands, had incurred much gratitude.

Plus there would be the funerals for his two old acquaintances, Detective Serge Cheklovich and Rene Kolldehoff, in the not too distant future, accompanied by their mutual friend, Michel Lomé.

Harry let out a sigh.

What a whirlwind of activity the entire past fortnight had been, and there were many things to take onboard, digest, and finalise.

Harry had barely returned to Norwich that morning at the Crane offices before they caught him up to speed on the new cases, plus those resolved in his absence.

Stephen Smith and the ownership of the painting, necklace and diary - which Michel Lomé had since mailed them - seemed the best case financially upon which Crane Investigation Services had ever engaged. Smith's desire for lucrative financial and social attention had made him a very happy man, he would be regaling his friends for months on this outcome and Harry's story, drinking the spoils of Harry's success.

Then there was Hayley Wilby's emotional breakdown following the media revelations after her husband Karl's suicide, and the clearing of his name from the murder of Caryn Krystyva, which was small consolation after everything she had had to endure. A sorry state of affairs to be sure with little to redeem them. Life's sordid cycle would continue unabated.

All these things seemed long past after the much more pleasurable reunion with Parisa that afternoon - she had demonstrated very expressively through her body precisely how much she had missed him - which brought Harry to his present, very chillaxed state.

"Dane." Harry said. "You didn't explain why your surname is Dane."

"I like Shakespeare." Parisa replied coquettishly.

Harry's grin could not be any cheesier.

He shivered involuntarily once more. Not because he was cold and naked, but perhaps through a combination of shocked remnants from the past fortnight, or maybe it was something far more erotic and primal which stirred his finer hairs.

Harry smiled at an errant thought.

"Happy?" Parisa asked, as if she needed to! She leaned forward and scooped up her wineglass.

"You might say that." Harry cocked an eyebrow and let out a further contented sigh. Their wine glasses touched in an unspoken toast. "I don't like to beat a familiar drum but I was just thinking how fortunate I am."

"Oh?" Parisa tipped up her wine glass, not taking her eyes off his, unintentionally seductive, and drank some.

"I don't wish to sound superficial but quick frankly I'm one lucky bastard!" Harry stated bluntly. "I'm not taking anything for granted, I know without a doubt how fortunate I am, because it's not everyone who has a gorgeous naked woman sitting on his lap on a spectacular evening like this."

Harry kissed Parisa slowly, deliberately, savouring the moment and the explosion of tastes and textures, and thoroughly enjoying his life to the max.

Also available from Amazon

BY
# PAUL R STARLING

The Scott Dalton adventure series...

Living On The Edge
Danger On the Edge
Over the Edge of the Abyss
British Bulldog

And

Life in the Shadows

HARRY KOVAC WILL RETURN

Printed in Great Britain
by Amazon